The Human Thing

Kathleen H. Nelson

www.dragonmoonpress.com

The Human Thing

Copyright © 1999 Kathleen H. Nelson

ISBN: 978-1-897492-34-5

www.dragonmoonpress.com

The Human Thing

Kathleen H. Nelson

Prologue

JILLIAN D'LANGE STRODE down the steel-enclosed docks of Calypso Station with a spring in her step. She had a three-day to kill, thanks to a client who was running late and willing to pay for the privilege, and she was readyreadyready to enjoy every minute of it. Three days without a care, she gloated, as she walked along. Three days without a cargo or a ship or a crew. It had been a while since she'd had any time to just fritter away.

She had her partner-in-frittering all picked out, too—Denis C. Latimer, captain of *Riff-Raff*, and her one and only lover for the past five years. He didn't know that she was on her way, for they'd expected to be two of those proverbial ships passing in the night at this conjunction, with no window for a tryst. But this pop-up three-day changed all that. DennyDennyDen was going to be *so* surprised.

She planned to jump him once or twice just to get his attention, and then talk him into going down to the moon for more of the same. Calypso was OK for a stop-over, but the atmosphere had very little going for it. It smelled of recycled air and propellant. And, from the inside at least, it looked like a cross between the mother of all motherships and a freakin' warehouse. Public flits and flatbed skimmers zoomed up and down the transport corridors, jockeying hard for right of way. The flits moved people, the flats moved cargo: mostly provisions and crewmen for the ships that were docked outside. Nothing exciting about that. She wanted a little glamour, a little adventure, a little gravity. Low-G sex and a grungy bar afterward got to be a bore after a while. A hawker flagged her down at the top of 'J' sector. She gave him the once-over, looking in vain for an SU emblem, then bought a sweet-and-sour pear from him anyway. It was sticky-sweet, with firm, pink, just-tart flesh. The flavor lingered in her mouth long after the fruit was gone. Denny would appreciate that, she thought. "Hey there," a flit-driver said, as she strode past his stand, "need a lift?" "No thanks," she replied in passing. Smart spacers kept themselves in good shape to avoid the bone and cardiovascular problems that were prone to the profession. And as humdrum as walking the ped-ways of Calypso was, it beat the hell out of a two-hour stint on *Zephyr's* treadmill. Besides, she enjoyed being physical— in every way. The thought shaped itself into an eager grin. The spring in her step became a hip-swinging saunter. A team of dockhands whistled their approval. She tossed her black, unfashionably long hair at them, and continued on her way.

'J' sector was the last of ten 'piers' that protruded like spokes from the station's domed hub. Station Control parked the biggest, ungainliest ships here: ore barges, flying factories, garbage scows, Denny's old tub of a salvager. When she thought of her *Zeph*, docked in a choice slip back in 'C' sector, she couldn't help but gloat to herself. *Zephyr* was everything that *Riff-Raff* wasn't: sleek and streamlined, fast as thought, a pleasure to operate and own. Or *almost* own, anyway. That was a major plus in *Riff-Raff's* favor: Denny held it, free and clear. She vented her superior conceits with a sigh.

She could see *Riff-Raff's* berth in the distance now. As she'd expected, the crew was taking on a load of fresh provisions. And as she'd hoped, Denny was not taking part in the job. She tracked down her lover's stevedore: a barrel-chested man by the name of Sam Quackenbee. He was standing next to the caterer's skimmer, checking his inventory against the auto-serv's.

"Bless these old bones!" he said, when he saw her. "If it ain't Capitan Jill, the best-damn-looking face in space. You here to try and steal me away from Denis again?"

"Would I stand a chance this time?" she bantered.

He gave his shaggy gray eyebrows a raunchy waggle, and then snorted so neither of them would take the innuendo seriously. "Nah. Put me on a cushy freighter like *Zeph*, and I'd be fatter than a Tuluvean houseboy in a fortnight. I need the abuse that salvaging dishes out."

"How'd you guys do this time out?" she asked.

"The hold's full," he said, in a much lower voice, "but on our way in, we found an ark—leastwise what was left of her. Damned pirates had blasted her full of holes. Denny was upset. Still is, for that fact."

"That's sad," she said, and it was. Arks were little more than prehistoric barges, throwbacks to, or occasionally leftovers from, the days when the fastest way between two points was still a straight line. As massive as they were, and as slow as they were, it often took them years to get from one solar system to the next. Like many spacers, Jillian had a sentimental attachment to those archaic rigs and to the legends that they'd inspired over the years. Hearing of one's destruction by pirates was like hearing of childhood-friend's death. "I think I should try and cheer him up. Is he around?"

He checked with his wrist-wiz. "Looks like he's in his quarters. Want me to ping him?"

"Negative," she replied. "I want this to be a surprise. Just open the walkway for me."

"Done."

"Thanks, Quackers. I'll be seeing you."

"Always a pleasure, Capt'n," he said with a grin, and returned to his work.

As she made her way over to the walkway, the airlock swept open and a stocky, copper-haired man clad in a spacer-blue flightsuit came barging out of the tube. He had frosty blue eyes and a deep dimple in his chin, but at the moment, his most distinguishing feature was the brand-new ridge of scar-tissue that ran all the way down the right side of his face. That was one of the hazards of salvage work, she thought. And a scar like that would be noticeable even after he had it sanded down.

"Stars!" she blurted, as she grappled for his name. Matthew? Mark? Something like that. "What happened to you?"

"I cut myself shaving," he said, and then shouldered past her. Too stunned to do anything else, she gaped at his retreating back. A moment later, he jumped into a passing skimmer's bed and was gone.

"Fuck you, too, space-for-brains," she grumbled, as she headed into the walkway. But as she passed through the access tube and into *Riff-Raff's* tarnished corridors, reason jumped to the man's defense. Salvage work could give anyone the growls, even when the run went right and well. And coming across a gutted ark would've ruined any trip.

The door to Denny's room came into view then; and just like that, she made the ark take a back-seat to lust. She raked her fingers through her hair, checked to see if she had slobbered fruit-juice down the front of her unitard, and then fed an access code to the wall-grid. An instant later, the grid flashed green and the door slid open.

She caught *Riff-Raff's* captain working, half-dressed, at his pull-out desk. Denny startled at the airlock's hiss, then hastily shoved the desk back into the wall and swiveled about to confront his uninvited guest. The ridges on his high, pale forehead started out as anger, but then arched into surprise.

"Jill?"

"Surprise," she said, as she sauntered toward him. "Happy to see me?"

"Of course," he said, though there was more bewilderment in his tone than delight. "But what are you doing here?"

"I'll give you three guesses." She ran her hands down his hairless, spacer-white chest, then caressed the bones of his pelvis. "And the first two don't count."

"Oh," he said then, and grinned.

"Finally," she teased, and grinned back.

The next thing she knew, they were a frantic tangle of sweaty flesh on the floor. His hands were callused; his lips, chapped. Her back arched to the thrill of rough edges. He rode her fast and hard—just the way she liked it the first time. Climax came quickly to them both.

"Damn!" she swore afterward, as her insides twitched and thrummed. "It's good to be alive."

"I'm glad you think so," Denny said, and then rolled out from under her just as she was starting to get comfortable.

"What's your hurry?" she asked, repositioning herself to give him a better view of her tall, angular, and very naked body. "I don't know about you, but once is definitely not enough for me."

"Sorry, Jillie-Jill," he said, as he collected the pieces of his cast-off clothing and started dressing, "but you didn't give me a chance to tell you. I've got some work to do this afternoon."

"What kind?" When he didn't answer immediately, her intuition kicked in. "This wouldn't have anything to do with that old barge you found, would it?"

He shot her a troubled look. "You know about that?"

"Nothing escapes me for long, lover. So what's the dish?"

"I won't know for sure until I've spent some time in the archives," he said. "But I have this high-velocity feeling that the union's in serious trouble."

Then hand the scat over to Barim," she said. "That's what we pay him for."

"If I'm right," he replied, glancing furtively toward the door, "Barim could be part of the problem."

Sweet, suffering mother! She didn't know what to think about *that*! But one thing was for sure: she didn't feel like being on her back anymore. She dove for her clothes. As she did so, a wrist-wiz pinged.

"Relax, it's mine," Denny said, and answered the page. "What is it, Trevor?"

"Time, Capt'n," came the reply. "You wanted me to remind you."

"Right. Is the shuttle ready?"

"Just finished fueling her up myself."

"Thanks. I'll be there in ten."

He turned to Jillian, who was now hastily stuffing herself back into her one-piece. His expression was one of amusement and rue. "Just because I have to go doesn't mean that you have to hurry off," he told her. "Take your time. Stick around if you want. If all goes well, I could be back before breakfast."

"Like I really want to spend a third of my three-day moping around on this grungy bucket of bolts," she jeered, and then began to pull on her boots. "I'm going with you."

"I don't know if that's such a good idea, Jill," he countered. "I could be sitting on a live round here."

She mocked him with her most lecherous grin. "Ooh, an element of danger. I like that. It'll make the sex afterward that much better."

"You're impossible," he accused.

"What's your point?"

He rolled his eyes, then strode over to his desk-slot. He eased it open, but only for a second; and as it slid back into the wall, she saw him slip a small, blackened disk into a vest-pocket. "Well," he said then, "since you're determined to tag along, let's get going. We're working with a small window of opportunity here."

"I'm right behind you," she said.

As they navigated the maze of corridors that led to *Riff-Raff's* shuttle bay, Jillian fingered her thoughts like worry beads. Barim, involved with piracy? It just couldn't be! He was the president—the freakin' *patron saint*, according to some—of the Spacer's Union. But Denny wasn't the type to voice accusations lightly. If he suspected Barim, it was for damn good reason. And although she had downplayed the dangers that came with playing cloak-and-dagger games, she was not so foolish as to think that they did not exist. Indeed, watching his back was one of her primary motives for tagging along. That, and it beat moping around Calypso.

"So," she said then. "What was that thing you slipped into your pocket anyway?"

"A memory disk that I recovered from the ark's auto-log," he told her. "It was damaged rather badly during the raid, but I'm hoping that it might still be able to tell us a thing or two."

"And where on Circe's II are you going to get the hardware to run something that primitive?" she wanted to know. "Ark stuff is *ancient*, lover."

He twitched a smug little smile at her. "As it so happens, the new data-library in Odysseus's Union Complex has a collection of antique computers on permanent display. And as it so happens, I've bribed the archivist to let me use one of them."

"Sneak," she said, in admiring tones, and then leap-frogged to her next thought. "But if you don't know what's on the disk yet, where'd the SU connection come from?"

They were closing in on the shuttle bay now. He sucked in a breath only to expel it again as a sigh. "I'll tell you all about it once we're moonbound, OK? For now, let's just say that space junk can be very telling."

Jillian harumphed: once at the cryptic remark, and then again as the bay's doors slid open and she caught sight of *Riff-Raff's* grimy work-horse of a shuttle. "Speaking of space junk," she said.

"Just because your shuttle can do everything but give birth doesn't mean that you can bad-mouth mine," he told her. "Besides, this baby's a classic."

"So sell it to a guy's-only museum."

She followed him into the cockpit, then flopped down in the co-pilot's chair. The bio-plastics in the seat conformed with her contours, creating an adaptable safety seal. As Jillian shifted, trying to adapt the seat's grip to her liking, he brought the shuttle's engines on-line. A high-pitched screech filled the cabin, then waxed ultrasonic. A moment later, the floor began to vibrate to a deep, synchronized thrumming. The sensation danced its way into her bones through the soles of her feet. It was an annoying little tingle.

"All systems green," she said, checking the monitors. "And all kidding aside, Den, this baby needs some work."

"I know," he said, and then jabbed at his wrist-wiz. "Henderson, this is Latimer," he said, as soon as the man responded. "I thought I ordered a tune-up for the shuttle."

"You did, Captain," came his crew-chief's reply. "And I put Marty Conrad on it. He said he'd have it done in time for your trip."

"Well, he lied," Denny said. "The number two resonator is still squealing like a pig in shit."

"Want me to ping him for you?"

"Hell, no! I want you to fire him."

"SU won't like that," Henderson warned.

"Fuck SU," Denny fired back. "They should never have certified the lazy bastard in the first place. You get him off my ship now, you hear, Frank? If he's still here when I get back, you'll be swabbing out the septic tank by hand."

"Wait a minute," Jillian said then. "Are we talking about a big, blocky guy with red hair and a spanking-new facial scar?"

Denny nodded. "He was barreling down the walkway just as I was coming in."

"He was probably on his way to meet some tart," he grumbled, and then switched back to his crew-chief. "You hear that, Frank? He left the ship without my leave. That's desertion. And that's a firing offense, even in the SU's book. So it's heave-ho and off he goes, mate."

"I hear you, Captain," Frank replied, sounding much more chipper all of a sudden. "Want me to send someone down to fix the resonator?"

"Negative. I can't spare the time right now and it's still reading green, so I'll just live with it as-is until I get back. Latimer out." An instant after he closed the connection, he pinged the bridge. "Trevor, this is Latimer. Do I have clearance yet?"

"That's a roger," came the reply. "Station Control has cleared you for a holding pattern over J-sector, and advises you to stand-by for your lane assignment to Cee-Two. Have a nice flight, Captains."Denny flashed her a conspiring wink, and then eased the throttle into drive. With a gut-wrenching lurch, the shuttle surged forward—out of the bay and into the velveteen blackness of space.

The first thing that spanned across the view-plate was the moon. Save for a small, white, polar tonsure, its face was brown and featureless—hardly Jillian's idea of how the most glamorous port in the galaxy ought to look. But Circe's II was the 'new' center of the galaxy; and it was power rather than appearances that fueled her glamour. Odysseus, the capitol, was home to the Galactic Council, planetary ambassadors, and the SU's high command. These people, plus their legions of flunkies and hangers-on, supported a city of service providers whose success encouraged droves of new arrivals who dreamed of striking it rich. Jillian shuddered at the thought of all those people living in one place. It might be good for business, but brr—! She needed more room to breathe.

The shuttle was swinging into its assigned holding pattern now. As it came about, a sliver of Circe's Moon I came into view, and then Circe herself; a gas giant, sullen and red. Although her hub star was a distant pin-prick, she radiated just enough heat to keep her two moons from turning into solid chunks of ice. And although her surface was pure poison, she was the only 'friendly' planet in the solar system.

And then there was Calypso.

On the grand scale of things, the station was nothing, just a flyspeck of debris in orbit. On a human scale, though, it was the umpteenth wonder, like the Great Pyramids come to space. It was so big and vast, it made the ships that were moored to its spokes look like cosmic sucker fish. And those ships were classed by the *giga*ton. When Jillian thought about where she stood in this scheme of things, she felt very small indeed.

A robotic voice spilled into the cockpit then, accompanied by a ration of static. " *Riff-Raff* shuttle-craft," it intoned, "this is Station Control. You have been cleared for Lane 2B to Circe's Moon II. Please observe the posted speed limit. The penalties for noncompliance are steep."

"That damned chip-wit could've cleared me ten minutes ago," Denny complained, as he angled the shuttle away from J-sector and toward its assigned zone. "There's hardly anyone out here."

"Except that big asteroid-eater," she said, pointing to a huge, slow-moving blip on the surveillance screen. "And we wouldn't want to get in that big boy's way, would we?"

His only reply was a grunt.

The view shifted from station traffic to Circe's II. Nothing, it seemed, stood between *Riff-Raff's* shuttle and that plain-faced moon. A smile crept across Denny's mouth like a crack in thin ice. And as soon as they cleared regulated space, he let the throttle out all the way. The shuttle shot forward with a throaty roar, prompting Jillian's seat to tighten its grip. She laughed— this was vintage Denny! When it came to going fast, he couldn't help himself. But her amusement was short-lived. An indicator flared suddenly yellow, and then began flashing red.

"I'm reading a twelve percent impulse power loss," she said.

"Is it the resonators?" he asked.

"Negative," she replied. "It looks like a problem with the thrusters—a clogged converter, maybe. Loss is up to eighteen percent now. Are you sure your monitors are trustworthy?"

"I'm sure," he said, and pulled back on the throttle. The ship did not respond as much as it should have. Damn it," Denny said, as he turned back toward Station. "It's going to take me days—not to mention another bribe—to set up another meeting with that archivist."

"Oh, well," she said, trying to sound casual in spite of the uneasy feeling that was creeping through her gut. "I'd rather stay in a pleasure-suite on the hub than a moonside resort anyway. Power loss at twenty-five percent now, and still climbing. We're starting to stray."

The station was expanding across the viewplate now. But even as the shuttle cruised toward it, she could feel their trajectory's quickening decay in her bones. If they continued to lose power at this rate, they were going to wind up in full free-fall through Station traffic, and that was an accident just begging to happen.

"Where's that big boy?" Denny asked then, as if he'd been listening in on her thoughts.

"Closing," she said. And a monster like that wouldn't be able to steer clear of a wayward shuttle—not in such tight quarters, on such short notice. "Regular traffic seems to be picking up, too. Power's down to forty percent and still falling, by the way."

He sighed. "You'd better call Station Control and arrange for a tow."

"Roger that," she replied, already punching in the priority code. "This is *Riff-Raff* shuttle," she said, as soon as she made contact. "We have a situation here."

"State the nature of your situation, *Riff-Raff* shuttle," a robotic voice intoned.

"Our thrusters are failing. We cannot maneuver. We request an immediate tow."

A maddening moment of silence ensued. She passed the time by glancing from the neon-green blip that was the asteroid-eater to the flashing red power read-out. The shuttle was losing direction as well as speed now. Denny had just set his third sight-line, and his grip on the steering U was white-knuckled. As hard as he tried, though, he could not contain the drift.

The commlink crackled then—Station clearing its voice. "*Riff-Raff* shuttle, your request has been approved. Our calculations have you passing over Service Portal DT-4 in three minutes, seventeen seconds. We will commence towing at that time. Power your vessel down now. Upon touching down at the portal, report directly to Security."

"They're going to fine your ass off for taking this hazard into public space," Jillian gloated, giddy with spite and relief.

"They're going to fine you, and I'm going to watch." Then she reached into an overhead compartment and grabbed a pair of safety helmets. "Which one do you want?" she asked him. "The one with the loose chin-strap, or the one that smells of rancid sweat?"

He scoffed at the offer. "We're just being towed, Jillie."

"A tow beam could shake this heap to pieces," she said.

"Yeah, right."

She didn't try to argue with him. She simply jammed the smelly helmet onto his head. He grumbled, but made no move to take it off.

The viewplate was all Station now—a vast expanse of sculptured metal. At their current velocity, its surface appeared as a blur encrusted with solar collectors and utility towers, cannon bunkers, ducts and cables. As she watched, a portal opened topside like a flower unfurling at high speed. A moment later, a fat band of brilliant blue light came streaking across the void.

The shuttle shuddered as the EM-beam slammed into its underside. An instant later, it began to buck and pitch like a wild thing that was on its way to be broken. Jillian swore. Her seat gave her a series of little squeezes. But Denny just sat there and laughed like a man gone mad.

"W-w-what's s-s-so d-d-damn f-f-funny?" she demanded.

"N-n-nothing," he replied. "J-j-just enj-j-joying m-m-myself."

Crazy bastard, she thought. But she had to admit—the ride wasn't nearly as bad as she'd expected it to be. The bio-plastic seats were absorbing most of the abuse. And at the rate they were being hauled in, they'd be down in record time. Which was funny in a way, since Station would never have allowed a shuttle to come in this fast under its own power. As she watched, they went scudding past the station's outer crust and through the open portal. The altimeter read fifty meters, then forty. She flashed a smile at Denny.

"M-m-must be a Union t-t-tech r-r-running the beam," she joked.

"Un-n-n-ion?"

"Yeah, one w-w-with a c-c-caffeine b-b-break c-c-coming up."

He started to laugh again only to be jarred sober by a bone-rattling shudder. An instant later, an enormous fireball came roaring into the cockpit. It hit them head-on, and kept on going. They both had time to scream before the viewplate exploded.

Chapter 1

DIAMONDS OF LIGHT invaded her sleep, pinging her back from a bottomless dream. She blinked. Darkness fragmented into static. She blinked again, kick-starting a thought: *she was Jillian D'Lange, class-one captain and owner of Zephyr.*

But she was not aboard her ship.

The room was small and off-white, a bare-bones compartment with a sterile glare. A holo-plaque of a comet streaking silver across a field of jet-black hung on the far wall. It was the SU emblem, and the only adornment in sight. The inscription read: *Research, Our Gateway To The Unknown.* So, she surmised, this was a research facility of some kind, probably a hospital.

But why was she here?

She pushed herself upright on her dense-air platform. So far, so good, she thought then. At least, nothing hurt. Then she saw her hands. Instead of spacer-white, they were tawny brown—not just in patches, but all over, fronts and backs and in betweens. It was the most elaborate syntheskin graft that she'd ever seen. As she gaped at herself, thinking what the fuck, she began noticing other things, too. Like: she had no fingernails anymore. And: the veins that had mapped the backs of her hands were gone, too. And her left ring finger, a crooked memento from the first and only time that she'd forgotten to use the rail while moving through a ship in flight, was vector straight now.

These weren't her hands!

But they did what she told them to do! She waggled her fingers—one by one, then altogether, translating her bewilderment into a sign language. Their responsiveness only fanned her confusion, for while she could see them moving, she couldn't feel them. There was no pain, no weakness, no sense of power.

Stars above! What had happened to her?

Her arms were the same color as her hands. So was everything else that she could see: breasts, shoulders, ribcage. She flipped back the bio-plastic coverlet that had pooled around her hips to find more bloody syntheskin. That, and big knees, and a hairless groin, and overly angular feet that only had four toes each. She clenched her teeth, and then her eyelids. A scream cycled furiously through her head.

What was going on here?

And where the fuck was her navel?

As she groped in vain for the memory that would explain her condition, she heard the door to her room whisk open and then shut again. Quicker than thought, she grabbed the coverlet and pulled it all the way up to her neck. Then she leveled a rancorous scowl at the balding, white-smocked man who was striding toward her.

"Hello, Jillian," he said, in a breezy tone. "I'm sorry no one was here when you woke up, but you weren't expected to regain consciousness for another three weeks yet. Personally, I'm delighted. Early revivification is always a good sign."

"Who in hell are you?" she demanded, heartened by the familiar rasp of her own voice. "Why am I here?"

"Charles M. Griffith, senior Bio-Phys Engineer, at your service," he replied, and then twitched her a smug, man-in-the-moon smile. "The Union's best for its own."

"Well, thanks heaps, Charlie," she said "but I don't want your freakin' service. I want answers. What *happened* to me?"

"You don't remember?"

"No, I don't," she said, resisting a sudden urge to jump out of bed and pound this self-important fuckwit to a pulp.

His pale, round face puckered with disappointment, but it was a fleeting thing. A moment later, he turned glib again. "Ah, well, I guess we can't have everything, can we, Jillian? Leastwise, not all at once. But not to worry. Partial amnesia is common in cases like yours. In time, and with a little therapy, you'll get your memory back. And all things considered, you're lucky. Some patients lose everything. Permanently."

"So are you going to tell me why I'm here or not?"

"Of course," he said, wringing his mouth into a patient, forgiving bend that was all condescension. "I was just getting to that." He pulled a hand-ledger from his pocket, then called up her file and began to read. "You came to this facility by Medi-vac on the ninth of February with a stunning array of injuries—"

"How did I get them?"

"All I was told was that you were involved in an accident on Calypso," he replied, frowning at the interruption. "If you want the specifics, you'll have to file a request for an accident report with the proper authorities. Now—as I was saying. When you arrived here, you had third-degree burns over ninety percent of your body. You also had breaks in both legs, a crushed pelvis—"

He rattled on, but she wasn't paying attention. She was dredging her thoughts for a memory that refused to surface. *An accident? What kind?* She hadn't crashed *Zeph*, had she? Pleasepleaseplease don't let it be so. She'd sold her past for a future with that ship. It wasn't just her livelihood. It was her life.

"—broken ribs, a perforated lung, liver and kidney damage—"

She'd remember if something bad had happened to *Zeph*. Wouldn't she?

"—injuries were so grievous, and so extensive, we had no choice but to construct a new body for you—"

Besides, Mr. We-Can't-Have-Everything said that the accident had happened *on* Calypso. That implied an absence of ships. Didn't it?

"—able to sustain your old body long enough to preclude the need for cryostorage. Which was extremely fortunate, for as you may know, cryostorage lowers the already low viability rate for this procedure—"

"Wait." Something horrible had wormed its way into her subconscious while she was worrying about *Zeph*. Now that something was trying to get out. "Back this bus up. Did you say something about constructing a new *body* for me?"

"I did," he replied, as matter-of-fact as an expert witness on the stand. "It was the only way to save your life. And we were told to do that by any means possible."

At that, a trapdoor in her universe snapped open, and she went fallingfallingfalling through it. As she fell, breathless with disbelief, shockwaves reshaped reality. "Cyborg," she whispered. "I'm a freakin' cyborg."

"That term isn't popular around here," Griffith said. "We prefer 'refabricated person'."

Jillian stared at her hands. They looked blurry, unreal, as things often did in a fall. She could've accepted them as prostheses—that seemed reasonable, given the extent of her injuries. She could've accepted the knees, the feet, and the syntheskin, too, because even then she would've still been herself, essentially whole and human. Now she'd never be human again.

"Cyborg," she repeated, perversely clinging to the word.

"Refabricated person," Griffith insisted. "And no ordinary one, either. Here, take a look. I think you'll be pleasantly surprised."

He pulled a small mirror out of his pocket and pressed it into her unready hands. Before she could look away, the reflection caught her attention. She recognized that face: the steely-gray eyes and full lips, the cathedral cheekbones and austere jawline framed by lengths of raven-black hair. No doubt about it—this was her face.

Except for the tawny brown skin.

"A stunning reproduction, wouldn't you say?" Griffith asked then, all but blushing with pride. "Anyone who didn't know better would have to say that this was the face you were born with. Technologically speaking, you're quite a breakthrough for us."

She set the mirror on her lap, glass-side down. Then, desperate for reassurance, even from a fuckwit, she asked, "Is there *anything* of the original me left?"

"Well, there's your brain—of course," he said, adding facetiousness to his list of crimes. "We also managed to save most of your spinal cord and your larynx. Everything else, however, had to be reconstructed.

"But you shouldn't let the extent of your refabrication distress you," he hastened to tell her. "Think instead of the tremendous advantages you have now because of it. Your vision extends into the infra-red, and your hearing borders on the ultra-sonic. You're five times stronger than you were before, and quicker, too. You'll never have to eat again—"

"I liked eating, Charlie," she said. "It was one of my favorite habits."

He gabbled on as if he hadn't heard her. "—never be sick. And think of the decades this has added to your lifespan. Why, with the proper maintenance, you could still be kicking two hundred years from now."

His enthusiasm galled her. She was used to being admired for her looks, her wit, her accomplishments. But this fuckwit saw her only as a *technological breakthrough*— a science project to showcase his Genius and advance his quest for vicarious immortality. She felt demoted, diminished, degraded. She wanted to be more; and much, much less. She willed her titanium-can of a body onto its side, putting its back to its maker.

"I've heard enough for one day, Charlie," she said. "Go away now."

"I understand," he said, in that condescending tone of his that she so despised. "You need some time alone to adjust." She heard him walk to the door, then half-turn like a man pretending to have an afterthought. "Your psych team is off-site for another week yet, but you need to begin therapy right away. So while I normally don't involve myself in this phase of recovery, I'm going to make an exception in your case."

He lingered a moment longer, clearing expect some response from her. When she denied him that satisfaction, he finally got the message and left.

In his absence, she closed her eyes and tried to will herself into an oblivious sleep. But a cyborg guarded that gateway, and would not let her escape.

Dammit! She hadn't asked for this! She didn't want it, either.

She thought about the few living cyborgs that she knew by name: Thomas Farrell, Ivan Duvall, and just plain Honey. They didn't come to Station often, and when they did, they never stayed long. Their constructs were clunkier than hers was, particularly around the joints, and their faces lacked depth and texture. People stared when they walked by, and then gossiped at their backs. How much of *him* is really left, they whispered. And: not worth it. And, of course: *poor bastard*. Jillian had been one of those.

But there were worse bigots than her in the galaxy. The Circe's II Coalition For Human Progress took moral and political exception to cyborgs, and campaigned to keep them away from their property and kids. Other fundamentalist groups shunned them like new-age lepers. And while ground-dwellers were often the worst offenders, the spacer community was by no means free of prejudice. Indeed, many old-timers refused to ship out with a cyborg. If asked why, Targon's name and legacy invariably came up.

Targon the Terror, they called him. After his construction nearly a century ago, he signed on with Gilda, a class-two asteroid-eater. He *seemed* normal, the wags would say later—a little aloof maybe, but then, weren't all cyborgs? How was anyone to know that he had Refabrication-Induced-Madness? Or that one night while in its grip, he would raid Gilda's small-arms locker and murder all his mates, and later, a salvager's reconnaissance crew. Thirty-one people had died before someone managed to put an AP bolt through his skull, the wags recounted. Was it any wonder that some men now thought twice about shipping out with *that kind*?

Resentment flared within her like a sun-spot. The RIMs was a rare, pathological reaction to being ripped out of one shell and spooned into another. It was also a risk that all refabs shared. But dozens of flesh-and-blood spacers had gone nova before and since Targon's time, so why was it still only bad luck to ship with a cyborg?

It was just so freakin' unfair!

And so...*permanent.*

She picked up the mirror that the fuckwit had left behind and studied his rendition of her face. The smile was weak at the corners. The nose was a tad too short. And the skin color was wrongwrongwrong. She hated that most of all, for it would never ever let her forget just how thoroughly, and how intimately, she had been compromised.

An urge to cry overcame her then. But it seemed that Charles M.Griffith hadn't seen fit to equip his technological breakthrough with something as frivolous as tear ducts. She snarled, damning the man for his presumptions, and then hurled the mirror across the room. It shattered against the far wall with a sparkling crash. She closed her eyes to the mess and waited for sleep to carry her back to oblivion.

୧୨

WAKING UP WASN'T the same anymore. Before, it had been a leisurely affair full of stretching and yawning and false starts. Now, it was like flicking a switch. One moment, she was asleep; the next, she was fully conscious. She couldn't tell how long or hard she had slept, either. There was no drool on the pillow or no tangled sheets, no sore muscles or tingling limbs. She had come awake flat on her back: the exact same position she had been in when she shut her eyes. It was depressing—moreso than she would've guessed.

She had roused for a reason, though: there was somebody in the room. She could hear the intruder breathing, in and out, in and out—a slightly congested, mouth-breather's purr.

She was almost sure that it was only Griffith, come to plug her into his pysch-tools, but on the off-chance that it might actually be somebody worth talking to, she cranked her in the direction of the sound. By slow degrees, a man came into view. He was small and wiry, a garden gnome perched on a visitor's pull-out. He had a disposable remote in one hand. His left leg was juking like a jack-hammer. And although his face was hidden by a cheap pleasure vizard, she recognized his slicked-back coxcomb of titanium-plated hair.

Well, color her surprised. Her half-brother had come for a visit.

He called himself Roadkill, which was, he had once explained, the term ancient Terrans had used for flattened, roadside remains. And as he himself conceded, he spent much of his time trying to be as obnoxious as his namesake. Jillian didn't know him well enough to say why. She wouldn't know him at all if he hadn't turned up by her elbow in a moonside bar one night shortly after her mother's death. He'd announced their kinship through a father whom she'd never met, bought her a drink that she didn't need, and then hit her up for a job. Drunk, depressed, and in desperate need of somebody to guide her back to her room, she'd signed him on the spot. That had been five or so years ago, and while there were times when she regretted that bleary event, this was not one of them.

"Hello, RK," she said softly, anticipating his surprise. "I'm back."

"I know," he replied, from behind his vizard, and then held up a hand to forestall further conversation. "Just a tic, OK? You wouldn't believe the boosters on this wawa."

Her tender feelings of a moment ago dissolved, but she gave him his tic and more. Eventually, he heaved a sigh and fingered the remote one last time. Then he brushed the viz away from his face and turned toward her.

"So what's up?" he asked, as if this were just another day.

As usual, he was wearing black-mirrored contact lenses. He said he wore them to protect his allegedly light-sensitive eyes.

Her best guess was that he did it just because he was warped to the core, and enjoyed looking like a skull with stubble. Either way, it was going to take her some time to get reaccustomed to the sepulchral lenses, especially since there was now a miniature image of her centered in each one.

"I'm a cyborg," she replied.

"I know. Griffith gave me your data disks to study—to get rid of me, I think. I don't know why he doesn't like me." He jammed a finger up his nose, wiggled it around, and then wiped his catch on the bottom side of the pull-out. At her sputtered protest, he grinned. "I've got quite a collection going here for some lucky soul. Remind me to show it to you later."

"You'll be happy to know that you can still turn my stomach," she told him, "even though I no longer have one to turn. And now that that's been established, why don't you do something useful and fill me in on a few things?"

"Like what?"

"Start with my accident, since I already know how that story ends."

He sighed—a sound as heavy as surf. His lacquered gaze became elusive. "Are you sure you wouldn't rather see my snot collection?" At her nod, he heaved another sigh and said, "All right then, if you're going to insist.

"It all started when you and Latimer—"

"Denny?" His toothsome image popped into her mind, but nothing else. "Denny was with me?"

"'Fraid so," he replied. "Apparently, you two were on your way to Circe's II in *Riff-Raff's* shuttle when engine trouble forced you to U-E. According to Station Control, you then requested, and received, an emergency tow. The tech running the beam that day said the shuttle was already through the portal and maybe fifty feet away from touchdown when it suddenly exploded."

She expected it all to coming rushing back to her then: the sights, the sounds, the billion different kinds of pain. But her mind remained a stubborn, infuriating blank. The memory was so thoroughly buried, she couldn't even get her imagination around it. She was so frustrated at the moment, she wanted to beat something just to feel it yield to her fists.

"So how's Denny taking all of this?" she asked instead, trying to distract herself from such violent cravings. "Has he come to yet?"

Her half-brother's stubbled face fell to half-mast. "Latimer didn't make it out of cryostorage."

That trapdoor to her universe snapped open again, spilling her into a void of black skepticism and grief. Denny was dead, killed in the same accident that had orphaned her. But it couldn't be. No freakin' way. She would've remembered something like that. She would have. She remembered everything about Denis C. Latimer—leastwise, everything that mattered. He had to be alive. *Hadtohadtohadto.*

Her denials generated drag, which slowed her nosedive to nowhere to a depleted crawl. And as she pulled out of that terrible fall, she looked for grounding from Roadkill. He was watching her as if she were a crack in the patch of ice on which he was standing; and while those black-hole eyes of his gave nothing away, the slight tic in his right cheek betrayed his anxiety.

"There's more, isn't there?" she said.

"It's about *Zephyr*," he replied in a hang-dog tone, and then hastily said, "She's fine, just fine, I swear," as she loosed an outraged shout. "It's just that it's been a horribly expensive eight months."

She shouted again. "I've been out of commission for *eight months?*"

He cocked his head at her like a dog who's trying to make sense of what it's just heard. "Yeah, give or take a few days. Didn't the pinhead tell you?"

"No-o," she replied, stretching the word into two bitter syllables.

"Sorry. Want me to leave you alone while you get over it?"

As tempting as the offer was, a part of her opposed it. Breaking down was a show of weakness, it argued. And weakness didn't inspire confidence. She needed to be strong from here on and hold steady—for her brother, her personnel, and herself. And besides, it added in a wryer tone, if she broke down over each and every casualty from this accident, she'd never get out of dry-dock. So she dismissed the loss of eight months with a flick of her fabricated wrist and then fixed Roadkill with a commanding stare.

"You were saying something about expenses?"

"Yeah, well," he replied, and his leg started juking again, "you know how much it costs to keep a ship at Calypsi. There's docking and maintenance fees, utility surcharges, bread, head, and water debits. I sold the cargo we came in with, but that didn't last, not after taxes, insurance, and Union dues. You gotta believe me, Jill—I tried, I really did. I even took a job hubside at Boomer's. But you know I'm no good with financial stuff—"

"Just get to the point, RK," she said.

"The point is, I fell behind on *Zephyr*'s payments," he said, almost cringing as he blurted the words.

"How far?"

"Three months."

"And what's the bottom line?"

"We have three standard months to cough up the back payments plus compounded interest," he said, less jittery now that he had unloaded the worst of the news. "And this month's payment has to be made *on time*. Failure to comply with one or more of these conditions will result in *Zeph*'s automatic seizure."

The ultimatum slung her into a possessive rage. Repossess *Zephyr*? Uh-uh. No freaking way. They'd already taken eight months from her, and a flesh-and-blood body. She'd fly *Zeph* into a sun before she let them take that away from her, too. And she still had three months to thwart the repo-man. She could do it. She knew she could. All she had to do was—

The door to her room opened then. An instant later, Charles M. Griffith made his entrance. He was carrying a boxful of paraphernalia and nipple-tipped wires. His smile was all for Jillian's face.

"Good morning," he twittered, as he hustled toward her. "And how are we feeling today? A little better, I hope."

"I don't know about her," Roadkill piped up then, "but I'm actually much better. I had terrible gas earlier. Too much beer at Boomer's last night, I reckon. Do the suds hit you like that, too?"

Griffith's smile crumbled like a ton of old brick. "Ah, yes, Mr. Roadkill," he said, in his coldest, most officious tone. "Do forgive me, but I must ask you to leave the room for the next few hours. It's time for Jillian's therapy session."

"Sorry, Charlie," she said then, "but we're going to have to reschedule this gig for a later date. Something urgent just popped up on my calendar."

He loosed a don't-be-silly snort. "You can't leave yet. We need to develop your psychological profile and smooth out any wrinkles that be hiding there."

"I don't have any problems that I can't handle on my own," she said.

"Oh? What about your amnesia?"

"She probably forgot all about that," Roadkill said.

"Shut up," she snapped at him, and then turned her scowl back to Griffith. "From what I've gathered about my little accident, I'd say the less I remember, the better. Now, be a right kind of guy and ping someone for my clothes."

But he just stood there with his boxful of toys and refused to be cowed. "You're not ready to leave."

"Yes, I am," she insisted, trying hard not to snarl. "Look here." She waggled her fingers, flapped her arms, then kicked her heels up under the coverlet. "See? Everything works, you've done a terrific job."

"Of course everything works," Griffith said, all condescension now. "We spent the last two months fine-tuning your physiological responses. But refabrication is a traumatic experience. A few bruises to the psyche are to be expected. We need to nose those bruises out and heal them before they deteriorate into more serious problems. Left uncorrected, the RIM's are lethal, you know."

"Ping someone for my clothes, Charlie," she repeated. "Otherwise, I'll walk out of here as is." She flung the coverlet aside, exposing the unnaturally brown stretch of her body. "After all, this isn't truly me, is it? It's just a sophisticated piece of bio-equipment. And there's nothing indecent about a naked machine, is there?"

His eyes narrowed. His mouth went suddenly flat-line. "That's exactly the sort of reasoning we need to work on, Jillian. And the anger that you're struggling with could be dangerous as well—to others as well as to yourself. Now please, be reasonable. You're not ready."

The hint of genuine concern in his voice left her wavering for a moment, but then she remembered *Zephyr* and all teetering stopped. Her ship came first. Period. End of discussion. So she vaulted out of bed.

As she landed, a strange and most unpleasant sensation overcame her. It was as if gravity was trying to slurp her out of her brand-new shell. She staggered a few steps, then went stock-still and tried to steady herself . A long moment later, the feeling went away.

"Jillian," Griffith said then. He was staring at her with a 'I-told-you-so' stamped into the folds of his doughy face. "Don't do this. Let me do my job."

Resentment crested within her, hot and rich. She let him have it with both barrels. "You had eight months to do your job, Mister," she snarled. "Oddly enough, I now have eight months worth of problems, and only three months in which to clear them all up. So if you really want to help, you'll stay the hell away from me.

"And in the future," she added, as he sputtered her name yet again, "I'll thank you to address me as Captain D'Lange."

She turned her glare to Roadkill, who was studying her with the sort of detached intensity that he usually reserved for porn. "Are you coming with me or what?"

Her brother shrugged, then stood up and started for the door. Griffith blocked his way.

"Talk to her," he said.

"I have," Roadkill replied, "and believe me, you've done a great job." He leaned closer, as if to confide a secret. "She's the same high-handed bitch she always was. I do have one complaint, however," he went on, in the same confidential tone. "It's about her ass. It doesn't jiggle. What's the point if it doesn't jiggle?"

With that, he shouldered past the BPE and then sauntered out of the room. Jillian followed on his heels, but soon found that she could not keep up with him.

Walking was an entirely different experience for her now— as effortless as taking a stroll in space, and twice as disorienting. For everything was so *visual* now. She could *see* her legs working, *see* the hallway growing shorter. But when she closed her eyes, she lost all sense of what was happening. The innocuous play of muscle over bone was gone, as was that burn that came from lactic acid and the warmth that came from friction. She felt weightless; adrift; detached. Vertigo sucked at her seat. She froze, fighting that gyre, and it reluctantly subsided.

Then Roadkill came scurrying out of a room and toward her with a white bundle tucked under one arm. She didn't recognize it as a laboratory smock until he presented it to her with a triumphant, "Ta-da!"

"After all, " he quipped then, "we can't have you scaring away the customers."

Even though she knew that it had been made in jest, the comment offended Jillian nonetheless. She was a cyborg, dammit, not some monster to be covered up and whisked away. If people couldn't bear the sight of her, tough titty—they could look the other way while she passed amongst them. But even as she went to tear the smock up in defiance of such fragile-minded fools, reason came to the rescue. Storming bare-assed across Circe's II was hardly the way to impress customers—fragile-minded or not, it reminded her. And right now, she needed their help more than they needed hers. So she swallowed her gripe and put on the smock. As she did so, a perverse part of her objected to being seen in such a shapeless sack.

"Where to now?" Roadkill asked then.

"To the shuttleport," she replied. "It's time to put *Zephyr* back in business."

Chapter 2

THE RIDE TO the shuttleport took them through the capitol of Circe's II. Odysseus was a perpetually cold, aesthetically challenged city with pop-up architecture, lousy food, and too many people. Much of it reminded Jillian of Denny. Coming up on the right was the club where they'd danced for twelve hours straight on a bet. And three blocks down from that was the shop where he bought all his clothes. He was everywhere, that Latimer: in viz-marts, on the ped-way, even in the thin air. She hunkered deeper into the back seat and tried not to look. Her dearest friend deserved an exclusive mourning, not one stained with other woes.

Up in the forward compartment, Roadkill and their driver were arguing about who was the better actress: Kandy Kross or Besame Belle. Jillian shook her head. This had to be an all-new low-point in her life, she thought—her riding in the back of a public flit that Roadkill had rented with pan-handled credit, listening to two horndogs debate the relative merits of their favorite viz-porn queen.

How far her fortunes had fallen!

Five years ago, she had been sitting sad but quite pretty as her mother's only heir. A comfortable line of credit had come her way, as had WaveDance, the class III freighter that eight generations of D'Lange women before her had been content to command. But Jillian was made of more ambitious stuff. So as soon as she qualified for the loan, she'd thrown tradition to the solar winds and used slow, antiquated WaveDance and the rest of her inheritance as a down-payment on *Zephyr*.

And *Zeph* was worth every credit. Bigger, faster, and better armed than most of the competition, it guaranteed her more first-rate work than she could handle. Denny had called it a credit-generator, the surest thing since white rice.

And now someone wanted to take it away from her!

"Speed it up, driver," she growled. "I haven't got a lot of time."

"Yeah, sure," he replied, and then went back to singing Besame's praises.

The flit skimmed past the city limits and over a maze of solar power stations and water reclamation plants—the industrial outlands. The collectors gleamed shiny black in the moon's long night. The ponds were all capped with a thin scum of ice. Jillian didn't remember the low-tide stink that went hand-in-hand with this scene until Roadkill made a strangled noise and tried to tighten the seal to his door, and by then, it should've been too late. It wasn't, though. She sniffed once and then again, but nothing came through. Her nose, it seemed, was strictly for ornamental purposes. She cursed Griffith for consigning her to such an impoverished world, and then turned around and scorned herself for getting nostalgic about the reek of shit.

The F. F. Waxman Municipal Shuttleport appeared in the distance. She noticed its brilliant blue guide-lights first—as always. She'd grown up on that color, and loved it like she loved the color of her mother's eyes. Then her infra-red vision kicked in and she saw an assortment of shuttles squatting on the tarmac like bizarre prairie-hens. Hers was parked on the port's back side, in the terminally blackened regolith of the public lot. On any other day, she would have been upset to find it there, for the dust wreaked havoc on the shuttle's scrubbers, but today, she was simply eager. As the flit pulled up to the sight, she broke into her first refabricated smile. *This* was the only kind of therapy *she* needed!

She ran up the ramp and up to the hatch, then slapped her hand to the red-eyed security pad. That eye flashed white as it scanned her only to fade back to a baleful red without admitting her into the shuttle. She jeered at herself then: *big freakin' surprise for someone with no fingerprints, aye, dummy?* She had a scathing thought for Griffith, too, for finding so many enduring ways to remind her that she was no longer human.

"I'll program the monitors to respond to your voiceprint as soon as we get back to *Zeph*," Roadkill said, as he reached past her and triggered the lock. "You'll be coming and going in no time."

"Thanks," she muttered, but it galled her to have to depend on somebody else for access to her own property.

Once inside, though, her mood took an abrupt upswing. Had it really been eight months, she marveled, as she made her way through the craft. It all looked the same— an iota less shiny perhaps, but still as new as yesterday. She touched the seats, the walls, and various instruments in passing, trying to catch up with everything by osmosis. With a lover's creamy sigh, she then settled into the cockpit. The bio-plastics in the pilot's chair gave her a little squeeze as if to welcome her home.

"Everything's battened down in back," Roadkill said, as he came striding into the cabin. "We're all fueled up, too, but it's cheap stuff, so—" He pulled to a sudden stop, seemingly surprised to find her behind the U, and then finished the thought in a distracted monotone. "—so don't be surprised if she runs a little rough. Want me to take us up?" he offered then. "After all, it's been a while since you last handled this bird. "

"Thanks," she replied, with a curtness that surprised them both, "but I'm perfectly capable of piloting a simple shuttle. So just take your seat and contact the tower."

"Aye, Capt'n!" he said, mocking her with a snazzy salute. "Right this instant!"

She curled her lips at his impudence, but declined to chew him out for it. Instead, she started the process of bringing the engines up to power. With the flick of a switch, a slow, swelling hum came into being. It was followed by the cycling, subsonic whine of resonators and then the muffled flutter of confined combustion.

"Tower's cleared us for lift-off," Roadkill said then. "We've been assigned to Lane 3C."

"Then let's get out of here."

"Roger that."

Jillian squared her shoulders, then cued the boosters. An instant later, the muffled flutter expanded into a deafening roar. The shuttle began to shudder then—slowly at first, and then with more intensity as it strained toward escape velocity. This shaking confused her. For one terrible moment, she thought it was Denny sitting beside her. *M-m-must be a U-u-union t-t-tech.*

"What was that, Jillie?" Roadkill asked.

"I don't remember," she admitted. "How odd."

"I wouldn't worry about it," he said, with a dismissive shrug. "It's probably just a little bug working its way out of your system. The data disks said that might happen."

"Good to know," she said. And it was. Because until she had *Zephyr* all squared away, she wasn't stopping for anyone—not even herself. "Retract landing gear. Prepare to engage main propulsion unit."

The shuddering intensified. It felt as if some unseen giant were trying to shake the truth out of her. *W-w-what's s-s-so f-f-funny?* Then, as the shuttle punched through the atmosphere's thin upper crust and into the frictionless expressways of cislunar space, the flight went as smooth as a Tuluvean love-song, and she forgot whatever it was that she'd been thinking.

"Leveling off," she said. "Easing into Lane 3C." A moment later, she announced, "We are now Calypso-bound."

"Welcome back, Capt'n," Roadkill said then.

"Roger that," she replied, and broke into a grin.

ↄ

"WHAT'S OUR ETA?" Jillian wondered. "Thirty standard minutes," her brother said, and then cast her an annoyed scowl. "That's the third time you've asked in the last ten minutes. You a little anxious or what?""Something like that," she replied. But in truth, what she was feeling was more like a nameless, sourceless dread. It had been with her ever since Station had come to occupy the whole of the viewplate; and seemed to grow more adamant with every passing klick. *Something was wrong.* She just knew it. She checked her monitors. All systems read green. Minutes later, she checked again. The read-outs remained the same.

"Go back and check the resonators," she told Roadkill. "Something doesn't feel right."

He arched a dubious eyebrow at her, but did as he was told. Moments later, he slung himself back into his seat with a sour hmph. "How's it feel now?"

"The same," she said.

"That's because there was nothing wrong in the first place. You're just rusty."

She dismissed the assertion with a snort. But as Station loomed closer and closer, her anxieties continued to proliferate. They urged her to out race the nameless danger that the monitors couldn't see. She shifted the throttle forward once and then again, but could not escape the sense that something terrible was closing in on them from the rear.

"Helmet," she snapped at Roadkill. "Get your helmet on."

"Since when do we pad up for a door-to-door?" he asked, in an incredulous tone.

"Just do it," she ordered, and then boosted the shuttle's output again. Moments later, she roared past another shuttle as if it were a lowly buoy. That was rudeness on her part, but she didn't care. "Call Station Control and tell 'em we have an emergency here."

"What did you say?"

The intensity of the question struck her suddenly sober, and then left her confused. Had she said something? She couldn't remember. Nor could she remember anything else that she might have been doing. She glanced at her monitors then, meaning to refresh her memory, only to receive another slap. *Shitshitshit!* Was she really going that fast in restricted space? Station Control could buy a whole new squad of robo-cops with the fine for such reckless flying. She hauled back on the throttle— too much, too fast. The shuttle bucked like a first-year flight-school skiff. Roadkill arched a sparse eyebrow at her.

"I guess I'm a little rusty after all," she said, in lieu of an apology.

"I guess," he echoed, righteously snide. "Want me to take it from here?"

"Thanks," she said, "but I think I can manage."

He harumphed. "Then maybe this helmet wasn't such a bad idea."

Although she knew that she'd just earned a fair measure of it, his doubt stung her nonetheless. As if he'd do any better after eight months on a lab-slab, she thought. As if he'd never made a mistake. So she issued her next order with more force than she might have otherwise.

"Just call in and clear us a lane for C sector. And ask for priority," she added, as she knocked the throttle back another notch. "I don't want spend half the day in a holding pattern."

"I'll call," he told her. "But just so you know—we're heading for J sector, not C."

"Why?"

"I had *Zeph* moved there a couple of months ago. The rates were cheaper."

He raised his chin to her then, daring her to find fault with him for that. She could not do so, but the thought of her beautiful ship docked alongside the grunge-heaps of the galaxy made her want to throttle the shuttle back into overdrive and go racing to *Zephyr*'s rescue. She did nothing of the sort, however—and not just because it was terribly illegal. Roadkill's confidence in her had already taken two minor dings during this flight. A third hit, intentional or not, might spook him into doing something rash. Like—reporting those little lapses to Station authorities. Or worse, reporting them to the crew. Or worse still, jumping ship altogether so he wouldn't have to crew for his half-sister the cyborg. All she had left of her old life was her ship, her career, and Roadkill. And for the moment, they were all jumbled together on the lip of a crumbly, man-made cliff. If one fell, the others would go with it, and then—well, sometime later, they'd find her dead in some moonside flop from a self-inflicted AP bolt to the head. And that wasn't the way she wanted to go out. So she continued to throttle down, and when her brother announced that they were clear for sector J traffic, she followed every picayune rule and reg to get there. Then, as she cruised along that mile-long spoke, her ship came into view. It was docked between a garbage scow and a toxic waste tanker. The sight both broke her heart and gladdened it.

"Hail the crew, RK. Let 'em know we're coming in," she said, almost singing the words.

"There is no crew, Jillie," he replied in a half-exasperated tone, as if he were tired of telling her things that would've been obvious to anyone else. "I couldn't afford to pay them, and they couldn't afford to wait, so they signed on with other ships."

Disappointment flared like a stubbed toe within her. Why did coming home have to be so freakin' complicated? "I wish you'd told me this before we came this way," she groused. "The public shuttle-bay is way the hell over on the other side of Station."

"So let it stay there. We won't be needing it today."

As he said this, he tapped a series of commands into his console. Moments later, a hatch in *Zephyr's* side swirled open. That appalled her for many reasons, but she could only put a name to one of them.

"If the insurance drones hear that you've fitted *Zeph* with remotes," she said, "they'll declare us high-risk for piracy. Our rates will sky-rocket. Our customer base will shrink. In no time at all, you'll be eating garbage out of the bins along with your buddies from Boomer's. Does that sound good to you?"

"I've heard worse," he tried to joke, and then immediately turned defensive. "But what else was I supposed to do for eight months—hire some security? Pay for long-term shuttle parking? Or maybe you think I should've stayed on the ship, hey? Well, forget it, Jillie-Jill. I did the best I could with what I had, and believe me, it wasn't much."

"I believe you, RK," she hastened to assure him. "I do. And although I haven't had a chance to tell you so yet, I truly appreciate everything you've endured for me and mine. All I'm saying is, now that I'm back, the remotes have to go. Is that clear?"

"Of course it's clear," he said then. "I'm not an idiot."

She guided the shuttle through the open hatchway then, and parked it squarely on its heat-shielded pad. An instant after she touched down, a smile spread across her face. Home at last! She could not wait to see the rest of the ship.

"Finish powering down the engines," she told Roadkill, "and then secure the craft. I'm going to tour the premises."

"Maybe you ought to begin with your quarters," her brother was quick to suggest. "You've got a serious backlog of work waiting for you there. The sooner you start on it, the sooner you'll finish. Here—" He tapped another command into his console. "—I'll turn the life-supports on for you. By the time you get there, the cabin will be all cozy and warm, just the way you like it."

"I don't have the capacity to enjoy ambient temperature anymore," she said, in a factual, flat-line tone. "And I won't be content until I've seen my bridge. Meet me there when you're done here."

He sputtered a word that sounded suspiciously like "Shit!", and then went to work at an energized pace. She shook her head, refusing to waste precious brain-power on the futile task of figuring him out, and then made her way out of the shuttle. A moment later, she found herself at the foot of the ramp, wondering what was so different. The bay still looked like the inside of a big metal blister. And as far as she could tell, Roadkill hadn't hocked any of the equipment for flit-fare. Then it hit her: the tang of burnt hydrocarbons was missing. Not gone, for she knew that *Zeph*'s scrubbers couldn't have cleared every trace of exhaust from the air already. She just couldn't smell or taste it anymore. It was funny in a sad sort of way, how much she wanted those senses back. She felt so isolated without them. But even as her homecoming mood started to decay, a tougher part of her stepped in to stop the slide.

"That's just the way it is now," she told herself, in a voice that sounded very much like her mother's. "So get over it already."

She moved on then, out of the shuttle bay and down the corridor. As she walked, she soaked up random details: the shiny beginnings of a path that she and her people were scuffing into the plasti-steel floor; a burnt-out runner-light; the crooked vent-cap over the engine room door. She wondered how many times she'd come this way without noticing these things, or if perhaps she *had* noticed them but simply couldn't remember. Just how partial was partial amnesia?

As she closed in on the lift, a sudden patter of footsteps called Jillian out of her thoughts. She came about, expecting to find Roadkill on her refabricated heels, but he was just now rounding the corner at the other end of the hall. Then she noticed that he was moving at an unusually brisk clip. He was also halfway out of his perpetual slouch. Her first thought was that he needed some kind of help.

"Is something wrong?" she said.

"Nope," he replied, slowing back to his usual shuffle as he closed the gap between them. "I was just on my way to the bridge. Thought you'd be there already."

"I'm headed there now," she said. "Did you finish stowing the shuttle already?"

"Oh, yeah. I got that down to a science now."

She summoned the lift. When it arrived a moment later, her brother held the door for her and then manned the control panel. "You want to check out the other decks before you go up? It's been a while."

"Bridge, please."

He pushed a tab. The lift shot upward. At that moment, he broke into a grin that easily qualified as desperate. "Look, Jillian," he said. "I didn't expect you back quite this soon. So if things aren't exactly as you left them, don't—"

The lift glided to a stop. The doors parted. Jillian stepped onto the bridge only to let out a horror-stricken shout.

The captain's station seemed to be ground zero. It had a thermal nap-sack slung over its back, several pieces of clothing dangling from its arms, and an ankle-deep ring of trash around its base. From there, the damage radiated outward in all directions: trails of empty food wrappers and discarded vizards; intermittent piles of dirty plates and laundry. The comm station was overrun, as was surveillance. Her truncated sense of smell seemed like a blessing now.

"After the crew quit," Roadkill said then, "I moved up here and cut life-supports to the rest of the ship to save money. It's really not as bad as it looks."

She had to agree with him there. It wasn't bad. It was infuriating. This was her ship, dammit, and he'd jerked off all over it. She wanted to shake him by the nape until something snapped. She wanted to bury him in his own crap. And while she knew that she was overreacting, a part of her wanted to slake these violent cravings just the same. She did no such thing, however. Instead, she kept her back to him and said, "Clean it up." Then, as he began scrambling after trash, she waded toward her chair. There, she sat down behind the crescent of her station and ran a hand over the plexus of equipment that defined her life. Her anger subsided immediately.

Hello, she thought. And: good to see you again. I've missed being here.

But the peace of mind that she attained through this was a very short-lived thing. The next thing she knew, she was already making a list out of all the work she had to do. And at the top of that list was hiring a new crew. She bit back a groan as she glanced at the array of deserted stations. Replacing one or two people would've been easy enough, for she had a good rep among junior techs—Union or otherwise. But a complete crew? Sweet, suffering mother! Where was she going to find the time?

By starting now, she told herself then. There would be time later for soaking up the atmosphere. So she vacated the chair that she'd been in such a hurry to fill, and then headed back toward the lift. Somewhere along the way, she abandoned her hard feelings for Roadkill, too.

"I'll be in my quarters if you need me, RK," she told him in passing. "But you'd better have a damn good reason for disturbing me. When you're done here, go and rest up. Tomorrow, you've got some recruiting to do."

An evil smile curved across his face. "Finally," he said. "Fresh meat."

☙

JILLIAN TOOK THE lift to sub-level one, and went directly to her quarters. As she fed her access code to the wall-grid, an image zipped through her head at light-speed: *Denny, half-dressed, seated at his desk.* It felt more like a premonition than a flashback. But the main cabin was empty when she entered it, and no one came striding out of the head. She was quite alone. She waited for the pang that should've accompanied that realization, but such pains were as beyond her as Den was.

The thought lapsed into melancholia as she prowled around the room. Everything was just as she remembered it: the electric blue safety webbing over her double bunk; her faux-wood lockers, sealed and secured; the neo-modern Goci holo-print above her desk. So how come she felt like an intruder? Did flesh make that much difference?

She was standing in front of her desk-site now. The indicator light by the pull-out lip told her that she had messages. "Ah, yes, the moment we've all been waiting for," she droned, and then slid the desk out of the wall. As soon as it was free, her keeper popped up, and chaos started scrolling down the screen— outdated shipping schedules and Union notices, business inquiries, voided contracts, and less-than-friendly reminders of payment past due. There was also an eight-month-long jumble of receipts, invoices, and personal mail. She cursed Roadkill for leaving her with such a mess, but immediately retracted the thought. Not his fault, she reminded herself. No one's fault. And no one to fix it but her.

So she pulled up a stool and went to work. And by the time she was done sorting through the flotsam of her shuttle-wrecked life, she had a better idea of how the next three months were going to be: all work, no play, and very little sleep. And *that* was only if she managed to scrape together enough business. After being out of commission for so long, she had no idea what kind of a client-list she had left. She scrolled through her directory, thinking to ping the top two or three on that list before they went home for the day. Then, as she went to switch her keeper to communi-mode, she caught sight of the chronometer. It told her that ten hours had passed—nine of them without her knowing.

The discovery rankled her. In the past, she'd known that it was time to quit when her stomach grumbled or her bladder cramped or that floating pain in her left knee kicked up. Now, it seemed, she could go on and on—just like a freakin' machine.

She snarled, rejecting the thought, and then shoved her desk back into its slot. It was too late to place those calls now anyway, she told herself. And unlike a machine, she didn't have to shut down until she was needed again. So she prowled around her quarters again, a restless search for distraction. The next thing she knew, she was standing in front of the larger of her lockers—the one that had a full-length mirror attached to the backside of its door. The old Jillian wanted to have another, closer look at herself. The new Jillian couldn't refuse. Despite her mood, though, she laughed at what she saw—a ragged caw of surprise. She had forgotten about the lab-smock. Its once starchy panels were wilted now, lending her the aspect of badly used goods. Had she really stormed down the streets of Odysseus like this?

Nothing indecent about a naked machine.

Her amusement withered. Before her courage could fail, too, she stripped off the smock and studied her reflection. This was what the psychologists called shock treatment, she supposed. Or was it habituation—the gradual deadening of a nerve by overexposure to harsh stimuli? She shrugged then. They could call it a blow-job, so long as it worked. And it did seem to help, leastwise to a point. The hands and feet and knees didn't bother her as much anymore. Neither did all of that syntheskin, though she still intended to keep most of it covered up. But that face—well, that was still a problem. Its near-perfection only made the tiny flaws more glaring.

She looked away from her facsimile. As she did so, she noticed the old-fashioned photograph that was lodged in the mirror's upper left corner. The man and woman that it portrayed were dressed in ponchos, ten-gallon hats, and gun-belts: garments from Terra's mythical Old West. They were standing arm-in-arm like the best of friends, and grinning obscenely at the unseen photographer. She was the woman. And that would-be cowboy beside her was DennyDennyDen.

Grief broke within her then: a dry, cerebral eruption. Some might've considered that a mercy, but not her. She wanted the tears. She wanted the heartache. She wanted to feel *human* again. So she reached into the locker and grabbed another memento from that long-ago fantasy camp: a two-liter glass jug of genuine gold tequila. She'd promised Denny that they'd drink it together. And so they would. Sort of. She twisted the cap off, then offered a toast to his picture.

"To you, lover," she said, and raised the bottle to her lips.

She remembered the blistering smell of mescal, and a taste like bitter fire, so when the liquor coursed down her throat like a shot of heavy water, she felt cheated once again. But that didn't stop her from taking another swig.

"For you," she said this time.

A tingle crept into her head. An illusion of warmth came with it. So, she mused, she could still get drunk. It hit her faster now, too. She smiled, then took another drink. At the moment, getting drunk seemed like the human thing to do.

An image came to mind then: *her naked on some floor, back arching to the rough thrill of chapped lips and callused hands.* She felt her nipples harden and her crotch go wet. Her hand strayed to her breast—an auto-erotic reflex. But cyborgs, it seemed, didn't need nipples. And when she slid her hand further south, down the slope of her navel-less belly and into the vee between her legs, she found she had no holes, either, fore or aft, just a tiny duct that leaked a drop of waste water when she probed it. Yet she was undeniably aroused. She could still feel those hands on her, fueling phantom excitement. Was that all she was to be allowed, she wondered: ghost feelings that she could neither counter nor control? That was just too fucking cruel.

She glared at her reflection now: at the bouncy breasts and their tattooed areolae; those grip-me hips; that impostrous face. They were all a lie to appease a fuckwit's sense of aesthetics! She would've been better off with a cruder form—something that wouldn't forever mock her with memories of what she once was and would never be again. If she ever got her hands on Griffith, she'd send him straight to the refabrication factory. And if he qualified for a penis, she'd find a way to make sure that it was very, very small.

Shitshitshit! How she hated being a cyborg!

She shut the locker with a savage kick, then staggered off to bed. She was asleep before her head hit the pillow.

෮

A STEADY PINGING snatched Jillian from her fade-away

dreams. The next thing she knew, she was standing next to her desk with the keeper switched to communi-mode— audio only. Her reply was as churlish as the thrumming that had taken up residence in her frontal lobe.

"What now?"

"Good morning to you, too," came her brother's maliciously cheerful reply. "You have a call from Circe's II."

"Take a message."

"It's Barim." He paused to let that little nugget sink in, and then added, "Shall I patch him through to your room?"

"Negative." She had a good idea as to why the president of the Space-Worker's Union wanted to have a word with her. And if there was ever a conversation that needed some prep-time on her part, this was certainly it. "Make my excuses, then ask him to call back in an hour."

"Be glad to, Capt'n."

"And RK—"

"Yes, Capt'n?"

"Be polite. No matter what else he may be, he's still president of the SU. And right now, we can't afford to pull the tiger's tail. Understood?"

"That's a roger," he replied, in that sweetly reasonable tone that always made her nervous.

In the ensuing silence, she shuffled into the head for a round of Nutri-tabs, water, and aspirin. Then, as the thrumming in her brain subsided into a fragile pulsing, she went looking for an outfit to wear. So, she mused, as she rifled through her locker, she was to have the executive treatment. Fuckwit or not, Griffith had pull. Too bad he didn't know that she and the head of the SU didn't get along.

Barim had been in office for over four decades now; and in that time, he'd steered a union with declining enrolment, lousy benefits, and low morale out of a potentially fatal slump and into one of the most lucrative eras in its history. The new police cruisers, with their massive fire-power and cutting-edge ship-to-ship communication systems, were a good measure of just how much the union's fortunes had improved. But while Jillian had no quarrel with Barim's success, she did take exception to his methods. He encouraged people to do things his way— the *SU* way. And when encouragement didn't work, he wasn't above harassment. She'd gone several heated rounds with him over her hiring of Roadkill, who was devoutly non-union. And the fact that she'd bought *Zephyr* instead of leasing a ship from the union's fleet was still a sore point between them.

Oh, well, she thought with a shrug. Those were the breaks. And she'd take *Zeph* over Barim any day.

She decided on a uniform then: her captain's dress-blues, with matching gloves and boots. The suit was high-collared, with full-length sleeves and old-fashioned slacks. It had been much too conservative for the old Jillian, who had only worn it once, and only then to please her mother. But the new Jillian craved a lower profile. The less syntheskin showing, the less questions raised—and the less she'd have to answer. And that was her best chance of getting back to business as usual. So she dressed—not for Barim, but for *Zephyr*. And when she was done, she combed her artificial hair and cleaned her artificial teeth and then headed for the bridge.

"A tad overdressed, aren't we?" Roadkill said, as she made her entrance.

"Just because you feel compelled to dress like a beggar doesn't mean that I have to," she replied, and then gave the bridge a critical once-over. All of the trash was gone now, and every bit of chrome had been restored to its former high gloss. "Looks good in here," she said, as she settled into her chair. "Let's keep it that way."

"Anything you say, Capt'n," he said, with an insincere smirk. And before she could take him to task for that, a sharp ping from the comm station distracted them both. "I'll give Barim this much," he said, as he ID'ed the call. "He's a punctual old fart. You want it over there?"

"Yes, thanks." She raked her fingers through her hair—an

old habit that no longer possessed the tactile power to soothe her. "Audio and visual."

"Coming through now," he said. And all at once, an image swarmed onto her station's utility screen.

Barim's facade was a study in contrasts: a generous forehead and a stingy mouth; ice-blue eyes and florid cheeks; thick brown hair that horseshoed his thin-skinned crown. "Captain D'Lange," he said, in a honeyed baritone, one of his subtler assets. "Your tech told me that you were indisposed earlier. I trust it was nothing serious."

"Nothing life-threatening, Mr. President," she assured him, with what she hoped was disarming candor. "It was simply a matter of getting back to a normal routine. I've been out of commission for a while, you know."

"I know," he said bluntly. "In fact, that's the reason I'm calling. Charles Griffith, the BPE in charge of—"

"I know who that mother-puffer is."

"Then you also know that he has some significant reservations about your current psychological profile. 'Repressed' was one term that he used. 'Ill-adjusted' was another. I want you to return to our facility for therapy."

"There's nothing wrong with me," she said. Then, as his forehead bunched into a range of contrary ridges, she hastened to add, "OK, I'll admit it—I've been a bit cranky these past few days. But I think you'd be cranky too if you woke up one day only to find that someone had repo-ed your body overnight. Now that I've had some time to get used to the deal, though, I'm ready to live with it.

"Does that sound ill-adjusted to you?"

"I'm not qualified to be a judge of that," he said, without inflection. "Griffith is. And you owe him and the union the chance to make your mind as sound as your body. A lot of hard work and SU credit went into your refabrication, you know," he went on, lecturing her now. "You're practically indistinguishable from anyone else on the street."

His attempt to prick her conscience jabbed her anger instead. "I don't spend much time on the street, so I don't know why I was tapped to receive such lavish treatment. But I do know this much, Mr. President: medical expenses are covered by union dues, and I'm currently all paid up. So I don't owe the SU a freakin' thing."

"That's a rather selfish attitude."

"I'm sorry," she said, a concession to the warning she read in his narrowed eyes, "but that's the way it has to be for now. My ship is three months shy of being confiscated, and—"

"You were the one who insisted on buying instead of leasing."

"Thanks for the reminder," she said, tossing him a smile that was as tight as a fist. "And while I'd love to sit here and rehash the rest of my failings with you, I'm afraid I've already made other commitments. I'll take your request under advisement and get back to you at a later, unspecified date. *Zephyr* out."

"Wait," he said, before she could sever the link. His angry flush was at odds with his conciliatory tone. "I need your help." When she didn't respond, he added, "You'd be doing Denis Latimer a favor as well as yourself."

Now there was a teaser she couldn't ignore, no matter how much she wanted to be done with this call. "Denny's dead. How is therapy for me going to help him?"

Her screen froze for a micro-second: Barim switching to a more secure channel. Then his image licked its sparse lower lip and said, "Station investigators found evidence of a bomb amidst the wreckage of his shuttle. Their guess is that it was meant to go off while you two were en route to Circe's II. In essence, engine trouble saved your life."

It took her a moment to make the connection, and when she did, it hit her like an electric current. All of a sudden, she felt confused; short-circuited. Who would want to kill her?

"Since Latimer was one of us," Barim went on, "Station handed the investigation over to my people. We didn't learn much else from the physical evidence, but one thing was clear: whoever made that bomb had access to union security explosives."

"It doesn't make sense," she complained. "Who'd want to kill Denny?"

"It's my belief that Latimer suspected someone in the union of criminal activity," he said then, as stiff-faced as an Odyssean telecaster. "It is also my belief that he was murdered for that suspicion.

"Why were you two going to Circe's II that day?"

"I don't remember," she said.

"Where were you going?"

"I don't remember that, either," she said, and then brightened as a ridiculously easy solution presented itself to her. "But why don't you give Sam Quackenbush of Denny's *Riff-Raff* a ping? He might be able to tell you. He and Den were like family."

Barim's perpetually red cheeks flushed even redder. "Quackenbush got drunk the night Latimer died and drowned in his own vomit. And none of Latimer's other crewmen could tell us much. Trust me, Captain: Security has spent the last seven months exploring every available avenue. Nathan Ross is overseeing the case personally. But we're still no closer to finding the culprit. Our one remaining hope is you. We need to know what you know."

The headache that had been simmering on the fringes of her awareness bubbled back to a slow boil. In the midst of its sullen percolations, she thought she heard a voice say, *"Barim could be part of the problem."* Her surprise must have registered on her face, for the SU president reacted immediately.

"Is there a problem, Captain?"

"No, thanks, everything's fine," she said. But all of a sudden, having these little memory spasms exorcised didn't seem like such a bad idea. "So how long would this therapy take?"

"A few months maybe, a year at most. Griffith can't say for sure. That's why you have to start right away."

"A year?" Her resistance to the idea stiffened again. "And what about my ship in the meantime?"

"The SU credit union can arrange a hardship loan fore you," he said then, with a confidence that bore the impression of documents already signed and sealed. "Minimum interest, deferred payments, guaranteed for as long as you need the credit."

"That's it?"

"Legally, I can't offer you anything else."

She let out a short, incredulous laugh. "So when everything's been done and said, you get what you want, and I get another creditor clamoring for my ship. That's not what I'd call a positive incentive."

His image went suddenly stiff. "You'd have the satisfaction of knowing that you helped a friend."

"Maybe," she replied, and then pinched the bridge of her nose in an effort to cut off the thrumming in her head. But the old trick didn't work anymore. Her mind and her body were now two separate things. "But maybe not. Den might not have said anything to me that day. Or, knowing us, we talked about lunch and sex and any number of other things that had nothing to do with anything or anyone but us. I might not know what you want me to know."

Barim might be part of the problem.

"I can't take that chance."

"I'm sorry, Mister President, but it's not your chance to take. And I'm not about to risk losing *Zephyr* on the basis of a mere maybe. You'll have my cooperation, but only *after* I've finished putting my debts in good order."

He shunted his frustration into a smoldering stare. "I can't compel you to do the right thing," he said, "but I do have other options at my disposal. Don't force me to use them."

She bared her teeth in a grin that had nothing to do with humor. "As always," she said, "it's been a pleasure chatting with you, Mister President. Give my best to Nate. I'd do it myself, but I've got work to do."

"I wouldn't be so sure of that," Barim replied, and then severed the connection.

The image winked out, leaving a solid gray utility screen behind. She stared at it for a moment, then swiveled toward the comm station. Roadkill was hunched low in his chair, apparently engrossed with his hangnails.

"I know you were listening," she drawled, "so you can quit the innocent act."

He looked up immediately. His grin both mocked and admired her. "Weren't you the one who told me not to pull the big kitty's tail?" he wondered. At her nod, he snorted. "I guess you wanted all the fun for yourself, hey?"

"If you think that was fun," she growled, "then you're even more twisted than I'd imagined."

He waggled his eyebrows like a redneck acknowledging an off-color compliment, but then waxed suddenly somber. "What do you think he'll do?"

"I don't know," she admitted. "And I don't want to stick around long enough to find out. So get moving, brother mine. I'm giving you just three days to round up a new crew. I know that doesn't give you a lot of time to pick and choose," she added, as he opened his mouth to protest, "but I went through the SU's most recent personnel listings last night and there seems to be plenty of juniors eager for work. I made a file of the best of them; it's in your wiz. That should facilitate the selection process.

"And while you're gone, I'll drum up some business."

"Does the first one done win a prize?" he joked.

"Will a three-month reprieve from destitution do?"

"Could be worse," he supposed with a shrug. Then he oozed out of his chair and shuffled over to the lift. "See you in three," he said, as the doors opened for him. "Don't wait up."

A moment later, she found herself alone with a heap of work to do and a headache that wouldn't quite go away.

Chapter 3

"YOU HAVE REACHED the private offices of Margaux Seville," a mechanical voice said. "State your name, and the nature of your call."

"This is Captain Jillian D'Lange," Jillian said, trying hard not to growl. "Tell the lady I'm calling about business."

"One moment, please. I'll see if she's available."

Jillian rolled her eyes. She'd been placing calls for almost three days straight, and was now thoroughly fed up with the consistent prissiness of robo-secretaries. Then again, she was fed up with just about everything at the moment—life, the universe, and fuckwits everywhere. And to make matters worse, all of that frustration and ire was accumulating in her frontal lobe. She could almost feel it bulging against her plasti-steel skull. It was a most distracting sensation.

After a noticeably long pause, an image finally appeared on Jillian's utility screen. Margaux Seville was a dainty woman with warm blue eyes and a crown of fiery red hair, but she exuded nothing but frost today. And her thin line of a mouth was crimped, as if she were keeping something unpleasant in check.

"Hello, Maggie," Jillian said, trying to sneak past these barriers. "Long time, no see. How's every little thing?"

"I thought I knew," the lady replied, in a voice as distant as her expression. Then she waxed sardonic. "I must confess—I didn't expect to see you again. Or leastwise not a 'you' that's so easily recognizable. The union did well by you. You must be grateful."

"Is that a supposition or a command?"

Margaux shrugged, a gesture that seemed to gall her as it did Jillian. That was a bad sign, Jillian thought, and part of a worse trend. There seemed to be no point in trying to tip-toe her way into a deal here, so she decided to switch to bluntness instead.

"I get the impression that you know what I want," she said, "and that you're not going to give it to me."

Margaux's only response was another shrug.

"Dammit, Maggie! It's me, Jillie-Jill—Myla's daughter. I've spent the last three days asking old friends for work, and all I've gotten for my trouble is the same stony look that you're giving me now. If I don't get some business in the next day or two, I'm going to lose *Zephyr* and everything else that matters to me. My mother helped you and Seville Exports through a rough patch a few years back. Won't you return the favor? Give me a chance to fight for what's mine."

A crack appeared Margaux's rigid facade. Jillian scrambled to widen it.

"Look. I know I'm putting you on the spot, and I'm sorry. But you have to know that I wouldn't do it if I had any other choice. Help me out here, Maggie," she urged. "If nothing else, at least tell me why I've been made *persona non grata* all of a sudden." She widened her eyes in appeal. "Is it because I'm a cyborg?"

"I'm sure there are a few fools out there who'd rather not hear from you for that reason," Margaux said peevishly. "But I'm not one of them. I think you know that."

"Then tell me what's going on."

The woman wavered for a moment longer, then abruptly pulled out the stops that had been holding her back.

"It's Barim," she admitted, in a tone rich with disgust. "I received a fly-by from his people three or maybe four days ago. And while the language used was beautifully ambiguous, the message was all too clear: If I assign you a contract, the SU will boycott Seville Exports." She leaned back in her chair then—as if to distance herself from Jillian again. The lines that fanned from the corners of her eyes were the stuff of hard decisions.

"This isn't like the old days when I could get by with a single freighter in my service, Jill. I've got a dozen captains working for me now, not to mention dockhands, shuttle pilots, and a host of other miscellaneous employees that all belong to the union. If they were to walk out on me, my competitors would be cracking my bones for the marrow within the week. I'm sorry, Jillie. I truly am. But whatever you did to piss Barim off, you did very well. And I can't jeopardize an entire company by hiring you, no matter whose daughter you might be.

"I can, however, float you a loan," she added in a rush, as Jillian went stiff with disappointment. "Enough to stay ahead of your payments, plus change to live on. And you wouldn't have to worry about repaying it until your financial situation improves."

Jillian was tempted to sneer at that. She didn't want some chicken-shit loan. She wanted cargo in her holds and a contract in her hand and more of the same waiting for her at the next stop. But since allies were as scarce as moon-water these days, and since she might actually need some hard, quick credit when it came time to reboot, she thanked her mother's oldest friend with a civil tongue and then let her off the hook.

"I have to go now, Maggie," she said. "You dared more than anyone else for me. I won't forget that."

"Give me a ping if you change your mind about the loan," Margaux replied, and then abruptly severed the link.

An instant after the utility screen went blank, Jillian's refabricated upper lip curled up in a snarl. So, she thought, Barim was trying to blacklist her, was he? Not just trying, either, but succeeding with a swiftness that left her dizzy. She'd never had cause to think about how much power that old bastard might own until she saw Maggie paralyzed in his grip. Her mother's old friend had built Seville Exports out of moon-dust and sweat, and was not a woman easily daunted. Yet Barim had cowed her with a piddling fly-by. That made Jillian mad. So did Mr. President's strong-arm tactics. If it didn't bend his way, it had to be broken—that was his unwritten motto.

KathleenH.Nelson

And Jillian wasn't bending. There were still other options available. There had to be.

In her mother's heyday, she would've had no problem finding customers who, for one reason or another, weren't interested in accommodating the SU. These days, though, the only independent operators left in settled space were those who transported hazardous wastes, high explosives, and the like—work considered too risky and low-paying by most union members. There were also a few worlds that Barim hadn't yet roped into the union fold, but those tiny havens were usually closed to outsiders.

She wondered how her new crew was going to feel about hauling toxic sludge for a credit-strapped cyborg.

Everything about that thought appalled Jillian. But from where she was standing now, it looked like her only other option was to chuck her law-biding life and go rogue. And that was no option at all. She came from a long line of hard-working women who believed that pirates should be exterminated on sight. Besides, she added wryly, given Barim's special interest in her, she'd probably get caught her first time out. She'd lose *Zeph* for sure that way, *and* do substantial time in a high-g penal colony. Her mother's ghost would haunt her forever.

As if in response to that thought, the lift doors whisked open. She started at the sound, then swiveled around in her seat. An instant later, Roadkill came staggering onto the bridge. His flightsuit was ripped at the throat and knees; the front of it was spattered with dark brown bloodstains.

"Knock, knock," he said, in a tone as rubbery as his knees. "Anybody home?" Then, as she came rushing to his side, he broke into a drunken grin. "I thought cha migh' be here."

Up close, she saw that the right side of his jaw was purple and swollen beneath its three-day growth of stubble. Old blood crusted the rim of one nostril, too. Only his eyes, shiny and all-black, showed no signs of abuse.

"Wanna hear my report?" he asked, as she ushered him into the nearest seat.

"I can hardly wait," she said. "By the look of you, the news is either very good or very bad. Which is it?"

"No good a'tall," he said, looking as sad as a black-velvet clown. "I started at the Union Hall down on Circe's II jus' like you tol' me to, but nobody there was innerested in talking jobs with me—not even the downy-cheeked juniors with zero experience. I didn't think much of it at the time cuz I've never been too popular with that crowd, but the same thing happened when I came back to Station and started cruisin' some of the better spacer hang-outs. I spent two whole days chasing down people who weren't there when I found them."

"So where'd you get that?" she asked, glancing at the bruise on his jaw.

"Boomer's," he said, and then loosed a belch that seemed to leave him stunned.

She should've known, she told herself. Boomer's was his favorite watering hole. It was also the vilest dockside dive in this sector of space, an unwashed armpit of a place where smugglers, sexual deviants, and drunks were considered high-class clientele.

"What happened?"

"I met this tech named Archie, who'd just lost his job on Vector—I forget why, some misunderstannin' between him and his captain. Anyway, he said he'd sign with us so long as we were pullin' out soon. I was all set to order him a welcome-aboard drink when this big guy with the hairiest knuckles I ever saw sat himself down at our table and asked Arch if he was crazy. When Arch denied it, the guy said, and I quote, '*Then why in hell do you want to crew for a cyborg bitch with mental problems?*' At which point, I hauled back and pasted the troll in the chops. People can say whatever they want about my sister, but *nobody* insults my captain. Leastwise, that was my thinking at the time. I changed my mind halfway through the pounding that Super-Knuckles then treated me to.

"Anyway, I woke up on the floor of a public toilet stall a

couple of hours ago. I don't know what happened to Arch." He rubbed his jaw then, as if to massage the pain there away, then added, "You gonna make me go out again?"

"No," Jillian replied—a distant, scooped-out sound. And at the moment, that's exactly how she felt—like a public urinal on the other side of Station, there to be pissed on by Barim and his proxies whenever they pleased. They'd hosed her down good this time, too. She'd never be able to assemble a crew while rumors about her sanity were being circulated. *And* enforced. That troll had probably been trailing Roadkill all along to drive away those candidates who were too drunk or desperate to be discouraged by mere scuttlebutt. She'd give Mister President one thing: he was a thorough bastard.

"Jillie," Roadkill gurgled. "*Zeph's* moving."

Zephyr wasn't, but he was—a slow, side-to-side wobble. His face was turning a bilious shade of green. She helped him out of his chair, then scooped him up and into her arms as his knees started to buckle. It took her a moment to realize that she was holding him. There was no strain, no sense of encumbrance, just the negligible fact of his weight. It was a strange feeling. Very strange.

"Put me down," her brother mumbled then. "I kin walk."

A moment later, he went limp and started to snore.

She carried him all the way to the infirmary. But while she didn't mind taking care of one of her own, what she really wanted to do was go out and find some stranger to hurt.

❧

JILLIAN SAT AT her desk and scowled at her keeper's screen. It was blankblankblank: no messages. No hope. No one wanted any part of her, not even the toxic sludge people. She sipped from a drink—her second already. The first one had disappeared without her noticing. As she sipped, the tequila worked on her like a massage, loosening the network of anger and tension that had a choke-hold on her mind. The pressure didn't completely dissolve—she'd need Barim's total capitulation for that, or perhaps a good braining. But at least she could think about her predicament without flying into a rage.

Not that there was that much to think about anymore. She'd rehashed her pitiful options a thousand times in the two days since Roadkill had returned from his disaster of a recruiting trip. And in the end, she always came to the same conclusion: have the stupid therapy, it was better lose *Zephyr* later than sooner. But dammit, she didn't want to make it that easy for Barim. She wanted him to fume and curse and fret over his decisions. She wanted him to be miserable—just like she was. Perhaps she ought to take Maggie up on that loan after all, if only to prolong the old bastard's wait.

The meanness of the thought startled her. Had she always been this spiteful? Or was she simply rising to the occasion? She couldn't remember.

And oh, how that rankled! She was *so* freakin' tired of those patches of glare ice on her neural pathways. She concentrated with all her might, straining for a melt-down or a breakthrough: whichever would set her free faster. But nothing came of it. She still had no clue as to why Barim was pressing so hard.

"Dammit, Denny," she growled. "What in hell did you get me into?"

Just then, her keeper pinged. She took another sip of tequila, then responded with a surly, "What?"

"There's a call for you," Roadkill replied.

"Who is it?" she said, and despite her mood, some incorrigibly stubborn part of her insisted on hoping for pay-dirt.

"Nathan Ross."

"Oh."

Nathan Ross was Chief of SU Security. The Torpedo, some spacers called him, because he was good at search-and-destroy. Jillian didn't know him all that well, but they weren't strangers. She had spent a couple of three-days with him back in her WaveDance years. It had been a casual alliance—

decent sex between consenting adults, and a friendly goodbye in the morning. They had not parted, *per se*, but simply gone their own ways.

"You want me to make your excuses?" Roadkill asked then. "I have a couple of new ones that I'm dying to try out."

"No, I'll talk to him," she decided, even though she had no doubt that the Chief of Security was only calling to accept her surrender. At this point, she welcomed the chance to argue with someone other than herself. "Patch him through to my room."

Then, because he was the union's top cop, and because what she did on her own time was nobody's business but her own, she set her drink on the floor. An instant later, Ross's image came streaming onto her screen.

His face was fuller than she remembered, and his neck getting thick, but even so, he was still a fine-looking man. Laugh-lines added depth to his piercing hazel eyes. The streaks of silver in his dark brown hair and eyebrows tempered the air of arrogance that he radiated even in his sleep. He smiled then, exposing a mouthful of perfect white teeth. Without meaning to, she smiled back.

"Hello, Nate," she said.

"Jillian! I'm so glad I caught you in," he replied, and then frowned at something that she couldn't see. "Tell your rodent of a brother to piss off. This is a private call."

Before she could say anything, a stripe of static sizzled across the screen. As soon as it disappeared, Ross's frown went away as well. "There," he said, "that's better. And before I get distracted again, Jill, just let me say this: refabbed or not, it's a joy to see your face. You're still the best-looking captain in settled space."

"You're wasting your breath with flattery," she told him, although some stubborn vestige of her former self branded her a liar for it. "And if you're calling on behalf of our beloved president, you're wasting your time as well."

"Barim doesn't know about this call, and if he ever hears about it, I'll be lucky if I only lose my job."

She resisted the urge to roll her eyes. One of the few things that came readily to mind about this man was his penchant for theatrics. "All right then, I'll bite. What's this all about?"

"It's the Latimer murder," he said. "The old man's obsessed with it." When she just sat there, deadpan, waiting to hear something she didn't know already, he hastened to say, "Don't get me wrong. I want to resolve the case, too. After all, an unsolved murder looks bad on my record, and that's not good for my career."

She remembered that about him, too: cut Ross, and he'd bleed ambition.

"But blacklisting a class-one captain just because she *may* know something about the matter is over the top," he went on, "an extravagant abuse of authority—even for him. I'm telling you, Jill: he has to be stopped."

"Sounds like you're running for office," she said.

He responded with a full-fledged grin. "You were always too clever by half. But yes, I'll admit to ulterior motives. By helping you, I'll be helping myself as well."

She hated the hopeful little flutter that stirred within her then, but it was as strong as a cyborg and wouldn't be squashed. The best she could do was smother it with doubts. "No offense, but I need work, not campaign promises. Moral support isn't going to keep the repo man away."

"I understand that," he assured her, "and believe me, I'm doing everything in my power to get you back into action. Just give me a few more days. Something will shake loose. I'm sure of it."

A few more days. It didn't sound like too much to ask—until she crunched the numbers. Then it turned into a very, very thin line. She factored a loan from Maggie into the equation. The line thickened into a thread: do-able, but ju-ust barely. Which was still better than what she had now. She decided to be grateful.

"Thanks, Nate," she said. "I appreciate your efforts on my behalf. And no matter what happens from here on, you've got my vote in the next election."

He raised a finger to his lips—the universal sign for hush. "Not a word about that or any other part of this conversation to anybody for now, please. If even a rumor of what I'm trying to do for you gets back to the old bastard, my good intentions could blow up in both of our faces."

"Bad analogy," she said, "but I take your point. As far as I'm concerned, this call never happened."

"Good. I'll be in touch. And if you remember anything pertinent to the Latimer case in the meantime, you will ping me, won't you?"

"You'll be the first to know," she promised.

He signed off then. Her keeper's screen went blank. She hummed a few bars of some nameless tune, and then hailed the bridge. As soon as Roadkill picked up, she said, "Did you miss anything?"

"Not a word," he boasted. "The Prince Of Snoops should've known that I'd be running more than one rat-trap on his call."

"So what do you think?"

"I don't trust him. He's been Barim's torpedo for ten years now, and the galaxy's biggest back-door man for even longer. There's gotta be something about this *campaign* of his that he's not telling us. Then again," he added, after a moment's thought, "what's a little political pony-shit between friends? If The Torpedo actually does pull a contract out of his hat for us, I'll join the freakin' union and vote for him, too."

It always surprised her to hear Roadkill voice opinions that mirrored her own. He was so peculiar, a smart-mouthed iconoclast who could rub even a cyborg raw. And yet those were her sentiments, exactly. She was prepared to put up with almost any indignity in exchange for a new lease on her life.

"I'm going to call a woman about a loan," she decided aloud. "Then I'm going to stock up. We need anything in particular?"

"How 'bout a crew?" he said.

"What's your second choice?"

"It's rather indecent. Are you sure you want to hear it?"

"Never mind," she said then, but she wasn't really that riled. Indeed, she was in a good mood—or at least as close to that as something with no physiological receptors for the state of goodness could get. "Ping me if you need me. Otherwise, I'll see you on the bridge in the morning."

"Roger that. Oh, and the catering unit needs to be refilled. Bridge out."

She shook her head at her half-brother's peculiarities, then retrieved her drink and downed it in one swallow. In honor of Ross and political bullshit, she then poured herself another.

℘

SHE BOLTED UPRIGHT in her bunk, electrified by a nightmare that began to erase itself from her memory even as she struggled to recall it. Denny had had a starring role in it— that much she remembered. There'd been a smell, too, something foul beyond imagining, and screaming. But everything else had already slipped back into that private black hole in her head. If it had taken her any longer to wake up, she might not have remembered anything at all.

Which didn't seem like such a bad thing anymore. Having dreams peppered with shrapnel from Denny's murder was distressing enough. If she recalled the primary event, she might never sleep again. And that was the last wholly human need that she could still satisfy. Pleasepleaseplease don't take that away from her, too.

She pulled the safety webbing aside, then slung herself out of bed. As she stuffed herself into her uniform, her head began to throb: a slow, steady pounding that seemed to reverberate down the length of her plasti-steel spine. The old Jillian would've diagnosed this as a hangover and sworn off alcohol for a while. But the new-and-not-so-improved model was coming to realize that liquor was the only thing keeping an even worse headache at bay. It was the suspense; the pressure; the fade-away dreams. When they went away, she told herself, so would the pain. Until then, she meant to cope by any means possible.

So she took a drink—a quick swig straight from the bottle that she'd left out last night. Afterward, she scolded herself for violating the first rule of ship-life: *stow it before it got broken, or broke something else.* In flight, such diligence was crucial. At port, it was a sensible habit. She pledged never to be that careless again, then stashed the bottle back in her locker and headed for the bridge.

The first thing she saw as she stepped off the lift was Roadkill. He was sprawled back in the comm-tech's chair, and thoroughly engaged with a viz. The promo-image on the face-shield was of some bare-boobed wawa. Annoyance flashed though her, hot and righteous. She marched over and yanked the vizard from his head. He loosed an instant howl of protest.

"Hey, wait your turn!"

She curled her lip into a scornful as-if, then said, "You know personal gear isn't allowed on the bridge."

He spun around to confront her. The bruise on his jaw was a sickly yellow now; the fact that he had shaved for a change suggested that he was fond of the color. "What's the big deal?" he asked, in a peevish tone that went well with those black-hole eyes of his. "It's just you and me."

"We're getting sloppy," she informed him. "And sooner or later, sloppy spacers are sorry spacers. I think we're sorry enough as it is. Don't you?"

"Oh, come on, Jillie," he complained, "give me a break. We're not in space at the moment."

"That's not the point, and you know it."

They stared at each other for a moment, but it was no contest. She could go all day without blinking. The instant after he broke eye-contract, she pitched the viz into his lap. "Look, RK," she said then, "I'm not trying to bust your chops here. If you've got a craving for this stuff, take the day off and have a viz-a-thon in your cabin. I can manage this shift without you."

"I don't want to go back to my quarters," he said, not at all grateful for the offer. "I'm a social creature. I like company every once and a while."

"Then get rid of the trash and come back," she said. "Because from here on, we're following the rules."

A nasty smile slithered across his mouth. The bruising on his jaw became a storm on the event horizon. "Can I get a copy of that rulebook?" he asked, all phony sweetness and reason. "I wanna see where it says that it's OK for you to have booze on your breath, but not OK for me to have a lousy viz on the bridge."

For one stunned moment, all she could do was gape at him. She'd forgotten that tequila had an aroma, and that people with their real, flesh-and-blood noses might smell it and jump to the wrong conclusions.

"I had a headache," she told him tersely, "so I took a drink."

"I had a hard-on," he retorted, "hence the viz. But you still haven't answered my question."

Several replies leapt to her mind: that she was the captain and would do as she pleased. And: every rule had an exception, and she was it. And even the simple truth: that she needed the tequila like he would never need a stupid viz. But before she could decide which tack she wanted to take, the comm-board buzzed. Her brother arched an accusing eyebrow at her, as if she had somehow arranged this diversion, but then shifted in his seat and became the very essence of a comm-tech on duty.

"*Zephyr* here," he said. "State your name, and the nature of your call."

"This is Tark cis Xamar, the Tolqan ambassador to the Galactic Council," came the reply. The speaker's accent was distinctive, lyrical and full like a poet's horizons— this despite an exceptionally bad connection. "Mine is a matter of the utmost urgency. I wish to speak to Captain D'Lange now."

"Please hold with I direct your call," Roadkill said, and then glanced at Jillian for instructions. She gestured toward the captain's station. An instant later, she was there, blank-faced and full of breath, but excited just the same. She'd never met a Tolq. She didn't even know what they were supposed to look like. But she had to admit: the idea of meeting someone from a foreign world wasn't nearly as exciting as the idea of doing business with him.

Pleasepleaseplease let this be the opportunity that Ross had promised to shake loose!

"Coming through to your screen," Roadkill warned then. "The visual is as bad as the audio—I'm not getting good resolution from either."

But despite the lousy visuals she had no trouble forming a first impression about her caller: *aristocratic* came immediately to mind. He was an older man with a striking, weathered look. His hair, equal parts of cinnamon and gray, was done up in elaborate braids like a Medusa's crown. His eyes, lively and deepset, reminded her of nut-brown ale. But what intrigued her most was the color of his skin: it was only a half-shade paler than her own synthetic hide! She pinched her wonder into a formal smile.

"I'm Captain D'Lange," she told him. "How may I help you?"

Surprise flickered in the ambassador's eyes—him realizing that she was cyborg, she guessed, and steeled herself for his immediate about-face. But he simply cleared his throat and pressed on.

"Please forgive my abruptness, Captain," he said, "but I have an emergency on my hands. One of the people on my staff has fallen desperately ill and must return to Tolq as quickly as possible. I've been told that your ship is for hire."

A thrill raced through her then, only to slam head-on into harsh reality. She never thought she'd hate the words that she heard herself saying now. "I'm sorry, Ambassador, but *Zephyr* is classified as a freighter, not a passenger ship."

He dismissed the distinction with an elegant wave of his hand. "Speed is the only luxury that matters right now, and I understand that your ship is fast. If you have room to accommodate three people—me, an aide, and our unconscious colleague—we'll manage without amenities."

"I'm also short-handed at the moment," she said, being compulsively honest with him because of the life at stake. "I wouldn't be able to provide care for the patient."

"We'll tend to him ourselves," the ambassador said, and then twitched her an odd, sardonic half-smile. "In fact, my aide wouldn't have it any other way."

Jillian blinked back a moment's astonishment. This guy had gone seriously out of his way to clear the obstacles that she'd thrown in his way! He must owe Nathan Ross a huge favor. She wondered what Nate had done to earn it, but only in passing. Now that her scruples had been appeased, she was eager to get down to business. She quoted the ambassador a figure—credit enough to cover operating costs, the SU's cut, and two loan payments, plus a little extra that she expected to lose through haggling. It was, she had to admit, an exorbitant sum for a no-frills, one-way, express ticket home—even if that home happened to be an out-of-the-way backwater like Tolq. So when Tark cis Xamar agreed to the price without so much as a raised eyebrow, she blinked again.

"I'll transfer the credit to your account immediately," he told her. "How soon can we leave?"

"That will depend on how fast you get here," she replied. "Five hours if you come to Station by Medi-vac. Eleven hours if I have to send my crewman down to pick you up. You'll have to pay Medi-vac for transporting you, but given your colleague's condition, it may be the wiser way to go."

"I concur," the ambassador said. "We'll come to you."

"Good. Tell your pilot we're in J sector, slot 4-B. We'll be ready and waiting."

"Thank you, Captain," he then severed their connection.

"No, thank *you*," she crooned to his afterimage, and then swiveled around to grin at Roadkill. "You hear?"

"Sure did," he replied, with a grin to match her own.

"The ambassador and his aide will want to be quartered close to the infirmary ," she said then, thinking aloud. "That would be Trine's old cabin. They'll need safety webbing and thermal nap-sacks on their bunks, a stock of D-drugs, and proto-fluids for afterward."

"I'm on it," Roadkill said, springing to his feet.

"Oh, and make sure everything in the infirmary is in good working order," she added, as he headed for the lift. "That's where our primary passenger will be staying."

He flipped her a cocky salute, then vanished from the bridge. In his absence, she grinned at empty space while her thoughts danced gleeful circles in her head. She'd done it! She was back in business! *So there, Mister President.* Still grinning, she accessed her credit account. The sum that blipped onto the utility screen was substantial. She savored this illusion of wealth for a moment, then proceeded to transfer most of it to her creditors' coffers. *Take that, Mister President,* she thought afterward. If nothing else, this contract guaranteed her a month's reprieve from his nasty little game. The improbability of such a respite made its achievement all the more satisfying.

Ready to start making flight plans now, she placed a call to Station Control. The comptroller was obviously aware of the conspiracy against her, and balked at her request for a departure time. But since she didn't owe Station any back-rent, and since he had— or so she guessed—no specific instructions to detain her, he finally assigned her a slot. It was later than the one she'd applied for, but earlier than the one she'd expected to get, so she signed off without a complaint and then accessed her star-charts. When she activated the search-engines, they came up with Tolq's coordinates and one thing more—a warning in big, bold print. *Restricted space,* it read. *SU travel advisories in effect.* She zoomed in on the red-flag, looking for specifics, but it didn't come with footnotes.

She shook her head, dunning herself for not expecting something like this. A gig this easy, this lucrative, and this damn timely had to have some kind of a catch to it. And *restricted space* definitely qualified as a catch.

"Damn it," Ross," she grumbled. "What've you gotten me into?"

Then it hit her: this job probably wasn't his doing after all. The ambassador had chartered her to take a sick colleague home. Nathan Ross couldn't have—or wouldn't have—engineered such desperate circumstances just to help her out. The political risks involved outweighed the possible benefits. She'd simply *assumed* that any work coming her way would be from Ross. She'd simply *assumed* that that work would be mundane. What had Griffith done to her, she wondered then. She hadn't been born this stupid, and certainly her mother had taught her better.

Still, she was luckier than she had a right to be. Restricted space wasn't the same as prohibited space, and besides, this trip was just a fly-by—fast in, fast out. With a little prep-work and some belated care, she could come out a winner on all fronts.

So she pinpointed Tolq on the star-map and then searched for clues as to why its space might be restricted. All she found, though, were unrevealing facts. Like: Tolq was a tiny orphan of a rock revolving around an aging yellow dwarf on the galaxy's distal tip. And: its nearest inhabited neighbor was over a hundred lightyears away. And: there did not seem to be a single space installation, commercial or otherwise, anywhere in its solar system. Just as she'd thought, she told herself then: a piddling backwater.

The encyclopedia was slightly more helpful. It described Tolq as a harsh desert world with just enough water and other resources to sustain a small population of human transplants. The original colonizers, it said, had been puritanicals searching for a simpler way of life. Their modern-day descendants were religious fanatics.

Jillian snorted. Religion? What a cack. Nobody was that naive anymore.

Nobody but the Tolqs, it seemed. They not only revered their desert-fired version of a supreme being, they also credited he-she-it with giving them extrasensory powers—a manifestation that probably had more to do with too much inbreeding than a god. But she could see how a people who didn't know any better might mistake one for the other. As a child, she'd believed in Spacer Nick—the jolly, white-whiskered fat man who left piles of presents on every good captain's bridge sometime during the wee hours of New Calendar Year's Morning. That's why her mother had always sent her and any other kids off to bed early on New Calendar Year's Eve. And Jillian figured that that was probably why the Tolq theocracy had restricted their space, too. They didn't want some jaded outsider wandering into the creche and spilling the beans about god.

The comm-board buzzed then. An instant later, a familiar image expanded out of the encyclopedia text on her utility screen. "Mister President," she said, as the lines of his scowl hazed into focus. "What a pleasant surprise."

"Where do you think you're going?" he demanded, in lieu of a greeting.

Technically, that was for her to know and him to find out. But all outbound ships, be they barges or union cruisers, were required to log a flight plan with Security before their departure. *In case of emergency*, the regulations read, but everyone knew that the data-base was used to keep tabs on who was going where and why, too. And since she was just about to place that call, she decided to be generous in victory.

"As a matter of fact," she replied, "I'm off to Tolq."

"That's not a good idea, D'Lange," he told her.

"Why am I not surprised to hear you say that?" she drawled.

"Tolqs don't like off-worlders," he went on. "And they like machines even less. That's two counts against you before you even open your mouth."

She gave her artificial hair an artificial toss. "I'm a cyborg, not a machine, Barim. A man of your reputed intelligence should be able to grasp the difference. But my clients are welcome to dislike me all they want, seeing as how they paid their bill in advance."

Barim's scowl intensified. "Over the past thirteen months, four union ships have gone into Tolq space and never come back out. We don't know what happened to them, because Tolq officials are refusing to cooperate with us; and because, by treaty, SU police can't enter that solar system. So it could be pirates. It could be crummy coincidence. Or, it could be the Tolqs themselves. As I said, they *don't* like off-worlders. My question to you, Captain, is: do you want to be the fifth ship to go MIA?"

"What were those ships doing in restricted space in the first place?" she asked.

He heaved a massive shrug, one capable of capsizing a lesser person's ego. "They all had their reasons—same as you. The only difference was, their intel wasn't as good as yours is. So be smart," he urged her then. "Learn from someone else's misfortunes for a change. If you compromise, so will I."

The concession galled her, for he was not a man who made them often. Now, no matter how contritely she phrased what she had to say next, he'd think that she was trying to spite him. She just couldn't win with this man.

Even so, she had to try.

"I'm sorry, Mister President," she said, radiating regret, "but like I said, my clients paid in advance. And I used that credit to pay off some of my debts. I'm committed to go to Tolq now, whether I want to or not."

His face turned a strokish shade of red. She could almost hear the blood backing up in his stringy old heart. "Very well then, have it your way—as you always must. But make no mistake here: running to Tolq isn't going to solve your problems. When you get back—*if* you get back!—you're going to either cooperate with me or lose your ship. If you want, I'll put that in writing for you, because we all know what shape your memory's in."

"Do what you feel you must, Mister President," she said, regretting her earlier attempt to coddle his ego. "I won't be bullied into reneging on a contract. Now, if you'll excuse me,

I have work to do. Perhaps we can talk again *when* I get back."

She mocked him a snappy salute, and then severed the connection. Then, as she returned to her charts, she thought: Ross was right. Barim was out of control.

Chapter 4

"ZEPHYR, THIS IS Medi-vac Unit One. We're closing in on your coordinates. ETA is seven point nine minutes. Where do you want us to drop your package—front door or back?"

Jillian thought about that for a moment. The ambassador was undoubtedly used to the formality of front door service. But that would necessitate the Medi-vac's landing at a service portal and then an ambulance ride to *Zephyr's* slip, and that would add another ten minutes to their ETA. If the ambassador's associate was ill enough to need an emergency evacuation, then every extra minute mattered.

"Bring 'em around to the back," she decided aloud. "The shuttle-bay doors will be open and waiting for you. Position yourself for slot two. Slot one's already taken."

"Roger that, *Zephyr*," the med-tech said. "See you in seven."

As soon as she severed that connection, she pinged her brother. He responded promptly: a pleasant surprise.

"Where are you?" she asked

"Fresh out of the shower. I had a feeling that I might need one, and no way it was gonna happen once we pushed off."

"Good thinking. Can you be decent in six minutes?"

"Depends on your definition. Why? The Tolqs here?"

"Yeah, they're coming in through the shuttle bay. And since I'm going to have to run the in-and-out from here, you're going to have to meet them."

"If you use my remote, you can be Miz Jillian-On-The-Spot," he told her, in a sly, dangling tone.

"I thought I told you to get rid of that," she said.

"You did," he conceded, and then hastened to defend himself. "But in order to do that, I'll have to go into *Zeph*'s datacore and pull the access sequences from her memory. That's a shut-down job, and you've had us on stand-by from the moment you got home."

"I see," she said. "So it's my fault that the remote's still intact."

"Essentially."

She knew she shouldn't be mad at him. She also knew that her anger was all out of proportion to the crime. And yet there was still a part of her that wanted to march right down to his quarters and smack the smart-assed smirk that she just knew he was wearing from his face. Fortunately for him, though, her presence was required here on the bridge.

"The next time I give you an order," she warned, "I expect you to carry it out or tell me there on the spot why it can't be done. Otherwise, brother or not, I'll—" *I want him fired.* "—I'll—" What had she been saying? "—oh, never mind. Just get yourself dressed and down to shuttle-bay. I'll join you as soon as I can."

Her brother made no reply. It was, she thought, a wise move.

There was a small, white blip skating across her screen now—the Medi-vac unit. She switched on *Zephyr*'s running lights, then opened the shuttle-bay's doors. A moment later, one of the med-techs announced their arrival.

"Roger that," she said, and then closed the doors behind them. "Hold fast until repressurization is complete. The O-2's going to be on the low side, so you might want to fit the package and his friends with re-breathers." As soon as she got a roger for that, she pinged her brother. "Move the Tolqs out of the bay as soon as you can," she told him, "so I can send the Medi-vac on its way and join you."

"I'm going in now," he said.

Minutes passed. The all's-clear never came. She used up what little patience she had, then pinged her brother again. He answered with a surly, "What?"

"What's taking so long?" she asked.

"One of these red-robed freaks is a colossal pain in the glutes," he replied. "First, he had a fit about the re-breathers. They're nikki-trikki-tavi, he said, or something like that. Then, when I explained him about the low O-2, he took a deep breath and tried to make it all the way across the shuttle bay on just that. He came up short, of course, and the med-techs wound up using a re-breather to revive him. At the moment, he's throwing a fit about that."

"Where are the Tolqs now?"

"In the hallway."

"And the techs?"

"They're climbing back into the ambulance even as I speak. Lucky bastards."

The comm-board buzzed then: the Medi-vac signaling its readiness to depart. She put them on stand-by while she dispatched a fresh set of instructions to Roadkill. "Escort the Tolqs to the infirmary. I'll meet you there."

"Hurry," he urged her, and for everyone's sake, she did so.

As soon as the ambulance was clear of the ship, she hit the lift. And as soon as those docks opened onto the main deck, she broke into a run. The next thing she knew, she was at the other end of the corridor. Her new track-time both amazed and appalled her. She had never been the pokey type, but this—this was unnerving. Especially since there was no fatigue, no quickness of breath, not even a drop of sweat to commemorate the effort. It didn't seem real. It didn't feel human. And she *hated* that.

Even as she thought this, she cleared another hallway.

She could hear muffled voices now. One of them was wild and thickly accented. The other belonged to Roadkill.

"Don't tell me," her brother was saying, in a beleaguered tone, "I'm just the hired help. Captain's the one who makes all the decisions on this ship. I'm sure she'll be here soon."

She took that for a cue, and went striding boldly into the infirmary. Her brother's face sagged with relief as she entered.

The ambassador acknowledged her with a nod and a cool half-smile. But the ambassador's aide lunged at her like a little, bald dog on a long leash. His red, full-length robe flapped in a breeze of his own making.

"He's to have none of your medicines, do you hear me?" he bawled, gesturing at the man on the floating gurney to his rear. "And none of your machinery is to touch him. Do you hear? None!"

"I hear you," she replied, in a calm, level tone, and then strode over to look at the patient.

He was a young man, thirty standard years old at most, and at first glance, he only seemed to be deeply asleep. Then she noticed his ragged breathing, and the too-taut cords in his neck and wrists. There was also a faint bluish tinge to his caramel-apple skin. Sick or not, though, his resemblance to the ambassador was obvious. They had the same sharp chin and high cheekbones, the same thick, red hair and full mouths. He was, she thought with a sudden wistful pang, quite attractive.

"Your son?" she asked the ambassador, standing beside her now.

"My son has no desire to leave his homeworld," he said, sounding aggrieved by that. "This is my brother's son, Ammas su Xamar, the future lord of our clan. And here," he went on, in a much droller tone, "is Zim, the keeper of my soul. Zim is an arch-liberal compared to most priests, Captain, but he's not at all happy to be on your ship. Might I suggest that we get underway before he changes his mind and bolts?"

"Of course," she said briskly, and then turned to her brother. "RK, escort these gentlemen to their quarters." As he curled his lip into a silent 'Thanks-a-lot!', she added, "While you're there, familiarize them the safety webbing and any other facilities that they may not know how to use."

"But what of Ammas?" Zim said. "He can't stay on this—" He gestured at the floater as if it were a cheap whore's unmade bed. "—on this Ni H'Nathelek *thing*."

"I'm going to transfer Ammas to a pull-out and then strap him down for the trip," Jillian told him. "You can stay and watch if you can't bear to trust me, but the longer RK and I are away from the bridge, the tighter our window of departure becomes. And your friend here doesn't look like he has a lot of time to spare."

Zim glanced from her to his unconscious ward and back again. His shaved head was ridged with misgivings. But even as he fretted over the appropriate course of action, the ambassador draped an arm around his shoulders and started to usher him toward the exit.

"Come along, Zim," he said, in a voice laced with sarcasm. "If we hurry, we may have time to offer one last prayer of expiation to H'Nath before The Great One sucks us into the eternal desert."

Jillian wondered who the ambassador had been mocking just then—the priest or himself. She didn't ask, though. It was none of her business, really, and besides, she still had Ammas to consider. So she drew a pull-out from its slot, then lifted the stricken Tolq onto it. He was dead weight in her arms, yet perversely feather-light. Despite the priest's adamant injunction against it, she was tempted to hook him up to the med-computer so it could maintain his vitals. After all, what could some backwater shaman know? But even as she started to succumb to her superior conceits, another internal voice warned her off. These Tolqs were paying her to get them home, not debunk their religion.

But poor Ammas! He looked so small and pitiful restrained to that pull-out, like a red-robed sacrifice on hold. She had to do *something* for him.

It was then that she remembered her stash of thermal blankets. They weren't as efficient as a med-computer for regulating body temperature, but they were considerably better than nothing. And not even Zim could consider a blanket profane. So she fetched one from a storage locker and spread it over him. Then, as she tucked the edge under his chin, their faces happened to align. He looked abandoned, helpless, and starkly beautiful. Driven by wistful impulse, she kissed him on the lips.

It was a bitter theft—a vacant micro-impression of pressure, and nothing more. Those subtle nuances of texture and taste that defined a true kiss were beyond her now. She mocked herself for being disappointed. What had she been expecting—fireworks? A symphonic tantara? That part of her was deaddeaddead. She was a machine cursed with human memories. The sooner she accepted that, the better off she'd be.

As she put herself back in her place, the headache that she'd been trying to shake for the past several days came inching back toward prominence. She scowled, resenting the intrusion. How perverse it was that she could still feel pain but not pleasure. And at a time when she could least afford such harsh distraction! She glanced toward her quarters, thinking tequila all the way. But before she had a chance to act on that thought, Roadkill came storming into the room.

"I'm telling you again, Jillie," he said. "These freakin' Tolqs are a pain. The priest all but swallowed his tongue when I offered to show him how to use the keeper in his quarters. I think he actually would've hit me if the ambassador hadn't chased me off. And that guy—" He pinched his nose as if it were the handle to a teacup and then raised his pinkie like a prig. "He thinks his shit don't stink, doesn't he?"

"I wouldn't know," she replied, "and I don't particularly care to find out." Then, as she ushered him out of the infirmary toward the lift, she added, "But he's probably just worried about his nephew."

His frown lost its intensity. "Poor bastard. Think he'll make it?"

"If he doesn't, it won't be our fault," she said, and she meant that as a promise of sorts. "Even if it *is* just the two of us. Can you manage both surveillance and comm until we get to the hole?"

He snorted. "The day I can't, I'll become a Tolq priest."

She snorted back. "I'll remember that." Then, as they stepped onto the lift, she added, "I'll need help some help at the entry-point, too."

"Is now a good time to talk about a raise?"

"Talk all you want," she told him, and then strode onto the bridge. As she did so, excitement welled up in her—the primal, wind-up thrill that visited her at the start of each new voyage. The obstacles that she'd cleared to get here lent that excitement an unusual sweetness, while the still-pending challenge of saving a man's life gave it an almost erotic edge. She didn't care that she was a free-floating brain in an ambulatory Petri dish at the moment. All that mattered was that she was here: on this bridge, in this chair, and on the verge of adventure.

"Ready to commence checklist," Roadkill said then.

"I'm with you," she said. Most captains considered the pre-flight check boring, and delegated the task, but it was part of a ritual to her—a psychic laying on of hands that reaffirmed the bonds between her and her ship. So she and her brother began a litany that not even death could make her forget. Drive generator, auxiliary engines, life supports— green lights all. Everything else on the list checked out, too. Satisfied with *Zeph*'s bill of health, she then proceeded to power it up, one system at a time. As the engines started cycling out of their slumber, their distant vibrations invaded her plasti-steel bones through the soles of her feet. A human would never have noticed such subtle reverberations, but sensation-starved Jillian did. They were as close to a tingle as she was ever going to get, and she was immensely grateful for them.

The comm board buzzed. Roadkill answered it, then relayed the news. "Station Control has cleared for us for departure."

"Ping our passengers," she ordered. "Tell them to web themselves in and stay put until we say otherwise." Then, while he was doing that, she began the separation process. "Vent airlocks," she recited aloud. "Seal outer hatches. Retract boarding supports." As these attachments between Station and ship disappeared, her excitement began to mount. "Reduce magnetic locks to half-power. Thrusters to stand-by. Reduce magnetic locks to zero-power."

Zephyr lurched as the locks lost their grip on Station's hide. A moment later, it began to fall away from its erstwhile berth like a chunk of moonbound sediment. Jillian fired the thrusters then, and steered her ship into an outgoing lane.

"We're away," she said.

"Any problems?" Roadkill asked, trying to sound casual rather than wary.

No clarification was necessary. She knew he was thinking about their last shuttle ride together. "No glitches so far," she told him, and then added, "It's good to be back, isn't it?"

"It beats mopping up barf at Boomer's," he said.

They were approaching open space now. She brought the drive-generator on-line, then asked for a report on any activity in the area. When he responded with an all's-clear, she killed the thrusters and engaged the drive-generator. The ship accelerated—a creamy smooth transition to near-lightspeed. She sat back to enjoy the ride then, but her pleasure was short-lived. For even as the excitement of setting out faded into a rosy afterglow, the ache in her head began to reassert itself. She tried to ignore the pain. She tried to pinch it back into its hidey-hole with a frown. Finally, she gave up and turned to Roadkill.

"Feel like making an aspirin run for me?" she asked.

"Why? You got yourself a little hang-over?"

"I don't think so," she replied, too distracted to take exception to his impertinence. "The timing's wrong."

"So what's the prob?" he said, switching to a tone with less finger-wagging in it.

"I don't know. I've had this freakin' headache off and on for almost a week now, and lately, it seems to be getting worse instead of better."

"Sounds like you popped a stitch or somethin'," he said, and then offered to scan her. "It won't take long," he promised, "and I still have Griffith's data-disks on me, so I have a pretty fair idea of what you're supposed to look like upstairs."

"You know we can't leave the bridge unattended," she said.

He shrugged. "The scanner's portable. I could do you right where you sit."

"All right then, go and get it. Bring the aspirin, too."

He was off and back again with surprising alacrity. "Now just lean back and stay still," he said, as he wheeled a tall, reed-thin contraption with a smoked-glass face toward her. "When I tell you to, close your eyes."

The big-drum thrumming in her head urged her to do as she was told. As she sat there, rigid as a Tolqan priest, she heard him program a set of parameters into the scanner and then fuss with some creaky, unseen appendage. "OK, close 'em." Now the clamor in her head was even louder—ka-boom, ka-boom, like cannon-fire. *Something was terribly wrong with her, she just knew it.* Then, through her eyelids, she saw a prolonged flash of bright, white light. It was accompanied by a high-pitched whine and a series of rapid-fire clicks. A moment later, the world went dark on her again, and the cannonade resumed.

"That's it," her brother said then. "I'll be back with the results in a few tics. Oh, and here," he added, tossing a pair of paper packets in her lap. "Knock yourself out."

"Thanks," she replied, and tore into one cache like a junkie long overdue for a fix. Six glossy gel-caps spilled into her palm. She popped all six into her mouth, then chewed them into a tasteless, textureless paste. If this didn't work, she thought, as she swallowed the emulsion, she was going to send Roadkill after the tequila. Screw the rule-book. She needed relief. Otherwise, she might just take her misery out on someone else.

Just then, the comm-board buzzed. She transferred the call to her station with an truculent flick, thinking: *what now, dammit?* But when she saw that it was coming from within the ship, her mood improved instantly.

"That was fast," she said, in lieu of a formal greeting.

"Captain?" It was Ambassador Xamar, sounding faintly amused.

"Yes?" she said, curt with him for having caught her off-guard. "Is something wrong?"

"It's Zim, Captain. He's almost frothing with concern for Ammas's soul. Might he be allowed to visit the lad? I fear for his sanity. And mine," he added dryly.

"I understand," she told him, although she had very little in the way of sympathy for any of the Tolqs at the moment. "As soon as my crewman is available, I'll send him around to escort your aide to the infirmary. Until then, though, you'll have to stay put. I can't have inexperienced non-personnel wandering around the ship."

"No, of course not," the ambassador agreed. Then, before she could sever their connection, he blurted, "Forgive me for imposing, but might I ask another favor of you?"

"Like what?"

Another voice erupted in the background then. The ambassador put her on hold for a moment; and when he came back on-line, there was a subterranean disturbance in his tone. "I beg your pardon for the interruption, Captain," he said, "but Zim gets frantic when I use offworld conveniences, even something so harmless as an intercomm. Might you and I speak face to face? I promise not to take up too much of your time."

She toyed with the idea of refusing him. She was still edgy from the pain, and the prospect of having to mind her manners for any length of time appealed to her as much as cryo-storage did. Then again, prudence argued, he *was* the one paying for this trip. And sooner or later, he was going to need a ride back to Circe's II. Perhaps *that* was why he wanted to talk to her. Perhaps he wanted to negotiate his round trip. The possibility, she decided, was too rich to pass up.

"I'll have RK escort you to the bridge after he takes care of Zim," she told him.

"Thank you, Captain. You won't regret it," he said, and then went off-line.

Her mood see-sawed again, tipping back toward excitement. If she could swing another paycheck out of this trip and then snap up the job that Ross had promised to line up for her, she'd be in fair shape for a re-match with Barim. She wasn't particularly keen on butting heads with him yet again, but there was a principle involved here. No one, not even the president of the Space-Workers' Union, was going to bully her into bankruptcy. If, on the other hand, he decided to be reasonable—well, she could bend, too. Anything to get rid of this headache.

If that was possible.

With that thought in mind, she pinged Roadkill. "Well, RK?" she asked, when he answered. "What's the verdict?"

"Just a tic," he replied. "I'm just finishing the data analysis now." The link went quiet for a long moment. Jillian tried to wring her arm-rest into a bottle-neck, but it kept plumping out again. Freakin' bio-plastics. "OK," Roadkill said then, "here's the scoop. Your scans came out clean. As far as I can tell, there's nothing wrong with you."

Relief washed through her like a balm. *Nothing wrong.* She'd never heard two sweeter words. *Nothing wrong.* Maybe she did have a hangover after all—the cyborg kind. *Nothing wrong.* All she had to do was tough it out.

"Thanks for the news," she said. "I owe you one."

"I'll just add it to the collection," he cracked. "Want me to bring you more aspirin on my way back?"

"That might save you a trip later on. Oh, and speaking of which, the ambassador needs an escort to the bridge. And Zim wants to visit the infirmary."

Her brother made a strangled sound. "Jillie, that priest is a lunatic."

"So maybe he can give you some pointers," she retorted.

"You've got a strange way of showing your appreciation for loyal service."

"Sorry. I'll make it up to you some day."

"Yeah, right," he said in parting.

Despite his griping, though, he returned with the ambassador in record time. As they stepped onto the bridge, a fair-sized scrap of the Tolq's robe got trapped in the lift's fast-closing doors. Roadkill freed him with a smirking flourish, then went scurrying back to his station for a semi-private snicker. Meanwhile, Jillian stood up to meet her guest.

"I'm always getting caught like that," the Tolq said, as he approached. "Although the priests would have you believe otherwise, the twarla's usefulness as a garment ends at the desert's edge."

"If you'd like, I could find a flightsuit for you," she told him.

He declined the offer with a polite half-smile. "My sincere thanks, Captain. But I am Tolq's representative; and tradition demands that I dress in Tolqan garb."

"As you wish, Ambassador."

"Please, call me Tark. I'm dreadfully tired of being addressed by a title."

"As you wish—Tark. And by-the-by, welcome aboard."

She held out her hand then: a spontaneous gesture of good-will to an immediately intriguing man. He pretended not to see it. Instead, he began to survey the bridge like an Inspector General on the job. His polite half-smile never wavered. His manner remained perfectly relaxed. And yet she got the distinct impression that she'd offended him. *Tolqs don't like off-worlders. And they like machines even less.* So, she concluded then, he probably knew all about her being a cyborg. She didn't know *why* that should bother her, but she told herself that it probably had something to do with Barim being right.

"So what can I do for you, Ambassador?" she said, pointedly resurrecting his title as a means of distancing herself from him. "No offense intended, sir—" Or maybe just a little. "—but this isn't the best time or place for a social call."

"No, of course not." He looked around for a place to sit down then, but she had already resumed her seat in the station's only chair. That, too, was deliberate on her part. If he wouldn't take her hand, then he could bloody well stand. But if he was discomfited by her little power-play, he didn't show it. He simply raised one foot and balanced on the other like a story-book stork. Then he said, "I came to make arrangements for Ammas's transportation from your ship to his father's estate."

She responded with a no-big-deal shrug. "Once we've established a stable orbit around your world, I'll ping your brother's stevedore, and he'll send a shuttle out to fetch you all. End of problem, no?"

"I'm afraid not," he said, and twitched her an apologetic smile. "Because you see, Captain, my brother doesn't have a shuttle at his disposal. Nor do any of the other lords. Such technology is Ni H'Nathelek, and therefore accessible only to the priesthood. And if it's all possible, I'd rather not drag the H'Nathma into this matter. They won't care that I chartered your ship to save Ammas's life, only that it's off-world and therefore corrupt. My nephew could die even as the priests argue over the best way to purify his soul.

"Please, Captain," he added, when she didn't respond right away, "don't turn your back on the lad. I'll see that you're well-compensated for the extra trouble."

She continued to study the backs of her gloves. Her thoughts were crackling like static. This wasn't the proposal that she'd been expecting. It was far less lucrative than a ride back to Circe's II; and far more risky. *Four ships lost in the past thirteen months,* Barim had said. And what better way to become the fifth than to put a nice, new freighter with no crew into orbit in restricted space? Still, she would've chanced it for the price of a return ticket. So why not for a bit of ferry service and a man's life? Roadkill could turn the trip in twelve hours, if he was properly motivated. That would give whatever predator there might be out there a very narrow window of opportunity in which to strike.

The risk seemed manageable enough. But before she committed herself to it, she wanted to hear what Tark cis Xamar had to say about the intel that Barim had passed her way. She knew from bitter experience that Mister President was capable of exaggerating the facts when it suited his purposes to do so. She wondered what an ambassador could do.

"I've been told that union ships have been disappearing in this sector," she said. "What do you know about that?"

"Every time something goes wrong in our space," he replied blandly, "the SU files a complaint with my office. So I imagine that I know as much about these disappearances as Union Security does, Captain—which is to say, not much at all."

"Then here's an easier one for you," she quipped. "What were union ships doing in restricted space in the first place?"

A corner of his mouth quirked upward—a gesture of dry amusement that could've been meant for her, the whole universe, or just himself. "Tolq has never been a bountiful world, Captain, and at the moment, it's in the middle of a particularly harsh cycle. Crops are failing, praxa herds are dying, our little ones are going to bed hungry. The H'Nathma has done little to alleviate the situation, so while it's expressly Ni H'Nathelek, a desperate few have resorted to private dealings with enterprising off-worlders."

"I see," she mused then. "So Tolq has a problem with boot-leggers."

"Actually," he said, perfectly deadpan, "it's the H'Nathma who has the problem, not Tolq. But that's splitting hairs, isn't? So sorry, Captain. It's an occupational hazard, I'm afraid."

Jillian didn't catch the apology. She'd already latched on to something else. "So tell me more about this H'Nathma of yours," she said. "Does it get rid of its problems by blasting them into debris?"

He laughed aloud at that—a loud, backhanded guffaw—and then apologized again as she went stiff-backed with affront. "But you'd laugh, too," he added, "if you knew the priesthood as I do. For one thing, its members are forbidden to do violence. For another, its so-called fleet consists of two hopelessly out-dated barges that were modeled after the vessels that brought my forefathers to Tolq. Arks, I believe you spacers call them—"

This wouldn't have anything to do with that barge you found, would it?

"—I'd like to see the straight-liner that could overtake a fast-running boot-legger's rig. They might actually be of some value then—"

Won't know for sure until I've spent some time in the archives.

"—as it is now, they're the next best thing to useless."

Won't know until—

"Captain?"

She smashed her fist into the armrest. "Damn," she grated, "I had something there for a moment. I just know it. Now it's gone again." If she could've cried, she would've wept herself dry. Instead, she took her frustration out on the armrest, striking it again and again and again. As she did so, she snarled, "I'm so *freakin'* tired of this!"

"Perhaps we should continue this discussion at another time," the ambassador said then. He'd taken a step back as if to remove himself from harm's way, and was eyeing her with a mixture of wariness and curiosity. "My apologies for upsetting you."

"Wait," she blurted. Then, inch by psychological inch, she backed away from the tantrum that had nearly swallowed her up. It was hard work, for her rage was strong and sticky like rubber cement, but she was embarrassed now, too—for losing herself *and* that moment in the ambassador's presence—and that seemed to grease the way. Indeed, she was almost glad that she had lost the capacity to blush.

Almost.

"It's not you," she assured him, as she stabilized. "It's just—" She groped for a suitable excuse. An instant after she touched on one, it flared into the truth. "It's just that I've had this dreadful headache forever now, and every once in a while it slips away from me."

As she said this, the Tolq's left hand strayed toward his throat, then closed around a reddish brown bead that was hanging there. It was a semi-conscious response, the stuff of old habit. A faraway smile crept across his mouth as he rolled it between his forefinger and thumb, and then turned bittersweet when he realized that she was watching him.

"It's called a quot'tl bead," he explained. "It's a piece of my world, and a token from my god. Every Tolq who survives the initiation rite wears one. It's soothing to the touch, and seems to have restorative properties as well. I find mine particularly effective for headaches." He glanced at her plasti-steel skull then, and made a rueful face. "But I fear it will not work for you."

"Are you sure about that?" she asked, only half-faking the desperate catch in her voice. "Because right about now, I'd trade you a free shuttle trip to your brother's estate for it."

He gave his crown of braids a sorry shake. "If this were any other possession of mine, I'd give it to you, with no expectations attached. But as it's my god's token to me, I must decline your most generous offer."

She was tempted to lash out and confiscate the bead anyway. But something held her back—amazement, or maybe a pole-axed sort of respect. "You really believe in this god stuff, don't you?"

"Life would be so much easier if I didn't," he said. Then, perhaps fearing that he'd let too much of himself show, he tucked the bead back into the folds of his robe and re-deployed his ambassadorial facade. "Now," he said, "about that shuttle trip, Captain. Ammas can count on you, can't he?"

"He can," she decided, "so long as someone's willing to pick up the tab. That'll include standard passenger fare for three, a flat mileage fee, and a hazardous conditions bonus for the pilot."

"Just ping me with the exact figure when you have it," he told her. "The House of Xamar will pay it." Then he slipped his hands into his robe's belled sleeves and hastened to make his excuses. "Do forgive me, Captain, but I had best be returning to my quarters now. Zim will be very mad at me for lingering so long in such Ni H'Nathelek surrounds, and there is, or so he warns me, a limit to his tolerance."

"As you wish, Ambassador," she said, hoping she didn't sound too relieved. But the strain of being on her best behavior was aggravating her headache, and she was glad to be rid of him. "My crewman will be happy to show you the way."

At that, Roadkill loosed a martyred sigh and peeled himself out of his chair. With a sarcastic flourish toward the lift, he said, "This way, you lordship."

In their absence, she chewed another packet of aspirin and then brought her flight plans back on-screen—anything to distract her from the strobing ache in her head. And it never hurt to re-check these all-important equations anyway. They spelled the fastest way to Tolq. They spelled the way to a wyrm-hole.

It wasn't a hole *per se*, but rather a point of tangency between this continuum and one of the nine separate, energy-rich dimensions that had been discovered and explored in the past five hundred years. These 'new' dimensions—or wyrms, as their lab-geek of a discoverer had labelled them—were supercoiled around the universe in mathematically predictable patterns. Hyperintegration of a wyrm's parameters in relation to points in real space yielded the location of two holes: the way in, and the way back out. And while the path between these holes was invariably an arc or a series of them, the vacuum-like nature of wyrms made travel impossibly fast.

And that could be dangerous.

Wyrm speed right, see Captain tonight. Wyrm speed wrong, Captain long-gone. That's how the old creche rhyme went. And she could walk into any spacer bar from here to mother Earth and hear at least one story about some near-virgin captain who'd failed to factor wyrm currents into his equations. The idiot's ship was usually found decades later, dead and drifting in some corner of uncharted space. But sometimes—or so the spinners said—they were never seen or heard from again. Jillian knew better than to believe that accidents in wyrm-space were *that* common. But she never forgot the current coefficient.

Just then, the lift doors whisked open. She started at the sound, then hissed as the sudden motion jolted her headache to fresh heights. She wanted to cry, to rage, to throttle something in effigy! She wanted—

"Everything OK, Jillie?" Roadkill said. "You look a little edgy."

Don't do it, she told herself savagely. It wasn't his fault that she'd been stuffed into a container that was a freakin' half-size too small. *Leave him alone.* It wasn't his fault that all she could feel now was pain. *Let it go.* But try as she might, she couldn't quite talk herself out of her violent cravings. She wanted to hurt him. She was going to hurt him.

"Jillie?" he asked again.

The semiquaver of alarm in his voice crippled the circuit that had been making her vicious, and just like that, she was back to normal—if a cyborg with a short temper and a raging headache could be called normal. But the spell left her badly shaken. She'd never been so aggressive in her human days. The pain was driving her to it. And she needed to fix that, by any means possible—before something terrible happened.

"Sorry, RK," she said then. "I'm not quite myself. Can you watch things here for a few minutes?"

"Sure," he said. Then, unable to contain his worry, he blurted, "If we have to, we can turn back, you know."

"No, we can't," she told him, as she headed for the lift. "I thought you understood that."

↜↝

THIRTY MINUTES LATER, the bridge seemed like a larger, brighter place to Jillian. She tried not to look too pleased with the difference, for she didn't want Roadkill to think she was drunk, but—damn! It felt *so* good to be rid of that booming in her head. She could think again. She could look at people without imagining their intestines in her teeth. Her only regret was that the effect wasn't permanent. And her only fear was that the tequila would run out before the trip came to an end. The bottle was definitely half-empty.

"ETA to hole, twenty-seven standard minutes," she announced. "Ping the Tolqs and tell 'em to web themselves in. I'll start prepping for entry."

The first thing she did was reduce *Zephyr*'s delta-vee. She did this in increments, percentage point by slow percentage point, so the excess velocity wouldn't pitch the ship around like an interstellar toy. As she worked, she listened to Roadkill's briefing.

"Some people see or hear things while they're traveling through a wyrm," he was saying now. "It's nothing to be afraid of, but if you're the excitable type, now's the time to swallow one of those sleeping tabs that I left for you. And don't worry about when to take the stim-tabs. When it's time, you'll *know*. Now sit back and enjoy the ride."

She smiled at that last comment. Out of the three Tolqs, only Ammas was likely to weather the wyrm well, and that was only because he was unconscious. Wyrm-space was weird-space, even for those who spent their lives popping in and out of it.

"ETA to hole, sixteen minutes and counting," she said. "Delta-vee holding steady at forty-five percent. How's it look out there?"

"All clear," her brother reported.

"Forward shields to max-cap," she ordered. "Disrupters to stand-by." A moment later, she added, "Switching to nav-computer."

A series of lights winked to life on her console. The yellow one represented the disrupters that would turn the tangency zone into a temporary entryway. The green one was for the shields that would protect *Zeph* from wyrm-radiation and other superluminal particles. And that flashing white indicator meant that the nav-computer was on-line and ready to tackle the nether-reality of another dimension. This was a very exciting point in the journey, a time of last-minute checks and helpless suspense; and she silently blessed the tequila for stiff-arming the pain so she could appreciate the moment.

"You OK now?" Roadkill asked, voicing a little helpless suspense of his own.

"Fine," she said. "ETA, five point seven minutes and closing. You secure?"

"Affirmative."

"Got your drugs handy?"

He confirmed that, too, in a more resigned tone. He knew as well as she did how brutal re-entry could be on a body.

"Good enough, brother," she said, choosing this last moment to acknowledge the blood they used to share. "See you on the other side."

"Not if I see you first."

She laughed. It was an old joke of theirs. "One point four minutes and counting," she said then. "Activate disrupters."

"Done."

The yellow indicator on Jillian's console went suddenly green and began to pulse like a child's ray-gun. She shunted *Zephyr's* controls over to the nav-computer, then bit her refabricated lip and finished the countdown. At point nine minutes, she saw a hole in space and time spin open. At point six, she caught her first glimpse of the wyrm. It was wondrous and horrible at the same time: an alien slipstream of pure, chaotic power. The ship shuddered then. A moment later, Jillian's reality unraveled.

❧

SHE FOUND HERSELF floating on a cloud of blue static. The sky all around her shifted and flowed like molten wax. As she gaped this way and that, trying to get her bearings, a flicker of white light in the distance caught her eye. An instant after she wondered what it was, it came zooming toward her— Denny at lightspeed, now naked, now not. He called to her as he drew near.

"Jilliejilliejill."

With a sob of wonder and joy, she flung herself into his arms. At his touch, every inch of her body bled soft colors and light. She sobbed again, and pressed herself closer. His musk smelled like roses. His sweat tasted like champagne. And the feel of him made her wet. They made love—a slow, shifting dance of hips and shoulders. Once, when she looked, she found herself clutching a dark-brown back and a handful of long, red hair, but when she blinked and looked again, all she saw was Denny's familiar blondeness.

Then, with no warning or transition, he was up and fully dressed. A small, plastic square floated in the air between them. She pointed to it, and in a little girl's lisp, asked, *"What's that?"*

"Memory disk," he told her. And: "Gotta go."

With that, he began shrinking back into the distance.

"Wait!" she cried, clinging to his shadow. "Where are you going? Take me with you."

He returned then, now larger than life, and extended a hand to her as if she were a space deb at her first social. As she took it, he sanctifed her with a tender smile and burst into a one-man firestorm. A scream boiled up her throat, then erupted from her mouth as a lava flow. And just like that, she was burningburningburning, too. She shrieked as her flesh cracked and blackened; she writhed as the blood boiled in her veins. The only thing she could smell was the sickly sweet stench of imminent death. The only thing she could feel was a thousand kinds of pain.

Those pains novaed, then abruptly winked out, leaving her to shiver and twitch in darkness. Then, when she finally dared to open her eyes again, she found herself floating on a cloud of blue static. The sky all around her shifted and flowed like molten wax. As she gaped this way and that, trying to get her bearings, a flicker of light caught her eye...

അ

ALARMS BLARED, AN urgent tantara: warning, danger, all hands on deck!

Jillian came out of her apocalyptic trance with a drowning man's gasp. Then, still wracked with phantom feelings, she reclaimed control of *Zeph*, and commenced re-entry procedures.

"Sensor report!" she said.

If there was anything in the vicinity—another ship, a chunk

of rock, even a cloud of dust—she had to know about it, ASAP. A ship fresh out of a wyrm was still moving at FTL speeds, and even the smallest of collisions could be fatal.

"All clear," Roadkill croaked in reply. The break in his voice spoke volumes for his energy levels, but she didn't have time for pity yet. There were only the two of them, and *Zephyr* needed all the help it could get.

"All shields to max-cap," she said. "Sit tight for primary vee-bleed."

She initiated the bleed then. An instant later, the ship began to pitch and buck as a turbulence born of discharged velocity enveloped it. She maneuvered around the worst of the backwash, but it was still a bone-jarring rodeo ride.

"C-c-coolant l-l-leak on l-l-level three," Roadkill reported. "I'm on it," he added, before she could ask. "L-l-looks like minimal d-d-damage."

As soon as *Zephyr*'s delta-vee returned to measurable percentiles, she executed a secondary bleed. This time, the turbulence was less intense—an irritable series of spasms that passed with no harm done. Afterward, she made a few minor course adjustments and then turned toward Roadkill. There were dark half-moons beneath the blanks of his eyes; and his stubbled jaws were slack. Even his titanium-plated hair-do seemed to droop with fatigue.

"Take a breather," she told him. "I'll run systems check solo."

"Thanks," he said, slurring the word like an old boxer who'd taken one punch too many. Then he groped for his cache of drugs. The brittle crackle of plastic reminded her of past voyages, when she had been just as desperate to relieve her hammering heart and aching bones, her dry-as-dust mouth and spinning thoughts. She had to admit: she didn't miss *that* part of being human. The only symptom that had followed her out of the wyrm was a residual feeling of ravishment.

But that was bad enough. She had never been so thoroughly traumatized by a trip through another dimension. The visions had been so vivid, so real. And the sensations— sweet Mother of Light! She'd had nerve endings again. She'd smelled and tasted things, too. And while most of those things had been truly terrible, part of her wanted to go back for more—because she'd felt so *alive*. How was that possible?

"Hey, RK," she said then.

"Whazzup, Jillie?"

Jilliejilliejill. She closed her mind to the images that tried to coalesce there. "Did you have weird day-dreams in wyrm-space this time?"

He stared at her for a long moment, as if he couldn't believe that she'd troubled him with such a stupid question. Then he curled his lip into a leer and said, "I have weird day-dreams all the time, Jillie—mostly about big-breasted women with beards. Wanna hear one?"

She rolled her eyes, then turned her back to him. A moment later, she forgot what they'd been talking about.

Chapter 5

TWO HOURS INTO Tolq's solar system, Roadkill suddenly started out of his perennial slouch and then peered at one of his monitors. A moment later, he announced, "Incoming message. It's general frequency, standard code, high static. Sounds like a repeater, too."

"Source?" she asked.

"Seems to be coming from a buoy in this sector," he said.

"Play it."

A translator chattered as if it were chewing up the transmission, then belched out static and a spew of hard-edged words. "...you have entered restricted space, and are in direct violation of Galactic Council treaty 60-TS6. If you persist beyond this point, Tolq authorities will take whatever measures they deem necessary to preserve the sovereignty of their solar system. Trespassers immediately forfeit the right to appeal—"

"I've heard enough," she said, and the message stopped in mid-threat. "Shields to half-cap. Laser cannons to stand-by," she added, even though she knew that they weren't going to be very helpful without a crew to man them. "Go and get the ambassador, too. I want to hear what he has to say about this."

In her brother's absence, she fumed to herself. *You'd laugh, too,* Tark cis Xamar had said, *if you knew the priesthood as I do.* But she didn't think that *authorities taking whatever measures necessary* was particularly humorous. And she had come away from their last encounter with a feeling that he'd been holding something back from her. At the time, she'd supposed that it had to do with her being a cyborg, but this—this could work, too. And may his god help him if he'd lured her into some kind of trouble.

The lift opened then, spilling Roadkill and the Tolq ambassador onto the bridge. Tark looked wrung-out. His robe was wrinkled; his crown of braids, slightly disheveled. He walked like a man in significant need of several joint replacements. In a spiteful sort of way, she was glad to see these chinks in his perfect facade. It made him more human, and therefore less daunting.

"You sent for me, Captain?" he asked.

She gestured at Roadkill, who replayed the message. Afterward, in the flintiest of tones, she said, "Care to comment, Ambassador?"

He mocked her vague suspicions with a shrug and a prim half-smile. "It's not our buoy, Captain. The Galactic Council put it there."

"I don't really give a damn who owns it," she saidd. "I'm more interested in the broadcast itself, especially that part about *whatever measures necessary*. What does that mean exactly?"

His reddish-brown eyes narrowed with exasperation, but he answered patiently, as if he were addressing a dear but daft old aunt. "The buoy records ID beacons, then relays them to Union Security data-sorters back on Circe's Moon II. Those ships that are found guilty of violating treaty law are censured, fined, and occasionally confiscated—or so I've been told. My government has nothing to do with the process or its decisions."

"And why is that, Tark? Do they prefer a more direct approach? Do they enjoy shooting trespassers out of the sky?"

"As I told you before," he said, "our god forbids us to do violence. A trespasser could run rampant through our system forever, and the Holy Seven wouldn't raise a finger against him. The only time they're free to take direct action is when they happen upon an intruder on-world without proper authorization. And even then, they're only permitted to give him over to H'Nath for judgment.

"But your worries are baseless, Captain. You're in Tolq space on official business, and have nothing to fear."

"Nothing, Ambassador?" she echoed, treating him to one of his own ironic smiles. "There isn't that much good luck in the universe. And while I don't doubt your sincerity, I still have reservations about this Holy Seven of yours. Therefore, I want you to place a call to one of them here and now, and request official authorization for *Zephyr*'s presence in Tolq space. I'm sure it's just a formality, but what the heck? I'm a rules-and-regs kind of gal." When he hesitated, she cocked her head at him. "Is there a problem here, Tark? These people have a communications system, don't they?"

He nodded glumly. "An old hyper-wave set. But—"

"I'm sorry, Tark, but I'm not accepting 'buts' today. If you refuse to place the call, I'll turn right around and head back to Station. I refuse to jeopardize the safety of this ship or its passengers simply because you have differences with your government."

His mouth puckered like a seam with a pulled stitch only to go flat an instant later. "Very well, Captain," he conceded. "I'll contact the H'Nathma. But mark my words," he added. "Little good will come of it."

She blithely ignored the caveat. "Go and give RK the code," she told him. "He'll put the call through for you."

It took Roadkill several tries and some under-the-breath swearing, but he finally established a link between *Zephyr* and the Tolq homeworld. As he handed the ear-jack and mini-mike over to Tark, he said, "Here you go, your lordship—audio only. Ask the holies what they're dishing up for dinner."

The ambassador donned the comm-set with the aplomb of an old pro, then began to speak in a low, urgent voice. Whispering did him no good, though. With her new and improved hearing, eavesdropping was as easy as breathing to Jillian, and she listened now with unabashed interest to the one-sided conversation.

"Yes, this is Tark cis Xamar....Why?....Because the captain of this ship refuses to return the ailing heir of Xamar to his father's estates without your official blessing....yes, I know I should've discussed something like this with you before now....yes, I know this is a Ni H'Nathelek ship....But Ammas su Xamar is dying, I was thinking of his soul, not my own....Yes, I know I go too far. I always do....Yes, I know H'Nath's mercy isn't infinite. May we proceed?....Thank you."

He thrust the comm-set back at Roadkill without so much as an acknowledgment of his presence, then aimed his now-smoldering gaze at Jillian. "You're clear to proceed, Captain," he grated. "One of the Seven will be on hand to meet us when we land. I want you to remember that that was your doing, not mine."

"I'm sorry I'll have to miss him," she said, lying through her false teeth. "But RK will be shuttling you down, not me."

"Out of the question," he said, flashing aristocratic colors again. An instant later, though, his perpetually self-composed alter-ego resurfaced. I beg your pardon, Captain," he said, "but few of my clansmen have ever seen an off-worlder. Your crewman's looks, as alien as they are, will terrify them—even as they terrify Zim. And frightened Tolqs are unpredictable, Captain. They could force your crewman to leave before I have a chance to draw up your voucher. Or, they could force him to face our god. I don't think your crewman would appreciate that, Captain. The desert is a most unforgiving place."

He gave her a microsecond to put her foot down then. When she didn't take it, he pressed on. "On the other hand, meeting someone like you would be good for my people. I want them to realize how similar off-worlders are to us. I want them to start outgrowing their age-old phobias.

"So please, Captain, do the right thing for everyone concerned."

"Jillie," Roadkill said then, in a bright, chipper tone. "Ix-Nay on you eyeing-flay the uttle-shay. I can handle it."

"Is there a problem?" Tark asked.

"No problem," she replied, looking at the ambassador, but talking to her brother. "I've got everything under control. And in the name of public relations, I'll be the shuttle pilot."

She knew why RK didn't want her to fly the shuttle: he still remembered their last jaunt together. She remembered it, too, and that was one of the reasons why she meant to go out again. Mind over matter—that was her new motto. Or, like Denny used to say: *if you don't mind, it don't matter.* And she desperately wanted simple things like her taking a shuttle for a spin not to matter—to her or anyone else.

Besides, she rather liked the idea of rubbing the ambassador's patrician nose in his own prejudices. Roadkill, too alien? What a cack! The old gent couldn't possibly know that she was a techno-horror then. Neither rumor nor Nathan Ross had brought him up to date. Too bad for him, she thought smugly. Now he'd have to learn the hard way, maybe just before she left Tolq with his credit voucher in her hand.

"I'll ping you when we're in a stable orbit around your planet," she told him then. "And now, if we're done here, I'll have my crewman escort you back to your room."

"Many thanks for your consideration, Captain," the ambassador replied, with an artful flourish, "but an escort isn't strictly necessary. I've traveled aboard Ni H'Nathelek ships once or twice in the past, and can find my own way."

She glanced from him to Roadkill and back again. "I'll admit, that would save us some wear-and-tear. But are you sure you can manage?"

He favored her with a blasé smile. "Captain, I have walked the desert seven times now. I believe I can find my way back to my quarters without mishap." He bowed again, said, "I'll be anxiously awaiting your ping," and then left the bridge.

As soon as he was gone, Roadkill swiveled around in his chair to face her. His mirrored lenses seemed to shimmer with the agitation that was rolling from him in waves. "Are you sure about taking them planetside?" he asked. "You know I can't pilot *Zephyr* by myself. If anything happens—"

"Nothing's going to happen," she assured him, in a too-brusque tone. Then, with less force, she added, "But I appreciate your concern."

"It wasn't concern," he said. "I just wanted a chance to stampede a whole village of Tolqs, that's all." Then he changed the subject. "We gonna stand down on this yellow alert now?"

"That's a negative," she replied.

Nothing was going to happen, she told herself. Even so, she wanted to be ready— just in case.

∞

ALTHOUGH ESTABLISHING A low, planetary orbit was a simple procedure, Jillian hadn't done it often. When not in transit, *Zephyr* was almost always docked at one space station or another. She had never appreciated the sense of security that came hand-in-hand with a sturdy metal berth—until now. She didn't like being parked in open space, exposed on all sides to all comers. She didn't like it at all. But the good news was, she didn't have to be here long. And the sooner she got going, the sooner she could be gone. So as soon as she was done settling she pinged the ambassador.

"This is Captain D'Lange," she said. "We're ready to transport your party to the surface now. Please report directly to the shuttle bay. I'll meet you there with Ammas as soon as I can. D'Lange out." Then she turned to her brother and said, "I switched most of the systems over to the auto-manager. You are, however, going to have to let me out and back in. And please—not a word about the remotes. As far as I'm concerned, they don't exist."

He muttered something about wasted time and talent then, but otherwise held his tongue. She tossed him a wave, said, "I'll ping you from the shuttle," and then started on her way.

Her first stop was the infirmary; and nothing short of a

live-feed from there to the bridge could've prepared her for the drastic change in Ammas's appearance. He looked like a fresh corpse now: blue-faced and stiff-limbed, with skin as brittle as parchment and hair as lusterless as hay. When she pressed her ear against his chest to make sure that he was still breathing, the occasional fluttering of his heart appalled her. It was a good thing that he believed in a god, she thought, as she shifted him to a floater. Because right about now, he was in desperate need of a miracle. She was almost willing to bet the whole ship that he wouldn't survive the last leg of this trip.

But while there was life, there was hope, she told herself. And as long as he kept breathing, she would do what she could to preserve him.

So she maneuvered the gurney into the hallway and began to hurry it toward the shuttle bay. It was high-quality, and didn't generate much resistance, so she was able to run. She glanced down at Ammas once, to see how he was doing. By chance, her gaze brushed into his lips. She thought of the kiss that she'd stolen from him then. It had been nothing—less than nothing. And yet for one irrational moment, she wanted nothing more than to steal another one. Then she scorned herself for a ghoul—a masochistic ghoul at that—and didn't look down again.

She came barreling down the home-stretch to find the ambassador and his priest waiting for her just outside of the shuttle bay's entrance. She didn't give them the chance to realize that she was moving much faster than any normal woman ought to be. Instead, she started shouting orders.

"Go on and get in the shuttle," she told them. "Don't worry, there's plenty of O-2 in the bay. Zim, I want you to take a seat and stay out of the way. Tark, stand-by in the cargo-hold. I want you to power down the floater and then secure it. While you're doing that, I'll get us ready to go."

They headed into the bay. A moment later, she caught up with them. Once again, she gave them no time to wonder about the swiftness of her pace. "Zim," she said, as she handed the floater off to the ambassador, "you'd best say a prayer for this man's survival. He's in a bad way." To Tark, she said, "Join me in the cockpit when you're done. I'll be needing you for coordinates."

She hurried off and to work then. By the time the ambassador finally poked his nose into the cockpit, she'd already fueled the shuttled up, disengaged the magnetic locks, and powered up the engines.

"Is everything secure?" she asked.

"Yes, Captain," he replied, so she pinged the bridge.

"We're ready for take-off," she told him. "Open up." The outer doors unfurled, revealing a star-freckled blackness beyond. As she eased the shuttle into drive, she said, "We're out of here, *Zephyr*. See you soon. Nobody in or out, you hear?"

"Bring me back a surprise, sister dear," he said, in a tone like a disembodied leer. "Something with big boosters would be nice. *Zephyr* out."

Tark shot her a scandalized look. "That's your *brother*?"

"Mind-boggling, isn't it?" They cleared the ship's hull then. A moment later, the upper third of a very large sphere appeared in the view-plate. Most of it was sullen and red, but there were a few curlicue swirls of storm-cloud to be seen as well. "We're in a low orbit," she told Tark, "so it's not going to take us long to hit Tolq's atmosphere. Be ready for a little jostling."

She thought she was prepared for re-entry, both mentally and psychologically, but as soon as the turbulence started up, her preparations failed her. All of a sudden, she was riding shotgun in a junky old shuttle, and the man sitting next to her was Denny. At first, she was glad to see him, but then that pesky memory disk came between them again and she got mad.

"What aren't you telling me?" she bawled at him. "What are you trying to hide?"

"I h-h-have no i-i-i-dea what you're t-t-talking about, Captain," Tark cis Xamar replied.

But she wasn't fooled by the disguise. That was Denny there, and he was saying something, something about barges and the union and—

"Dammit, man! Speak up! I can't hear you."

Just then, the turbulence died back down. With its passing, her reality straightened itself out. She was flying *Zephyr*'s shuttle, Tolq was drawing closer, and Tark cis Xamar was sitting next to her, looking somewhat put out.

"And what exactly would you have me say?" he was saying.

But that reality came at a terrible price. Her headache was back now, bigger and meaner than ever before. Her grip on the U quickly became a stranglehold. If she didn't get some relief, she'd be frothing at the mouth by the time she landed. A drink would've been ideal. But she'd settle for whatever distraction she could get at this point.

"It doesn't matter," she told him, trying not to grind the words between her teeth. "I was only trying to pass the time. Maybe you could start by telling me something about your world."

The ambassador shot her a wary look, which didn't surprise her at all. She knew she was acting oddly—by anybody's standards. But he made no mention of her behavior. Instead, he shrugged as if to dismiss his suspicions, and then said, "There's really not that much to know, Captain. Tolq is a world dedicated to simplicity in all of its forms."

He had a wonderful voice, very deep and tranquilizing. She fished for a topic that would keep him talking. "So what's this god of yours got against technology?"

That wrung a sardonic half-smile out of him. "If you were to put that question to Zim, he would tell you that H'Nath has no room in his all-giving heart for technology. If you were to ask Zim, he would tell you that technology corrupts, and that the children of H'Nath are better off without it. But since you asked *me*, I'll let you in on a little secret. H'Nath doesn't really care one way or the other about technology. But The

H'Nathma does. It's been trying to hold the modern age at bay since the dawn of wyrm-travel."

"But why?" she wondered aloud.

His tone became mordant. "So the priesthood can remain in control—why else? The Holies have always known that a primitive society is easier to dominate. They know that keeping our society isolated from the rest of the galaxy works to their advantage, too. They're so desperate to stay in power, they've actually deluded themselves into believing that isolation equals independence. And that's killing us, Captain—as a people, and as a culture. Tolq cannot survive in the past."

Just then, the shuttle broke through a thick gray cloudbank, and Jillian got her first clear look at Tolq's surface. All she saw for miles on end was red sand, juts of rock, and lengthy, violet shadows. Heat shimmered on the horizon. Nothing else moved. Now she understood why Tark had described his home as an unforgiving place.

"Is all of Tolq like this?" she asked.

"Not all," the ambassador said, in a melancholy tone. "The land to the north of here is cooler and less sandy. Clans Jamal and Doba raise grains for bread-food and kluur there, and praxa for meat and milk. If we were to fly over their estates, we'd see fields of fat-capped purple grasses rippling in a breeze, rust-colored herds grazing in the wadi, and children who still have some flesh on their bones.

"If we went south, however, we'd see mountains. H'Nath's Crown, the range is called; and I've been told that the highest of its peaks can actually be seen from low orbit. Many creatures live in that land of perpetual shade, including predatory nammas, and wo, the giant, light-sensitive spiders that spin the sturdy red silk that clan Krystan then weaves into twarlas.

"As it happens, though," he added then, "we're heading west."

She shook her head at the desolate view. "I can't believe that people actually live down there. I've seen airless moons that looked more hospitable."

He snorted then: an oddly indelicate sound coming from such a polished presence. "Your pardon, Captain, but no one lives *here*. This is H'Nath's testing ground, his maker and breaker of hearts. This is where we're sent to atone for our sins. This is where we're sent to suffer. Clan Xamar lives in another, less hostile part of the desert."

"If it were me," she said, "I'd consider relocating."

"The desert has been Clan Xamar's home for a thousand years," he said, as if that were a reasonable excuse for staying. "We need its sands for our crystal, and its wildness for inspiration."

She smacked her forehead then, almost expecting it to ring hollow. "You're *those* Xamars? The Xamar crystal Xamars?" At his nod, she said, "Yowza, Tark. That's some of the finest artwork in the galaxy. Some of the most expensive, too."

"Indeed. Tolq is not a poor planet, only a poorly managed one. The clans need to become more involved in their own government. They need to realize that the H'Nathma are god's servants, not gods themselves. They—"

He slammed on the verbal brakes. She could almost see the words pile up in his mouth like derailed box-cars. "My apologies, Captain," he said then, showing her a smile stiff with self-mockery and rue. "But I'm famous for my diatribes—as any priest on Tolq will tell you. They've tried to shut me up seven times now. And seven times, H'Nath has sent me back.

"I am a prophet, Captain. That can a very difficult thing to be."

Jillian made no reply. She didn't believe in this H'Nath of his. The concept was archaic; infantile; inane. Gods had no place in an age where men could make things like herself and get away with it.

Just then, a reddish spire in the distance snagged her attention. It was glinting and flashing in the late afternoon sun like a child's kaleidoscope. She pointed it out to Tark, wondering what it could be. He squinted in that direction for over a minute before finally making the connection.

"Your vision is remarkable," he said in passing, and then identified the tower as H'Nath's Throat. "It was crafted by my ancestors as a tribute to H'Nath's greatness," he told her. "And sometimes, during the Season of Storms, he sings to us through it. It is a horrible, haunting sound—the music of divinity and despair. The only thing worse than hearing it on a stormy night is never hearing it at all."

Then, without permission, he flicked the intercom switch and said, "Good news, Zim. We're almost home."

Now she could see a series of mounds nestled in the sand. They didn't look tall enough to be dwellings, but as she watched, a red-robed figure emerged from one like an ant from its hole. It hit her then. Xamar estate was like a desert iceberg—only the tip of it showed on the surface. The rest was buried beneath the sand, where it would be cooler. Rather ingenious, she thought, and then noticed another curiosity in the distance. At first, she'd mistaken it for an outcropping, for it was made of stone, but as she drew nearer, it morphed into a two-story building with a monstrous smoke-stack. She was just about to ask Tark what it was when the rose-tinted sky-lights of Xamar estate began to wink and glimmer in the setting sun's light. It was a dazzling display, like a nest of dragon's eggs.

"How beautiful," she said.

"It is, isn't it," Tark agreed, with none of his usual irony. Then, as the light-show sparkled to a close, he pointed toward the out-building. "There's a large bed of flat rock over by the glassworks. It's no shuttle-pad, but at least it'll keep a little bit of the desert out of your intake valves."

"Thanks," she said, and then veered north to skirt the estate. No point in stroking the whole warren out, she decided—although the temptation was definitely there. When Tark realized what she was doing, a curious look of wonder and something more spread across his face.

"Thank you, Captain," he said. "You're quite remarkable. I believe I'll miss you when you go."

"Kind of you to say so," she said. "I'm just sorry that we had to meet under such harrowing circumstances."

"If not for the circumstances, I doubt that we would've met at all. I regret that."

She had a long shoal of purple bedrock in her sights now. It was large enough to accommodate either a vertical or a horizontal landing. The vertical would be more efficient fuel-wise when it came time to take off again. The horizontal would be less bumpy now. She went with less bumpy, and told herself that it was for Ammas's sake.

So she cut back on the throttle and raised the braking flaps. As the shuttle nosed its way toward the ground, a miniature sandstorm rose up in its wake. She braked again, then lowered the landing gear. Moments later, the shuttle touched down and then skipped along the bedrock. Sand coated the view-plate. Sensor-panels flashed. She applied the brakes one last time, then smiled at Tark as the shuttle came to a grudging stop. The Tolq had gone quite pale beneath his perennial tan.

"Welcome home, Ambassador," she said, and then cut power to stand-by. "You can disembark whenever you're ready."

The Tolq was out of the co-pilot's chair in an instant, but his knees were stiff from sitting in one place for so long and he could barely move. As soon as he realized this, he shouted for Zim. The priest poked his shiny head into the entryway as if it were the door to hell.

"Start Ammas on his way to Elyn's quarters," Tark commanded him. "I'll let her know that you're coming. I'll also arrange to have other lifters meet you along the way."

"Lifters?" Jillian echoed, as Zim ducked back out of sight.

But Tark forestalled her with an upraised hand. There was a sudden, strained look about him now, as if he were on the verge of inspiration or a seizure. As she watched, the tension within him mounted—once and then again. A moment later, he let out a gasp and grabbed the back of his chair to steady himself.

"What was that all about?" she asked.

"I'll explain later—"

I'll tell you all about it once we're moonbound, OK?

"—right now, we need to go and meet our welcoming committee."

"Excuse me?" she stammered, and then hastened to add, "I thought I'd wait here while you got the voucher."

He nixed that plan with a tight little smile. "Financial transactions are forbidden after sunset, Captain. You'll have to wait until tomorrow for the voucher. And I won't hear of you spending the night here in the shuttle. You are my guest."

"Ta-ark," she said, stretching his name into a complaint. "I wish you had told me about this financial taboo before the fact. My ship's sitting up there in orbit with a single crewman aboard. I need to get back to it. Can you direct-deposit the voucher into my account?"

His tight little smile grew even tighter. "I'm afraid we don't have those kinds of facilities here on Tolq, Captain. But come now. What difference will a few hours more or less make to your crewman?" Then, before she could tender one or two of the more outstanding possibilities that sprang to her mind, he went on to say, "This is your chance to show my people that offworlders are normal human beings, not demons to be feared. And you cannot leave with giving the lord of Xamar a chance to thank you for saving his son's life. He would be mortally offended."

She groped for a way out of this ironic web. Posing as a human among backwater techno-dopes had sounded like a surefire cack back on *Zephyr*, but now that she was here, it didn't seem so funny. Because conniver or not, Tark's heart was in the right place. She didn't want to sully his intentions with unspoken lies. But it was either that, or 'fess up to the truth. And once she did that, she could kiss that voucher goodbye. She had come this far for it. She might as well go one step further.

"All right," she said, not bothering to make her resignation look like anything else, "you win. I'll call my change of plans in. But just remember," she added, "this was *your* idea."

"I'll meet you outside," he replied.

Roadkill wasn't pleased to hear from her. "What do you mean, you'll be delaying your return till tomorrow?" he said. "Have you forgotten that I'm up here on my own?"

"My memory's not *that* bad," she replied. "But there's been a foul-up with the voucher. If I leave now, there's a good chance we'll lose it. And in case *you've* forgotten, we're hurting for credit."

"I know, I know. But I still don't like it. Being up here all by myself give me the big-time creeps."

"As soon as that voucher's in my hand, I'm out of here," she promised him. "I'll give you a ping just before I take off."

"Roger that," came his sour reply. "*Zephyr* out."

She powered down the shuttle then, all but the security systems. Better safe than sorry, she thought—even amongst the anti-techs. Then, as she headed toward the hatch, she noticed the floater. It was still bracketed to the cargo-hold wall. She tsked to herself: stupid Zim. He was probably dragging Ammas through the sand by the hair.

"That floater belongs to you, you know," she told Tark, as she came striding down the gangway. "The Medi-vacs wouldn't have left it behind if they hadn't charged you for it."

"Consider it an eccentric gift from me to your ship," he said.

"What about Ammas?" she asked. But even as the words left her mouth, she realized that Ammas was nowhere in sight. Zim was gone, too. Impossible, she thought. That spastic little runt of a man couldn't have carried a lunch-sack that far already, never mind a full-grown, dead-weight man. "Where'd they go?"

"They're well on their way to a healer's care," he said.

"But how—"

"Zim is a lifter, Captain," he explained, half-smiling at her confusion. "He has the power to teleport heavy objects over short distances. He and others like him are floating Ammas to Elyn's. When there is need, they can work quite fast."

"But—"

"H'Nath gives each of his children a gift upon their coming of age, Captain. Zim received the power to move things with his mind, for example. Elyn received the power to heal. We're given these gifts so we might better turn our backs on technology's sordid temptations and lead a purer lifestyle. Or so the priesthood says."

"And speaking of priests," she said, glancing over the slight stoop of his shoulder, "here comes one now." Then, although she could tell already, she waited a long moment before adding, "It's a woman."

The ambassador's half-smile hardened into something more official and somber. At the same time, he tucked his hands into his robe's belled sleeves and turned to watch the red-robed figure march across the sand and toward them. Her carriage was stiff with purpose; her close-shaved head reflected the sunset's fading light. It wouldn't take much for her to be beautiful, Jillian mused. All she'd have to do was lose that ferocious scowl. It was puckering her delicate features into an array of hard lines. But her expression grew no brighter as she drew closer. If anything, it became more rancorous. She lashed Jillian with an outraged glance in passing, then plowed to a stop in front of the ambassador and lumped her fists against her hips

"Tark cis Xamar," she said.

"Micca de H'Nathmaza," he replied, with his usual ironic inflection. "I should've guessed that the Seven would elect you to adjudicate this matter. How very good to see you again, child."

She ignored his banter. "I can't believe you chartered a Ni H'Nathelek ship to transport the heir of Xamar home. Is there *no* end to your audacity?"

"I had to do something," he said. "Otherwise, Ammas would've died. Surely H'Nath would rather have him my way home than yours. Or do you think The Great One enjoys prayers for the dead?"

The priestess flushed. Her light brown eyes narrowed to slits. "Don't tempt me to add blasphemy to your list of sins, Tark, because I'd just as soon drive you into the desert as look at you right now. You and your son could beg H'Nath's mercy together."

As Micca had reddened, so Tark now paled. "Tobia?" he asked, a hint of dread or menace in his tone. "Tobia has nothing to do with this." He scanned the horizon as if in search of a familiar outline, but there was no one to be seen. "Where is he?"

"Ten days ago, he and a man from clan Jamal were caught trying to make contact with an off-world profiteer. Their intention was to buy Ni H'Nathelek goods with Xamar crystal. Tobia freely admitted his guilt at the truth tribunal. The H'Nathma had no choice but to sentence him to the desert."

"For how long?"

The animosity drained from her face all at once, leaving puddles of rue and regret behind. "He was sent to do a two-day penance five days ago. A storm came through on his first night out."

"I see," Tark said, in a funereal tone, and then turned to Jillian. His brown eyes were glassy with grief and rage, but he tried to wring his mouth into a smile nonetheless. The result was more frightening than anything else. "Come, Captain," he said. "Allow me to show you to your quarters—"

Micca cut him off with a scandalized hiss. "Have you completely lost your mind, Tark cis Xamar? This, this—" She looked Jillian up and down as if she were a pregnant super-roach, but failed to come up with a suitably awful description. "—this *person* can't stay here!"

"Clan Xamar is in Captain D'Lange's debt," he replied. "Until that debt has been paid, she is to be our honored guest."

"You can't offer hospitality without Lord Xamar's consent," the priestess argued.

He despised her with that bland half-smile of his—an almost superhuman feat, it seemed to Jillian, considering his emotional state. "Saj is my brother. He doesn't have to speak his thoughts for me to know them, especially when they concern his son. Captain D'Lange saved Ammas's life. Saj will welcome her as his guest. I'm as sure of that as I am of the blood we share."

"We'll see about that," Micca said, as icy as he was mild. "But just remember, Tark: the desert is an unforgiving place."

At that, the priestess whirled on her heel and marched back toward the estate. Tark glared at her receding form until it vanished in the fast-fading twilight, then gave his robe an irritated flick and headed that way himself. At a loss for something better to do, Jillian followed.

She saw the estate long before she set foot in it. The glass-capped mounds that she had flown over earlier were now spilling rose-colored light into the darkening sky. It looked as if all of Tolq were a lantern, glowing from within. On some other evening, she might've enjoyed the spectacle. But tonight, the only thing that she could appreciate was Tark's fey mood. His pace was brisk; his conversation, clipped. As they strode down a half-hidden ramp and into the estate's red-tinged interior, the only advice he gave her was not to touch anything. She didn't press him for more. She knew how loss worked.

Ahead, she heard a door creak twice and then click. An instant later, somebody went scurrying down the hall in his or her bare feet, whispering, "Gather your young ones and lock your doors! The off-worlder's coming this way!"

Jillian regarded the alarm-raiser's fear with a degree of wonder. All that hubbub just for one lousy offworlder? Sweet, suffering mother! She couldn't even imagine what the poor bastard would do if he knew what he was *really* running from.

Just then, Tark came to a stop in front of a door that looked no different from any of the others that they'd passed already. Without ceremony, he pushed it open and said, "This is one of the places that I'm permitted to call my own when I'm here. I hope you'll find it to your liking."

She stepped across the threshold, then froze, overwhelmed by what she saw. An antique divan of leather and brass occupied the center of the room. It was surrounded by cushy pillows and a low-slung table. Abstract tapestries adorned the walls. Black Florian carpets hid the floor. But what awed her most was the collection of Xamar crystal. She'd seen a piece on display in The Museum of Post-Modern Art on Circe's II, but it had only a passing glimpse, and only from a laser-enforced distance. Now she understood what all the fuss had been about.

There were five pieces in all in the room. Each had been exquisitely crafted from glass that blushed deep red at its core; and each had a personality of its own; but Jillian's eyes kept straying toward the two-meter high statue near the door. Twisted and bent at uneasy angles in some places but then emphatically straight in others, it reminded her of a complex and not entirely pleasant thought. She tried to work through the snarl, but it lost her somewhere in the middle, and then dared her to try again. She would have made the attempt, too, if Tark hadn't intervened.

"I'm flattered by your interest in my work, Captain," he said. "I hope it will keep you amused while I'm otherwise detained. If you get tired, feel free to stretch out on the couch or the pillows. The necessities room is through that door to your right. I'll have a tray of food and water brought to you."

"Ta-ark," she protested, daunted by the room's opulence, "I can't stay here."

"On the contrary," he told her more ironic than usual. "You can't stay anywhere else. Most of my people would sooner open a vein than let you into their homes. But tell me what it is about the room that displeases you. Is it that statue? I can have it removed. I only keep it around to remind me of my limitations."

"We should all be so limited," she mused, glancing at that oh-so-compelling piece again. Then, aware of his need to be gone, she added, "But don't worry about me, Tark. I can manage by myself. Go and take care of the things that need your attention."

He bowed to her, a gesture steeped in genuine gratitude, and then took his leave. The door was still closing behind him when she heard Micca's buzz-saw of a voice erupt in the hallway. Although the priestess spoke softly enough, her tone cut through sand and glass with ease. Jillian didn't have to work hard to eavesdrop.

"Where do you think you're going, Tark cis Xamar?" she asked.

"Literally or metaphysically?" the ambassador drawled in reply, and then sighed into a hostile silence. "I weep for you, child. You're too young to be without a sense of humor." More silence followed. "Very well," he said then, "if you must know. I'm off to greet my brother, and then to look in on Ammas."

"What a coincidence," she said. "I've just come from Ammas's healing."

"Is all well with him?"

"It was a near thing, but yes—he's going to live. Are you disappointed?"

He mocked the question with a derisive snort. " I risked H'Nath's wrath to get the lad to a healer as fast as possible. Why in The Great One's name would I be disappointed to hear that my gamble was not in vain?"

"A rescue attempt that failed by minutes would've made you seem like quite the hero in clan Xamar's eyes," she speculated. "They might've believed you when you told them that you could've saved their fair-haired son only if you'd had a Ni H'Nathelek ship at your immediate disposal. They might've followed your lead when you started agitating against the H'Nathma. If Ammas had died, you would've had a nice little power base all ready and waiting for you to step in and claim it."

"You have a remarkable imagination," he said.

But she pressed on as if she hadn't heard. "But Ammas lived, Tark. And Elyn says his sickness was caused by poison, not disease. What do you know about that?"

"Poison?"

Jillian's eyebrows arched just as Tark's tone had. This was getting interesting.

"Elyn says it was nammasting," Micca continued, becoming suddenly lavish with her contempt. "Who but you had access to such an indigenous toxin? Who but you had a motive to use it?"

"Your logic is flawed from start to finish," Tark said, sounding both amused and annoyed. "I cherish Ammas as I do—did—my own son. And I have no wish to be Lord of Xamar."

"Save your lies for the truth tribunal, Tark cis Xamar. I'm on my way to arrange for it now."

"The only truth you're likely to expose is the extent of your own foolishness," he warned.

A moment's silence ensued. It was broken by an ominous snick at Jillian's door, and then a sugary, "You're next, Tark."

The ambassador loosed a martyred sigh. "Honestly, Micca. There's no need for any of this."

"I was appointed to be the judge of that," the priestess replied. "And I say you and your offworld collaborator are to remain confined to your rooms until the tribunal is ready to convene. If you resist, I'll call a mind-bender."

Tark sighed again, then receded beyond earshot. A moment later, Jillian heard a single twarla go swishing past her door. She waited until she was certain the hallway was clear, and then tested the door. It was locked.

"So much for being an honored guest," she said.

Her irritation was instant. No one kept Jillian D'Lange against her will, especially not some backwater priestess with a bad attitude. She nudged the door with her shoulder. It shuddered—and rightly so. Because it wouldn't take much more than a nudge from her to bring it down. And once she was free, there was precious little these Tolqs could do to stop her from blowing this gig. The only thing holding her back was the voucher, and she was starting to wonder how much aggravation one lousy little credit slip was worth.

Shit! Now her head was starting to hurt again, too.

Just then, a rich, baritone voice said, *"Captain. It's me—Tark cis Xamar. Don't be alarmed."* The voice sounded so real and so close, she actually glanced from side to side to make sure she was alone. She was. But it didn't seem to matter. *"The ability to mind-speak is my gift from H'Nath,"* the voice went on. *"But while you can hear me, I cannot hear you, so you must listen now and ask questions later.*

"As I predicted, involving the H'Nathma has complicated matters. Micca is no Zim to be bullied and bluffed into submission, but one of the Holy Seven's most trusted servants. As such, she has a great deal of personal power that she may dispense as she sees fit. Unfortunately, she has a suspicious mind. She also has an active dislike of me. I'm telling you this because she's raised some accusations against us—accusations that only a truth tribunal can resolve. Don't be alarmed by anything you might see or hear during this tribunal—we're in no danger. And when we've been vindicated, the rest of Xamar will apologize to you even as I am now. Until then, Captain, I can only ask you to be patient."

The voice retreated then. In the ensuing silence, Jillian paced the floor and tried to ignore the throbbing in her head. *No danger, no danger, no danger,* Tark had said.

But what did he know?

Chapter 6

A LOUD KNOCK rattled the door. Jillian winced at the sound. She'd stretched out on the davenport, hoping to lull her headache back to quiescence, but that time-honored trick didn't work for cyborgs, and now her plasti-steel skull felt like a decompression chamber. The door rattled again. Beyond it, she heard the shuffle of feet.

"Go away!" she shouted.

A lock clicked. The door swung open. A pair of shiny-headed priests planted themselves just beyond the threshold. Their strong-man stances and flinty stares made it clear that they were unhappy to have drawn this duty. She didn't feel the least bit sorry for them. Indeed, she intended to make them downright miserable—simply because she wanted the company.

"Why'd you bother to knock if you were planning to barge right in anyway?" she drawled, glaring at them from the couch.

"We are H'Nathma," the larger of the two said, though he wouldn't quite meet her eye. "The adjudicator sent us to escort you to the tribunal."

"And what if I don't want to go?"

He fingered his quot'tl bead as if it were a source of strength, then said, "We will compel you if we must."

She flashed the pair a vicious smile, then flowed to her feet—a seemingly graceful unfurling that left her teetering on the brink of vertigo. She grabbed the back of the couch to steady herself, then smiled again.

"All right, here I am. Who's going to try and compel me first?"

The priests tensed like frightened hares. Their fear antagonized her. She took a step toward them, projecting menace. She could almost see their soft brown flesh turning to a frothy pulp beneath her pile-driver fists. She could almost hear their bones snapping.

Almost.

And *almost* wasn't good enough anymore.

The unmitigated savagery of the thought triggered a series of internal alarms; and for one horrified moment thereafter, all she could do was stand fast and gape into empty space. She'd actually intended to hurt one or both of those priests. She'd been looking forward to it with the same sort of glee that she'd once reserved for sex. And even now, part of her couldn't understand why she'd changed her mind. But that was OK, she told herself, because the spell had passed.

She glanced at her escorts then. Both of them were still braced for contamination or perhaps damnation—whichever came first. This time, though, the sight provoked only grief. She raised her hand, motioning for peace, then said, "Just kidding, guys. Come on, let's go and check out this tribunal thing."

"A wise decision," the spokes-priest said, and then positioned himself to her rear. The other one took the lead. Neither of them, she noticed, came within an arm's length of her. She couldn't say that she blamed them.

As they herded her from one subterranean corridor to the next, the booming in her head began to mount again. She clenched her false teeth, and wished for a swig of tequila or anything else that could silence the ache. Then, for no apparent reason, she thought of Targon. Maybe he'd been in near-constant pain, too, she mused. Maybe that's what had driven him right out of his mind. But she was quick to reject the theory. Targon had had the RIMs. She was suffering from an overdose of stress and aggravation. As soon as she had a chance to equalize, the pain would disappear. No other alternative sufficed.

The priest in the lead strode up to a pair of double doors

then, and drew them open with a Spartan flourish. "Go in," he told her. "The adjudicator is expecting you."

But Jillian didn't trust Micca to play fair, so instead of walking all the way in, she merely crossed the threshold. The hall in which she found herself then was spacious—a dining area perhaps, or some sort of classroom. Although it was dimly lit, she could see three people sitting at a table that had been set up along the wall across from her. One of them was Micca. Another was Tark. And while Jillian didn't know the older, lock-jawed man seated in the middle space, there was no doubt in her mind that he was Xamar's lord. His resemblance to both Ammas and Tark had survived the graying of his rusty braid, and the gradual petrification of his deeply tanned face. He projected pride rather than hauteur.

But it was the other way around with Micca.

"You there—off-worlder," the priestess called out, in the snottiest of tones. "We have some questions to put to you. Come forward."

Jillian did so at a leisurely pace, a calculated act of insolence. It pleased her to see the woman's scowl harden into a glare. It revived her craving for blood.

"Close enough," Micca said, as Jillian came within a meter of the table. "If you wish to sit down, you may pull up a chair."

"Thanks," Jillian replied, "but I think I'll stand. That way, you won't have to destroy the chair afterward." Then she took another step forward— just to tweak the priestess's pert little nose. Afterward, she asked, "So what now?"

In reply, Micca waved a small, wafer-thin woman with heaps of auburn curls out of the shadows. This waif approached Jillian with a wary sort of shyness, as if she were expecting to be outright rebuffed. Jillian did her best to be civilized. Micca was the one who rankled, she told herself. Micca was the one to spite.

"Are you ready, Gev?" the priestess asked then.

"Micca," Lord Xamar said, before Gev had a chance to respond, "The captain has no knowledge of our ways. Tell her what's going to happen here."

Jillian modified her scowl, a gesture of respect for the old man's unexpected show of fair-mindedness. Micca glowered, too, condemning the request as a waste of time, but she didn't contest Saj's right to command her in this.

"Gevera's a mind-seer," she said, addressing Jillian as she might address an idiot or some knuckle-dragging barbarian. "She'll be monitoring your thoughts as you answer our questions, so we'll know if you're telling the truth or not."

Jillian continued to scowl at the priestess, but inwardly, she was glaring daggers at him. *No danger, huh?* What the fuck did he think this was? She couldn't afford to have an alien telepath poking around in her head. If Gev discovered that she was a cyborg, she could forget about her voucher. And if she stumbled onto something else—like whatever it was that was causing this damned headache!—the stars only knew what would happen. She had to get out of here. She had to—

A faint pressure on her shoulder startled her out of her snowballing thoughts. To her surprise and momentary confusion, she realized that it was Gevera, trying to comfort her. The telepath's touch was gentle. Her smile was bittersweet.

"I understand, Captain," she said. "All people, no matter how good, have secrets. But do not be afraid. So long as they don't pertain to this tribunal, those secrets are yours to keep. This I swear to you by H'Nath."

Secrets? The word buzzed through Jillian like a swarm of bees. Did Gev know? Had she already seen? Did she need—shutting up? But even as paranoia scrabbled for a fingerhold within her, reason intervened. The telepath had sworn by her god not to pry, it argued. Such oaths were sacred to Tolqs. And besides, Gevera wouldn't have touched her if she knew the truth. If anything, she would've run screaming from the room.

"Thank you, Gevera," Jillian said, grateful in more ways than one. Then, feeling suddenly better about this ridiculous situation, she returned her attention to Micca. "All right, let's get this show on the road."

A moment's confusion deepened the priestess's seemingly perpetual scowl then. But the lord of Xamar knew what the antiquated expression meant, and was quite ready to go with it. He clapped his hand against the table three times, and then said, "This truth tribunal is now convened.

"We are here because Ammas su Xamar was poisoned on Circe's Moon II; and because his healer determined that the poison came from Tolq. We are here to learn the poisoner's identity if possible, and to consign him or her—" He glanced at Jillian, but not his brother. "—to the desert, if necessary.

"Micca, you may commence with the questioning. May H'Nath's wisdom guide your thoughts."

"My thanks for your prayers, Lord Xamar," the priestess said. "I trust H'Nath to guide and nurture all of us." She turned to look at Jillian then. As she did so, a predatory half-smile spooled across her tight-beam of a mouth. "Now tell us truly, off-worlder: did you know of Ammas su Xamar's poisoning before you heard of it in this room?"

Jillian glanced at Tark, who tipped her a supremely confident nod. His smugness irked her almost as much as Micca's vulpine simper did. She decided to throw them both for a little loop, and so answered with a big, bold, "Yes."

"Truth," Gevera said, in a voice like distant windchimes.

Tark's jaw dropped like an old-fashioned draw-bridge. For one stunned moment afterward, all he could do was glance from Jillian to Gevera and back again. He found no answers there, though. The mind-seer's eyes were closed. And Jillian refused to meet his gaze. Let him wonder, she thought.

Meanwhile, Micca grew more intense. "Tell us when you first heard of it."

"It was approximately one standard hour ago—just before you locked me in my room," she said, oozing phony earnestness. "I couldn't help but overhear you and Tark talking out in the corridor. My hearing is quite good. But prior to that, I knew nothing of Ammas's poisoning. I didn't even know Tolq produced poisons."

"All true," Gevera announced.

Only then did Jillian deign to look at Tark; and it was obvious by the amused light in his eyes that he had forgiven her for her little trick. She couldn't tell what Lord Xamar thought about it, for he remained as straight-faced as a statue, but Micca looked ready to rend and tear.

"Have you conspired with Tark cis Xamar in any way?" she asked

Jillian wanted to bait the priestess again—just because it was so freakin' fun. But she couldn't think of a clever response off-hand, and the pounding in her head precluded a more in-depth search, so she dismissed her druthers with a shrug and said, "None that I know of."

"Truth."

"Then why did he charter your freighter rather than a smaller, faster ship?"

"Objection," Tark said then. "The question calls for speculation on the captain's part."

But Jillian answered anyway. *Nobody* was going to make *Zephyr* sound like some second-rate tub, especially not a neo-Stone Age priestess. "My ship is faster than a lot of private skiffs," she said, "and much better-armed as well. Both features come in handy in a sector of space where Ni H'Nathelek vessels have been disappearing. So while I can't say for sure why Tark hired me instead of someone else, maybe it was because he wanted the best transport available for his nephew.

"And before you ask," she added, "I took the contract because I need the credit."

"Truth," Gevera confirmed.

Micca was all but fuming with frustration now. She turned to the lord of Xamar as if he were her last hope and said, "Do you have questions for the off-worlder?"

"No," he said, with a delicate wave of his hand. "Question Tark cis Xamar now."

Jillian marveled at the old man's control. Here he was, sitting in judgment over his only brother, yet both his tone and his expression remained strictly neutral. If Jillian hadn't known better, she would've mistaken him for a cyborg. Too bad he wasn't, she mused in passing. She would've enjoyed a little company.

Meanwhile, Micca went over to Gevera and gave her shoulders a gentle shake. The telepath blinked, then swayed as if she'd suddenly been released from a stasis field. Micca held her in a light embrace until the spell passed, then asked her if she was strong enough to continue.

"We can call another mind-seer to take your place if the off-worlder's thoughts have left you in need of rest or cleansing," the priestess added.

"I am quite well," Gev assured her. "Just give me a moment to recollect myself." Micca nodded, then started toward the table. As soon as her back was turned, Gevera dared to touch Jillian again. "I was not spying," she whispered, "but some things cannot be shut out. That headache will consume you if it isn't remedied soon."

"I know," Jillian said. It certainly felt like she was being eaten alive—bite by saw-toothed bite. "I'm taking care of it as soon as I get home."

"Good," Gevera said, and then added one thing more in parting. "You aren't at all what I expected. I am glad of that."

Moments later, the tribunal recommenced; and this time, Tark was in the hot seat. To look at him, though, a person who didn't know better would suppose he was taking in a seminar with friends. He sat calm and poised with his hands folded on the table in front of him. His eyes took everything in without giving any of his thoughts away.

"Tark cis Xamar," Micca said, "did you poison Ammas su Xamar?"

"I did not."

"Truth," Gevera said, and Jillian saw the iron rod of Lord Xamar's spine relax a notch.

"Do you know who did?" Micca asked then.

"I do not."

This time, Gevera remained silent. When prompted by the priestess, she frowned as if she were trying to see beyond the obscure twists of Tark's thoughts, and then droned, "Not entirely true. While he knows nothing for certain, I sense that he suspects somebody very strongly."

At that, Micca swiveled toward Tark like a gunboat turret and opened fire. "Tell us who you suspect, Tark cis Xamar. Otherwise, I'll send for somebody who can compel you to the truth."

Annoyance spasmed across the ambassador's sun-browned face. He shifted in his seat, but when he could not escape Micca's stare, he heaved an exasperated sigh and said, "Ammas. I suspect Ammas."

Both Saj and Micca blurted, "What?" At the same time, Gevera said, "Truth."

"But why?" Micca demanded then. Her predatory smile was gone now, upended by pure consternation. "He had no reason to murder himself. And he knows that H'Nath forbids suicide."

"Why indeed?" Lord Xamar echoed—a deep, troubled rumble. He looked much older now than he had a scant moment ago. His shoulders were slightly stooped now, and his face seemed eroded rather than aged. "Gevera," he said then, "go and get Ammas su Xamar from Elyn's quarters. I had planned to let him sleep after his ordeal, but it appears that he is needed here to solve this matter."

Gevera went scurrying out of the hall. In her absence, no one spoke.

Jillian's head was pounding like heavy surf now. She glared at the now-pensive priestess through her false eyelashes and fantasized about slapping her: once for dragging a patently innocent offworlder into this peculiar witchhunt; again for not having the grace to be embarrassed by the enormity of her mistake; and once more just for fun. Her fists knotted of their own accord, ready to transform fantasy into irrevocable fact.

She forced them open again, then loosed an inward groan. Stars above! She could sure use a drink right now. In addition to being stupid, these Tolqs were miserable hosts.

Just then, a red-robed silhouette stepped into the hall through a side-door. The newcomer was too tall and masculine to be Gevera, and too shaggy to be a priest. He hurried over to the table, then executed a deep, respectful bow in front of Lord Xamar. Afterward, he said, "You wanted to see me, Father?"

Saj made some reply, but Jillian didn't hear it on any conscious level. She was still trying to come to grips with what her eyes were telling her. But that was impossible, she thought, as she stared at Ammas's back. A few hours ago, that man hadn't been fit to breath, never mind stand unassisted on his own two legs. The healer who had tended to him was nothing short of a medical genius!

Her wonder gave birth to sudden inspiration: if this Elyn could restore somebody as far gone as Ammas to health, then surely she could banish a simple headache. Perhaps Tark could introduce her to the woman. *Meeting someone like you would be good for my people,* he'd said. And even if he'd changed his mind since then, he owed her big for getting her involved in this stupid tribunal.

Another quote bubbled out of her memory then, a rider to the first: *I want them to realize how similar off-worlders are to us.* And just like that, reality crushed her infant hope beneath its heel. Any healer of Elyn's caliber would notice the differences between syntheskin and real flesh immediately. And if she had a chance to look closer than that— well, the cyborg would definitely be out of the bag. So as much as it pained her to do so, she was going to have to endure this damned headache until she got back to Circe's II.

"Yes," she heard Ammas say then, "it's true. I poisoned myself."

She turned her attention back to the table just in time to see Lord Xamar blanch. An instant later, his eyes went dark and narrow with anger. "Perhaps you would care to tell us why," he rumbled.

Although she couldn't see his face, she could tell that the question made Ammas uncomfortable. He shifted his weight from one foot to the other, then combed his fingers through his long, sleep-disheveled hair and cleared his throat. The excuse he offered then was low-voiced and feeble.

"I needed to get sick."

Micca sputtered then—a sound of disbelief and fury. "You took nammasting to make yourself *sick*? What in H'Nath's name were you thinking, Ammas? Even children know how deadly that poison is."

"That's true," Ammas conceded. "But I also know that healers sometimes use it in tiny doses to lower a person's metabolism. I thought I could do the same sort of thing. Unfortunately, I miscalculated the dose and wound up a victim of my own cleverness."

"But why, my son?" his father asked again, in a voice that rippled with confusion. "If you wanted to come home, all you had to do was tell someone. Proper arrangements would've been made."

Ammas shrank into the folds of his robe, as if he were trying to duck the question. In a hushed, semi-pleading tone, he said, "Must we discuss this now, Father? Believe me, I didn't mean for any of this—" He gestured at the table then, so they'd know that 'this' meant the tribunal. "—to happen."

"But it did," Saj said. "Now you must answer for it."

"Very well." He drew himself back to his full height like a man preparing to face a firing squad. "I did it in the hope of securing clan Xamar an off-world contact. I did it in the hope that Captain D'Lange would want to be a go-between for us and the granaries of New Georgia."

Micca loosed an outraged hiss. "You risked your life? To involve your clansmen in forbidden matters? Great H'Nath!" she prayed then. "Give this man his brains back!"

"And what was I supposed to do?" Ammas asked, in a surprisingly fiery tone. "Let my family and friends starve?

You know as well as I do that there's not going to be a Blessed Distribution Day this year. The inbound ship was destroyed by pirates almost nine months ago, and the outbound ship has barely set sail."

The priestess hissed again. "Ammas! That information is *not* for off-world ears."

At the same time, Jillian said, "That ark was *yours?*"

All eyes turned her way. She didn't notice at first. She was desperately trying to recover the memory that had nearly surfaced at the putt-putt's mention. *Denis was upset. Still is for that fact.* But there was more than that. She could *feel* something stuck inside her—something small and square, a curiosity of some kind. And: *let's just say that space junk can be very telling.* But the harder she tried to force these fragments into a coherent package, the harder her head pounded. Finally, she had no choice but to let the fragments go.

It was then that she realized that everyone was staring at her. She wondered what she'd done or missed. Micca was quick to clue her in.

"What do you know about that ship, off-worlder?" she asked, in a voice brimming with suspicions.

Jillian frowned, trying to squeeze her thoughts past the white-hot fishing-hooks of a full-fledged migraine. "Nothing," she said. *Space junk can be very telling.* "A friend of mine found the wreckage, is all. He's dead now." *DennyDennyDen.* "Maybe Union Security can be of more help. I know someone at the top if you're interested."

"I am not," Micca replied coldly, as if Jillian had just offered her a grievous insult. "H'Nath commanded his children to be independent. We'll solve our problems without Ni H'Nathelek help."

"And how will we do that?" Tark asked then, in that dry, mocking voice of his.

"We'll persevere," the priestess said. "And, as always, we'll pray."

Before Jillian could scoff at such a useless strategy, Ammas said, "Perhaps we've been praying for the wrong thing."

"Oh?" Micca's tone arched like a cat's back. "And what do *you* think we should be praying for, Ammas su Xamar?"

"Forgiveness," he asserted, and then smiled at the priestess's uncomprehending scowl. "Because if you think about it, we as a people have sinned."

"How so?"

"H'Nath's first commandment to his children is to be independent," he explained. "We aren't, though—leastwise, not when it comes to daily life here on Tolq. We depend on the H'Nathma for everything from grain allotments to production quotas. We let them solve our problems for us. That's neither good nor right. If we're going to honor the first commandment, then we need to start taking a more active role in our destinies. We need to share the burdens of government more equally."

Micca whirled to address Lord Xamar. A dusky flush gave color to her outrage. "I warned you not to let Ammas go off-world with Tark," she said. "Now you know why. Your brother is a master of seduction, and he's done his work well." Then she rounded on Tark. "First your son, now your nephew. How many lives must you lose to the desert before you quit preaching corruption?"

"My views are my own, not my uncle's," Ammas said, reddening in his turn. "And if it's corrupt of me to want to feed hungry people, then I'll gladly walk the desert a dozen times. Captain D'Lange could be Xamar's salvation, Micca. If you won't give her ship your blessing, then at least turn a blind eye to it. Please?"

Although Jillian could barely hear over the hammering in her head, she waited for the priestess's reply nonetheless. Any deal involving Xamar crystal would be, by its very nature, a profitable undertaking. One gig could pay a lot of bills. A repeat engagement or two would make serious inroads into getting Barim off her back forever. And it wouldn't even be boot-legging—not if Micca gave the project an official nod.

But Micca wasn't the obliging type.

"The off-worlder's ship is Ni H'Nathelek," she said, lobbing the words at Ammas like missiles. "Neither you nor any other Xamar may avail yourselves of it. At the proper moment, great H'Nath will show us a proper solution to this problem. Until then, though, we must abide by his laws."

Jillian's disappointment was instant. So, it seemed, was Ammas's. "You priests make the rules," he said churlishly, "not H'Nath."

Micca's eyes narrowed. "Up until now, Ammas su Xamar, it's been my intention give you an easy penance because it seemed to me that H'Nath had already punished you enough for your transgressions. But if you continue to spew borderline heresies, I'll have no choice but to consign you to the desert.

"And if *you*," she went on, bringing her big guns to bear on Lord Xamar, "allow your heir to proceed with this misbegotten scheme despite my injunction, the Holy Seven will censure your entire clan. One out of every three will be taken to other estates, where they will function as servants for a season. Another third, you and your son included, will be sent to the desert for a week of introspection. And you will give the H'Nathma a third of the crystal that you would've otherwise handed over to the off-worlder.

"So, Ammas, heir to Xamar who cares so much for his people and their welfare: what do you have to say now?"

Jillian wondered if Tolqan priests were allowed to marry. Because if they were, she wanted to introduce this bitch to Barim. They *deserved* together.

Meanwhile, Ammas deflected Micca's glare with a defiant half-smile and said, "If it were my decision, I'd brave your threats simply because sooner or later, someone must. But Saj du Xamar is the lord here, not me, and I'll abide by his decision." He squared his shoulders, then pivoted toward the old man. "Father?" There was no shred of entreaty in his tone, only pride. "What say you?"

Lord Xamar met his son's gaze with a nod of respect. "Your concern for our clan is admirable, son. But while I laud your compassion, I must side with Micca. We cannot traffic with offworlders. I say this not out of fear of reprisals," he hastened to add, casting a severe glance in the priestess's direction, "but out of respect for H'Nath. Our first duty is to him, not to our own physical comfort."

Ammas bowed. His back was to Jillian now, so she couldn't read his expression, but his body language proclaimed his disappointment. Micca simply looked vindicated— leastwise until the old lord turned to Jillian. Then she went all prickly and stiff, too.

"Captain D'Lange," he said. "Although it was done with the noblest of intentions, you were dealt with falsely and then falsely accused. I would like to apologize for that. I would also like to invite you to be our guest at tomorrow's god-day gathering. There will be food and holy entertainments; and maybe you'll gain a better understanding of what it is that we Tolqs are trying to preserve."

Jillian had no intention of accepting the invitation. It was a poor consolation prize for the poor off-worlder—she'd shipped fossilized quava bones with more meat on them. But even as she opened her mouth to say so, Tark's voice bloomed in her mind.

"This unprecedented invitation is more than just an apology, Captain," he told her. "It's Saj's way of asserting Xamar's autonomy. If you turn him down, Micca will humiliate him for his daring. 'You can't trust off-worlders,' she'll tell everybody. 'Or those who deal with such scum.' He'll lose face with his clan and the other lords. The priests will hound him into abdicating. So please, Captain, accept his invitation, if for no other reason than to deny Micca that much power over him."

The thought of staying on just to spite the priestess appealed to Jillian for less than a heartbeat. Wasn't little miss Micca an integral part of this society? And wasn't society what Lord Xamar was so determined to preserve? As long as the people of Tolq insisted on hosting a parasite that thrived on their fear, they deserved whatever happened to them.

"Thanks, your lordship," she began, and then froze as she happened to catch sight of Ammas. He smiled as their eyes met. An electric thrill skated through her. Before she could stop them, the wrong words tumbled past her lips. "I'd be honored to be your guest."

"So be it," Lord Xamar said, and then swiveled his head toward Micca. "Have all your questions been answered?" When she responded with a sullen nod, he smacked the table-top three times and declared, "This tribunal is adjourned. All praise to great H'Nath for guiding us to the truth."

He stood up at that and held out his hand. Micca took it with ceremonial respect, then allowed the old lord to escort her out of the room. As soon as they were out of sight, the heir of Xamar came hurrying over to Jillian like a puppy in need of a belly-scratch.

"Captain D'Lange," he said, as he approached, "what a joy it is to finally meet you face-to-face." Out of reflex, she offered him a handshake. He accepted it without batting an eyelash. Afterward, he said, "Thank you for saving my life."

His proximity provoked an excited flutter in her. She crushed it with the memory of that stolen kiss, and then fed the pulp to her headache. "You're welcome," she replied. "And the ride comes with a word of free advice: the next time you get the urge to arrange an under-the-table deal with an off-worlder, try asking the off-worlder first. Poison is too drastic an approach."

"But if you'd known of my plans," he countered, "you could've been accused of conspiracy. I kept you and my uncle ignorant for your own protection."

"I see. So you think it's better for someone to be charged with attempted murder than conspiracy to defraud a foreign government. What curious priorities you have."

But his crestfallen look brought her more guilt than satisfaction

"You said something about finally meeting me face-to-face," she said, hoping to change the subject. "Have we met in some other context then?"

He brightened instantly—like a puppy who'd just been forgiven for shitting on the Corellian carpet. Her fingers twitched with a sudden urge to pick him up and cuddle him: to rub his belly and tickle his ears and stroke his long, red hair. She lambasted herself for entertaining such fantasies. Didn't she have enough pain in her refabricated life already? What was this maddening compulsion to court more?

Meanwhile, Ammas proceeded to answer the question. Most of what he said fell on self-absorbed ears—until he mentioned somebody named Ross. That got her attention in a hurry.

"I'm sorry," she said then, "but what was that again?"

Ammas did not mind repeating himself. "I said—I was preparing for a briefing in the next room when I overheard Security Chief Ross telling my uncle about you. He said you were looking for work, and that it was now or never. I knew then that I had to find a way to take advantage of the situation.

"I only wish that fortune had brought us together in some other way," he went on, in a more flirtatious tone. "I had no idea that you were a woman—or so beautiful."

"Xamar blood must be nine-tenths charm," she retorted, and then high-tailed it for safer ground. "So. Nathan Ross and Tark are great friends, are they?"

"Ammas exaggerates," Tark said drolly, suddenly cropping up at her other elbow. "Nathan and I are more like comfortable acquaintances. He drops by the embassy every month or so with his latest version of a Tolq-SU compact, we have a glass or two of kluur and talk about the weather, then I reject his latest proposal and he goes home.

"And speaking of which, Captain, allow me to walk you back to your room. It's late; and despite his vigorous appearance, my nephew has not yet fully recuperated from his ordeal."

She thanked her lucky stars for the intervention. A minute or two more alone with Ammas, and she might've started flirting back. As it was, she had to focus on the ache in her head just to keep from smiling when she turned to look at him.

"Thanks for the company," she said. "Pleasant dreams."

"Likewise, Captain," he replied, and then bowed to his uncle. A moment later, he was gone.

Tark talked incessantly on the way back to Jillian's room. He complimented her on her conduct at the tribunal; and on the way she handled Micca; and on that little laugh that she'd had on him. But she scarcely heard a word. Her head was full of hot, broken glass, and her only thoughts were of Ammas and a king-size glass of tequila.

Chapter 7

A SERIES OF distant taps invaded Jillian's murk-infested dreams. An instant later, she was lying wide-eyed on the shores of wakefulness and wondering where the fuck she was. Everything was *redredred*—the walls, the ceiling, the divan. Maybe her fabricated eyes were bleeding in their fabricated sockets, she thought. Maybe she had died of blight in her sleep and gone to cyborg hell. Or maybe—

The tapping continued, light but insistent. It drew her gaze toward the door. She saw Tark's crystal statue then and remembered where she was—cyborg hell was as good a name for it as any other.

Taptaptap.

"Wait a minute," she said, then gave herself a quick once-over. Her pants were wrinkled. Her tunic was skewed. But no more than a glimpse of syntheskin was showing anywhere below the neck. Good cyborg. Clever cyborg.

Taptaptap.

"I said *wait*, damn you!"

She stood up. Vertigo sucked at the base of her brain for a moment, then abruptly novaed into thought-warping pain. She winced. She cursed. She wondered how she was supposed to function when her foremost desire to do was lash out at everything within her reach. Meanwhile, her body headed for the door of its own accord.

Her caller was Ammas. The sight of him standing there at the door, grinning like a schoolboy with a big, fat crush, sparked a moment's delight in her which then ignited a firestorm of mixed emotions. The new Jillian wanted him to go away so she wouldn't be tempted to forget who she was. The old Jillian wanted him to stick around for the exact same reason. If only she'd met him before the accident, she mourned. Or, barring that, never at all.

It seemed like all of her wishes were futile these days.

"Hello, Ammas," she said, deflecting his admiring gaze with a variation of Tark's bland facade. "I hope you're not here to bring me to another truth tribunal."

He laughed—a bright, hearty sound. "In that case, Captain, your prayer has been answered, for I only came by to see if you've had anything to eat yet. If not, I'd be glad to break fast with you. The Gather-meal is still a few hours away, and of late, it's been more ceremonial than substantial, so it's best not to wait if you're hungry."

"Thank you for the invitation," she said, "but I don't take breakfast as a rule."

"I don't either," he confided. "But I was willing to make an exception just this once. Perhaps you'd care to tour the estate instead. It's really quite beautiful."

"Thank you again, but Tark showed me around yesterday."

"I see." His schoolboy grin twitched at the corners. "A most thorough man, my uncle. Did he show you the glassworks as well?"

She didn't have enough mental agility to keep dodging him—it was all she could do to hip-hop from one half-truth to the next without getting lost. Yet she couldn't bring herself to summarily dismiss him, either. She didn't want to be alone with a cannibalistic headache. She didn't want to be alone, regardless. And the glassworks sounded like a decent compromise. It was a place public enough to distract them both.

"As a matter of fact," she said, "he didn't get a chance. Other things came up."

Triumph danced its way into his engaging brown eyes. "If you'd like, I could give you the tour now. It's god's-day, so there won't be much activity, but that could work to our advantage."

"OK, if you're sure you don't have anything else to do."

She started through the door then, only to pause as the statue in the corner caught her eye again. There was just something about it that demanded attention. When Ammas saw what the hold-up was, he nodded like a mechanic who knew what the problem was, and said, "My uncle is a man of many talents, isn't he? He calls that a failed self-portrait. I call it a masterpiece."

They started on their way then. Jillian wanted to travel topside—anything to get away from the color red!—but Ammas insisted on taking her through the estate's buried byways. It was cooler this way, he told her, and less dusty. That, and he wanted people to see her. Like she was some kind of science exhibit, she thought. Or a sideshow freak. She stepped up the pace, once and then again. Her would-be guide was hard-pressed to keep up. Then they rounded a corner and came nose-to-nose with Micca. Jillian avoided a collision with refabricated ease, but Ammas's momentum carried him a step too far. He caught the priestess by the waist to keep from bowling her over, then spun her in a dancy little circle just for fun. Her hood flipped back, exposing her shaven head. Her hand flew up for balance. But she didn't protest until Ammas whirled her out of his light embrace.

"Have a care," she cautioned him then, scowling as she fussed with the folds of her hood. "We aren't children anymore."

"I miss those days sometimes," he said.

"You should be grateful that H'Nath allowed you to escape them unscathed," she fired back. " Not all are so fortunate, heir of Xamar."

"I *am* grateful," he said, refusing to be cowed. "I simply choose to savor the things that I've been given rather than mourn the things that I've lost. You would do well to do so, too." Then, before she could rebuke him for presuming to advise a high priest, he said, "But never mind, Micca. Everyone faces their namma in their own way. Captain D'Lange and I are on our way to tour the glassworks. Will you join us?"

Micca's frown deepened as she glanced at Jillian. "No. I have duties to perform before the gathering starts. And if I were you, Ammas, I'd think twice about parading the offworlder around the estate. Her immodesty is an affront to H'Nath."

"Sorry," Jillian sneered, oozing insincerity and itching for a fight. "Next time, I'll remember to pack my twarla."

"There will be no next time, offworlder," the priestess hissed, and then turned to Ammas again. "First Tark, and now a godless alien. Your taste in companions has hit the rocks beneath the sand, Ammas su Xamar. I pray that H'Nath leaves the rest of your judgment intact. Elsewise, you're likely to die in the desert."

With that, she continued on her way, her red robes streaming like rage behind her. Ammas stared after her for a moment. His expression was a blend of bile and rue. Jillian stared, too, clenching and unclenching her fists all the while. Oh, how she wanted a piece of that pompous bitch. She wanted to bend her; break her; make her bleed. She wanted to stuff a freakin' twarla down her throat and then make her run naked through the houses of the so-called holy.

"I hate that woman," she said aloud, trying to bleed off some of the pressure. She wasn't going to let a puny little nobody like Micca nudge her over the brink of reason, she told herself. She was stronger than that. Stronger. Smarter. Better. "You gotta wonder why no one's strangled her in her sleep yet."

"Tolqs are forbidden to do violence," Ammas said, in a sad, faraway voice. "And she wasn't always so mean-spirited."

"I'll just bet," Jillian said.

"No, really, it's true," he insisted, rousing out of his funk. "We were first-loves in the days before adulthood changed our lives, and what a joy she was back then—clever, quick to laugh, and eager to do great things. We used to lay together at night and dream aloud about the gifts we were going to receive from H'Nath. I wanted the healer's touch, so I might help other people. And Micca wanted the far-sense."

"What's that?" she asked. "The ability to see into other peoples' living rooms?"

He shook his head, but it was hard to tell whether he was discounting the guess or Jillian. "Far-sensing is the holiest of gifts. Those few who receive it are able to guide our solar schooners through the deserts of space without technological assistance."

If Jillian had been able to shudder, she would've done so then. The mere thought of faring into deep space without a first-rate nav-computer scared her. She couldn't even *imagine* having to depend on some human's sense of direction to keep her on course. It was beyond risky, and even beyond foolhardy. No wonder Tark preferred to travel with offworlders.

Meanwhile, Ammas rambled on.

"I know it's hard to believe now," he said, "but it's true: Micca had a wish to see the stars. And for a while, it seemed as if her wish had been granted. She tested positive for the far-sense when she returned from her coming-of-age walk in the desert. And the priesthood welcomed her into its ranks with open arms. Ten months before I was called to my own rite of passage, she was offered a training berth on an outbound schooner. I still remember how happy she was at our parting.

"She was gone for over two years. And when she returned, she was as she is now: angry and bitter, closed to all who had once held her dear. She wouldn't tell me what had happened, but I've since learned that she spent most of that voyage in her room. Her gift, it seems, is hopelessly skewed. It consistently drew her the wrong way. And she slipped so readily into trance, she couldn't even serve as crew. The H'Nathma had no choice but to ground her.

"Now, ten years later, she's well on her way to becoming one of the Holies—the youngest ever to achieve such heights. I'm glad for her, but worried for the rest of Tolq. Because I think that Micca's come to believe that H'Nath punished her for her childhood aspirations, and therefore, that dreams of any kind are now a sin. And I don't know how to persuade her otherwise."

Jillian understood Micca better now. Some people were born to be spacers. It was a life-long obsession, and enough to cripple the lightest of hearts when thwarted. But she didn't like the priestess any better for knowing the source of her anger. Disappointment was a hard fact of life. Any cyborg could tell her so.

They went topside then. The unmitigated brightness of the day sent fresh splinters of pain lancing through her head, but Ammas mistook her garbled curse for an expression of awe.

"It *is* rather impressive, isn't it?" he asked, grinning at the huge stone building that stood some fifty meters away. "My ancestors carved each of those blocks from H'Nath's Crown, then hauled them across two hundred miles of desert. I thank H'Nath daily that I wasn't born back then."

The sight left Jillian uninspired. One building seemed much the same as the next to her, especially when her brain was throwing itself against its plasti-steel playpen like a sugar-crazed child. Suffering mother! Why hadn't she thought to ask Ammas for a shot of hard drink before they started on this jaunt? Why wasn't she asking him for one now?

Because it was too freakin' late, she told herself. They were already closing in on the glassworks. She could see its walls clearly now. Wind-driven sands had blasted them to an unnatural smoothness. Now she was impressed. Now she was appalled. Because that's what the inside of her skull felt like.

"This way, Captain," Ammas said, and then ushered her into the glassworks.

An instant after she stepped inside, a creeping sense of dread possessed her. She looked up and down the corridor that ran from one end of the building to the other. It was little more than a broad rut striped with well-greased tracks. Nothing alarming about that, she told herself. And the few Tolqs in the vicinity posed no threat. Even so, she couldn't ditch this niggling urge to turn and bolt. She forced herself toward the tracks instead. As she did so, the unpleasant fluttering in her ears became a faint, vaporous roar. It stopped her in mid-stride.

Ammas touched her lightly on the shoulder. "Captain? Is something wrong?"

"That noise," she said, groping for its name even as she tried to block it from her mind. "It's coming from over there." She pointed at a set of huge steel doors to her left. "What's back there?"

"The furnaces," he replied.

"Furnaces?" she echoed, trying in vain to make a connection.

"We use them to melt the sand," he explained. "They're kept running all the time, even on god-days, because our glass is notoriously temperature-sensitive. It's funny how the sound caught your attention, though. I can barely hear it from here."

"That's because you've lived with it all your life," she said—a wan diversion that might've even been true. She didn't care one way or the other. Her circuits were on the verge of overload.

"Maybe so," he granted. "But this is nothing compared to what you'd hear if you were on the other side of that door. It's as noisy as a shuttleport in there. And hotter than sin. Fortunately, H'Nath has blessed us with a high tolerance to heat. We can practically wallow in fire."

Something shot out of her memory at wyrm-speed then—a nearly colorless flash that left a slick scab of mind-numbing fear in its wake. It was so intense, it shut down her fight-or-flight response and left her flat-out stunned while Ammas chattered on.

"We don't sweat, either," he was saying now. "I didn't even know what the word meant until I went off-world with Uncle. It took me some time to get used to the smell."

"Ammas," she said, from a pit deep within herself. "I need to be somewhere else. I need—

'To go', was what she was thinking, but before she could convert the thought into words, an unseen bell clanged three times. At the sound, Ammas quit his yammering and grabbed her elbow.

"This way," he said, then ushered her across the tracks and onto the knee-high platform that stood on the other side. "Now you'll get to see how the sand gets to the furnaces."

As if on cue, a rumbling like heat thunder erupted at the far end of the glassworks. An instant later, an old-fashioned ore cart heaped with sand come rolling down the tracks. Jillian was desperate be somewhere now else. It was too loud here, too painful. And— the doors to the furnace room were starting to swing open! She didn't want to see what was behind them. She didn't want to experience that colorless flash again.

The doors opened wider, then wider still. The furnace's roar expanded. She felt herself grow warmer and warmer: phantom heat that left her sweating inside. *Don't look*, a little voice begged her. *Don't look away*, urged another. But even as she made up her mind to be brave, the cart went rumbling past the doors, which then started to close again. She was both relieved and dismayed.

"Are we done then?" she asked.

"Not quite," Ammas replied, and ushered her in the direction from which the cart had come. "My family's workshop is down here, and while I don't claim to be talented, I'd like to demonstrate a few techniques for you."

She went along with him—but only because that was the path of least resistance. Her head was pounding. It hurt to think. All she wanted to do was collect her credit and go home. Instead, she wound up in a dimly lit doorway. Ammas had been standing there a moment ago, but she hadn't noticed that he'd stopped and so plowed right into his back. The collision sent him stumbling into the studio. It also snagged Tark's attention.

The Tolq ambassador was standing behind a waist-high workbench. A glob of half-molten glass spun on a wheel in front of him. His expression was feral, a disturbing amalgamation of grief and hate. He stared at them like a man who's just been stabbed.

"I beg your pardon, Uncle," Ammas said, backing toward the door. "We didn't mean to intrude. I didn't think anyone would be in here today."

"I was trying to craft a memorial for Tobia," he said, in a shattered tone, and then glanced down at the wheel. It had wound to a stop. The half-molten blob had collapsed. "I guess I'll have to try again."

Ammas took another step back and then cupped Jillian's elbow. "We're leaving, Uncle. I wish you an easy end to your grief."

Tark returned to his work. Ammas hustled Jillian out of the room.

"I'm sorry," he said, as he hustled her farther down the corridor. "This tour hasn't exactly turned out the way I'd wanted it to. But I hope you'll be patient with me for just a few minutes longer. There's one more place I'd like to take you."

She shrugged. He led her to the end of the corridor and up a double-width flight of stairs. There was only one room up here, and it was filled with crystal. Much of it was tableware and such, intended for domestic use, but there was also an array of artwork— fluted spires and inverted spheres; Klein bottles, Escheresque figures, statuary that shifted in the beholder's eyes a like living thing. Each piece was as unique as a fingerprint. Each piece was as alluring as a siren's song. The spectacle was too much for Jillian. Her head screamed for relief. Vertigo tugged at her like an undertow. She looked for a safe place to keep her eyes, and wound up looking at Ammas. His expression was anxious, like that of a father showing off his baby for the first very time.

"I know several people who would kill for the chance to see a collection like this," she told him.

"I'd like you to select a piece for yourself," Ammas said then. "As a token of my apology for getting you involved in Tolqan politics."

"I can't," she said, refusing to encourage him. Or herself. "That's too extravagant a gesture."

His mouth acquired a beguiling curve. "Nonsense, Captain. Until it leaves Tolq, it's just glass." When she continued to hold out, he switched tactics. "All right then, I'll pick out something for you." He was off before she could stop him; and the swiftness of his return gave her the impression that she'd been outmaneuvered again. "I made this the last time I was home," he said, as he presented the melon-sized piece to her. "I must've had you in mind."

The core was a solid globe, blushing deepest red at its heart as all Xamar crystal did. A multitude of urchin-like spines rayed from its surface. These spines were so fine, and so delicately tipped, they created a pinkish aureole around the globe. It was, Jillian thought, the most exquisite rendition of a starburst that she'd ever seen.

"Please," Ammas urged, when her hands remained limp at her sides. "I want you to have it."

She took the sculpture in both hands and then held it up to the light, a gesture of admiration that she performed strictly for his sake. She'd been wrong, she thought. This wasn't a starburst. It was a backwoods-burr, one that could penetrate even her synthetic hide. Damn that fuckwit, Griffith! He should have tossed her emotions out with the baby and the bath water. Because all they did now was cause her grief.

"Thank you," she said, not quite meeting his eyes. "Now, if you don't mind, I'd like to return to my room. All of a sudden, I'm quite tired."

"As you wish," he replied.

They headed back downstairs.

There was a bounce in Ammas's steps now: a light-hearted, low-g spring. Jillian wasn't happy to see it, for she remembered enough about men to know that it was for her. Her little deception had him fooled. He thought she was human; all flesh and red blood; a right and proper woman. She knew she ought to say something to set the record straight, but she couldn't bring herself to think that bloody hard. And anyway, she'd be gone in a few hours. Her leaving would resolve all sorts of problems.

Just then, the ground beneath her feet began to vibrate. She snapped out of her daze to find herself on the sand-wagon tracks. She couldn't remember how she'd gotten there. Nor could she recall hearing a warning bell sound. But it must have, for there was a wagon coming her way. She'd mistaken its rumbling for the noise in her own head. It was already close enough for her to discern individual rivets in its heavy, metal seams. It was moving fast enough to cause significant damage.

"Runaway cart!" someone shouted then.

Ammas appeared at her elbow, shouting something like "Go!" or "Save yourself!" She slung him up and onto the platform like a duffel bag, then vaulted after him. The cart clipped her right heel in passing, but she felt no pain, only a distant thud and then a lumpy softness beneath her. Four impossibly slow heartbeats later, a resounding crash sounded in her ears.

To her utter amazement, the noise didn't spur her headache. Indeed, the pain had receded, leaving nothing but an acrid memory of suffering behind. What an extraordinary relief! She was back to normal!

And she meant to keep it that way.

She snapped to her feet, ready to do whatever the Tolqs needed her to do: dig through wreckage; resuscitate victims; perhaps beat the culprit's head in. The cart was now resting against the furnace-room doors in jagged folds. Red sand was spilling from its wounds; the floor was already thick with it. But while people were racing toward the mess, their alarm lacked the frenzy that fallen comrades inspired.

Ammas staggered to his feet beside her. His robe was torn at the knee, and his hair was disheveled, but the frown that seamed his dusty face belonged to a man whose dignity was intact.

"Are you well?" he asked her.

At her nod, he started toward the scene of the accident. Jillian followed in his vapor-trail, clenching and unclenching her fists He walked with a slight limp and some pain now, but he didn't let that slow him down. And everyone in front of them cleared out of the way.

"Is anyone hurt?" he asked.

A ragged chorus of denials rose up around him. He eyeballed the crowd like a suspicious mind-seer, then singled out a well-muscled man with a humpback nose and a thick jaw. "Clem," he said. "What happened here? Why wasn't the warning bell rung?"

Before Clem had a chance to say a word, Tark pushed his way to the forefront of the crowd. His breath was in tatters. His brow was knotted with worry.

"Ammas," he panted. "Were you hurt?"

"Not really, Uncle," he said, and then turned his attention back to Clem. "You were saying, my friend?"

"I don't know what happened, young lord," Clem replied, nervously fingering his quot'tl bead. "I was in the sand room earlier—Kai and I had words this morning, and I came here to work off my anger. But I went home over an hour ago and returned just in time to see the cart hit the doors. And if you're wondering why I'm back again so soon, well—" He cocked his head a sorry angle. "—Kai and I had more words."

"Is it possible that you forgot to set the brake before you left?" Tark asked.

"I've been a sandman for twenty-one years now," Clem said, stiff-backed with affront. "Not once in all that time have I ever forgotten to set a brake."

"I meant no offense, my friend," Tark countered, managing to sound soothing and amused in the same breath. "Could it have been brake failure then?"

The sandman stroked his chin like a magic lamp, and then nodded. "It's possible. But I doubt that anyone save almighty H'Nath will ever know for sure," he added, casting a meaningful glance at the crumpled heap of metal. "The damage is extensive."

"See what you can find out from the wreckage," Ammas told him, "and then bring what you've learned to me." Then he turned to address the rest of the crowd. "Praise be to H'Nath for showing mercy to all of us. If anybody knows anything about this mishap, I urge you to stay here and talk to Clem. Everybody else may return to whatever they were doing before the excitement."

As the crowd started to disperse, Ammas trained his somber gaze on Jillian. "That's twice that you've saved my life, Captain—"

"Are you sure you're all right?" Tark butted in. "I can fetch Elyn if you need her."

"I'm fine except for a scraped knee and a curiously sore arm," Ammas assured him. Then he pushed his belled sleeve up, revealing a set of deeply purpling bruises on his biceps—the cyborg's equivalent of fingerprints. In a tone that was only half-teasing, he said, "That's quite a grip you have."

"Oops," she said, and flashed him an embarrassed smile.

"Thank H'Nath that she *is* so strong," Tark said then, displaying a surprising lack of composure. "I don't know what I would've done if I'd lost you as well as Tobia."

Ammas folded his uncle into an embrace. Jillian averted her eyes, respecting their privacy, and happened to notice the starburst's shattered remains glistening on the tracks. Disappointment tried to gel within her, but she would have none of it. *Zeph* was no place for something that fragile anyway, she thought. And cyborgs had no need for art.

Leastwise, that's what she told herself.

"I'm taking Captain D'Lange back to her room now, Uncle," Ammas said, as he and Tark pulled away from each other. "Will you join us?"

The ambassador shook his head. He'd recovered his poise, but still looked a bit peaked. "You go ahead," he said. "I still have some cleaning up to do. But Captain," he added, as she turned to go, "I'd like to call on you before the gathering if I may. I believe we have an account to settle."

"I'll be waiting for you," she promised.

The walk back to the estate started out slow and quiet. That was fine with Jillian. Pain-free for the moment, and on the verge of collecting a debt, she was in a good mood, content to stroll idly along while Ammas hobbled. The heir of Xamar, on the other hand, looked preoccupied.

"You're thinking of the accident," she guessed.

"We're a meticulous people, Captain," he said. "I cannot understand how failing brakes could've gone unnoticed."

She shrugged. "It happens sometimes."

"Not here, it doesn't," he argued.

"Then maybe it wasn't the brakes."

"There's very little else that can go wrong with a sand-cart, Captain."

She shrugged again, then proposed a different theory. "Then maybe it wasn't an accident."

His eyes narrowed. His nostrils flared. He looked angry, shocked, and offended. "Do you accuse Clem of lying?"

"Not necessarily," she countered blandly. "But you can't discount the possibility that somebody might have been trying to kill you. Or me," she added, as an afterthought.

"N'Hath forbids his children to do violence," he said, as if that were the end of *that* argument.

She jeered at his naiveté. "That commandment has been turning up in holy books ever since man learned how to write, Ammas. And for every follower who obeys it, there are at least seven or eight who see fit to ignore it. And—if you look at it in the right way, it would've been the cart doing all the violence."

His shock intensified, bleaching the boyishness from his face. "Now I understand what the prophet meant when he said, *'Corruption often wears a pretty face'*. You should be ashamed of such thoughts."

Radiating indignation, he pulled ahead of her. Taken aback by his attitude, she let him go. So, she thought, as the gap between them widened. She was corruption—simply because she was willing to consider humanity's darker side. Silly boy! If he knew what a bogeyman she really was, he'd burst a vessel in that pretty little head of his.

Ammas was closing in on one of the estate's half-hidden entrances now. But even as he started underground, Micca came marching topside. The dyspeptic look on her face turned even more bilious when she saw who it was that was suddenly in her way. Ammas didn't seem to notice, though. He was too intent on his own agenda.

"Micca, " he said. "You're just the person I was hoping to see. Have you heard about the accident in the glassworks yet?"

"I'm heading there now," she told him. "The Holy Seven will want a full account of this incident."

"It was an accident," he chided, "not an incident."

But she refused to stand corrected. "It was an incident, Ammas su Xamar; and as far as I'm concerned, it was all your fault. You tempted H'Nath's wrath by flaunting your off-worlder under his nose, and he answered you—in a most compassionate way, I might add, since you're obviously still in one piece. Keep *that* in mind the next time you decide to defy our god, Ammas su Xamar. He isn't always so merciful.

"We'll speak more of this and other matters at the gathering," she went on. "Until then, though, I bid you to stay out of my way."

Micca started toward the glassworks. In passing, she scorched Jillian with a look. In turn, Jillian passed that look on to Ammas.

"I seem to be a grain of sand in everyone's eye today," he said.

Although she heard the apology behind the words, Jillian wasn't ready to forgive him yet. So she shrugged and elbowed her way past him. As she headed down the stairs, she said, "Corruption thanks you for the tour. Corruption can find corruption's way back to corruption's room from here."

He sputtered a protest, but she was already underground.

&

LESS THAN AN hour later, a knock sounded at her door. Finally, she thought, as she went to answer it. Her mood was starting to fray at the corners now, and she wanted to be done with Xamar before its host of petty aggravations could unravel it completely. "Good afternoon, Captain," Tark said, as he came sauntering into the room. His hair was freshly braided. His twarla looked new. He had a swan-necked decanter in one hand, and two crystal snifters in the other. "I was wondering if you'd care to have a drink with me before we head for the gathering. This is an excellent year for kluur."

"Don't mind if I do," she replied, and then wondered where he and his decanter had been last night.

He strode over to the divan and sat down. Remembering his aversion to personal contact, she remained standing. He started to unstop the decanter, then thought better of it. She was about to bark at him for teasing when he reached into his robe and withdrew a thin metal slip.

"First things first," he said. Then, with a flourish, he handed her the voucher. "For services rendered. In addition, please accept my thanks for everything, including your patience."

"You're quite welcome," she replied, and tucked the marker into her hip pocket without pausing to check the figure in the credit column. At this point, she didn't care if it was right or not. All she wanted to do was go home—after a drink or two. And Tark was already working on the latter wish. She watched intently as he poured a measure of pale pink liquor into each of the snifters. His precision bordered on ritual.

"To a job well done," he said afterward.

But he didn't drink right away. He had to admire the kluur first. He held it up to the light to admire its color, then raised it to his nose and sniffed. Jillian did likewise, but it was all an act. The subtleties that might've distinguished this from any other fermented drink were forever lost to her. Still, it went down easy enough. She copied Tark in that, too: a quick snap of the wrist; a hard swallow; and then a satisfied, "Ah."

"Here, let's have another," he said, refilling her glass before she could refuse him. Not that she would have. "It's the perfect drink for a long afternoon—mild and sweet."

"Speaking of which," she said, as he poured. "Is there anything special I should know about this gathering of yours? Do's and don't's—that sort of thing?"

"That's a very good question," he replied, and his mouth acquired an ironic kink. "If you had asked me yesterday, I would've advised you not to speak unless spoken to, and to keep your hands in your pockets. But Xamar's attitude toward you has changed, Captain. Everyone knows you risked your life to save Ammas this morning. Because of that, many are now willing to overlook the unfortunate circumstances of your birth."

"How liberal of them," she quipped and then knocked back her refill. Like the first, it slid down her throat without creating an impression. Her mood began to improve again. "In turn, I'll overlook their obsession with the color red. But sweet suffering stars, Tark," she added, in a beleaguered tone, "haven't you people ever heard of dyes?"

"Red is H'Nath's color," he replied. "We use it when we can to honor him." Then he set his empty snifter down with a sigh. "I believe it's time to go."

Just when things were starting to look up, she thought.

༄

HE ESCORTED HER to the tribunal hall. It was better lit than it had been last night. It was also brimming with red-robed people. The crowd fell quiet when Jillian appeared in the doorway, but only for a moment. The next thing she knew, her name was flying from mouth to mouth at a frenzied pitch. It was a heady experience, but somewhat unnerving, too. She felt like a first-class fraud. They were closing in on the head table now. As before, Saj occupied the center chair. Micca sat to the left of him; Ammas, to the right. The two end chairs stood empty. Jillian's fists knotted at the thought of having to sit next to that bitch of a priestess for any length of time, then relaxed again as Lord Xamar motioned her toward the seat next to his son. Had he read her mind? Or had he heard about the antipathy between her and Micca the old-fashioned way? She decided she didn't care. Mercy was mercy—no matter who engineered it.

"Better you than me," she whispered to Tark in parting.

A muscle in Tark's jaw twitched, telegraphing his dismay. He headed toward his assigned seat with the dignity of an innocent man on the way to the gallows.

"Uncle Tark's no fun at a gathering anyway," Ammas told

Jillian as she sat down, taking up her personal space like an intimate. "He gets all grumpy and impatient." When she refused to respond to his banter, he shed his happy-go-lucky facade and said, "Please forgive me for being so rude to you this morning. My only excuse is that I was upset."

"Nearly being crushed does tend to have that effect on a body," she said.

"So does the thought of a Tolq attempting murder," he added. "And one of my own people, no less."

"Forget about it," she said, and then forgave him with a smile. "It was probably just a fluke." Anger shorted out a bunch of circuits that she couldn't afford to lose. And besides, this was good-bye. There was no harm in them parting as friends. "Accidents happen sometimes, even under the best of conditions."

"So I've heard," he said.

Just then, Lord Xamar slapped the table-top with his hand. Silence swept across the hall. All eyes turned toward the head table—and Jillian. The scrutiny left her uneasy. She wondered how many telepaths there were in the crowd, and how many of them were delving into her thoughts. She wondered what they would do when they hit pay-dirt. She wondered what she would do.

Kill them.

She drove the thought away with a frown, then told herself to quit being paranoid. Gevera had said that her secrets were safe. And no one had given her any reason to think otherwise. She folded her hands together then. For one disoriented moment thereafter, it felt like Ammas was holding them instead. She drove that notion away, too.

Saj was on his feet now. In his upraised hand, he held a snifter that could've been a sister to the ones that she and Tark had used earlier. His expression was stern, but pride danced in his eyes.

"My people," he said, glancing slowly around as if to make eye-contact with each and every Tolq in the room, "we have earned a place in the Tellings today. For among us sits the first off-worlder to take part in a gathering since the prophet

Jamallad's time. Her name is Captain Jillian D'Lange, Xamar, and it was she who saved your young lord-to-be. I wish her long life and happiness. Will you join me?"

"Long life and happiness," came the answering chant. It wasn't a deafening roar by any stretch of the imagination, Jillian mused, but it wasn't half-bad for a tough crowd, either. Lord Xamar snapped his drink back then. His people followed. The bottoms of their glasses flashed red as they tipped them. It looked like a micro-fireworks display.

"Aren't you going to drink yours?" Ammas asked then, glancing at the snifter that had miraculously appeared by her elbow. "You can have water instead if you want it, but kluur's the better drink for a long afternoon."

"I seem to remember hearing that somewhere," she said, and then knocked the drink back before she had a chance to wonder whether it was a smart thing to do to or not. Afterward, she smacked her lips. A luxurious phantom-sense of warmth was seeping into her thoughts now. She would always remember that as the taste of kluur.

Now Micca was standing up in Lord Xamar's stead. With her hood gathered in folds around her long, nut-brown neck like a wattle, and her glabrous head, she reminded Jillian of a species of desert vulture. She couldn't understand how Ammas could've ever found her attractive.

"Clan Xamar," the priestess said, "let us give thanks to H'Nath. Without him, we would be lost in a galaxy that's more unforgiving than any desert. Do not be misled by the off-worlder's presence here today. Her ways are not ours, nor will they ever be. We are the children of H'Nath. Our duty is to him alone.

"To god and duty, Clan Xamar."

Everyone in the hall echoed that sentiment—everyone but Jillian, who maintained a discreet silence instead. She did, however, down her kluur when it came time for that part of the toast. Immediately afterward, Ammas refilled their glasses yet again from one of the pitchers that studded the table.

"Your turn," he prompted then, grinning like a loon as he urged her to stand.

Kluur smothered the gust of stage-fright that blew through her. And she snuffed out the spark of anger that flared in its wake. This was an honor, not an indictment, she told herself. None of them knew what she really was. So she rose to the occasion with a glass in her hand and a game smile on her face. Out of the corner of her eye, she saw Micca tense as if bracing for a string of off-world heresies, but Jillian decided not to give her that kind of satisfaction.

"Clan Xamar," she said in a ringing voice. "Customs differ from world to world, but it is said that friendship is universal. Thank you kindly for your hospitality. Long life and happiness to you all."

The response came much closer to a roar this time. She sat down feeling quite pleased with herself.

"Enjoy the gathering," Lord Xamar urged his clan then, and the hall erupted with festive noise.

Food began circulating from table to table, and from hand to hand: thin slices of roast praxa; yellow, sponge-like tubers studded with herbs; and flat discs of crumbly red bread. Although the cooks had tried hard to disguise it with decorative tricks, the lack of bounty was evident. Jillian took as little of everything as was possible—except for kluur. Funny how there was always enough grain for alcohol, she thought, even when there was none for anything else. Funny but good—leastwise as far as she was concerned.

"Is something wrong?" Ammas asked then, suddenly noticing her lack of appetite. He had just finished wolfing down his plate of food, and she could tell by the gleam in his eye that he was still hungry. "I can have the meat cooked more if it displeases you. Or, if it's overdone, we can call for slices closer to the bone."

"Everything's fine," she assured him, and then sipped from her kluur to satisfy the anxious host in him. "Unfortunately, I'm not supposed to eat solid foods before a flight." Then, before he could question the lie, she slid her plate toward him. "I'd appreciate it if you'd finish this for me. There's no point in it going to waste."

"That would be a sin, wouldn't it?" He made the leftovers disappear in an instant, then reached for the nearest pitcher. "I feel wonderfully light-headed," he said, as he poured for them. "It must be your company."

"Flattery will get you everywhere," she said—a flirty line out of her past. Alarms went off in a distant corner of her brain then, but she told herself that she was just having a little harmless fun, and made no attempt to modify her behavior. All work and no play made JillieJillieJill a dull cyborg.

"I wasn't flattering you," Ammas said, edging closer to her. "I was simply trying to express my appreciation for a most remarkable woman. I'll be returning to Circe's II to continue my education," he continued. "Maybe we could meet for kla or something at the embassy sometime."

"Or something," she echoed.

Just then, a series of notes from a low-throated flute pierced the shell of privacy that they'd erected for themselves. Jillian glanced toward the center of the hall, and saw a rag-tag group of musicians starting to warm up. As they fussed with their exotic glass instruments, Clem and several other burly fellows worked to make room for a dance floor. Tables were carried to the furthermost corner of the rooms. Chairs were swept against the walls. As they worked, the music became more cohesive. It was slow and lonesome— an ache with crystal wings. Jillian closed her eyes to better savor the sounds.

Some time later, a faint yet familiar pressure closed around her hand. She didn't know whether she wanted it to go away or stay forever, so she tried to ignore it instead. But Ammas wouldn't let her do that. He leaned in close and whispered in her ear.

"Do you like what you're hearing, Captain?"

"It's like a dream," she replied, without opening her eyes. "A beautiful dream."

"I had a most unusual dream not too long ago," he told her. "It came to me during my poisoned sleep. I dreamed that I was floating in a steel chamber, and that my body lay below me, strapped to a bed. It looked cold and stiff; and a great sadness filled me, for I thought that I was dead. Then, as I hovered above myself, waiting for the hand of H'Nath to take me home, a beautiful woman strode into the room. She was dark-haired and lean, with a look of magic about her. And to my amazement, she kissed me. Feeling the brush of her lips across my own, I knew I wasn't dead after all. Then, as she left the room, the dream came to an end.

"What do you think about that, Captain?"

"I think poison does strange things to a person's body," she replied, hiding her chagrin behind the blandest of tones. "I think this music is divine."

"I see," he said with a mysterious smile, and then gave her hand a squeeze. She'd forgotten that he'd been holding it. "Would you care to dance?"

Jillian glanced toward the dance floor. It was sprinkled with mismatched couples now. And contact between partners was limited to the hands and eyes. That seemed safe enough— another round of harmless fun. And she was desperate to escape the specter of that stolen kiss.

"Why not?" she said.

They danced by fingertip, an adagio waltz that spun time to a standstill. As he led her where he would, she remembered other dances on other worlds, dances where all of this flirting would've been a mere prelude instead of the grand finale. Back in those days, she'd never considered herself a romantic. Now, as a cyborg, it seemed like her greatest failing. Bitterness stained her thoughts yellow. She wanted to be a woman again—to flirt and to laugh and to fuck if it pleased her. She wanted to be alive or dead, not trapped in a plasti-steel netherworld where she would never truly be either. Was that so freakin' much to ask?

Not today, it wasn't.

So she danced. And she laughed. And she batted her artificial lashes in Ammas's admiring face. She felt so good, so deliciously *real*, that she almost cried aloud when the music finally swirled to a stop.

"Ask them to play one more piece," she entreated Ammas.

"There will be more music later," he replied, as he led her away from the dance floor. "Right now, though, it's time for the Telling."

"This telling isn't being done on my account, is it?"" she asked, all petulance now. She wanted more music, another dance, some more time to pretend. "Because I wouldn't want to put anyone out."

"You aren't putting anyone out, Captain," he assured her. "Tellings are a part of every gathering. You are lucky, however. Our tellers are the best on Tolq—even Micca says so. You're bound to enjoy their work."

How nice that one of them thought so, she sulked.

He urged her toward a patch of floor near the front of the room. She had to wade through a crowd of Tolqs to get there. Some of the elders still recoiled as she passed, but others— mostly the young—looked up at her with curiosity and awe. A few of them even touched her in passing. Although the faint voice of reason argued otherwise, it seemed to Jillian like they were checking for the catches in her disguise—cracks that would open up and devour their souls. The thought spoiled her buzz; the illusion; her mood. She wished that they'd just bring the damn music back.

The gas-lights dimmed then, plunging the room into near-darkness. As she and Ammas settled onto the floor, someone announced, "Today's Telling comes from Chapter One of the Book of Tolq."

Oh shit no, Jillian grumbled to herself. They were going to make her sit through a catechism lesson! She definitely wasn't in the mood for this. But even as she considered offering her excuses and heading out, a disembodied voice called out in anguished tones.

"Tolq!" it cried. "Have we follow'd ye t' our doom? This world be a lifeless hell. How will we n' our children survive?"

A candle flared then, casting a halo around the head of a hawk-faced man. His features were composed, a mask of certainties, and his eyes were like polished obsidian.

"My friends," he said, "despair not. This planet be not lifeless, merely wild. Tha desert sun will purge us of the ills that have poisoned our souls, and tha work that awaits us will make us strong. Our pleasures will come of our own making, n' they will come in plenitude as our labors revive tha pride in us. Take heart, I tell you, for we have found a new home."

Another candle sputtered to light, and lent the old woman who bore it a pasty aura. It cast shadows on those who rallied behind her.

"Questions remain, Tolq," she said, aggressive with doubts. "Where will ye have us live? What will ye have us eat? My family will na' get fat on words."

Her supporters echoed agreement.

Tolq frowned, a fatherly reproach. "We'll build our own homes n' grow our own food—just as I promis'd we would ere we fled our old lives. Ye were one of tha first to embrace my vision, Kara tik Xamar. How came ye to be so frightful of it now?"

"I'm na' speaking for myself now," she argued, folding her arms across her chest, "but for them who trusted me when I yoked them to your visions of a new and better life. This world is na' their idea of better, Tolq, and there be more than a few here who fear ye as mad for claiming it so."

"Fear be a healer, for it sharpens the wits," Tolq countered. "And we'll be better off for such an edge in the days to come. We did na' cross the galaxy ta resume our old, decadent ways on a new world, did we? No. We came ta forge a new purpose for one and all. N' so it will be done. Starting here. Starting now.

"Tell *that* ta them who trusted you. N' while you're at it, tell them ta start trusting themselves as well."

He started to walk away from the crowd then. As he did so, Kara demanded, "Where'd ye be going?"

"Your doubts have left me sad n' restless," he replied. "I need a walk in the desert to set me right again."

At that, his candle winked out. A moment later, so did Kara's.

Not a moment too soon, Jillian thought then. She had no interest in the cast of characters. And their archaic language rankled her ears. Still, the telling had done one thing for her—it had stalled her fascination with Ammas. She could leave now, with no regrets other than the ones that had been soldered into her, and no lasting damage done. She turned to Ammas with a goodbye in her mouth only to fumble it as he smiled at her. Up until now, he'd been part of the game—an obliging stand-in for her cyborg fantasies. But now that the game was over, she realized that she'd made a mistake. She'd grown attached to him. Seriously attached. She railed at herself: *stupidstupidstupid!* Never mind that she knew next to nothing about the crown prince of Xamar. Never mind that they frequented different solar systems. She was a cyborg. He was all human. It simply wouldn't work. No how, no way. Never.

"Is something wrong, Captain?" he whispered then.

"I need to be going," she replied, carefully avoiding eye-contact.

"Stay just a little longer, won't you?" he asked. "The second part of the telling is just about to start."

As if on cue, a candle flared in the teller's circle. Ammas squeezed her hand—a further entreaty. Although she knew better, she stayed.

Kara tik Xamar was in the limelight again. This time, she and several companions were ringed by a mob of angry faces. The candle's glow lent their frowns an unflattering depth.

"It's been a week now, and Tolq still has na' returned!" one man said. "Nor have our searchers found any sign of him. He canna' still be alive. I say we get back in tha ships and get off this miserable rock ere tha desert eats us all."

"I agree!" another shouted. "Tha only thing for us here be death by thirst and heat exhaustion. Our food and water rations be getting low already. Best we leave ere they're gone completely. One of tha settled worlds will have us as immigrants."

But Kara stood adamant. "Those worlds are shadows of tha same corruption that we left behind in our youth. Would ye trade one brand of slavery for another, Thom? We must stay here and make a new beginning, even if Tolq be lost."

"Ye ha' come ta be as crazy as he was!" Thom said, and his fellows cheered him on. "And if ye will na' listen to reason, then perhaps ye'll respond to force."

The mob closed in around Kara and her few supporters. She commanded, then bellowed, and then finally begged for a return to sanity, but the human noose around her and the others grew ever tighter. Jillian clenched her fists, caught up in the drama in spite of her mood. But even as Thom was about to strike the first blow, a voice knelled from out of nowhere.

"Violence is forbidden!"

A moment later, Tolq came shouldering through the mob, deaf to the angry buzz that rose up at his back. That buzz grew louder and meaner as he planted himself in front of Kara.

"Where would ye be coming from?" she hissed.

He didn't seem to hear her. His hair was disheveled; his clothes, in tatters. The milky light from Kara's candle cast dark shadows on his inappropriate grin. He raised his hands as if for silence. He looked wild and exultant, and there was madness in his eyes.

"People!" he cried, in a tone as compelling as a whip. "Put aside your doubts, for I ha' found hope beyond measure in the desert. Na' only will we dwell on this world, we will thrive!"

"More promises, Tolq?" Thom jeered.

"Aye," Tolq replied, "but none of my making. From here on, I speak for H'Nath, the god of New Beginnings—"

"A god, you say?" someone scoffed, over an outbreak of harsh laughter. "Well, that be proof enough for me, my friends. The strain of being homeless ha' joined hands w' tha desert's infernal heat ta addle his wits."

"Hear you me," Tolq insisted then, in a tone that flattened the laughter like a foot flattens grass. "There be nothin' wrong w' my wits. What I am saying be true. H'Nath came to me in a dream while I was lost in tha desert. He called me his child, and said he would make me strong. He promised me and mine a life worth living."

"Tha nursery 'bot used ta tell us stories like this ere it tucked us in for the night," a woman said, sweetly sarcastic. "What be tha difference between them tales and tha one ye be spinning now?"

His supporters squirmed as if their innermost thoughts had just been broadcast without their permission, but Tolq paid them no heed. He was still reliving in his vision. "H'Nath bestowed gifts upon me as a token of his commitment," he claimed. "He will give them to ye and yer descendants, too, if ye cleave to him."

"What gifts?" Thom demanded. "I dunna see any gifts, just a dirty old mad-man."

"I went seven days in tha desert with only one sip of water from H'Nath's pool to succor me," Tolq bragged. "Yet I be neither sweat-stained nor parched to near-death like a man of my age should be."

"Then no wonder ye be seeing things that na' be there." Thom said. "T'is better ta sweat than ta stew in yer body's own poisons. But I'm as fair a man as tha next, Tolq. If ye wanna believe in this god of yours, ye be welcome ta go back ta him. Ye can take your lackies w' ye, too," he added with a contemptuous nod toward Kara and the others. "Tha damn desert ought ta be big enough for all of ye."

Kara's candle went out like a snap. A moment later, a sound like a fully loaded sand-cart came rumbling out of the dark. Jillian recognized it as Tolq's voice, but not by much. It was amplified in an eerie, out-of-phase sort of way.

"Ye ha' despised H'Nath and his prophet twice now," he said. "I will overlook yer disrespect this one last time for ye dunna yet understand that which ye mock, but ye'd best mind yer hearts in future. I say again that ye ha' been chosen. N' if proof be what ye need, then proof be what ye shall receive. See for yourself the sign of H'Nath."

Then, with a soundless whoosh, the shadow that was Tolq burst into flames.

Fire!

Jillian screamed. The viewplate exploded. The next thing she knew, Denny was gone, blown clear of the cockpit, and she was burningburningburning. Her face blistered in an instant. The breath in her lungs turned to ash. And shitshitshit—she hurt so bad! There was no pain left in the universe; it was all coming to a boil in her body.

Then she saw a man-sized torch of red flame in the distance. *Denny,* she thought. And: *must help.* She started toward him, dragging herself along the ground with hands that were twisting into blackened claws. The stench was phenomenal: roasted flesh and shuttle propellant. It was the quintessential smell of pain.

"Captain," someone shouted, from a million miles away. "What's wrong?"

"Denny!" she sobbed. He was burningburningburning. And so was she. Where was the freakin' rescue squad? "Help him!"

She clutched Denny's leg, then hauled herself to her feet. But by the time she got there, her dearest friend was gone. An older, red-robed man stood in his place. He was gaping at her in horror. She didn't understand. This man had been on fire a moment ago, she was sure of it. Yet there wasn't a mark on him. She touched his face. It was smooth and brown. His hands showed no sign of scarring.

"Is this your idea of a joke?" she demanded. Flesh burned. Fire killed. This man should be deaddeaddead like Denny. "Do you think this is funny?" She grabbed him by the throat then. The fear that flooded his eyes filled her with fury and savage glee. "Let's see how you like my sense of humor."

"Please don't do that, Captain," Ammas said, as she began to squeeze. "Bo didn't mean to scare you. Let him go."

"You're next," she told him, and meant it.

He touched a hand to her temple then. An instant later, she blacked out.

Chapter 8

JILLIAN CAME AWAKE with a mental gasp to find herself sprawled belly-down on the floor. She couldn't say how she had gotten there. The last thing she remembered was—

Fire!

An stark echo of fear gusted through her, baring memories like half-buried bodies: shots of kluur, a dance with Ammas, a man bursting into flames. *Shitshitshit.* Even now, this far after the fact, she couldn't bring herself to re-visualize that moment. She was too afraid of triggering another of those devastating episodes. *Fire!* No wonder she'd been in so much pain. All of hell had taken up residence in her head.

It wasn't her head that was bothering her now, though, but rather a creeping sense of mortification. She felt like a drunk after her third or fourth black-out—she didn't want to admit that something might be wrong, but it sure fit the pattern. Now suddenly seemed like a very good time to apologize to her hosts, pay for any damages done, and get the hell out of Xamar. So she flipped herself over and then snapped to her feet. To her surprise, she found herself surrounded by wary-eyed priests. The rest of the hall was deserted.

"Where'd everybody go?" she said, voicing her first thought aloud.

The nearest priest turned his back to her without saying a word. His companions did the same. Jillian's mortification soured into dread. No doubt remained—she'd done something. Something wrong enough to clear a room. Sweet, suffering mother. And she didn't have to tiptoe too far back into the minefields of her memory before that something clicked. The crazy bastard, the one who'd torched himself—she'd attacked him. Killed him, for all she knew. But even as she shouldered the awful responsibility of the crime, a feral voice within her spurned it. *He was on fire. He had to die.*

She tapped a priest on the back. "How's that man? Is he going to be all right?"

He didn't answer, but someone else did—someone who was just now stepping into the room. "If you mean Bo," Micca said, "he wasn't breathing when you finally let him go. Fortunately, Elyn is a master of her gift."

"I'm truly glad he's going to live," Jillian said, as the priestess approached. "And before you kick me out of here, I'd very much like to apologize to him as well as to you, Saj, Tark, and Ammas."

"We have no use for your apology, offworlder," Micca told her. "And you aren't going anywhere until you've answered to H'Nath." She split the circle of priests into two groups with one gesture, then beckoned to Jillian with the next. "Now come, the tribunal awaits you. Do not try to resist. We can force your compliance."

"I have no intention of resisting," Jillian said.

The squadron of priests escorted her to the adjudicators' table. The lord of Xamar and his two kinsmen were already seated there. All three had a betrayed look about them, although Tark wore it better than the others. Ammas looked heartsick, too, and refused to make eye-contact with her. Micca acknowledged the men with a curt nod, then instructed her underlings to stand guard at Jillian's back. She was already headed for her seat among the tribunes when Gevera stepped out of the shadows and bowed to her.

"Thank you for coming, Gev," Micca said, though she was clearly surprised to see the other woman. "But you need not stay. Your services are not required here today."

"I think otherwise," Tark asserted. "Captain D'Lange has the right to defend her actions with the truth."

"There is no defense for attempted murder," the priestess argued. "Furthermore, we were all witnesses to the crime."

"You presume to judge where you have no authority to do so," Tark said. "I want to hear what the captain has to say."

"I concur," Lord Xamar said. "We must attend to all aspects of this tribunal, not just its resolution. And Gevera has told me that she is willing to do her part."

Micca made a disgusted sound under her breath, then conceded the debate with a churlish wave. She didn't sulk in silence for very long, however. As soon as Lord Xamar officially proclaimed the tribunal to be in session, she snapped to her feet and fired off her first question.

"Offworlder," she asked, regal with disdain, "was it your intention to kill Bo?"

"It was," Jillian said.

"Truth," Gevera intoned.

Micca glanced at Tark with a 'what-more-do-you-want' in her eyes. To her deep disgust, he donned a gentle smile and asked, "But why, Captain? Why would you want to do a thing like that to a man you don't even know? Did he do something to offend you?"

"No. Not exactly," she replied, trying to pick through the pieces of that memory without looking at any of it. "It's just that he was on fire. And I'm—" She paused for a moment, then blurted the newfound truth. "I'm deathly afraid of fire."

"That's no excuse for trying to strangle a man," Micca said.

"You don't understand," Jillian objected.

"So enlighten us."

"I was in an accident not too long ago—a shuttle-craft explosion," she appended, because *accident* wasn't nearly explicit enough for these truth-loving sadists. "My friend was killed. And I—" In spite of herself, she glanced at Ammas. He was looking at her with a massive ache in his eyes. She forged ahead before her courage could fail. " I was burned alive."

"Truth," Gevera said then, and although she was in a trance, her voice still rippled with twinges of awe and fear.

"But how can that be?" Ammas blurted, now flat-out staring at her. "There's not a scar on you."

"The lad raises an interesting point," Tark said, and then turned to Jillian with a peculiar gleam in his eyes. "Answer him, Captain. How *did* you manage to survive?"

Astonishment crashed through her like a rogue wave. She couldn't believe it—he had jammed her straight into a corner. One false word now, and his attempt to familiarize his clansmen with offworlders was going to take an even nastier turn. And the bitch of it was, he didn't even know what he was doing..

"I spent eight months in a SU rehab facility," she replied, as if that were the whole story.

"Truth," Gev said. But just as Jillian was about to release the thought that she'd been holding like a baited breath, the telepath added, "There's more that she's not telling, though."

"Let it go," Saj said. "It has no bearing on this case."

"I'm not so sure about that, brother," Tark was quick to argue. "It could tell us much about her state of mind. And that, after all, is what she wants us to understand."

"A valid point," the lord of Xamar conceded, and then looked to Jillian with a hint of regret in his eyes. "You will tell us what we need to know, Captain."

But even as he urged to her open up, the windows in her mind were ramming shut. She could hear them quite clearly. *Bang. Boom. Blam.* Just like that, her headache was back. Resentment flared alongside it. Stupid Tolqs. She was tired of tapdancing around their delicate sensibilities. She was sick of the masquerade. If they wanted the truth, they could have a shuttle-load of it. And *fuck* them all for asking.

"So what exactly do you want me to tell you?" she asked, looking squarely at Saj. "That over ninety percent of my body was broken and burned? It was. In fact, it was so badly damaged, it eventually died."

"But—" Ammas began, a garbled croak. And while he couldn't bring himself to finish the question, Jillian knew exactly what he was asking. His mind was like a pane of glass to her now; and out of pure spite, she chucked her next brick of truth right through it.

"What you see here is a refabrication," she told him. "My healers constructed it in my image. It holds my brain and a few other organs. It's not real meat, but at least it gets me where I need to go." Then, just for fun, she stripped off one of her gloves and showed the nailless hand to everybody. "See?" she asked, taking a perverse pleasure in the horror that coagulated on their faces. "I'm a technological breakthrough."

Ammas recoiled then, but even so, he couldn't seem to stop looking at her. His skin was ashen now. His eyes were glazed. As he gaped, he began to rub his hands on his robe as if he were trying to wipe his palms clean. Micca and Saj were doing the same thing.

But not Tark. He was sitting perfectly still. His mouth was a flat, bloodless line, but he wasn't oozing shock like the others were. Indeed, he seemed quite well-adjusted for a Tolq who'd just seen his first cyborg. But then he'd probably been exposed to far worse on Circe's II. She caught his eye, meaning to see where she stood with him now. He looked away—too fast and yet not fast enough. She realized then that he'd known about her all along. Ross must've told him. That's why he'd been so scrupulous about not touching her.

But if that was so, then what the fuck had he been thinking when he backed her into that confession? And—*bang, boom, blam*—why did this freakin' headache have to come back now?

"H'Nath forfend us all," Micca breathed then. "We have an abomination in our midst."

"I'm a cyborg, not an abomination," Jillian told her. "There's a difference."

"Not in our eyes, there isn't," the priestess said archly, and then rounded on the three Xamar lords. Father and son looked like they'd just been clubbed in the jewels, but Tark's bland mask was firmly in place. "I warned you not to welcome this, this, *thing* into your home," she said, "but you ignored me. Now Clan Xamar stands on the brink of damnation. 'Suffer not the machine in your midst,' Tolq said, 'for it will seduce ye, body and soul, and ye shall be lost.' I only hope that H'Nath will be merciful with you."

Jillian snorted. "You've used a radio, Micca. I hear you've done a tour aboard a solar schooner, too. So how come H'Nath hasn't punished you for your sufferances yet?"

"Pay no attention to the abomination's words," Micca instructed the three Xamars. "It seeks to cloud the issue, and thereby further its unholy cause. It doesn't need to know that I only use machinery that has been sanctioned by H'Nath."

"Yeah, right," Jillian said then, growing more belligerent by the second. "Like a supreme being wouldn't have better things to do with its time."

But Micca refused to snap at the bait. Instead, she said, "Saj, Ammas, Tark: your duty is clear. You must rescind your offer of hospitality and then join me in banishing the abomination to the desert for final judgment."

Jillian snorted again. *Banishment?* Like hell! Who did these backwater nabobs think they were?

"Sorry, people," she said, with an ultra-tight smile, "but the only place I'm going is back to my ship. If you want to have me punished, give Union Security a call and I'll surrender to them as soon as I return to Circe's II. They'll prosecute me for assault, I'll make restitution, and you'll never see me again."

"That is not our way," Saj told her, even though he drew a frown from Micca for talking to Jillian. In the face of such fairness under duress, she decided to tone down her own attitude.

"Look," she said. "I'll take full responsibility for my actions. I promise. But I've got a ship and one crewman parked about two hundred miles straight up from here, and if I don't get back to them in the very near future, the consequences could be dire."

"The abomination should've thought of *that* before it decided to try and pass itself off as human," Micca argued, with a barrister's zeal. "It should've thought of *that* before it violated Xamar's trust and tried to strangle poor Bo. Now is too late, Saj. Now it must answer to H'Nath for what it is and what it's done."

"I agree," the lord of Xamar replied, although he appeared to take no pleasure in saying so. "The law must be upheld. The cyborg known as Captain D'Lange will be sent into the desert for a period of three days—"

"Three days?" Tark echoed, an incredulous outburst. "Brother, what can you be thinking? Tobia was sent out for three days for the petty crime of bootlegging; and I, myself, have been given longer penances. Surely that *thing* deserves the very worst that you can give it."

Up until now, Jillian had considered Tark an ally. Indeed, somewhere in the back of her mind, she'd rather expected him to step forward at the very last moment with some clever loophole that would absolve her and embarrass Micca at the same time. She knew better now, though. *That thing.* She had never heard so much loathing in his voice. He must've hated her right from the start.

But if that was so, then why had he talked her into coming down to Xamar?

The answer came to her as an intuitive whisper: *he wanted to kill her.* That same sad voice then reminded her of the runaway sand-cart. She'd told Ammas that it had been no accident. But it was surprisingly painful to learn that she'd been right.

"...I understand your concern, brother mine," Lord Xamar was saying now. "But the Season of Storms is upon us now; and the law clearly states that no sentence shall last for more than three days during this time. If we mean to hold the off-worlder to our laws, then we must hold ourselves to them as well."

Tark scourged Jillian with a look, then folded his arms across his chest and grated, "Three days, thirty days—it matters not. It will only take a minute for H'Nath to swallow her up."

His sudden antagonism toward her continued to confuse and aggravate Jillian. What had she ever done to him, she wondered. And: what could he possibly gain by having her killed? As she glared at him, trying to glean a motive from the ridges of his frown, she thought of something else. Maybe Micca had been right all along. Maybe there was more to Tark's hiring of her than met the eye.

Meanwhile, said priestess continued with her poll. She was badgering Ammas now. He didn't want to look up from his hands. When pressed, though, he groaned, "I agree as well. The law is clear. Captain D'Lange must walk the desert."

Tark's betrayal had confused her. Ammas's made her mad. *Care to dance?* How could she have been so fucking stupid? *I feel wonderfully light-headed.* What made her think that he was any wiser than the average Tolq? *It must be your company.* She was so mad, she wanted to march right over there and—

Her spine tensed. Her fists knotted. Then she choked back an incredulous laugh, because despite all the hurt that he'd just heaped upon her soul, some tragically naive part of her still wanted to kiss rather than kill that red-haired moron. Sweet, suffering mother! How she hated this planet. It was driving her crazy. She *had* to leave. Now.

"But what if Captain D'Lange doesn't want to walk the desert, aye, Ammas?" she asked, mocking him with her version of his sorry-ass tone. "What if she wants to bid you holier-than-thou humans a less-than-fond farewell and go home? You know how fast and strong she is. What's to stop her?"

"I could," he replied wanly, "if she forced me to. H'Nath has given me the power to control minds. I have used it to stop her once already this day."

"And if that doesn't sway her," Saj added, "then perhaps this will."

She glanced toward the old man. He was holding a lively little tongue of orange flame in the palm of his hand. Her thoughts broke into a cold, teeth-chattering sweat at the sight. An instant later, her field of vision went red.

"Bad move," she rasped, struggling for self-control. "Make it go away."

With a regal nod, Saj did so.

But he was already too late. She was caught in an undertow, and it was dragging her downdowndown to that murderous place where Targon The Terror must've gone just before he raided Gilda's small-arms locker. There was no denying the truth any longer— she was weak. Flawed. Defective. She had the freakin' RIMs. Thirty-one people had died by brother Targon's hand. She had a chance to top that record. The prospect both appalled and delighted her.

"Ammas," she panted, just barely clinging to the last frayed threads of her sanity.

"Yes, Captain?" he replied, all misery and hope.

"You'd better do your thing," she told him. "Otherwise, I'll kill you all."

"Truth," Gevera intoned.

A sense of soothing coolness came over her then. It felt like a mother's hand on her child's fevered brow. At the thought, Myla's stern but loving image took shape in her mind. She was smiling. Jillian smiled back. A moment later, the world went black.

ᴄ๏

FOR THE THIRD time in a singularly hellish day, Jillian woke up not knowing where she was. It was darkdarkdark now—a black-cherry night with few stars and a tiny slip of a moon. All she could see for miles around was shadowed rocks and sand. It came back to her then: *the cyborg known as Captain D'Lange will be sent into the desert for a period of three days.*

"Bastards!" she howled.

She scrambled to her feet, then craned her neck for recognizable landmarks—the glassworks, H'Nath's throat, anything that would get her back to Xamar Estate. Because she had absolutely no intention of spending the next three days out here in the desert. She was going to find her shuttle, lock the doors, and blow this freakin' rock. And if anybody tried to mess with her along the way, she'd squash them like bugs and good riddance.

A large, thumb-shaped boulder in the distance caught her eye. It looked vaguely familiar, so she started toward it. As she walked, she sputtered to herself. Stupid Tolqs. What were they thinking when they *dumped* her out here? That she couldn't or wouldn't her way back? That this H'Nath of theirs would protect them? She snorted. Their myths were no match for her. She could survive anywhere.

"You hear me?" she bellowed. "Anywhere!" She punched the night air with her fists, then turned a defiant circle. A vanguard of violet shadows copied her every move. "What do you say to that, H'Nath of the New Beginnings?"

Nothing stirred. She snorted her contempt, and then continued on her way. That knobby cluster of rocks in the distance was further away than she'd first guessed, but she wasn't concerned. She had plenty of time, and plenty of energy. And someone had once told her that flat land played tricks with the eye.

The next thing she knew, she was thoroughly lost.

As soon as she realized that she'd been blending her landmarks, she turned around to retrace her footsteps, but the sand hereabouts was fine and shifty, and refused to hold a track. *Shitshitshit,* she thought. And: *now what?* The one time that she'd gotten lost on Calypso, all she'd had to do was ask someone for directions. And she'd never been lost on solid, uninhabited ground!

Don't panic.

That had been her mother's first rule of survival. And rule number two was: *see rule number one.* The unsolicited memory gave Jillian a little boost—just enough for her to see a way out of this dismal Tolqan sand-trap. All she had to do was wait until the sun came up. Knowing east, she could then use the coordinates that Tark had given to her on the shuttle-ride down to find Xamar estate. And then—

"I'm going to kill you, Tark cis Xamar!" she cried. "You back-stabbing bastard!"

She fantasized about that murder. It would be a slow, intimate affair, punctuated by his pleas for mercy. She would peel away his secrets like layers of skin and leave him as raw as wind-blasted bone. *'Why?'* she would ask, wearing a bland smile in his honor. And: *'Why me?'* Why hire her, then semi-befriend her only to try and kill her—not once, but twice now? He didn't strike her as a paid assassin. His attempts were so...so sloppy and happenstance. One used an AP bolt to kill a cyborg, not a cart filled with sand. And there was no way that he could've known what the sight of a man on fire would do to her.

She blocked that memory and its half-buried associates with a scowl. A moment later, her head began to boom like a doom's-day cannon. It was the fire trying to get out, she thought. All she had to do was let it go, and the headache would disappear for good. As pained as she was, though, she couldn't bring herself to release that genie. It was too powerful, too devastating. It was also the only thing keeping the RIMs at bay.

And she wasn't ready to go irretrievably insane just yet.

So she held those terrible memories in check and started walking again—this time in fat, loopy circles that overlapped like waves. Her only goal was to keep her mind from the pain. RIMs, she thought. It rhymed with BRIMs. And GRIMs. She wondered what nickname the tavern wags would give her in the years to come. D'Lange The Destroyer? Jillian The Juggernaut? Bastards. They ought to be pickled in their own—

Something hard collided with her boot, then went skittering across the sand like a whirligig. She glanced after it—an automatic reaction. To her surprise, it was a rib-bone. A human rib-bone, she appended, noticing the rest of the skeleton. It was strewn across the ground in ignoble bits and pieces. The stark-white skull had been cracked open like a large nut. So, she mused. This was what became of those who failed the desert's test. And this was what Tark had in mind for her. She imagined some red-robed sinner from the future bumping into her plastisteel frame. The stooge would no doubt see it as a sign, she mused, the bones of a saint or maybe even H'Nath's. She laughed aloud. Her death would breed the ultimate joke.

Echoes of her laughter were still rippling through the night when the ground to her left erupted. Sand sprayed everywhere. An odd clacking sound rattled in her ears. She sprang away from the disturbance like a startled cat, then knuckled the grit from her eyes. As her field of vision cleared, the blur before her became a creature from a Tolq's worst nightmare.

It resembled the tattoo that Roadkill had on his back. A scorpion, he'd called it— a Terran bug with lots of attitude. But Jillian would've been willing to bet that there was nothing quite like this thing back on the mother of all homeworlds. It was as long as she was from head to multi-spiked tail, and perhaps half again her weight. It had six jointed hinter-legs made for traveling over sand, and two forelegs tipped with claws. A wicked set of mandibles protruded from its small, neckless head. Two pupilless eyes stared at her from reed-like stalks. It looked hungry.

She laughed again. "The joke's on you, old boy. I'm a miserable mouthful."

It scuttled toward her—a wary start and stop. Although she could've easily outrun it, she only backed away. And she only did that because she was still looking for its weak spots. She'd been more of a lover than a fighter in her human days, but she *had* learned a trick or two in the rougher alleyways of Station. And she meant to take this would-be god of new beginnings down.

"C'mon, H'Nath," she said, as it advanced toward her again. "Let's you and me mix it up—right here, right now. If I win, I get to be god for a day. If you win, well, poor you—you're stuck with Micca for the next hundred years."

It clacked its mandibles at her, then surged forward yet again. To her surprise, she realized that it was trying to trap her against a large, horseshoe-shaped outcrop to her rear. She came about to keep the open desert at her back. As she did so, the creature charged. In spite of its size, it was surprisingly quick. Few people would've reacted fast enough to save their lives.

But Jillian did.

She dodged one set of snapping pincers, then the other. Faster than conscious thought, she then snaked past its guard and ripped the right eyestalk from its socket. It loosed an almost ultrasonic screech of pain and fury, and then thrashed at the air with its forearms.

"You're gonna have to do better than that," Jillian said, standing just out of range of its claws.

She didn't see the tail arching out of the darkness until it was too late.

A spike slammed into her thigh. The force of the blow knocked her from her feet. The shockwaves from that ass-first landing drove the pain in her head to excruciating new heights. For one interminable moment, all she could do was watch as the creature closed in on her. Thick, green ichor oozed from its wounded socket. White foam dripped from its mandibles. It stalked her slowly now, with more caution than hunger. It seemed ready to take all night. But Jillian was no longer in the mood for games.

"Piss off, you big ugly bug," she shouted, and tried to wave it away. It sank into a crouch as if threatened. "Go on, you can keep your godhead." It clacked its mandibles at her. "Don't give me an excuse—"

It sprang.

"—to do this."

Rage bloomed, hot and ready. A berserker's instincts took over. The next thing she knew, she was somersaulting backward and onto her feet. The creature landed in her dust. She raced around to its blind side, then used one of its rear legs as a step-up to its back. It reared. It shuddered. It flailed its claws and tail. She ripped the other eyestalk out with no regret. She would've continued to mutilate it, too, until there was nothing left but a gooey, green carapace, but it plunged headfirst into the sand and started to burrow. Moments later, it was gone.

"Fuck you, H'Nath!" she shouted after it. "This is my gig now."

And the truth be told, she *was* feeling rather godly at the moment. The headache had vanished. So had the rage. The only thing left was this minor, matter-of-fact craving for violence. That seemed like a reasonable trade-off to her, but she was fairly sure that Tark wouldn't see it that way. Leastwise, she hoped not. Because she was ready to go back to him now, readyreadyready to teach him the essence of respect. She turned in a slow, lock-jawed circle, hoping for a glimpse of dawn. It had been dark for so long now. She had been gone for so long.

But the horizon remained all black. She sputtered an impatient curse, then picked a direction at random and started walking again. Although she knew that staying put was a better idea, she had no intention of camping out here and maybe giving H'Nath another shot at her. And speaking of which—

She glanced down at the leg that the creature had struck with its tail. To her utter surprise, there was a huge gash running down the length of that thigh. It wasn't messy. It didn't hurt. It was, however, quite eye-catching. She could see synthetic muscle, sheaths of tubing and circuitry, even a glimpse of plastisteel bone when the limb was flexed. And everything was all studded with black, viscous droplets. Venom, she guessed, and tensed with sudden apprehension. She didn't *think* that she could be poisoned like this, for there were no blood vessels or nerves in her legs—nothing to aid or abet a toxin's spread. But if it was corrosive, it could cripple her whether it went systemic or not. That would never do. So she stripped one of her gloves and began dabbing at the wound. The beads came up, but only grudgingly. What she needed was water.

The thought triggered a sudden awareness in her: she was thirsty. Not in the dry mouth, shriveled stomach sense of the word, but in a primordial, neurochemical way that was no less compelling for its being so intangible. That fight with H'Nath, combined with all the kluur that she'd knocked back earlier, must have dehydrated her. She had to find water, and soon.

But where?

Xamar Estate came immediately to mind, but she dismissed the possibility with a scowl. She didn't know where the settlement was yet, and besides, they'd probably salt the wells as soon as they saw her coming. But one of the other estates might take her in. A fox's smile curved across her face. She thought: why not? She had passed for a Tolq once. Why not twice? She'd slip in, drink her fill, maybe crack a few skulls on her way back out.

She *liked* the sound of that.

So she ripped a long strip of cloth from her already torn uniform and wrapped it around the gash in her thigh, then drew her glove back on. Disguise complete, she then started walking again. She paid no attention to where she was going. Tark had told her that there were estates to the north, south and west. She was bound to hit one of them.

"Can't get away from me," she mumbled, though it sounded quite loud to her.

The skyline was growing more distinct now. If she stared really hard, she could see silhouettes in the distance—rock formations, a petrified tree, the faintest suggestions of a far-off mountain range. Then the sun's first rays spilled over the horizon. Magenta streaks appeared in the night-stained sands. The sky turned lavender and mauve. Jillian was transfixed. Spacers like herself didn't catch many sunrises, and this one, the desert's child, was the most spectacular that she had ever seen. As she watched, the pain in her head fell mute. A moment later, a sense of perfect peace came over her. She closed her eyes to better savor the feeling. It felt very good to be here in the dark. It felt very good to relax—

She didn't realize that she'd fallen asleep while standing up until a nagging sense of thirst woke her up again. And an instant after she opened her eyes, a full-on beam of harsh, yellow light spearheaded a new onslaught of pain. She winced, then whimpered to herself. How had it come to be so late in the morning? She had only closed her eyes for a minute!

And oh, how tempting it was to close them again. She was tired, so tired—not in body, for that knew no better, but in mind. She was tired of cycling pain and hate and the hope of murder around in her head. She was tired of this world and its ocean of red sand. Redredred—it was the newest freakin' curse in her vocabulary. It tinted her thoughts like a menstrual flow. But she wasn't going to get away from it by sleeping all day. Nosirree. She had to keep going, westward-ho—on to Xamar, water, and revenge.

So Jillian set off once again, this time with the sun to her back. Or leastwise, that was the plan. Sometime later, she came awake again, and the sun was directly overhead. Not good, she thought, all groggy and slow. She'd fry her brain this way. Her peripheral vision was already starting to blur. Water could wait, she decided. A snooze in the shade could not. And fortunately, there was a fair-sized formation nearby. She trudged toward it, thinking *sleepsleepsleep* all the way. As she drew closer, she saw that it was more like a hedge of loose boulders than a true outcrop. She looked for tell-tale bones. There were none. That was good enough for her.

But even as she closed the gap between her and her would-be refuge, she caught a flicker of movement through a crack between two towering stones. She pressed an eye to the cranny, but all she saw was an indistinct glare. *Shitshitshit.* The last thing she wanted to do now was face-off with another of Tolq's horror-viz denizens. Or so she told herself as she took a fist-sized rock in each hand.

"Leave now," she yelled, "and I'll let you live."

The desert responded with silence.

She prowled along the hedge until she came to a gap large enough to let her pass. Then, armed with a few stones and a berserker's rage, she charged through the opening—

"Ready or not, here I come!"

—and nearly had herself a splash-landing on the other side. As she pulled herself up short, sunlight shimmered on the pond's calm surface like laughter. That's what she'd seen through the crack.

"Water!" she exclaimed. It dazzled her red-weary eyes like a sheet of diamonds.

Her thirst reasserted itself immediately; and she had to force herself, one grudging step at a time, to secure the rest of the outcropping before she dropped to her belly on the pond's sandy shores. She stripped off both gloves then, and poked a finger into the drink. Nothing out of the ordinary happened, so she scooped up a handful and took a small sip. Again, nothing happened—no dizziness, blindness, or sudden death. So she cast caution aside and drank until that sense of thirst retired. Afterward, she shifted back into a sitting position. The sound of so much water sloshing around in the holding tank that passed for her stomach brought a faint smile to her lips.

Her amusement vanished as soon as she removed her makeshift bandage, though. For despite her precautions, the gash was now infected with sand as well as venom. She muttered a curse, then tore off another strip of trouser and began sopping up the poisoned grit. As she worked, she began to see just how lucky she had been. If the creature's tail had struck her at any other angle, it would've separated one or more quadriceps from the bone and thereby taken the whole leg out of commission. As it was, she had escaped with only a large but inconsequential vertical tear in the primary muscle-bundle construct.

She snorted at the thought. *Only?* If she'd been anyone else, she would've bled to death by now from an *only* like that—*if* the venom hadn't killed her first. She snorted again. If she'd been anyone else, she wouldn't have been dumped in no-cyborg's land in the first place.

Her thoughts began to tailspin then—a slow, downward spiral that robbed her of all ambition. She dabbed at the wound one last time, then tore a third strip from her pants and fashioned it into a bandage. That would do until she got back to the ship, she thought drowsily. Then Roadkill would make it good as new.

An image of her half-brother drifted ghost-like through her mind. By now, he had to know that something was wrong. She could see him pacing across the bridge with his hands knotted in his titanium-plated hair. She could see him bombarding the H'Nathma with communiqués that were liberally sprinkled with threats and obscenities. *Good man. Good brother. She'd have to—*

"Have to what?" she gasped, even as she started awake again. She was tired, so tired. Her thoughts were mired in quicksand. "Oh yeah, I remember," she muttered then. "Have to give RK another half-share in the ship. He'z a good man. Good brother—"

She fell fast asleep in mid-mumble.

❦

A STEADY, LOW-THROATED moaning crept into the cushy blackness that held Jillian in its grip. The sound started out as part of a nameless dream, but then it burrowed deeper into her subconscious and set off a primordial fight-or-flight alarm. Her body responded immediately. The next thing she knew, she was on her feet. At first, she was so groggy, she could barely focus beyond her refabricated nose. But the moaning persisted, on and on—a raw, undulating sound that churned a previously undiscovered sense of stomach in her. It overrode the mental static and turned her toward the west. Even so, it took her several moments to notice the seething, red-tinged cloud on the horizon. It was so big and so dense, she'd mistaken it for a mountain's side.

And it seemed to be heading this way.

She remembered then. Saj had said something about this being the Season of Storms. Therefore, that dreadful noise must be coming from that crystal spire back at Xamar. What had Tark called it—H'Nath's Throat? Sweet, suffering mother! How could anything that far away be so freakin' loud?

"Shut up!" she shouted, clamping her hands to her ears. "Just shut the fuck up!"

Her head started to ache again. *No, not now*, she begged herself. She needed to have her wits about her. That sandstorm was closing in a hurry. The wind had already picked up, giving rise to an army of infant dust-devils. And the western sky was growing ever darker. By her reckoning, she had less than an hour to figure out what she was going to do to protect herself. Running was out—the storm-front was too damn big. And lying down along the outcropping's lee-side only seemed like a good idea until she realized that wind wasn't going to be the only problem. There'd be sand, too, as much in the air as on the ground. She could be blinded by it, or suffocated, or even buried alive. She needed a shelter of some kind, someplace where she could curl up like a Terran black bear and nap the bad weather away.

Unfortunately, the outcropping didn't have any cyborg-sized crannies.

The realization didn't bother her. She was still imagining that black bear, all nice and snug in its cozy little cave. *Mmm, sleep,* she purred to herself. She could do with a little of that now. It felt like she hadn't had more than an hour of it in the past few weeks, even though she knew full well that she'd slept the better half of today away. She nodded off only to bolt awake again a moment later in the grips of absurd inspiration. There were plenty of loose stones in the vicinity, she told herself. All she needed to do was pile them into a couple of walls perpendicular to the lee, then stretch her uniform over the top like a tarp. She'd have a little cave of her own in no time.

She threw herself into the project with childish gusto, but her enthusiasm had a very short half-life. For gathering stones was tedious work; and that pile-driving ache in her head made it hard. She thought of that Terran bear again, of curling up and sleeping through the pain and this stupid storm. The noise from H'Nath's throat became a *lullaby, close your eyes, time to dream spacer dreams.* The bruise-colored sky reinforced that narcotic suggestion. She started to drift off only to start back awake as the rock that she happened to be carrying shimmered into an odd-shaped skull.

"There's work to be done," it scolded, in her mother's voice. "And no one to do it but you."

She dropped the skull. It landed in the sand as a rock. She picked it up and toted it over to her haven-in-progress. One of the proposed walls stood knee-high already. The other came to mid-shin. That surprised her. She didn't remember being that far along. A few more trips, and she'd be done.

So she pressed on. Lift, carry, stack. Lift, carry, stack. It was appropriate work for an automaton, she thought. It was work fit for a *machine.* Sand began to ping into her face—fleeting, micro-dot pressures that made her think of desert kisses. Lift, carry, stack. The kisses intensified—*Lift*—becoming harder— *Carry*—and more urgent. *Stack.* The moaning in her ears became a lover's croon that carried her away like a bride. She helped the hands that were now tearing at her clothes. And afterward, she allowed them to thrust her into a bed of sand. She was excited now, hungry for sensation. But when she opened her eyes to look upon her deep-throated lover, the desert sand-blasted them. The sky was the color of old blood now. The air was thick with sand. Yet there she was, stretched out on the ground with her uniform pulled down over her boots.

What in hell had she been thinking?

She glanced toward the shelter. One wall bulged outward in the middle; the other had a noticeable slant, but that was OK. At least they were both standing. She heaved a relieved sigh, then finished stripping. The uniform snapped and writhed in her hands like a frantic wild animal, so instead of trying to fashion it into a tarp, she wrapped it over her head and then laid down in her would-be cave with her face to the outcropping.

The wind began to roar—louder and then louder still, until she could no longer hear H'Nath's Throat. And the sand began flying so fast and furious, she could almost feel the sting of it as it tried to embed itself in her exposed syntheskin.

"Are you afraid?" the storm howled at her.

"Why should I be?" she howled back.

At that, a cyclone sucked her up and spun her into a wyrmhole. There, it dumped her on a cloud of crimson static and then disappeared. She turned in a slow, dazed circle. Vertigo lapped at her toes. She was about to call out for help when a pair of disembodied eyes winked into view right in front of her.

"Abomination," a voice like scraping scales whispered.

"No," she whispered back. But the denial lacked conviction.

Her scrap of a bandage burst open of its own accord then. A moment later, the syntheskin around the wound began to peel away in all directions—down her leg, up her belly, across the isthmus of her sexless groin to her back-side. She wanted to resist, but couldn't move. It was if she had been disconnected from her body. Abominable indeed, she thought, and then there she was, peeled clean like a cocktail shrimp. There were four eyes glowering at her now. As she glowered back, they multiplied again, becoming eight and then sixteen. Her muscle-bundle constructs began to spring free of their attachments then—one right after the other. Her right leg collapsed. So did her left. Yet she stayed upright—upright, alert, and appalled, even when her bones dissolved and trickled away like red hour-glass sand.

The universe was all eyes now. And she—she was a mass of pulsing gray tissue tucked away in a plastisteel shell. She cried aloud at the sight. The eyes started to bleed tears. Then the cyclone reappeared, and she was sucked back into the void.

She landed, fully re-assembled, back on Station. *Zeph* was caught in a monstrous, titanium-plated web down on Circe's II. She ran here and there, desperately trying to find a way to get to her stranded ship only to be blockaded by a fat, frog-mouthed man with an ice-blue glare. He came from out of nowhere to stand just beyond her reach, then wagged a finger at her as if she were a naughty child.

"No, no, Jillie," he said. "The ship's mine now."

"But I can pay!" She pulled an impossibly large number of credit vouchers from a pocket that hadn't been there a moment ago. "Here," she urged, "it's all yours."

The man laughed, baring nasty yellow teeth and gray gums, then undid his fly and pissed on the vouchers. They flashed white, then fluttered from her fingers as snowy ash. An instant later, she went up in white-hot flames as well.

Her eyeballs boiled in tears; her heart, in blood. The pain was intense; absolute; all-encompassing. She could think of nothing else. But even as death was about to take her into its bony palm, someone else screamed, and The Reaper left her for another day.

"No, wait!" she begged, and bolted upright.

That was when she saw Denny.

He was standing in the distance, burning as brightly as a bonfire. As she gaped at him, horribly transfixed, he screamed again; and although she couldn't make any sense of the words, she knew he was begging her for help.

"Hang on, lover. I'm coming!" she cried, without a second thought. And just like that, her charred lump of a body sprouted new legs.

She stood up then and kicked her way out of a half-ruined tomb. The world was completely black now except for Denny; and that blackness was the enemy. It scratched at her eyes, and roared in her ears, and stole one step back for every three she took. She pressed on, though, because her lover was burning and bleeding and howling for god, and she had to save him. He reached for her then, one fiery arm extended. She choked back a sob of terror and remembered pain, then slung him over her shoulder. At his touch, she ignited with a whoosh. Now both of them were burning, suttee for two, and the stench of pain was everywhere.

"Stay with me," she panted, as she hauled him through the blackness. "Hang on."

Zephyr swooped out of a fold in space and snatched her away, leaving Denny to blaze in her wake. She wailed, a soul-stricken, "No-o!" and then frantically tried to turn the ship around. But urgency rendered her fumble-fingered, and *Zephyr* shot forward at wyrm-speed instead. A massive ball of fire bloomed on the view-screen. It mirrored the one in her head. She screamed and wept and tried to change course, but *Zeph* would not respond.

"Relax, Jillie," Roadkill said from his station, as blasé as a Tark with death's-head eyes. "It's just a star."

At that, *Zephyr* shifted into high-speed reverse. The fireball on the view-screen shrank to the size of a Tolq's fiery head, and then to a shining speck of white, the merest pinprick in an infinite field of black. A tear dripped down her cheek. She laughed for joy and understanding.

She'd always loved the stars.

Then she was on a beach with Denny by her side. They watched as dawn spilled colored fire into the sky, then hugged each other close and fell into a peaceful, dreamless sleep.

Chapter 9

SLEEP RECEDED IN layers—a slow, co-mingled progression of consciousness and memory. *She was Jillian D'Lange, class-one captain...*

...There had been a terrible, terrible storm...

...Something was pinning her right arm to the ground.

An instant after that realization sunk in, her eyes snapped open. All she saw was a gritty, dark-red blur. *Sand,* she thought. *She was buried in sand. And shitshitshit,* she added, as the weight on her limb lurched closer, *something was buried with her.* She rid herself of that pressure with an emphatic jerk, then scrabbled her way out of her would-be grave. As soon as she broke the surface, she was on her feet and ready to repel whatever came scrabbling after her. But the only thing that followed was a feeble human groan.

"What in hell?" she sputtered.

She dove back into the mound that she had so hastily vacated and started digging with both hands. Tattered bits of a twarla appeared, then a rat's nest of dull red hair. A moment later, she hauled a man's head onto her lap. His thin face was wind-burned, and pocked with dozens of tiny, sand-studded scabs. A gummy ooze sealed one eyelid shut. The other twitched frantically. With a curse as dark as the day was bright, Jillian dragged the rest of his body out of the sand, and then scooped him into her arms. He was as light as a dried corn-husk, and appallingly limp.

She set him down on the banks of the pond, then scavenged a scrap of cloth from his twarla and started to clean his wounds. As she worked, questions buzzed her thoughts like flies. Who was he? Where was his home? And how in hell had he managed to wind up in her arms? Her memories of the storm were distorted and bizarre. She remembered multiplying eyes and brutal darkness and reaching for DennyDennyDen, but even now, by the harsh light of day, it was hard to tell what had been real. Everything seemed like part of a long, drug-induced dream. Had she really tried to build herself a cave? A glance at the mound ended all doubt. Two sloppy, knee-high walls protruded from the outcrop— or leastwise, what was left of them. One had a large breach in the middle now, as if it had been kicked in. Was that the stranger's doing? Or had she done it in her dreams?

Just then, the man stirred. A moment later, his one good eye fluttered open. She could tell that he wasn't fully conscious. His pupil was dilated; his stare, unfocussed. He mumbled something unintelligible.

"Shh," she crooned, and cupped water in her hand for him to drink. Most of it dribbled down his chin, and the one sip that he did manage to swallow left him strangely restless. She remembered something that Tark had told her then, and patted him down for his quot'tl bead. As soon as she popped it into his mouth, the gleam in his eye grew less frantic and his breathing slowed down. He sucked on the stone until it had satisfied some inner craving, then let it fall out of his mouth and lifted his gaze up at her.

"H'Nath—" he slurred.

"Guess again, friend," she replied. She tore another strip from his twarla, dipped it in the water, and then knotted it around his brow to keep him cool. He didn't seem to notice. "What's your name?"

"Friend," he said.

"Can you walk?" she asked then.

"Walk?" He giggled, a pitiful sound. "Walk?"

"I see," she said, with an inward scowl. Not only was the desert unforgiving, it had a vicious sense of humor as well. She wondered which of them was supposed to be the butt of this particular joke. She eased his head from her lap to the ground, then stood up. When he tried to follow, she gently pressed him back into the sand. "Stay there and rest for now. We've got a long trip ahead of us."

"Trip," he echoed solemnly.

Sympathy welled up within her only to give way to surprise. Here she was, trying to figure out how she was going to get this poor bastard to a healer, while only yesterday, she would've cheerfully finished what the desert had started. Where had that craving for murder gone? She ran a systems check on herself, searching in vain for pockets of latent violence. As she did so, she realized that her headache was gone, too! She felt nothing, absolutely nothing, and it was a *glorious* feeling. She let out a joyous whoop. It startled the Tolq, and he began to tremble.

"Don't worry, friend," she said. "This is your lucky day. Or rather, *our* lucky day."

She gathered up the remnants of her uniform then. Everything was in sorry shape, but she dressed anyway. Her returning to Xamar was bound to shock the whole clan as it was. Her returning naked, with a storm-damaged Tolq in tow and a foot-long gash in her reconstructed thigh would probably be interpreted as a harbinger for the end of the world. Anyone stout-hearted enough to look could still see the gash through the tear in her pants, but that was just tough titties. The last bandage that she'd fashioned for herself had come off sometime during the storm, and any spare material that she had left was strictly for the Tolq. She offered him a hand then. He took it with a child's trust.

"Time to go," she said, as she hoisted him to his feet.

"Go," he repeated firmly.

They headed westward, toward the setting sun and Xamar. The Tolq started out slow but semi-steady, but his condition deteriorated as they walked, and by dusk, he was flapping his arms and babbling inanities like a madman.

"H'Nath!" he shouted, with a drunk's broad grin. "Saved! Me! All praise—to him!" He tittered at her. "And to you, strangerfriend. H'Nath shines within you, oh yes, it's true. Saw him, I did, bright as day in the heart of darkness. Saw you. One eye short and still I saw." He knuckled the injured eye, then blinked at her. "Think it'll ever open again?"

"Not if you keep messing with it," she said.

Under different circumstances, she might've found his chatter amusing, but now it only framed her worries. She wondered if she should've left him there by the water-hole and gone for help by herself. Or maybe they both should've stayed put for a while— until he recovered a measure of strength. But no, she decided then. He needed a healer badly, and food in his gut. As hard as this march was for him, it was his only hope of surviving the desert.

Twilight came and went. A half-moon climbed its way into the evening sky. The Tolq was staggering now—an extravagant, drunken reel. If Jillian hadn't been holding on to the back of his twarla, he would've surely wandered off. She tugged him to a stop, the fourth one this hour. But as feeble as he was, he could not sit or stand still. He threw his arms around her waist and clung to her, his backside swaying like a metronome.

"Who you be, strangerfriend?" he asked, grinning up at her. "You need a name."

"I'm Jillian," she told him. "Jillian D'Lange."

"Jill-ian. Jill-i-an. Jilli-an," he said, playing with the pronunciations like a man trying to find the perfect angle for his hat. "Strange name. Strange times. I was dead, you know," he went on, in a more confidential tone. "Dead of sin until H'Nath sent you to bring me back. Plucked me right out of the storm, you did. Won't forget that, no, I won't. But I'm tired, Jillian. So very tired. Would you mind if I went—"

He crumpled to his knees in a faint. She scooped him into her arms and began to run.

Miles passed. The Tolq remained insensate. He'd be OK, she kept telling herself. *She'd* been in and out of her mind just a few days ago, and *she'd* survived. The argument was lame, though, and she knew it. *She'd* survived because she'd been engineered to take physical punishment. This poor bastard was mere flesh and blood.

A wry half-smile tugged at the corners of her mouth. A year ago, she would've scorned such a thought as a cyborg's superior airs. A week ago, she would've scorned herself as well, and seen her man-made strength as another stigma designed to segregate her from the rest of humanity. Her attitude had undergone another yet change since then, though. And her new motto, just now conceived, was—so what? So what if this wasn't the body that she had been born with? So what if she wasn't her old self anymore? She still mattered: to *Zeph*, to RK, and to this sorry son of a Tolq in her arms. She wondered what his clan would do when they heard about his Ni H'Nathelek savior. Probably send him back into the desert so the next storm could sand-blast his soul clean. It was a bitter thought, one that she might've riled her yesterday. But not today. She'd been in enough foul moods since her revivification. She wanted to live in the doldrums of inner peace for a while longer.

"Jillian?" the Tolq mewled then. He sounded lightyears away, and lost. "Jillian? Where are you?"

"I'm right here, friend," she said, and then tightened her grip on him as he started to squirm. "Just relax. Everything's going to be fine."

"Can't see," he complained, and continued to fidget until his head dangled in open air. He let out a blood-curdling shriek then, and pointed wildly at an outcropping of rock in the near distance. It looked very much like the place where she'd encountered that big, ugly scorpion-thing. "Nammaden, nammaden! We're too close to it," he gabbled, almost panting with urgency. "They live by the rocks where it's shady. Nammas don't like light. Or water. No water here, though. Call your fire, make us safe."

As he said that, a tiny flicker of blue flame appeared in the palm of his hand. She started at the sight, but felt no fear. *Amazing,* she thought. And: *just what she needed, a half-crazed pyropath.* She blew the flame out like a birthday candle.

"But—"

She shushed him with a sound that her mother used to make and then said, "Don't worry, friend, we're safe. Look, the nammaden's already far behind us."

He dared a peek over the round of her shoulder. His good eye went round with childish wonder and surprise.

"So far, so fast," he said. "How can that be? Are we flying?" Before she could think of a reassuring answer, he went on to say, "My father wanted me to fly, but I didn't because I was afraid. I'm not afraid anymore. Why is that, Jillian?"

"I don't know."

"I'm not dead, am I? My father says only the dead have no fear."

"No," she said softly. "You're not dead. You're flying. Remember?"

"Oh, yes. That's right. Flying. Thank you." The tension oozed from his body all at once. A moment later, he buried his face in the fold of her armpit and passed out. She ran on, her ears attuned to the fragile rhythm of his breathing. The miles continued to pile up behind her.

ᎯᏉ

SUNRISE CAME AND went. Sometime later, a large, thumb-shaped boulder appeared in the distance. She recognized the formation. It had been the first, and was now the last, milestone in this round-trip tour through madness. "You see that, friend?" she said, jostling the Tolq's too-limp body. "We're almost home. C'mon, time to wake up." But he'd never woken up from his last faint, and she had her doubts as to whether he would ever do so. Nevertheless, she maintained speed and course. As she sped across the sands, searching for signs of Xamar, a red tatter caught the corner of her eye in passing. A twarla, she thought, and then rolled her eyes. *Another* twarla. Stars above! However did these Tolqs manage when she wasn't here to haul their sorry asses out of the sand? She grudgingly doubled back for another look-see. And just as she'd thought, it was indeed a Tolqan robe that she had seen. Its owner was sprawled face-down in the sand, and did not stir as she approached. None too gently, she jammed the toe of her boot into a section of cloth most likely to contain ribs.

"You there," she said. "Are you all right?"

Scarlet silk snapped and billowed. A moment later, she was staring into Ammas's astonished face. He looked haggard and dusty—a combination that made him look much older than she knew him to be.

"You!" he blurted. "How—?" His eyes darted from her face to the back of her Tolq's matted head. "H'Nath forfend! Who's that? What have you done to him?"

She tried not to be wounded by his misplaced suspicions. After all , she'd given him ample cause to doubt her. But she hadn't been expecting to meet him here and now, or anywhere else for that matter, and her defenses were down. Accordingly, the blow hit a rare nerve.

"I don't know who he is," she said brusquely. "And he was already like this when I found him in the desert. If he doesn't get help very soon, he's going to die."

Ammas shed his mistrust immediately. He pointed her in one direction, saying, "Head for the estate! I'll go and fetch Elyn." Then he sprinted off in the other direction, shouting, "The healer! Get the healer!"

She caught herself listening for his voice long after he was gone from sight. That surprised her, too. She remembered wanting to kill him for deserting her; she recalled the hate, the grief, and the rage. All of that was gone now, but it seemed that she had retained the masochistic capacity for impossible yearnings. She began to understand why cyborgs kept mostly to themselves.

A wary crowd was already gathering on the outskirts of Xamar estate by the time she got there. Most of the faces were unfamiliar, a blur of red hair and troubled eyes, but she spied a few that she knew: Gev, Zim, and Micca in the background, racing this way as if to a five-alarm fire. Then she spotted Tark in the crowd's midst. His brow was seamed with worry. And with good reason, she thought. For while the desert had taken her rage away, it had left her grudge against him intact. She projected a message at him: *soon, you bastard, soon.* He disappeared from sight.

"Which way to the healer's rooms?" she asked then, loud enough for everyone to hear.

A distressed buzz rose up from the crowd. A moment later, Zim stepped forward and held out his arms. "I'll take him there," he volunteered. When she balked, he added, "Have no fear, offworlder. He will not suffer in my care."

She held on to the unconscious Tolq for a moment longer, strangely reluctant to give him up. Then, realizing that she could do no more to help, she handed him over to the priest. As she did so, his head lolled back, exposing his face. Zim let out a stunned gasp.

"Great H'Nath!" he blurted then. "It's Tobia!"

Tark appeared from out of nowhere to frame the stricken man's wind-scourged face in his hands. A moment later, his stony facade cracked. Disbelief and joy tugged at the corners of his mouth. A shimmering of tears glazed his eyes.

"Take him to Elyn's," he urged Zim. "Hurry." Then, as the priest and a swarm of concerned friends headed for the housing complex, Tolq's ambassador to Circe's Moon II prostrated himself at Jillian's refabricated feet. "Please forgive me, Captain," he said, in a shattered voice. "I am in your debt."

A clutch of hard words stuck in her throat. She'd imagined a variety of different confrontations with this man, but none of them began like this! She wanted to kick sand in his face, grind her boot into the back of his neck, tear him apart like a namma.

But she couldn't—not while he groveled on her shadow. And she couldn't forgive him, either.

"I didn't do what I did for you," she said.

"Nevertheless, he is my son, and I owe you his life." He patted the ground next to her feet. Even now, he wouldn't touch her. "I have a confession to make."

"Tell it to someone who cares," she said. "I'm leaving."

But even as she was about to step over him, he scrambled to his feet and planted himself in front of her. The look on his face was one of desperate determination. "I must insist that you hear me out, Captain."

"You're pushing your luck, Tark cis Xamar," she warned. "Just because I haven't broken down and strangled you yet doesn't mean that I won't. Now get the hell out of my way."

He didn't budge. "Don't you want to know why I did it?"

She loosed a snarl and clenched her fists. Why couldn't he leave her alone? Why these freakin' mind games, even now? All she wanted to do was get back to *Zephyr*. But she couldn't leave now—not without hearing him out. The bait was too perfect.

"All right, Tark," she said, "I'll listen to what you have to say. But not right this moment. I need to call my ship first. And if anyone tries to stop me, I'll twist his or her head off."

Up until then, she hadn't noticed Micca standing in the background. But now the priestess stepped forward and said, "No one's going to stop you, Captain. You're free to come and go as you please until you depart. H'Nath, for reasons of his own, has granted you that privilege, and no one here would dare to gainsay it."

The woman's tone was level. So was her gaze. But beneath that aloof facade, Jillian sensed turmoil. The abomination's return must've contradicted H'Nathma dogma in a dozen different ways. It would probably take the Holy Seven *years* to come up with a suitable interpretation, she mused. Fortunately, she'd be long gone by then.

With that thought in mind, she went in search of her shuttle.

ം

AT HER TOUCH, the shuttle's hatch hummed open. She stood in the doorway for a moment, absorbing the unobtrusive colors of home, then made her way into the cockpit and brought the comm-board on-line. The crackle of static suddenly became one of her favorite sounds. "*Zephyr* here," RK said, answering on the first ping. She could hear the tension in his voice. It was both electric and raw. "State your name and your business."

"*Zephyr*, this is *Zephyr* shuttle," she replied, trying to keep her tone light. "How's the weather up there?"

A moment of silence followed. It ended with a incredulous, "Jillie? Is that really you?"

"Who else would it be?" she quipped, trying to joke her way past his distress.

"Where the fuck have you been?" he bellowed then.

"Sorry, RK. It's a long, weird stor—"

But he wouldn't let her finish. With less volume and more speed, he proceeded to chew her out. "Do you know how long it's been since I last heard from you? *Six* fucking days. I thought you were *dead*, dammit! I thought I was stranded up here, *by myself*— easy pickings for whatever happened along. The friggin' H'Nathma wouldn't answer my calls. And you *know* I can't fly this rig. So I—" He gulped down a deep breath as if to calm himself. "So I sent out an SOS. It should've gotten to SU-HQ two days ago."

"What was that last part again?" she asked. She'd gotten stuck at the six-day bit, and was just now catching up. *Six* days? She would've guessed three, maybe four at the most. That must've been one bitchin' nap by the water-hole.

Her brother repeated himself, and then sullenly added, "I'm sorry. I didn't know what else to do."

"There's no need to apologize. You didn't have much of a choice. And no one's going to respond anyway. Barim made it abundantly clear that he wouldn't violate a treaty on my account."

"So what's the deal?" he said then. "You staying down there forever or what?"

"As a matter of fact," she replied, "I'll be taking off sometime within the next hour. While you're waiting for me to get there, send out a retraction of that SOS, and then power up all systems. We're going back to Circe's II."

"Ah, civilization at last," he drawled, slathering the reply with reassuring sarcasm. "I'm having wet dreams already."

"Just don't stain the upholstery," she drawled back. Then, because she was truly sorry for all the anxiety that this trip had caused him, she warmed up her tone and added, "I owe you one, brother."

"That's the understatement of the year. *Zephyr* out."

She switched the shuttle to stand-by, then went to find Tark. A part of her didn't understand why she was doing this. Sitting down, locking up, and blasting the hell out of here certainly sounded like a better idea. But she didn't understand why Tark was doing this, either—and that was the freakin' hook. She wanted to know why a virtual stranger wanted her dead. She *had* to know.

To her surprise, she found Ammas waiting for her at the foot of the shuttle ramp. She arched an eyebrow, questioning his motives. He turned an uncomfortable shade of pink and wrung his hands.

"My uncle and a few others have gathered in the meeting hall," he said. "If you can stomach my company, I'd be glad to escort you there."

"I don't have much in the way of a stomach, Ammas," she told him, half-teasing but half-testing, too. "So I guess you're in luck. Lead the way."

He did so, but he wasn't his usual animated self. He shuffled along with his head bowed and his shoulders slumped—like an old man. Or a condemned one. Every now and again, he peeked at her out of the corner of his eye and then fingered his quot'tl bead. Jillian had a fair idea as to what was going on with him, but was in no great rush to set his mind at ease. Those feelings were a lesson that she wanted him to learn. But the silence between them was suffocating, and she eventually took pity on him.

"Did you have something on your mind, Ammas?" she asked.

He took a shallow breath, then turned to her with shipwrecked eyes and said, "I'm so ashamed of the way I behaved at your tribunal, Captain. I knew you couldn't be the abomination that Micca said you were. But I condemned you anyway, because I was stunned and confused and—" He groped for a word that wouldn't come to him. "—and confused. I've been begging H'Nath for forgiveness ever since we gave you to the desert. That's what I was doing when you came upon me."

"You followed the teachings of your religion," she told him, in a tone like a shrug. "And the irony is, you did the right thing."

"No, I didn't," he argued miserably. "I should've gone with you into the desert."

She dismissed the notion with a snort. "I would've killed you, Ammas. You and anyone else who came along. Do you understand? I had some kind of brain sickness."

But apparently not the RIMs, she added to herself. Refabrication madness wasn't curable in its last stages. She must've had something else—post-traumatic stress perhaps, or some other syndrome that six days in a desert could heal.

Meanwhile, Ammas continued to despise himself. "I deserved to be killed for the way I behaved. I'll let you kill me now if you still want to."

"Sorry," she replied, "but I'm over that now. It's time for you to move on, too." He started to say something then, but she silenced him with an upraised finger. "You've apologized, and I bear you no grudge. All things considered, I'm glad you got a chance to see that conscience and religion can be two very different things.

"Now let's move on, shall we?"

They were standing in front of the dining room's double doors now. They'd been there for well over a minute now.

Ammas looked like he wanted to continue pleading his unworth, but Jillian refused to hear it. Her injured pride was healing up nicely now. Too nicely, in fact. She didn't want to get sucked up into any more bittersweet human games. So she went barging into the meeting hall. Heads turned as she entered. She recognized Micca, Zim, Gevera and Saj. But she only had eyes for Tark. He'd been marooned at a table of his own. He looked like a broken man.

"Start talking," she said.

"You must understand that everything I did was for the people of Tolq," he began, glancing from her to Saj and back again. "I wanted them to be warm and comfortable and well-fed. I wanted them to take their proper place in the galaxy. But much to my shame, I was seduced into believing that such a lofty goal justified any means."

He coughed—a dry, self-conscious clearing of the throat. Then he met Jillian's unforgiving stare head-on. "My nephew told you that Nathan Ross and I were friends— '*great friends*,' I think he said. But a better word for what Nate and I are is conspirators. Our mutual dream was to end the H'Nathma's choke-hold on Tolq's future."

Micca sputtered then, but before she could put her outrage into words, Jillian cut her off with a steely hiss. "This is *my* gig, sister," she said. "You can have him when I'm done." Then she waved an imperious hand at Tark. "As you were saying, *Ambassador*."

"The idea was straightforward enough," he told her. "Take away Tolq's food and starve the people into revolt. H'Nath had already set the stage by subjecting us to six lean years in a row. And once Ross removed the Distribution Day grain from the equation, all we had to do was keep bootleggers away and wait. Hungry people are quick to lose faith in their leaders, my great friend said. He said their pinched bellies would keep them up at night and get them to thinking about food that was only a wyrm-hole away, food that their young ones had to do without because the H'Nathma was so stiff-necked. He said they'd grow angry—man by man, then clan by clan. And he was right."

"How did Ross get our Blessed D-Day grain from the pirates?" Ammas wanted to know.

A smile that had nothing to do with humor curved across Tark's mouth. "My dear boy, don't you see? Ross and I *are* the pirates."

For one long, incredulous moment, all Jillian could do was gape into empty space and think: *that bastard. That miserable, shit-eating bastard.* And this time, she was thinking of Nathan Ross. She couldn't believe how dirty he was, or how well he hid that grime. *No matter what happens from here on, you have my vote in the next election,* she remembered saying to him. Stars above, how he must've howled inside. She started to count the black marks against him: the Tolq's ark, at least four Union ships, and who knew how many people. She remembered something else then, too: *Denny slipping a small, blackened disk into his pocket.* A memory disk, he'd called it—the one he'd recovered from *the barge's auto-log.*

"Shit," she swore then, as pieces of a vast and puzzle finally clicked into place. "Denny was on to your scheme, wasn't he?"

"Who?" Tark asked.

His ignorance outraged her. If nothing else, he should at least know the names of his victims. "Denny," she repeated, with exaggerated care, as if he were deaf, or an idiot. "Denis C. Latimer, first-class salvage captain and the erstwhile owner of *Riff-Raff.*"

"Ah yes, the man who found Blessed Venture's auto-log," he recalled then. "Ross was very upset about that."

"How did Ross *know* about it?" she demanded. "Denny didn't tell *anybody* about that, not even me. And I was his best friend."

An instant later, she realized what she had said; and what it meant. Her memory was back. She could finally look back on that fateful day and honestly say that Barim had hounded her for nothing. She didn't know squat.

But Tark knew rather a lot.

"One of your friend's crewmen was on Nate's payroll," he told her. "He was also the one who planted the bomb on that shuttle—per Ross's instructions, of course."

She ground her teeth as if she had already that crewman's bones between them. "His name," she said, in a low, deadly tone. "I want that crewman's name."

The Tolq absorbed her anger without flinching. "Sorry, but Ross never volunteers that kind of information. And I make it a habit not to ask."

"Then I'll just have to wring it out of the man himself," she said—a promise to herself. "Now go on with what you were saying."

He shrugged. "There's really not that much more to say. Ross wanted you dead from the moment he heard that you'd been found alive in the shuttle-wreckage. He bided his time at first, expecting you to perish from your injuries. Then your doctors turned you into a cyborg." He grimaced as he said the word, as if it were distasteful to him. "Nathan tried to get an assassin into your room then, but you were being monitored far too closely. So he watched. And he waited. Then you woke up and almost instantly landed yourself on President Barim's black-list. My great friend saw a chance to be rid of you then, and called me. I agreed to lure you to my world and then arrange a suitably fatal accident for you."

"But it was my idea to poison myself," Ammas blurted. "You had nothing to do with that."

Tark flashed his nephew a rueful half-smile. "You're bright and well-intentioned, my boy, but terribly susceptible to suggestion. *I* planted the idea of securing an offworld contact for Xamar in your head. *I* told you how it would have to be done. The only thing that you came up with on your own was the nammasting— and I truly wish that I'd been more specific about that, too."

"And what about the runaway sand-cart, brother mine?" Saj asked then, in a voice as raw as the look in his eyes. "Was that your idea, too? Does your nephew's life mean that little to you?"

"I didn't see him there on the tracks, Saj," he said. "If I had, I swear to you and H'Nath that I would never have let the cart go. But all I could see was Captain D'Lange. The abomination. The *thing*."

He turned to Jillian then. "I had second thoughts about killing you after you saved Ammas from my error. For it was getting harder and harder to think of you as a machine, and I couldn't see you as anything else and still justify your death. Then you went berserk on Bo at the gathering, and I couldn't refuse the opportunity. It was a sign from H'Nath, I told myself. *He* wanted you destroyed. *He* wanted you gone. I left you in the desert with a sense of relief.

"But H'Nath spared you," he said, in a voice that still rippled with wonder. "And you brought my son back from the dead. Even the chill in *my* blood has its limits.

"Apologies are meaningless, so I won't make them. And that's all I have to say."

Silence settled over the room like a pall. Not even Jillian knew what to say. Tark had fooled everyone with his wry, compelling charm and intricate lies. No doubt about it, she thought. He was one of the most deceptive men in civilized space. And he had been tutored by Nathan Ross, a grand-master if ever there'd been one. *It's a joy to see your face, Jill. I'm in a position to help you, Jill, but mum's the word for now, OK?* And all the while, he'd been setting her up for her own murder.

All because he thought she knew something.

An ironic smile crept across her refabricated mouth. At moments like this, she thought, she could almost believe that there really was a god. Because she knew more now than she had ever known then. And now it was pay-back time.

"Get up," she said, gesturing to Tark. "You're going back to Circe's II with me."

"Out of the question," Micca said. "Tark cis Xamar has much to answer for, both to the Holy Seven and to H'Nath. He must stay here and atone for his sins."

"Feeding Tark to the desert isn't going to help anyone but Ross right now," Jillian argued. "I need him to come back with me and tell the Galactic Council everything he knows about Ross and his operations. Otherwise, nothing's going to change—leastwise, not for the better. If this H'Nath of yours is as righteous as you say he is, he won't mind waiting an extra month or so for his pound of flesh."

"Who are you to say what a god will or will not mind?" Micca railed. "You're an outsider, here strictly on our forbearance, and have no right to be making demands. Tark is staying here."

"You're not speaking for H'Nath right now, you're being stubborn and arrogant," Jillian accused then, growing louder now, and more impatient. "Because this is precisely the solution that you and your fellow skin-heads have been praying for. Tark's testimony will send Ross to a penal colony for the rest of his twisted life; the disappearances in your space and mine will come to an end; and the bastards who killed your ship and its D-Day cargo will be caught and punished.

"But we've got to act now. The longer Nathan Ross is at large, the more damage he can do. And my guess is that he doesn't mean to stop until he has everything: the SU, your government; me."

Then, from out of the blue, it hit her: Roadkill's SOS. As soon as Ross got word of it, he'd head this way to take care of any evidence that his great-friend-in-crime might have missed. She believed that with every fiber of her refabricated being. Ross wouldn't want to risk another screw-up, not this soon after the memory disk scare. And that meant that he was already en route. *Shitshitshit.* She couldn't let him catch her. Not now, not when she was so close to bringing him down. She had to get out of here, quick—*with Tark.* And she was going to do it even if she had to knock a few heads to have her way.

"Look!" Ammas exclaimed then. "H'Nath's fire!"

She tracked his gaze back to her hands. To her utmost surprise, she found them encased in cool blue flames.

Chapter 10

FIRE?

Jillian's mind went blank, but old memories and panic didn't come rushing in to fill the void. She remained curiously detached, buffered from fear by a glimmer of stars and sunsets. The smokeless little fire danced in her palm like a pet. It left no pain, and no residue behind. When she made a fist, it squirted past her knuckles like juice. This sudden mastery over her nemesis amazed her almost as much as her newfound ability to generate it.

H'Nath's fire.

But she didn't believe in gods. Did not. They were a delusion, a false sense of security in an age that knew better. Yet she had no other answer. Not yet anyway.

"H'Nath forgive me for my pride," Micca muttered then, and ran a hand over her shaven head. "I saw this moment in my dreams, but didn't want to believe it. The end of the world as we know it is at hand."

"And we'll be able to tell our children that we were there to send it off," Ammas said, in an awed, reverent tone.

"Is someone going to tell me how to put this out?" Jillian asked then. None of the Tolqs responded, though. They were still all gawking at her hand-fire. Annoyance flared within her. The flames grew higher, and acquired orange streaks. She tried to extinguish them with a vigorous shake, but they refused to be smothered. She asked for advice once again, and then wondered, "Or am I going to look like a leaky acetylene torch for the rest of my life?"

"H'Nath's fire will respond to your will, Captain," Lord Xamar said then. "If you want it to disappear, you need only to concentrate on that desire."

Jillian did as he suggested. The flames guttered, then winked out, leaving no sign of their existence behind. When they didn't return, she favored the Lord of Xamar with a relieved half-smile.

"That wasn't so tough," she said. "But what's to stop the fire from coming back? Walking, talking torches don't play well in a lot of places, you know."

A glimmer of amusement flashed in the old man's eyes then, but he didn't allow it to infect his tone. That remained a solemn drone. "At its most primitive level, H'Nath's fire is a defense mechanism, Captain. Unchanneled anger and fear will trigger it, as will panic. If you wish to avoid these accidental manifestations in the future, you must learn to prevent your passions from merging with your will."

"So basically, you're telling me that I need to have more self-control."

He rewarded her perspicacity with a nod and the faintest hint of a smile. "That is essentially correct." With his next breath, he added, "I'd be honored to teach you more about the gift we share if you'd care to remain here for a time."

"You rescinded your offer of hospitality," she reminded him, just to see how sore a spot that was between them.

"It had to be done, Captain," he said, refusing to apologize. "You gave me no choice. But you're a child of H'Nath now, one of us; and that distinction has its rewards as well as its burdens. You have a home here in Xamar for as long as you live. You may also come and go as you please."

Just then, a door creaked open. No one else heard it, but Jillian did. She turned toward the sound to see Tobia heading toward her. She was amazed to see him walking on his own soon after such a harrowing ordeal, but at the same time, it was obvious that his healing had been rushed. Dozens of tiny scars dappled his cheeks and forehead, and his wind-burned flesh hung slack on his bones. But both of his eyes were open now, and he was squinting at her with a look of budding wonder.

"Jillian?" he said, and then broke into a lopsided grin as he drew nearer. "Jillian! It *is* you! H'Nath be praised! You weren't a dream after all."

"*Jillian?*" Ammas echoed, in a voice rich with shock and indignation. "You call her Jillian?"

His cousin shrugged and rolled his eyes, but before he could put his nonchalance into words, Micca interrupted. "What brings you here, Tobia cis Xamar? You should be in bed, resting up after your experience."

"And that's where I was," he told her, "right up until a few minutes ago. But then my father Called to me. He told me he was going back to the embassy on Circe's Moon II. I came to say goodbye—"

The priestess didn't hear that last sentence, though. She was already rounding on the ambassador. "You presume too much, Tark. That decision has *not* been made yet."

Now it was Jillian's turn to butt in. "Then quit your jawing and make it already," she snapped. "Because I have to leave. Now. With Tark. If Ross catches up with me before I reach Circe's II, we're all going to have serious problems in the very near future."

"I don't understand," Tobia said. "What's wrong? What's a Ross?"

But his uncle talked right over him. "I fail to understand your urgency, Captain," he said, with just a twinge of exasperation in his tone. "This Ross person cannot possibly know what has happened here yet."

"Yes, he can," she countered. "My crewman sent out an SOS while I was MIA. He says it should've reached Circe's II two days ago. An outback patrol could've picked it up even earlier."

Tark paled at that, then turned to his careworn brother. "I know Ross, Saj. He'll come. He's already on his way. If you don't let me go with Captain D'Lange, I'll have to leave with him. He won't have it any other way. And sometime in the foreseeable future, he'll use that SOS as an excuse to come back and make Tolq space safe for all law-biding spacers. He'll do that by removing the H'Nathma from power, and he won't care how he does it.

"So let me leave now, brother," he urged. "Give me the chance to set things right. I swear by H'Nath that I'll return for my day of judgment."

"Don't trust him, Saj," Micca warned, but the Lord of Xamar cut her off with an upraised hand.

"This is no longer a matter of trust, young one," he countered. "It has become a matter of faith. We must take the signs that we've been given today to heart, and dare to embrace the answer to our prayers."

The old man squared his lean shoulders then, and aimed his pride right at Jillian. "Captain D'Lange, I grant you custody of Tark cis Xamar, a traitor to his people. Treat him with as much kindness as you can muster, for he was once a great man. And when he has served your purpose, return him to us. He must be given to H'Nath for judgment. Elsewise, clan Xamar will never be rid of the shame that we bear in his name."

"As for you, well—we have treated you badly. Such is ever the lot of prophets. In apology, I offer you this." He looped his quot'tl bead necklace over his head, and then held it out to her. "A taste of Tolq for when you're far from home," he told her. "Sample it when you feel H'Nath's restlessness inside of you. It will help you control your gift."

Unexpected affection rolled through her like a ground-swell then. It went a long way in restoring her faith in the goodness of Tolqs. She bowed so Saj could slip the thin leather strip over her head. He did so with solemn pomp, as if he were awarding her the Tolqan medal of honor. The bead was smooth and finger-oil-shiny from countless years of use. Its weight was so slight, she couldn't feel it against the center of her breast-bone.

"Thank you, Lord Xamar," she said, with equal gravity. "I hope the Tellings remember you as fair as well as bold. I know I will."

He favored her with a rare half-smile. "It is my hope that the Tellings will be kind to us both. Fare well, Captain Jillian D'Lange, and swiftly."

Then he turned to Tark, and that half-smile faded into something sad and pained. "For better or ill, you are my brother, and I love you," he said, all the sterner for the ache in his eyes. "If you conduct yourself well in Captain D'Lange's service, perhaps H'Nath will spare you the worst of his wrath. I will pray that it happens so."

"Thank you, brother," Tark said, and then creaked to his feet, old with resignation. His parting bow displayed none of his usual flair. "I'll try to live up to your prayers."

He hobbled his way over to Jillian, flanked by his son and nephew. She offered the cousins an awkward, farewell hand-shake, but Ammas declined it with a somberness that must've done his father proud.

"No need for goodbyes just yet," he told her. "We're going with you."

"No, you're not," she said flatly, and turned her back on them to close the subject. "Come on, Tark, we've got a shuttle to catch."

"Yes, we are," Ammas said, as he and his cousin circled around to block her way. "You need us. Uncle says you have no crew."

"Uncle also says a great big union cruiser crammed to the crawl-space with heavy artillery is headed this way. You *don't* want to be aboard *Zephyr* when it gets here. And I definitely *don't* need a crew that doesn't know the first freakin' thing about technology. So run along, fellows. If nothing else, it's been educational."

But Ammas persisted. "I've used a comm-board at the embassy. I can fetch and carry, too."

"And I'll look after my father," Tobia added, "so you won't have to."

Aggravation welled up within her like a drum-roll, then burst from her fingertips as tiny blue flames. As she reined in her temper, she thought: just once, she'd like to do something around here without a Tolq complicating it tenfold! She pivoted toward Lord Xamar then, her arms open wide in appeal.

"Would you please send them to their rooms or something?" she asked.

Saj folded his arms over his breast and slowly shook his head. "If they wish to go, I won't gainsay them. You shouldn't have to stand alone against an adversary common to us all."

Up until now, Micca had been gripping her quot'tl bead in thoughtful silence. But all of a sudden, she snapped to her feet and said, "I'm going with you, too.

"I've trained aboard a ship, so I'll be of some use to you in that regard," she went on, defending herself against Jillian's incredulous stare. "I can also keep a close watch on Tark. He may have seduced you all into believing that he's a new man, but I see the same old honey-tongued scoundrel. I'll make certain that he doesn't talk his way out of the trip back to Tolq.

"And besides, one of the H'Nathma should be present on such an unprecedented voyage."

Jillian ground her teeth against an urge to scream. These stupid, stupid Tolqs had no clue as to how very dangerous this trip could be. And she didn't have the time to spell it out for them. Or argue. The best she could do was give them one last warning.

"Once you're on board," she said, "you're mine. You'll do what I tell you to do, when I tell you to do it. No questions. And no arguments," she added, looking squarely at Micca. "If you can't do that, then do us all a favor and stay here. This is *not* going to be a pleasure cruise."

"We understand," Micca said, apparently speaking for all of the volunteers. "And we will not disappoint. We're the vanguard of H'Nath's new age."

Jillian wondered if the priestess knew what a truly scary thought that was.

❧

THE RIDE BACK to *Zeph* proceeded without major incident. Somebody in the main cabin spewed—once during take-off, then again while the shuttle was shuddering its way through the last few strata of Tolq's outer atmosphere—but Jillian didn't count that as an untoward event. Lots of people puked in smaller spacecraft, especially people who were flying in one for the first time. Many had anxiety attacks, too. But not her. Not anymore. Her stay on Tolq had set a good many things right with her. She never would've guessed it. *Nevernevernever.*

The planet was hundreds of miles behind them now: a bright red globe basking in its star's distant light. *Zephyr* was a sleek, silver gleam in low orbital space. She smiled at the sight, then called her brother. He answered on the first ping.

"It's about time," he said, and then immediately switched to a slyer tone. "Did you remember my surprise?"

"I've got a whole slew of them for you," she replied, stealing a glance at the main cabin, "but I doubt that you'll find any to your liking."

"Feel free to explain."

"We're bringing four Tolqs back to Circe's Moon II with us. One of them is the ambassador, and he's going to be traveling in the security cell."

"What?" he squawked, venting surprise, doubt, and just a scintilla of amusement all at the same time. "What's going on?"

"I'll brief you on the specs just as soon as I'm back on board," she told him. "For now, let's just say that Tark's ass is in a king-sized sling. And so are ours," she added, as an afterthought, "so don't start gloating quite yet."

"You take all the fun out of life."

"This time, it's not my fault."

Zephyr's steel-gray hull dominated the view-plate now. She was so happy to find it alone and in one piece, she almost burst into song. So far, so good, she thought instead. Maybe Ross wasn't coming for her after all. She knew better than to put any faith such a whopping big maybe, though. *Expect the worst*, her mother used to say, *and all of your surprises will be pleasant ones.* Therefore, Ross was coming. And she was out of here. With that thought in mind, she throttled back and hit the brakes, slowing the shuttle down for its first and final approach.

"OK, RK," she said then, "open up. We're coming in."

The hatchway swirled open. Neon guide lights appeared in the textured darkness beyond. She leveled off, then activated the landing gear. A moment later, she snuffed the engines and coasted into the bay. The shuttle screeched as its wheels touched down, then jerked to an emphatic stop as the braking catches engaged. She heard someone throw up yet again at that. But she felt just fine.

"Repressurization of the shuttle-bay is now complete," Roadkill announced over the commlink, as she was locking down. "Where do you want me?"

"The infirmary," she replied.

"Wha—?" he began, and then tsked irritably. "Oh, never mind, I'll find out soon enough. See you there."

She headed into the main cabin to round up the Tolqs, and as soon as she saw them, she knew who'd been doing all the spewing. Tobia's eyes were blood-shot and glazed. His windburnt skin had a sick, greenish cast to it. *First-timer*, she thought, full of a born-and-bred spacer's superior conceit. *But at least he'd used the plasma bag.* And the rest of the troops looked OK—a little frazzled by the day's events maybe, but still functional. Which was good, because she didn't have time to coddle them.

"I hope you're all quick studies," she said, as she ushered them toward the exit, "because you're about to get the crash course to end all crash courses on the good ship *Zephyr*."

They walked down the ramp and into the dimly lit hangar. Its sheer, man-made dimensions seemed to spook Tobia, and he fingered his quot'tl bead constantly. Micca and Ammas were round-eyed as well, but Tark looked blasé, as if he'd seen it all before.

"This is the shuttle bay," Jillian told them in passing. Unless instructed otherwise, you have no business in here."

As they approached it, the door to the hallway opened with a hiss. Tobia jumped backward at the sound, as if he'd just stepped into a nest full of nammas. Micca gave him a reassuring pat on the shoulder and said, "We have such things on our ships, too. They are not Ni H'Nathelek."

"You may need to get somewhere in a hurry before this trip is over," Jillian told the group then, "so memorize the ship's lay-out as we go along." As an afterthought, she pointed to the hand railings that protruded hip-high from the walls. "And always hang on to one or the other of these things when you're moving about the ship. If you don't, and *Zeph* hits a patch of turbulence, you'll fall until something—usually a wall—stops you. I learned the hard way. I don't recommend it to others."

Tobia, Ammas and Micca all made a grab for the railing.

Tark tried to share a knowing look with Jillian at that, but she wouldn't have any of it. One smile would lead to more smiles, which would lead to friendly words and then avuncular advice, and the next thing she knew, he'd be eating bon-bons on the bridge and acting like nothing had ever happened between them. No way was she going to let it play that way. So she put him back in his place with a look like daggers, then motioned for the Tolqs to follow her. As they walked, she directed their attention with flicks of her wrist.

"The galley is that way: one corridor down and two doors to the right. And it's every human for himself. There's a head that way, too, and a lavatory, but I doubt that you'll have time for a shower on this voyage."

She came to a stop in front of a door that had a small transom near its base, then fed its security grid an access code. "And this," she said, as the door swooshed open, "is where Tark is going to stay until we get to Circe's II."

"This isn't necessary, you know," he said, as she waved him into the cell.

"Once bitten, twice shy," she replied, and engaged the lock. As the door whisked shut on his unhappy scowl, she added, "See you on the other side."

Tobia looked at her with wounded eyes. She softened her hard-line stance, but only a little. "The access code is ten-twelve-double-seven-forty. You can visit with him to your heart's content. You can take him meals and look in on him while he's sleeping. But he *stays* in the cell, friend. All the time. If you don't think you can play by my rules, just say so, and I'll lock you up in there with him. There are worse places to be."

"That won't be necessary," Tobia replied. "Your rules are fair. It just grieves me to see him so sorely reduced."

They continued on their way—down the corridor and into the crew's wing. "Pick a room, any room," Jillian said, and then caught Ammas by the hand as he headed toward the nearest door. "My brother lives in there," she told him, "and while you're welcome to share his space, I don't think you'd enjoy it. Personally, I'd rather sleep in a nammaden."

"I see," he said, and followed Micca down the hall.

"There should be flightsuits in all of the lockers," she called after them. "Anyone who intends to work a shift on my bridge is required to wear one."

Micca disappeared into a cabin only to come bursting back out a moment later with a flight-suit clenched in her fist. Her expression was a comical blend of indignation and rue. "This isn't going to fit over my twarla," she said.

Jillian shrugged. "So take the twarla off."

The priestess glanced from Jillian to the close-fitting uniform and back again. Her indignation was fast paling into horror. "I couldn't do that. I'd be all but unclothed. And immodesty is an affront to H'Nath."

Jillian shrugged again. "Then stay down here on the lower decks. I'm sure Tobia will appreciate the company."

"But—"

"The matter isn't open for debate, Micca," Jillian said. "Because, as an ex-friend of mine once told me: a twarla's usefulness as a garment ends at the desert's edge. They catch in airlocks, snag on expensive equipment, and restrict movement. Any one of those events could be disastrous at the wrong moment. So you can either dummy up and follow orders, or ride out the trip in your room. You decide. And do it now."

A whole marathon of emotions ran across Micca's face: resentment, reluctance, and fleet-footed flashes of anger. But a driving need to be in the thick of things won the race. She squared her shoulders to Jillian like a general who was surrendering her sword but not her commission, and said, "I'll dummy up, as you say."

"Then go and change," Jillian said. Then, because she knew that Micca needed to give orders as well as take them, and because a good captain wasn't above delegating, especially when she was short on time and other options, she put the priestess in charge of the other Tolqs. "Once everybody's all suited up, report to the galley and find yourselves something to eat. If we run into trouble—" She said 'if', but thought *when*. Her mother cropping up again. "—you might not get another meal. When you're finished, clean up, batten everything down again and then report to the infirmary. It's down this hallway and to the left. I'll leave the door open so you can find it easier."

Micca glanced at the sand-encrusted gash in Jillian's thigh out of the corner of her eye--almost but not quite against her will. "Does it hurt?"

"Not in the torn tissue sense of the word," Jillian replied. "But it won't mend on its own. And it wouldn't take much to make it worse. And the thought of my movements being restricted at the wrong moment causes me mental anguish, so I guess you could say it hurts in that way."

A peculiar look crept into the priestess's eyes. It was the look of someone who's just been turned upside down and shaken by the ankles. She gave Jillian one last puzzled look, then started toward her cabin. As she departed, Jillian heard her praying under her breath: "I beg thy patience, Great One, and thy pardon. I am slow in getting used to this."

For some reason, that satisfied Jillian. She had the impression that something had changed within the priestess, or leastwise shifted. That feeling stayed with her all the way to the infirmary, then deepened into genuine affection as she caught sight of Roadkill. He was perched on a pull-out, idly scratching himself. She couldn't remember when she had been so glad to see his lacquered scruffiness.

"You've got a lot of explaining to do," he said, as she entered the room. Then, as she locked the door in its open position, he arched an eyebrow at her. "So I won't make a scene?"

"It's for the Tolqs," she replied. "I told them to report here for their assignments." Her brother made a strangled sound. She gave him a reassuring pat on the back and said, "I'll tell you all about it while you're patching me up."

"What's the problem? You strip a gear or something?"

She ripped the remnants of her trouser-leg away from the gash then. His mirrored eyes went wide, exposing a rare glimpse of the whites. His admiring whistle sounded low and long.

"Well, I'll be damned," he said, as he jumped down from the pull-out. "Looks like you might have a decent story to tell after all. I was half-convinced that you'd gone on a week-long bender. But never mind. Hop on up and let the tech take a look."

"You'd better use gloves," she warned, as she lifted herself onto the pull-out that he'd just vacated. "There was some kind of venom involved, and I'm not sure I got all of it out."

"Venom, hmm? Better and better, Jillie." He grabbed a pair of disposables from a nearby drawer and snapped them on with an old-time surgeon's flair. "Holy shit-balls," he said, as he poked at the wound. And: "Will you look at that?" But he was grinning by the examination's conclusion. "The wiring's intact," he told her, "which is good, because neuro-bundles can be tricky things to repair. But your muscles need work. In addition to the original damage, there's been some secondary stress tearing."

"Can you fix it?" she demanded.

"Yeah, sure. Synthetic muscle is remarkably resilient stuff."

"Then do it. Quickly."

"All right, all right, don't get your circuits in a twist. Hang on, I'll be right back." He shuffled off to another part of the infirmary and began rummaging through an unseen locker. As he did so, he called out, "By the by, how's that headache of yours?"

The question confused her for a moment. How did he know about that headache? She'd been on Tolq for the worst of it. Then she remembered complaining about the pain on the bridge one day, the same day they had started out on this convoluted misadventure. Stars above! That had only been a week ago. It seemed more like a lifetime!

"It's gone now," she replied. "For good, I think."

Despite that assertion, he returned with the scanner in tow.

"We haven't got a lot of time, RK," she said, as he wheeled the machine toward her. "I wouldn't even be bothering with this leg if I weren't afraid of it cutting out on me at a bad moment."

"You gotta sit here while I'm working anyway," he said, and pressed the back of her plastisteel skull up against the screen's smooth face. "If there's any difference in your scans, I might be able to tell what was causing the pain and therefore how to prevent it in the future." The machine began to thrum then. Its vibrations traveled down the length of her spine to shiver her toes. "You can talk as long as you keep the rest of your head still," he told her. "And I would very much like to know what the fuck is up."

"Nathan Ross is a big-time bastard," she told him then. "He had Denny killed. He wants me dead, too. Tark was working for him all along."

"I told you there was something dicey about that red-robed freak," RK sneered, and then powered up a micro-laser. As he brought its thin red beam to bear on her thigh, he went on to say, "But never mind about my superior instincts for now. I want to know how you managed to get a copy of your death warrant."

Over the scanner's visceral hum, and the faint, white-smoke pop and sizzle of fusing proto-muscle, she gave him a much abridged version of the story. He made no comment until she was done.

"So you're *sure* The Torpedo's coming?" he asked then, as he applied quick-set skin cement to the dermal layers of her wound.

"I'm positive," she said. "He's gone much too far to take a minor detail like my survival for granted."

"I see." He pressed the torn edges of her synthetic hide together, then waited for the quick-set to bond. "So we're about to make the most desperate run of our lives, and all we have for crew is three landbred technophobes."

"You got it." She wasn't pleased with the thick, rubbery scar that he was leaving on her leg, but that was the drawback to field-medicine. And she supposed that she could always find someone to sand that nasty seam down when she got back to Circe's II. That was the nice thing about syntheskin. It could wait when you couldn't. "Are we done here yet?"

"Yeah. The quick-set wasn't meant for syntheskin, but it should hold until we get back to Circe's II." He reached past her to switch off the scanner, and added, "*If* we get back." And he never knew her mother. "Do me a favor and clean up here, would you? I want to have a look at the scanner results before the new meat comes toddling in."

Some captains would've pulled rank and refused such a presumptuous request, but Jillian merely hopped down from the pull-out and got to work. The way she figured it, she owed her brother some major slack for all that he'd endured in her name over the past year. And besides, *someone* had to do it. So she picked up the gritty fabric swabs and squeezed-flat Quick-set tube, the spent laser cartridges and discarded Disposos. As soon as she was done with that, she wheeled the scanner back into its brackets. She was just locking everything up when she heard her brother whistle.

"What is it?" she asked, more curious than alarmed.

He looked from her to the graphic in his hand and back again. "Are you *sure* your headache's gone?"

"Yeah." Frowning now, she closed the gap between them. "Why? What's up?"

"See this?" He pointed to a small, kidney-bean speck nestled in the holo-image of her cerebrum. At her nod, he said, "Well, there's nothing like it in your last set of scans." He activated another graphic and pointed again. "See?"

Vertigo lapped at the base of her brain-pan—dread looking for a fingerhold. "So what is it? A tumor?"

He dismissed that fear with a shake of his head. "Infra-red patterns indicate a totally independent organism. Looks like you picked up some sort of a parasite while you were on Tolq."

"*A parasite?*" Her jaw dropped—unhinged once by disbelief and a profound sense of cosmic persecution, and then again by a spasm of intuition. "I knew there had to be a logical explanation for it!"

"For what—your headache disappearing?"

"That, too—maybe. But I was thinking of Tolqan psychic abilities. Every adult is said to have one—telepathy, telekinesis, the power to heal, and so forth. This parasite has to be some kind of catalyst or facilitator."

Her brother was quick to draw the right connections. "And now that you've got a bug in your ear—"

"—I can make fire," she told him, then closed her eyes and imagined it happening. She didn't need to peek to know that she'd been successful. Roadkill's gasp said it all.

"Any chance of me scoring one of those bugs?" he asked.

Just then, she heard footsteps out in the hallway. A moment later, someone called her name. She extinguished her hand-fire with an overkill of thought, then harpooned her brother with a sharp look and whispered, "Nothing about this to the Tolqs."

He sniffed like a wounded child. "You never let me have any fun."

Micca nervously sidled her way into the infirmary then. Although the flight-suit that she had on now was two sizes too big and nowhere near form-fitting, the priestess acted as if she were totally naked. Her arms were crossed over her breasts. Her knees were clenched together. As soon as Roadkill saw her, his face lit up like a retro-pinball machine on a bonus play.

"Jillie!" he crooned, as he started toward the priestess. "This is the best surprise ever. C'mere, darl—"

Jillian caught him by the wrist and squeezed—a none-too-gentle call for decorum. He skidded to a stop with a squawk, but continued to ogle Micca from afar. The priestess turned a mortified shade of red.

"Where are the others?" Jillian asked her.

"Tobia wishes to remain in his room," Micca replied, trying hard to overcome her self-consciousness. "He is having—difficulty—adjusting to his new circumstances."

"And Ammas?"

Her forehead bunched. She glanced here, then there. "He left the galley while I was trying to ease Tobia's mind," she said then. "I thought he was already with you."

Roadkill jeered. "Want me to send out a search party?"

Before Jillian could reply, the object of her brother's scorn came plodding into the infirmary. His complexion was pasty. His eyes lacked their usual luster. He strode over to Micca and draped an arm across her shoulders like the last man to finish a foot-race.

"What's wrong?" Jillian asked.

"The food," he said, not quite meeting her eyes. "It did not sit well in my belly, and I was sick. It will not happen again."

"Do you require medical attention?"

He shook his head. "It was just a spell. I'm feeling better already."

It didn't look that way to Jillian, but she didn't have the time or the inclination to fuss over him or anyone else, so she just monkey-barred on to the next subject. "All right then, listen up and listen good, because all our lives may depend on it. Ammas, Micca, this is my second, Roadkill. If he gives you an order pertaining to this ship's *business*—" And she stressed the word for everybody's sake. "—you are to obey it with all possible haste. If you have a problem with something, bring it to him, not me. Any questions?

"Good," she said, when no one spoke up, and then went on. "You two are going to take turns manning the comm-station. Micca has the first four-hour shift. Ammas, you take the second. When you're not on the bridge, feel free to get some rest or keep Tobia company.

"Roadkill is going to show you around the rest of the ship now. Crew dismissed."

"Let's go," her brother said, waving the Tolqs toward the door. Then, as they disappeared into the hallway, he added, "Micca, you shiny-headed darling you—stick close to your old Uncle Roadkill. He's got lots of things to show you."

As her would-be crew headed toward the bridge, Jillian made a fast-break for her quarters. There, she hastily stripped off her tattered uniform. She knew it was foolish of her, but she couldn't bring herself to start what could very well be her last voyage looking like a piece of space trash. She grabbed another uniform out of her locker at random. It was a spacer-blue unitard with a low neckline, tight sleeves, and crimson piping down the legs. It had been one of the old Jillian's favorite outfits. The new Jillian was fairly happy with it, too—and not just because Micca was sure to swallow her tongue when she saw it. The days when she tried to camouflage what she was were gone for good. For better or worse, she was Jillian D'Lange, class-one captain and—cyborg.

She drop-kicked her balled-up trousers toward the recycler then. As she did so, a thin metal slip dropped out of a pocket and onto the floor. Amazing, she thought, as she picked the credit voucher up. She'd never even thought to see if it had made it out of the desert with her. This was a good sign, she told herself, as she stashed it in her keeper. It had to be. She *was* going to live to cash it in.

She looked in the mirror then. The face that looked back at her was dusty and wind-blown and much too brown—not her, exactly, but damn close. She smiled. The reflection smiled back. They each admired the other's style. But while she reached into her locker for a hairbrush, her reflection seized upon something else: the bottle of tequila. Out of habit, she pulled it out.

Just one for luck, she thought, as she uncapped the bottle. Just one, she thought, to steady her nerves. But even as she raised the bottle to her lips, she spied herself in the mirror and froze. She didn't have nerves, or believe in luck.

Nor did she need a drink.

She resealed the bottle and put it away. The pride that welled within her then was stronger than any tequila and twice as sweet.

Chapter 11

Z EPHYR TORE THROUGH Tolqish space like a Oort-cat with its tail afire, and with each passing moment, Jillian dared to grow a tad more hopeful. For even if Ross was already in this solar system—and that was *not* a given—he'd be looking for *Zeph* in orbit around the Planet of New Beginnings, not racing toward the wyrm-hole that would carry her back to Circe's II. She'd have a chance in Union space. There were more places to hide there. And more witnesses.

Just as that thought crossed her mind, Roadkill piped up. "I'm picking something up on long-range scanners. It's small. Man-made. Could be junk."

Or a scout-ship, she thought, and began to bring the ship's weaponry on-line. As she did so, she called for a comm-report. If it was a scout, it would probably be squealing for mama right about now. And if it *was* squealing, she was going to silence it. Forever.

"Any time now with that report, Micca!" she said.

But before the priestess had a chance to respond, Roadkill sang out again. "Relax, Jillie. I got it scoped now. It's another GC commsat—like the one we passed on the way in. Remember?"

She remembered. And she was truly relieved to hear the news. But that peace of mind soured into irritation as soon as she recalled how poorly her would-be comm-tech had performed in a potentially critical moment. As an exercise, she ordered Micca to run the commsat's message through the translator and play it for the bridge.

Again, the priestess failed to respond.

Jillian's irritation sky-rocketed. She swiveled her chair toward the comm-station and barked, "I thought you said you knew how to use that equipment. RK, see what her problem is."

He shuffled over to the comm-station and draped a quasi-avuncular arm across the back of Micca's plasma chair only to snap out of that huddle an instant later. "You're not going to believe this," he exclaimed then. "This crazy bitch is *sleeping!*"

"So wake her up," Jillian ordered, and willed back a flicker of hand-fire. This was the freakin' Voyage of the Damned, she grated to herself. Anything that could go wrong, had to. And her brother was quick to encourage the theory.

"I got her to open her eyes," he said, "but I don't think that's going to matter much. She's so zoned, she looks like she's in another dimension."

"How long has she been gone?" Jillian asked.

"How would I know?" he fired back, countering her irritation with sarcasm. "You forgot to tell me that I'd be responsible for periodic bedchecks on this run."

"A fine excuse that would've been if something other than a bit of luck had snuck up on us while she was out," she said, and then pinged Ammas's cabin. He answered with a heavy grunt, as if he were half-asleep. "Report to the bridge, ASAP," she told him. "Something's wrong with Micca."

"On my way," he said.

Long minutes later, the lift spat him onto the deck. He looked awful—disheveled and red-eyed, as if he'd been tossing and turning in his bunk since the moment they broke orbit. His mouth was a thin, slack line.

"Is your stomach still giving you problems?" she asked, as he approached.

"No, Captain," he replied, in a dreary monotone. "I am well. What ails Micca?"

"We can't wake her up," she replied, pointing toward the comm-station.

He glanced that way, then back again. As he did so, his sleepless look acquired a gloomy patina. "I'm sorry, Captain," he said. "I was afraid this would happen, but Micca wanted to believe that things would be different in a Ni H'Nathelek vessel, so I didn't say anything."

"So say it now," she told him. "What's her problem?"

"She's slipped into a far-sensing trance."

"Can we get her back?"

"You can't," he said. "But I may be able reach her. Would you like me to try?"

"Either that," Jillian said, "or get her ass below-decks. I can't have unresponsives on my bridge at this particular point in time."

The heir of Xamar strode over to the comm-station. Jillian trailed after him, only to wish that she'd stayed put a moment later. For she hadn't been expecting Ammas to cup his ex-lover's vacant but still lovely face in his hands, or to plant a tender kiss on her brow. She averted her eyes then, fiercely glad that she could no longer blush. And when she dared to look again, she kicked herself again, for now both Tolqs had that vacant-lot look. *Shitshitshit,* she thought. And: *now what?* But before she had a chance to come up with a solution, Ammas let out a drowning man's gasp and then tottered backward. If Jillian hadn't been there to catch him, he would've landed on his backside. And that was another reason that she should've kept to her chair.

"Now what?" she asked, for Micca hadn't stirred.

"Give her a minute," Ammas panted. "She was very far away."

She sat him down on the floor so he could catch his breath. And it was as he said it would be: a moment later, Micca surged back to wakefulness with a garbled croak. She was disoriented at first, psychically dazed, but her confusion turned to urgency as soon as she saw Jillian's too-close, scowling face.

"Are we heading in the right direction?" she asked.

"Of course," Jillian replied

"And there's some kind of a gulf ahead of us, isn't there?" she said then. "An 'otherworld' through which we must travel."

"It's called a wyrm-hole," Jillian told her.

At that, Micca's perpetual half-frown blossomed into a reverent O. She bowed her head, then clenched her quot'tl bead and murmured, "Forgive me for doubting you all of these years, Great One. I should've known. I should've believed."

"What are you going on about?" Ammas asked then, in an unusually harsh tone.

"I far-sensed our way," she said, growing excited now. "I saw it as clearly as I'm seeing you now. Do you know what that means?" Before he had a chance to answer, she sang, "It means that everybody was wrong about my gift. It isn't warped. It's unique. It means that Tolqs can now traverse these otherworldly wyrm-holes in H'Nath's name."

Jillian rolled her eyes at the thought. She had no way of telling *what* Micca had sensed while entranced. She knew it must've been *some*thing, for there was no denying that Tolqs had psychic abilities, but a way through wyrm-space without a nav-computer's guidance? It didn't seem likely, especially not in the light of Roadkill's recent discovery. Why would a parasite impart that kind of specialized ability? What was the evolutionary advantage? And besides—wyrm-space was already dangerous enough without a bunch of unschooled fanatics blindly popping in and out of it.

Meanwhile, the priestess babbled on. "Things are changing, Ammas-sa," she was saying now. "A new age has begun. Will you join me in a prayer of thanksgiving?"

"A ship's bridge isn't the place for that," Jillian interjected then. "And given your tendency to trance out on the job, I'm afraid that it's not the place for you, either, Micca. Turn your station over to Ammas and then—"

"Please, Captain," Micca begged, "don't exile me to my cabin. I can be of use to you here. I know I can."

Before Jillian could insist that Micca leave for the good of the ship, RK piped up. "Something just came up on the LRS. And if it's what I think it is, we're going to need every hand we can on deck."

She bulled her way over to his station, thinking, *Shitshitshit*. And sure enough, there was a blip on the long-range scan. She could tell at a glance that it wasn't a buoy, or space debris, or even a bootlegger's furtive rig. This blip was *big*. And closing fast. Only Union cruisers and pirates did that. Therefore, it had to be Valiant, Ross's ship. Freakin' Ross, she fumed. He didn't deserve to be so goddam lucky all the time.

"Time to intercept?" she asked.

"One point three six standard hours," RK replied, after crunching a set of numbers. "At present course and speed."

"And ETA to our hole?"

He called up more data. "One point two standard hours."

"That with the delta-vee reduction?"

"Of course."

It was going to be close, she thought, as she juggled the numbers around in her head—horribly, teeth-grindingly close. But they could still make this hole. They had to. It was their only hope of long-term survival. Her nerve hardened. Her thoughts became a high-intensity slipstream. She snatched a packet of stim-tabs out of the comm-station's utility drawer and handed it to Micca.

"Swallow the whole dose," she said, "and then take second seat on surveillance. I may need Roadkill elsewhere during this part of the trip, so be ready to take the station over at a moment's notice. Ammas, you're on comm. The first thing I want you to do is ping your cousin and uncle and tell them to web up. After that, I want you to try and get that ship's ID number. RK," she added, as she headed back toward her chair, "just stay with me, OK?"

"Fat lot of choice I have," he grated. A sullen moment later, he issued an update. "Blip's gaining on us. Time to intercept is now one hour."

"Did you get an ID yet?" she called to Ammas.

"No-o," he replied, in a harried tone. "I can't seem to find the right frequencies."

"It's running silent," RK confirmed, "but its emission patterns are consistent with those of a Union cruiser. It's headed right for us, too. It's gotta be Valiant."

"Time to hole?"

"Zero point nine standard hours."

Shitshitshit. Zephyr was quick for a freighter, but that cruiser was just plain *fast*. If she didn't do something in a hurry, they'd be hitting that wyrm-hole piggy-backed. So she checked the time again, juggled a few more numbers, and then boosted the delta-vee to an open space percentile.

"Are you out of your mind?" Roadkill said, when he realized what she'd done. "If we hit the hole at this speed, we'll lose our disruptors. We'll be trapped in wyrm-space, and that's as good as dead."

"We still have twenty-seven minutes of good, hard, running time left," she told him. "And I mean to use every second. Don't worry, brother, I know what I'm doing."

But while neither said so aloud, they both understood that knowing was one thing and doing was another. She'd have to reduce *Zeph*'s delta-vee in one great lump rather than by steady increments, and if her timing wasn't spot-on, all of that displaced velocity would get sucked into the hole on their wake and create a drag. Her calculations would be useless then. They might emerge from the wyrm in another galaxy or an asteroid field or perhaps even a sun's corona. At the very least, they'd be terribly, terribly lost. But if she didn't hold off until the very last minute, they'd all be dead of an AP bolt to the head before the day's end—and that seemed far worse to her.

"Call coming through," Micca said then. "Audio only."

Jillian jeered. Even now, this close to the kill, Ross and his pack of feral bastards were afraid to show their faces. *Cowards!* Their mothers would be *so* ashamed of them. "Play the message for the bridge," she said. "Give it to the data-core as well."

A ration of static crackled over the intercomm. An instant later, a woman's lilting voice said, "This is SU Security calling *Zephyr*, registration number 671K20-H83N. You are in restricted space without proper authorization. We are ordering you to disarm your weapons and power down."

As if Ross didn't have enough advantages already, she thought, and then decided to give him a taste of his own brazenness. "SU Security, this is Captain Jillian D'Lange," she said, borrowing Micca's haughtiest tone. "*This* ship is on legitimate business. Your vessel, however, is in clear violation of Galactic Council treaty. State your commander's name for my data-core, and his reasons for running silent in Tolq space."

"We have reason to believe that you aren't who you claim to be," the comm-tech replied. "That's all you need to know. Now power down and prepare for boarding."

"I'm afraid I can't do that until you identify yourselves," she fired back. "Who's commanding that rig?"

She heard a definitive snick, and then a ration of static. An instant later, Roadkill announced, "We got a pair of Sunbursts heading our way."

"Aft shields to max!" she ordered, and then took quick stock of their situation. It didn't look good. They were still losing ground to the cruiser, even at this headlong pace, and once they slowed down for the hole, Ross would easily close the gap between them. She considered sending Roadkill to man the cannons, but even as she did so, she knew it wouldn't help. *Zephyr*'s weapons were strictly short-range, and no match for Valiant in any case.

Just then, the Sunbursts caught up with them. The first one hit the shields without exploding. But its mate left *Zephyr* shuddering—an appalling combination of sounds and sensation.

"Damage report!" Jillian said.

"All minor," Roadkill replied. "But we've got more incoming. A whole freakin' volley this time. And they don't have as far to travel."

She masticated a curse between her man-made teeth. *A whole volley of big-bang torpedoes?* There was no point in trying to stay ahead of that barrage, not when they only had ten minutes of hard running time left on the clock. And foregoing the wyrm-hole was *not* an option. Her one hope was to take those Sunbursts out of the equation. And to do that, she had to let them catch up. She made the decision to do so in a blink.

"Hang on, people," she said. "The ride's going to get a little rough."

Then, all at once, she hit the brakes.

The ship loosed a horrible, stressed-metal groan as it was shorn of its momentum. A moment later, it began to buck and pitch in the grips of its own displaced velocity; and the bridge became a violent blur. Jillian barely noticed the commotion, though. She was focused on the helm now, intent on keeping *Zeph* on course. This stunt would be futile as well as crazy if they strayed too far from their wyrm-hole.

"S-s-s-unbursts s-s-s-till c-c-c-losing," Roadkill said, and then let out a shout. "B-b-blammo! One d-d-d-own, s-s-s-ix to g-g-go! The t-t-turbulence is s-s-s-screwing up their S&D s-s-systems."

He continued to report good news—two down, then three and four. As he did so, *Zephyr* cleared the worst of the turbulence, and the ship-quaking began to subside. Jillian stole another peek at the chronometer then. They were into the final countdown now, but still twenty-three minutes away from the safety of wyrm-space! Dread eddied through her like vertigo. Maybe braking early hadn't been such a good idea after all. A police cruiser could chew up a serious amount of space in twenty-three minutes. Maybe she should've gone with the ten extra minutes of running time.

"Red alert!" Roadkill shouted then. "Two torpedoes made it through the wake. Prepare for impac—"

A monstrous boom cut him off, so loud and virulent as to shiver Jillian's eyes in their sockets. *Zephyr* lurched. The bridge-lights dimmed, then flared again as if the ship were trying to blink back the stars in its eyes.

"Damage report!" she bellowed.

"Aft shield's been breached," RK replied, a staccato outburst. "Cargo Hold One took the hi—"

Another blast rocked the ship. An instant later, an indicator on Jillian's console began flashing, red and compelling like panic. "Nav computer's down!" Roadkill yelled then, confirming the disaster. "Extent of damage unknown."

"Get on it!" she yelled back. "Forget everything else."

She checked at the countdown then, and suffered a ghost pang of nausea. For while her brother was a champion tech, she had her doubts as to whether even he could find and cure the nav-computer's problems in a paltry thirteen minutes. And they had to hit the wyrm. It was their only chance of escape now.

"Micca!" she barked, trying hard not to think about the decision she'd just made. "Get over here. Hang on to the railing. Ammas, send out an SOS—multiple frequencies, repeater beacon. Say we're being attacked by an unidentified union cruiser."

She knew that the distress call wouldn't get anywhere in time to make a difference here and now. But it could make things awkward for Ross later on. *If* she didn't survive to do the job herself. And she wasn't giving up on that 'if' just yet. That was why she'd called Micca.

The priestess was standing at her elbow now. Her cinnamon-colored eyes were glassy with stimulants and fear. Her grip on Jillian's armrest was white-knuckled. Jillian flashed her a brief but sympathetic smile, and told her to take the co-captain's chair. As Micca did so, Jillian quipped, "Not quite the ride you expected, aye?"

"Not quite," Micca echoed. "But H'Nath will see us all through it nonetheless."

"Can you communicate with others while you're in trance?" Jillian asked then.

"I have never made the attempt," she admitted. "But the far-sensors who guide the H'Nathma's ships do it. Therefore, I should be able to do it, too. Why do you ask?"

"Because if RK doesn't get the nav-computer back on-line in the next—" She glanced at the clock for an up-to-the-millisecond update. "—nine minutes, you're going to have to take us through the wyrm." In the background, she heard Roadkill groan and step up his diagnostics. She knew exactly how he felt, but pressed on with the proposal nonetheless. "I haven't got the time to show you how to work the equipment," she said, "so we'll have to act like a tag-team. You tell me when we've reached the entry-point to the 'otherworld' as you call it, and I'll let us in. Then all you'll have to do is let me know when it's time to re-enter normal time and space. Can you do that?"

"H'Nath will guide me," Micca said.

"Then go ahead and get yourself into a trance."

The thought of popping in and out of a wyrm at a mere human's say-so would've Jillian paralyzed with fear if she'd had a spare micro-second to dwell on it. But there was tons of prep work to do before the moment of intrusion, and no one to do it but her, so as soon as she gave the priestess the go-ahead, she turned her mind to other things.

"Ammas," she said, "take a peek at RK's monitors and see if Valiant has cleared the cloud of turbulence yet."

A long moment later, he replied, "Almost. But not quite."

That was a tiny break in their favor, she thought, for Ross wasn't the wasteful type. He wouldn't send any more Sunbursts after her until he was sure that they'd fly true. So she raised the forward shields at the expense of the afts, and then brought the disruptors to stand-by. Her console was flashing like a child's light-board now, but the one indicator that she wanted to go white remained stubbornly red.

"Got a line on that problem yet, RK?" she asked then.

"Not yet," he rasped in reply.

"What are the odds of it happening within the next five minutes?"

"About as good as the odds are of you getting pregnant."

"Then pack it in and get ready for wyrm-space. You, too, Ammas."

As they battened down their stations, she grabbed a pack of stim-tabs from an old cache beneath her seat and gulped the whole ration down. She needed to remain awake in the wyrm so she could hear Micca when it came time to return them to normal space. She snuck a peek at her unlikely savior, then did an immediate double-take. To her profound dismay, the priestess was still bright-eyed and much too lucid.

"You're supposed to be in trance!" she said.

"I'm trying," Micca told her, "but the pills you wanted me to take are interfering."

"Here, stare at a monitor," Jillian urged, pointing her toward the utility screen. "It seemed to work for you last time."

Just then, Ammas said, "Valiant's cleared the cloud."

Shitshitshit, Jillian thought. The freakin' hits just kept on coming. Maybe she'd gone crazy back on Tolq after all. Maybe this was just another of those terrible dreams that she'd forget as soon as she woke up. That wouldn't be so bad. At least she never died in her dreams. She glanced at the clock again: three minutes to entry. But being on time wouldn't make a lick of difference if they weren't in the right place. She peeked at Micca again. Her eyelids were closed now but twitchy, so there was no way to tell what in hell was going on behind them. And Jillian didn't dare to ask for fear of disturbing the priestess at a potentially critical moment.

"We got a fresh round of Sunbursts heading our way," RK said then.

Sweet, suffering mother, Jillian thought. Had she really said that *Zephyr's* bridge was no place for prayer? She'd shave her head and eat sand forever if it would get them out of this fix.

Two minutes and counting now. If she didn't hear from Micca in the next forty seconds, she was going to fire the disruptors blind and hope for the best. If they were on course,

the wyrm would swallow them up, and all they'd have to worry
about was getting out again. If they were off-course, well, the
torpedoes on their tail would make quick work of them.

Tee minus one hundred. She said, "See you on the other
side, brother."

Tee minus ninety-five. He replied, "Not if I see you first."

Neither of them laughed.

Tee minus ninety now. She fingered the disrupter switch.
But just as she ticked off the last few seconds in her own private
countdown, a ghostly little voice said, "Adjust heading two
point two degrees to starboard."

Without pausing to wonder or doubt, Jillian did as she was
told. A moment later, Micca said, "We are at the door."

Jillian fired the disruptors. Zero point nine seconds later, a
hole appeared in the pure black fabric of space, and *Zephyr* was
sucked into the veins of another dimension.

ৎৎ

JILLIAN'S THOUGHTS CAME and went like quicksilver:
a slow, wyrm-space parade of shimmering beads. Whenever she
tried to pin one down, it squirted off in all directions, creating
offshoots that invited pursuit. She chased a few of them, but
never too far. She had to be readyreadyready for Micca's cue. She
turned, a slow-motion maneuver, to look at the priestess. Her
face seemed distorted now, fish-like—hilarious and disturbing
at the same time. It was, Jillian mused, an accurate portrayal of
hope. The doubts that she had cordoned off during that frantic,
pre-wyrm countdown were all loose now, free-floating globules
of scintillating disbelief. Had she really given her ship over to a
woman who navigated from a trance? A woman who claimed a
supreme being as her guide? What had she been thinking?

The answer came to her in a word: escape. She'd been
thinking of escape. And if hoping was anything like praying,
then she believed in a god, too. *Pleasepleaseplease, let this insane
stunt work. Pleasepleaseplease, let Micca know what she was doing.*

The fact was, she didn't care who got the kudos—H'Nath or parasite or plain dumb luck—so long as they all made it back to Circe's II alive.

Is it time yet, Micca?

As she studied the priestess, she found herself wondering about Ammas. He'd been acting strangely ever since he set foot on *Zephyr*, especially when Micca was in the vicinity. He was unabashedly tender toward her now, as solicitous as a suitor. And that swoony kiss that he'd planted on her entranced lips right here on the bridge had spoken volumes: now that Micca had regained her spiritual self-worth, he wanted her back in his life. Jillian could see why he might wish such a thing. Micca was beautiful, even without hair, and there was a rich history between them. How had he described her back in their first love days—*a joy? Clever, quick to laugh, eager to do great things?*

A thought intruded, uninvited: *if that was what he valued, then why wouldn't a cyborg do?* She knew better, though. Love was a human thing, a tangle of arms and legs as well as of hearts. She couldn't compete with flesh and blood. It was demeaning to try. And Micca would be good for Ammas now that she was no longer consumed by grief.

The concession left Jillian sad. She thought about closing her eyes, of yielding to the dreams that were gnawing on the tips of her awareness. But dreams were no escape from her pain. She'd learned that on Tolq. So she swallowed another pack of stim-tabs and blinked back futile cyborg wishes.

Now, Micca?

Time passed, unmonitored and thus undefined. Jillian dropped two more stim-tab packs, days or perhaps hours apart, because her thoughts were turning from quicksilver to quicksand. It was hard to stay awake now. She trawled up memories to keep the dreams at bay. She remembered her mother and her wild, Wave-Dance days; *Zephyr*'s purchase, her brother's first hair-do; the mad-cap times that she and Denny had shared. Then, when the images trickled to a stop, she started on equations, tables, and the names of stars. She was in the middle of deriving Princess Abby's Transdimensional Theorem II from scratch when a tiny voice intruded with a single word.

"Now."

Poised at the console since the moment they'd entered wyrm, Jillian plunged *Zeph* back into real time and space.

ക

ALARMS SHRIEKED AND indicators flashed red, reminders that all was not well. Over the din, Jillian heard her brother groan and then rip into a stim-tab packet. She knew how he felt, but could cut him no slack. For *Zephyr* was blindly barreling through an as-of-yet unidentified sector of space at near-FTL speeds, and *that* was a disaster just begging to happen.

"RK, Sensor report!" she said.

"All clear," he croaked, and sounded dully amazed to find himself still alive.

"All shields to max-cap."

"That's a roger on the forwards," he said. "But the afts are down to half-cap."

"That'll have to do," she said, thinking aloud. "I'm going to do a primary bleed, then coast on the residuals until we get some idea of what's been done to us. I'll need a damage report, ASAP. And Ammas, see if you can pick up any loose chatter on comm. That should give us some idea of where we are."

She initiated the bleed then, only to regret it an instant later. For the backwash of displaced velocity was vicious this time around, and *Zephyr* was no shape to withstand it. The ship shuddered and moaned as the turbulence buffeted it, then suddenly listed sharply to starboard. At that, a new round of sirens began to wail.

"Number four stabilizer's down!" RK shouted. "Number three's failing."

Zeph was falling through space now—a tight, downward spiral. Jillian was forced to do a secondary bleed to slow the ship down. They lost the disruptors in that backwash, and a swath of insulation tiles, and while she managed to wrangle *Zephyr* to a standstill, it insisted on hanging in space like a crooked holo-frame. Finally, she gave up the fight and slung herself deep into her seat.

"Damage report," she said then.

Her brother rattled off a whole list of casualties in a weary, much aggrieved voice. She anticipated most of the news, but some of it, such as the pressure leaks in both cargo bays and a near-breach in the hull, came as an unhappy surprise.

"Poor *Zeph*," he said in conclusion. "She just wasn't built to take a pounding like that."

"Captain," Ammas said then. "My uncle and Tobia. Are they—?"

"The grav's a little on the low side below-decks," Roadkill reported, before Jillian could ask. "But aside from that, life supports are still all running in the green."

"Go ahead and ping Tobia's cabin," Jillian told Ammas, happy to throw him that little bone. "RK, while he's doing that, run some diagnostics. I need to know how soon *Zeph* can be up and running again."

Her brother snorted, but went to work without a word. Meanwhile, Ammas made the call. Someone answered immediately, but it wasn't Tobia.

"Uncle?" Ammas asked. "What are you doing there?"

Jillian's temper flared like a stubbed toe. Damn that man, she fumed, and tapped into the conversation just as Tark was saying, "Tobia was sitting with me in my cell when the excitement broke out. He was ship-sick already, and unsure if he could make it back to his cabin on his own, so I went along just to be sure. Then I thought it best to stay with him during the ride through wyrm-space. It was his first time, you know."

"How is he now?" Ammas asked then.

"Tired, scared, and still rather ship-sick," Tark reported, his tone as wry as ever. "Can we dare to hope that the excitement's over now?"

At that point, Jillian cut in. "No, we can't, Ambassador. And we have your great friend, Nathan Ross, to thank for it."

"I thought as much," he said. "Have we lost him?"

"Who knows?" she grated. "I don't even know where *we* are at the moment. And by the way, you're supposed to be locked up." He started with his Tobia-needed-me spiel again, but she cut him off. "I don't have time to play games with you," she said. "In fact, until I have some idea as to what's what, I don't have time to deal with you at all. So I'm putting you on your honor, Tark. I'm trusting you to *stay in that room* until someone tells you to get out. If you disappoint me in this, I swear I'll vent you."

"That won't be necessary, Captain," he assured her.

"I hope not," she said, and then severed the link. But before she had a chance organize her thoughts, a distant voice said, "We are falling off-course. Adjust heading."

She smacked herself on the forehead as if to shake a frozen circuit loose. With so much else going on, she'd forgotten that Micca was still in her far-sensor's trance. And if what she'd just heard was correct, then they'd emerged from wyrm-space right on target. She wished that she could take some sort of pleasure in that, but the sorry fact was, they would've been better off being lost. Because Ross was bound to come looking for them, and she'd bet her little brain-bug that he'd search the Circe sector first.

That meant that he was on his way. And that made *Zephyr* a sitting duck.

"Ammas, come and wake Micca up," she said, as she came to terms with this new reality. Then, to RK, she said, "Go and fuel the shuttle up."

"But I haven't finished ye—"

"Can you fix both stabilizers within the hour?" she snapped. He shook his head— *no*. "Can you bring the nav-computer back on-line?" Another head-shake. "Then go and fuel the shuttle up."

"Oh," he said then, and went slinking off to the lift without another word.

Ammas was in deep rapport with Micca now. Jillian stared at them for a moment, envying that intimate connection and their future. Then Ammas's eyes popped open, and he pulled away from the priestess with a lover's gasp. An instant later, his knees buckled. Once again, Jillian was forced to catch him. He seemed to sense, if not comprehend, her irritation.

"I'm sorry to inconvenience you," he said, as he struggled to catch his breath, "but mind-touching is draining work. It's H'Nath's way of preventing abuse." A strange, sour look flashed across his face then. It could've been fatigue. It could've been gas. "Or so I was taught," he added, and then extricated himself from her grasp as Micca stirred.

As if he didn't want the priestess to get the idea that there was anything between him and the cyborg-captain, Jillian thought. The rejection hurt more than she'd imagined it would. Fortunately, those things didn't show on her face anymore.

"Go and keep an eye on the scanners until Roadkill gets back," she ordered him, in what she hoped was a neutral tone. "Let me know if anything suddenly turns up on any of the screens." Then she turned her attention to Micca. The priestess looked dazed, but not wasted like some people who came out of wyrm-space without drugs. "How are you feeling?"

Micca blinked, then ran a hand over her now-stubbled scalp as if collecting data for a report. "I am tired," she admitted, "but that will pass. Why have we stopped?"

"*Zephyr*'s in a bad way," Jillian told her. "Now tell me—as far as you know, did we come out of wyrm on target?"

"My far-sense is true," Micca declared, flushing with pride. "Circe's Moon II is a day away, provided that you correct the deviation in our present course."

Jillian had to believe in Micca's unlikely ability now. There was no other way that a non-spacer could've known where Circe's II was with respect to this particular wyrm-hole. And with belief came resignation. She began shutting *Zephyr* down. The bridge went dark save for the scant light of those few monitors she intended to use until the end. The thrusters that kept *Zeph* from regressing into a spiral droned to a standstill. The running lights stayed on, though. They were the spark of life in the opossum's eyes. Enough of a spark to give Ross pause—she hoped.

Her brother reappeared on the bridge just as she was powering down the last few sections of the ship. He glanced this way and that as if he were at a darkened crosswalks, and then asked, "Don't you think the seance angle is just a bit premature?"

"Is the shuttle ready?" she asked, unable to rise to his bantering tone. At his nod, she said, "Good. Now you can pilot these Tolqs, and the Tolqs below-decks, to Circe's Moon II. It's a two day shuttle-ride from here. Micca can give you the coordinates. Try not to take a direct route. When you finally do get to Circe's II, go directly to the Galactic Council. Ross probably has spies everywhere."

"You make it sound like you're not coming with us," he said, in a half-joking, half-accusatory tone.

"I'm not."

"And why not?"

"I'm staying here—to wait for Ross. He'll have to contend with me. I'll see to that. And that will give you more time to get away from his long-range scanners. Once I'm sure you're safe, I'll lure the cruiser into *Zephyr's* detonation zone and then key the destruct. I might not take the bastard out, but I'll sure as hell slow him down. Now go on and get out of here. I wish I could say that it's been fun."

"I got a better idea," RK said. "How 'bout we all stay right here with you?"

Ammas and Micca nodded agreement. Jillian got mad at them for making her articulate certain galling thoughts. Like: "As it stands now, *Zeph* hasn't got a chance." And: "But we *need* to bring Tark before the Galactic Council so he can testify against Ross and the rest of his SU conspirators." And, most galling of all: "You're my only chance of beating him now. And I want him to pay through the ass for everything he's done."

Roadkill exchanged a glance with the two Tolqs, then returned his mirrored gaze to her. His face was tense now, a battlefield for warring emotions. Jillian had never seen him struggle so hard for control. Then he peeled his lips back in a big, psycho-lecherous leer. It would've broken her heart if it had still been human.

"Do your worst, Jillie," he told her. "I'll clean up the big chunks after you."

"Thanks," she said. "See you on the other side."

He shot her a disgusted look and snorted, then abruptly headed for the lift. Micca bowed to Jillian—a first-time gesture of acceptance and respect. Then she followed after RK. She held her hand out to Ammas in passing, but he blew her a tender kiss and stayed put. Seeing that out of the corner of her eye, Jillian stropped her tone and said, "We don't have time for long good-byes here, Ammas. Just pick yourself up and go."

"Nathan Ross is as much my enemy as he is yours," he said.

"I know. Now run along, you're holding up the others."

"I'm not going with them."

Frustration and fear bubbled up within her like peroxide bubbled up in a cut. She rounded on him with a snarl. "You dolt! Weren't you listening? I'm going to blow *Zeph* halfway back to Tolq. I don't want you around when it happens. How much plainer do I have to get?"

"I deserted you once in an hour of darkness," he stated, ultra-calm in the face of her fury. "I will not do it again."

She scrabbled out of her chair then, meaning to drag him all the way to the shuttle bay by the scruff of his neck. But even as she stormed toward him, she saw a neon-green blip pop suddenly into being on the long-range monitor behind him, and her anger turned to dust.

So soon?

She ducked into the comm-station and pinged her brother. "Hurry it up," she said, as soon as he replied. "Ross just came out of wyrm."

"That's a roger," Roadkill replied. "By the way, there's no need to open and close the hatch for me. I've got the remote."

"RK—"

"What are you gonna do, fire me?" he cracked. Then, in the same half-mocking tone, he said, "Gotta go, Jillie. We'll be running silent, so this is it."

She thought about saying something horribly sentimental like 'I'll miss you,' or 'I love you,' but such phrases didn't come easily to her refabricated tongue, and then it was too late. He sundered the link. She suddenly felt very alone. She hadn't expected that.

"Captain," Ammas said. "Another blip just appeared on-screen. It's smaller than the first one. And slower."

"That would be *Zephyr*-shuttle," she said, and then joined him at the surveillance station.

The larger blip was the more noticeable one. It was streaking across the screen— a fast-moving series of fade-away stitches that marked Valiant's post-wyrm trajectory. In contrast, the smaller one looked like it was coasting, if that. But at least it was coasting away from the cruiser. By the time Ross bled his delta-vee back to reasonable percentiles and doubled back this way, the shuttle would be well into open space. He'd know it was out there, for his long-range sensors had no doubt picked it up as he'd gone streaking by. But he'd have to stop and deal with her before he went chasing after it. And she meant to be difficult. Very difficult.

"Get on the comm and send out an all-frequency SOS," she told Ammas. "Make sure you mention that we're being attacked by an unidentified union cruiser."

"Do you think help will come?" he asked, from the other station.

"No," she replied—brutal, dead-pan honesty. "My comm-unit isn't sophisticated enough to attract instant, long-distance attention. But the longer we scream, the better our odds of someone hearing. Ross will know that, and move in to shut us down. While he's doing that, the shuttle will be slipping further and further away."

"I see," he said, and then turned up at her elbow a moment later. "And what's this that you're doing now?"

"I'm rigging a self-destruct," she told him, as she tapped commands into the main computer. "So when I finally have Ross where I want him, all I'll have to do is enter my access code into a console and then hit 'End'. The code is nine; thirteen; twenty-seven." Her mother's birthday. "Can you remember that?" He answered with a nod. "Good. Because if anything should happen to me in the meantime, you're going to have to do the job for me."

His jaw dropped. His eyes went round with shock and disbelief. But she didn't give him a chance to cough up the protest that had lodged in his throat. "Sorry, Ammas," she said, "but there's no one else to impose on. And staying on was your idea, not mine."

She glanced at the scanner again. The shuttle had cleared the detonation zone and a little more. The cruiser had completed its primary bleed, and looked to be getting ready for a second. It wouldn't be long before Ross had all the maneuverability that he needed, she reckoned. It wouldn't be long before this end-game began in earnest. She took one long, last look about the bridge that she had loved so well, and then motioned to Ammas.

"Come on," she said. "It's time to man the cannons."

The lift spilled them onto Level III. Several rooms down here had been sealed off to contain pressure leaks. The overhead indicators that warned of this filled the darkened corridors with a murky, red-cola light. It grieved Jillian to see *Zeph* so sorely reduced. It had been more than a ship to her, more than a career. It had been her whole goddam life. Her one consolation was that they were checking out of this continuum together. And her one remaining ambition was to take Nathan Ross with them.

The plasma cannons were located amidships: four turrets, two on each side. All four were humming to themselves—the sound of fire-power on stand-by. She strode up to the first turret, then motioned Ammas to take it. As he climbed into his seat, she said, "I don't suppose you know how to use one of these things."

"You suppose correctly," he replied. He looked small and out of place behind that big, shielded barrel. He looked like a lost child—miserable and afraid. "I've never even dreamed of using something like this."

"First time for everything, I guess," she said. "And these babies are fairly easy to operate." She reached past him then and turned on his visuals. A holo-grid flared up in front of the shield. It contained two blips. One was inching toward a set of cross-hairs; the other was moving away. She pointed at that one and said, "That's our shuttle. Under *no* circumstances are you to lob a shot at that. Clear?"

He nodded glumly. She proceeded with his education. "All you have to do to get a fix on your target is move these handlebars in the appropriate direction. Then, when the target appears in these cross-hairs—" She pointed to the holo-grid. "—press the trigger next to your right thumb. If the shot is good, the blip in question will break up on-screen. If it stays whole, target it again. And don't worry about wasting ammunition. We're not saving anything for a rainy day here."

"Should I start shooting now?" he asked.

"Negative," she replied, glancing at the holo-grid again. "The cruiser's still out of our range. For now, all you need to do is sit tight and wait for my command. If things go as planned, you won't have to fire a single shot." He looked so relieved to hear that, she couldn't bring herself to remind him that that plan entailed blowing the ship and everyone on it. Instead, she signed off with, "I'll be next door if you need me. Stay alert."

He opened his mouth as if he wanted to say something in parting, but then ground the thought between his teeth and hunkered deep into his chair. She didn't blame him for his reticence. Last words embarrassed her, too.

The first thing Jillian did when she got to her turret was boot up her visuals. For while she'd told Ammas that Ross was still out of their range, she'd neglected to mention that they were now well within Sunburst range. But she was betting that he wouldn't use torpedoes this close to inhabited space. Any duds or shrapnel found in the same vicinity of the resulting wreckage would be easy to trace and hard to explain. He'd come closer and use ubiquitous plasma cannons.

Or so she hoped.

The cruiser continued at advance at a cautious clip. She watched and waited like a cyber-cat in tall grass—willing her prey to come closer and then closer still, thinking of nothing else. A faint yellow line sizzled across the holo-grid. It was followed by another and more. Cannon-fire, she thought, and was dully satisfied to have anticipated Ross for a change. Moments later, the shots slammed into *Zeph*'s hull. The sound was deafening.

"What's this horrible noise?" Ammas asked then, shouting over their comm-link.

"Cannon-fire," she shouted back. "But don't sweat it. It's coming from too far away to do any major damage. Ross is just poking *Zeph* in the ribs to see if we'll jump. He'll lighten up soon, then come in closer to board us."

"Why would he do that?" he wanted to know. "Why wouldn't he just destroy us and be done with the deed?"

"Because he needs to pull *Zeph*'s data-core and any other incriminating evidence that he can find before he blows us to space rubble," she replied. "And because he needs to know where I am. There's no point in collapsing a nammaden if the namma isn't in it. So we'll continue to lay low and keep Ross guessing until he's well within our detonation zone."

Even as she said this, the barrage died down. And for a moment or two thereafter, it seemed as if Jillian had anticipated Ross correctly once again. But just as a grim sort of smugness began to set within her, the cruiser's holo-image shed a series of fly-speck blips that then went swarming across the grid. And to her jaw-dropping surprise, they weren't swarming toward *Zephyr*. *Shitshitshit*, she thought, as she frantically brought her weapon on-line. She'd forgotten that a police cruiser had the capacity— and the resources—to do several missions at the same time.

"Ammas," she yelled then, "those specks on your grid are scout pods. And small as they are, they're more than a match for the shuttle. So as soon as they come into range, fire away. We need to get them before they get to the shuttle."

"I'll try," came his wan reply.

Ross would pull back as soon as they started firing, she predicted, pull back and pound poor *Zephyr* to space rubble ASAP instead of later. Yet she had no choice, none at all, because her hopes were all riding in the shuttle. So she whittled her world down to the space within a laser-cannon's cross-hairs and waited for the first pod to come within range. But the cruiser's cannonade had knocked *Zeph* out of its precarious standstill and back into a slow, downward spiral. Just as she targeted her first victim, *Zephyr*'s rotation took her out of the would-be fire-fight. Swearing gustily, she slung herself out of her seat and across the hallway to a starboard turret. An instant later, she fired the first shot.

A scout-pod crumbled on the grid like a Tuluvean fortune-cookie. She hooted, a cry of vengeance and savage glee, then targeted the next pod. As she did so, Valiant launched another cannonade. The shots slammed into *Zephyr*'s hull like high-G rain, and accelerated the ship's tailspin.

"Fire away, Ammas," she said, as the rotation took her out of the fight. "Shoot those bastards down before they get to the shuttle." A moment later, she told him to open fire again.

"I cannot," he half-groaned and half-gasped in reply. "There are people in those pods. They'll be killed if I fire."

"And the people in our shuttle will die if you don't!"

To no avail. The holo-pods on her grid were closing in on the shuttle, and Ammas was doing nothing to stop them. She loosed a curse that would've blistered old paint, and went tearing out of the turret. As she did so, *Zeph* took a harsh shot to the chin. The ship lurched like a stumbling old drunk. Caught in mid-stride, with no grip on the railing, she went half-falling and half-flying down the hallway. Her last thought, before she slammed head-on into a pressure-sealed door, was one of sheer amazement for her own stupidity.

Chapter 12

JILLIAN WAS FLOATING on a cloud of red-hued static when a voice called to her from a distant event horizon. She'd never known a voice quite like it. It was intuitive, soundless beauty; and as compelling as a tap on the shoulder or an outstretched hand. She couldn't resist its allure.

The next thing she knew, she was awake.

The world looked much like it had in her dreams: black and red and textureless. But here, the darkness sheered off into seamless, close-set walls instead of a black hole; and here, she wasn't alone. Ammas was kneeling on the floor next to her bunk. His face looked gaunt and strained. Her infra-red lenses gave him the aspect of a photo-negative.

"Where are we?" she asked him, for she could tell by the powerful reverberations that were strumming through her body that they weren't aboard *Zephyr*. And even as she asked, she remembered that the both of them should be dead. "What happened?"

Although it was clear that he was glad to see her awake, there was little joy in his face. Indeed, he looked haunted, as if he'd done or endured something that would leave him scarred forever. "I think you hit your head and gave yourself a concussion," he told her glumly. "Leastwise, that's what Ross's men figured when they found you."

That sorry little statement did nothing to improve his stature in her eyes. Not only had he not blown *Zephyr* like she'd told him to, he'd allowed the ship to be boarded and them to be captured. She crushed her hopes for the shuttle then—a mercy killing if there had ever been one. And yet she couldn't stop herself from asking.

"What about the others? Did they get away?"

He squeezed her hand, telegraphing his misery, and then blurted, "I so wanted to help them—you must believe that. But I couldn't do it. I couldn't bring myself to press that trigger and take some stranger's life."

"So that stranger pulled his trigger and killed our people instead," she said, in a brutal tone.

He nodded wordlessly. Then tears began to drip from his tormented eyes, and he made no effort to hide them. Jillian lost another chunk of respect for him. "One moment, the shuttle was creeping toward the edge of the grid," he told her. "The next, it burst into tiny pieces. I didn't know where you were or what to do, and before I could get my mind in order, a stranger grabbed me by the hair and dragged me out of my turret. That's when I saw you."

"Lucky me," she growled, indifferent to his pain. He should've blown the ship, dammit! At least he should've tried. Now Ross had it all. "How long have I been out?"

"I don't know," he replied, "but we've been in and out wyrm-space once already. I tried to call you back to consciousness before we went in, but you needed a healer more than a controller."

"Aren't much good to anyone, are you?" she asked, out of sheer, vindictive spite. She was *so* angry with him, and *so* disappointed, she was surprised she wasn't bleeding blue fire yet. "You really should've stayed home."

He hung his head—a despairing acknowledgment of his inadequacy. That made her want to ladle another helping of abuse on his soul. Before she had a chance to do so, though, the wall in front of them disappeared with a hiss. A stocky shadow-man stepped into the resulting patch of artificial light. Jillian was quick to note the anti-personnel rifle in his hands. He was almost as quick to brandish it.

"On your feet," he said, and his raspy tenor voice begged for recognition. "Both of you."

"Why?" Jillian asked.

"Because I said so," he replied, and once again, she got the feeling that she knew this man from somewhere.

That sense soon grew to a near-certainty. For as she filed past him, his features emerged from the shadows. She remembered the cleft chin and cold blue eyes, the red hair and that kicked-dog snarl. But what she remembered most was the mean-looking scar that ran down the right side of his face. He'd had it sanded since she'd seen it last, but it was still quite recognizable.

She slammed him into the wall as the memory came sizzling out of cold storage, and then pinned him there by the throat with his own rifle. Blood pooled in his face. His eyes bulged. She leaned in close like a lover. Like a rapist.

"Hello, Marty," she said, in a stropped whisper. "Blown up any shuttles lately?"

The business end of another AP rifle appeared at her temple. It was, she noticed, already primed for firing. She would've gladly risked its payload to repay the man who'd killed her once already if not for one hard, cold fact: she wanted Ross more. So she gave Marty one last body-check into the wall and then surrendered herself to his crewman. As she stood there with her hands over her head, Marty bashed his rifle butt into her left side, precisely where her kidney used to be. She scorned him with a glance.

"Asshole," she said. "Did you think that a cyborg with tits would be easier to beat up than a cyborg without them?"

Blood colored his scar like mercury in an old-fashioned thermometer. He stalked over to Ammas and punched him twice in the stomach, glaring daggers at her all the while. "Maybe you can't bleed anymore," he said, as the Tolq gagged for air, "but your pretty friend here can. And if you so much as look at me wrong from now on, I'll mess him up good."

"Do your worst," she said. "If he had followed orders, we wouldn't be here now."

"Hard to find good help these days, huh?" he quipped, and then gave her a shove. "C'mon, let's go."

He and his partner marched her and Ammas through a long series of hallways and lift trips. She paid attention to every stop and start, hoping to find an advantage in one of them, but the only thing she learned was that police cruisers were *big* suckers, and mostly teeth. Finally, they came to a secured lift. One of the guards there looked at her as if she were already dead. The other averted his eyes. She wondered if he was ashamed of what he'd become, or simply of getting caught red-handed. Not that it mattered, she supposed, as Marty prodded her onto the lift. Either way, his secret was apt to be safe with her.

The lift delivered them unto a small antechamber. There were guards here, too—a crack team of assault troopers. "Surrender to me now," she said in passing, "and I'll say a good word for you at your trial."

Ammas took a shot in the ribs for that. She didn't feel at all sorry for him.

The antechamber opened onto the bridge, and it was truly a beautiful thing—the best of everything, and a first-class captain's wettest dream. She glanced from station to station, mentally fingering the equipment, and for one awed, envious moment, she forgot why she was here. *Stars above*, she thought. *The places she could go with this ship!* Then she remembered her own poor *Zeph*, and the fabulous took on a perverted glare.

Ross was waiting for them at the captain's console. He even dared to flash her a toothy smile as Marty herded her toward his chair. At that moment, she would've traded a thousand fortunes for a single gob of spit. As it was, all she could do was scorn him with the iciest look in her repertoire. It had no impact on him.

"Hello, Jillian," he said genially. "You're looking splendid—as usual." He gave Ammas a sly, passing glance, and then added, "I see your taste in men has changed."

"After you, it could only improve," she said.

He deflected the insult with a polished laugh. "You were always a quick-minded minx, Jillian. That was one of the things that I liked about you. But let's stop wasting time, shall we? There are a few details that I'd like to clear up before I retire your file."

"Such as?"

"Such as who was on that shuttle," he replied. "In addition to your techno-horror of a half-brother, that is."

"I'm sorry, but I don't know what you're talking about," she said, refusing him the answer simply because he wanted it.

"No?" One eyebrow arched like a fishhook. "Are you sure?" When she refused to budge, he cocked a smile at her and said, "Maybe I can jog your memory. I understand you've had problems with it lately."

Ross nodded at Marty, who then left the bridge. When he returned a few minutes later, he had someone with him—an older, twarla-clad man with braided hair and a slight limp. This man tipped Jillian a mocking bow in passing, nodded to Ammas, and then sat himself down in the co-captain's seat. Ross greeted him with a smile.

"Tark," she said then, finally finding her voice. A stunned moment later, she asked, "But how?"

"I'm afraid I didn't stay in my cabin when you told me to," he replied, wide-eyed with phony innocence. "Instead, I called Ross via your shuttle's comm and let him know that I was aboard your ship and in dire need of rescue. Then I hid. Micca and the others searched for me as long as they dared, but finally had to leave without yours truly."

The confession only exacerbated her confusion. Her circuits were so scrambled, all she could do at the moment was gabble. "But—but you were going to testify."

He scorned her with that infamous half-smile of his. "For somebody who's seen and done so much, Captain, you can be incredibly naive. I *volunteered* to go with you simply to make sure that you headed for Circe's II rather than into hiding. I knew Nate would catch up with you before I ever had to say a word."

"He caught up with Tobia, too," she pointed out. Her daze was gone now, burnt off by a flash of righteous ire. And grief made her mean. "It doesn't surprise me that you could send my brother and Micca to their deaths without batting an eyelash, but your own son? Sweet, suffering mother, Tark. You must mainline anti-freeze."

His half-smile flattened into a thin, bloodless line. His eyes went flinty. "My son was a tragic casualty. I will mourn his passing for the rest of my days. But he believed in Tolq's Reformation, Captain. And as you well know, he had the desert-scars to prove it. Had he lived, he would've become my right hand man in the government-to-come. As it is, he'll serve almost as well as an inspiration to others."

A sly gleam sidled into his eyes then. He cocked his head at someone to her rear and said, "And how about you, nephew? Are you inspired?"

"I don't take your meaning, Uncle," Ammas replied.

"I'll need somebody whom I can trust at my side in the days to come," his uncle explained. "I was rather hoping that that someone might be you." When Ammas didn't respond right away, he gestured at the bridge like a ringmaster. "Look around you, lad. All of this and more can be Tolq's if we remove the H'Nathma from power."

"And seize it for yourselves," Jillian said.

Ammas took a kidney punch for that. Tark complained to Ross immediately. "Is that necessary?"

Ross shrugged. "I'm sure Marty has his reasons. But if you ask him nicely—" He exchanged a smirk with his enforcer then. "—I'm sure he'll back off."

Tark did as Ross suggested, but even the Great Pretender himself couldn't entirely conceal his distaste for Marty and his thuggish manners. In turn, Marty didn't seem much inclined to do favors for the high-handed ambassador. But before either of them could go to work on Ammas again, the young Tolq let out a strangled gasp and then knotted a hand in the back of his twarla as if to hold himself upright.

"Ammas!" Tark said, springing to his feet. "What's wrong?"

"Hurts," Ammas grunted, and then began to crumple. Jillian reined in the impulse to catch him, and he slumped to the floor in a faint.

Ross signaled Marty to investigate. The synthe-scarred man poked his rifle-barrel into various parts of Ammas's motionless body, and then made his diagnosis. "He'll live. He just can't take a punch, is all."

That seemed to satisfy Ross. "OK, Neil," he said, addressing Marty's counterpart, "go ahead and take him back to lock-up. When he comes to again, feed him. Maybe that will keep him on his feet."

"Why don't you put him in my room instead, Nate?" Tark suggested then. "After all, he's one of ours now."

"That hasn't been decided yet, Tark," Ross replied, with a tight, naughty-naughty smile. "And until it has, he'll stay in the brig. He'll appreciate freedom more after a taste of the alternative." He paused to watch Neil sling Ammas over his shoulder like a sack of dirty laundry, then turned to Jillian and said, "I guess that leaves only you, aye, Jillie?"

Although shaken all the way down to the last brain cell by Tark's latest betrayal and three more personal and oh-so senseless deaths, she refused to break down in front of Denny's killers. She'd swallow her refabricated tongue first. So she drew a corner of her mouth upward in a cocksure dare and said, "Aren't you going to try and persuade me to work for you, too, Nate? I'm pretty good with my hands."

He flashed her the same tight smile that he'd showed to Tark. "I'm sure you are," he said. "But I'm afraid I already have other plans for you."

"I figured as much," she said dryly. "In fact, I was rather surprised to find myself still alive this morning. Did someone goof or what?"

"The mix was all wrong," he said, casually, as if they were talking about brands of shuttle propellant. "But don't worry. You'll get your chance to go down with the ship."

"Let me guess. You're going to plant me on something you've already torpedoed and then let some poor salvager find me there. After a lengthy investigation, you'll blame me for everything that you and your gang of thieves has been doing for the last decade or so and declare the piracy problem solved."

"Nice idea," he told her. "But I see you being discovered in your own ship."

"You lost me there."

He pressed a perfectly manicured hand to his cheek, affecting a mildly scandalized look. "Did I neglect to mention that we have what's left of *Zephyr* in tow? How careless of me."

Her thoughts soared. *Zeph? He had Zeph in tow?* For one crazy, out-of-body moment, she actually entertained hopes of escape. *All she had to do was*— Then reality reasserted itself. Even if she somehow managed to break out of a freakin' *police* cruiser and find her way back to her ship, she wasn't going anywhere with blown stabilizers and no crew. She was stuck here. Period. Still, it was heartening to know that *Zephyr* was back there, hanging on against all odds. She suddenly felt much less abandoned.

"I wasn't sure that she'd make it through a wyrm," Ross confided then, "but she's a surprisingly sturdy vessel."

"Or at least she used to be," she drawled, and then tried to milk him for more info. It wasn't hard to do. All she had to do was appeal to that towering ego of his. "But I'm still not following you, Nate. Why move *Zeph* at all?"

"Because her original SOS came from Tolq space," he said, all but jumping at the chance to show off his brilliance. "And that's where this cruiser is going to find her, dead and adrift. A search party will find you in front of a spent cannon with an AP bolt in your head. Your crew will be missing and presumed dead. But there will be one survivor: the ambassador of Tolq."

"*And* his nephew," Tark firmly appended. Then, before his co-conspirator could contradict him, he went on to say, "I'll be so upset and incensed by the attack, I'll invoke my personal authority and demand that Ross pursue the pirates immediately. In doing so, he'll eradicate one stronghold in Tolq space and uncover evidence of several others. I'll insist that Ross present his findings to the H'Nathma immediately. Those priests who do not wish to listen to him will be taken to the desert for a time of reflection."

Jillian despised him with a look. "Why don't you come right out and call it mass murder, Tark? Because that's what it'll be."

"On the contrary, Captain," he said, deadpan as ever. "Those priests who submit to reformation will be welcomed back to society with open arms. And those who don't— well, all worthy causes have their casualties. I'll just have to take comfort in the fact that my new government will bring an end to Tolq's hungry years and thereby save more lives than it's forced to take."

"A masterful bit of rationalization," she told him, and then rounded on Ross. "So what do you get out of all this, Nate— aside from first dibs on the plunder, that is."

He leaned back in his chair and grinned at her. "Do you know how many people have tried to bring Tolq into the union over this last century? Do you have any idea how much credit, and how many jobs, a planetary membership like that pulls in? I'm going to be a hero, Jillian. And that's just for starters. I really do plan to unseat Barim in the next election."

"You think honest spacers are going to vote for you over Barim after you break a long-standing GC treaty and invade a low-tech nonaligned world?" She jeered at that. "Get real, Nate! You can't run a union from a penal colony."

She was trying to sow kernels of doubt in him now. For as she knew all too well, a troubled mind often made mistakes. And right now, a mistake on his part was her only chance of getting out of this mess alive. His self-confidence, however, was impregnable. He'd always been that way. The bastard.

"Tolq's new government will refer to us as guests, not invaders," he said. "And the slap on the wrist that I'll get from the GC for treaty-breaking will generate excellent publicity. Once people hear that I: one, torpedoed the pirate ring that was driving their insurance rates up; and two, established Tolq as an open market; and three, violated a treaty to try and help one of the union's own, there won't be a spacer left in the galaxy who'll vote for Barim. I'm going to be one of the most powerful men in human history, Jillian. And I couldn't have done it without your help."

The thought appalled her. Was she really *that* predictable? *That* freakin' easy to manipulate? She had to give him the chance to deny it. "You can't tell me that you had this incident planned from the first time we talked."

He snorted. "Don't be absurd, Jillian. You were just a minor glitch in the original works. But the set of circumstances that boiled up around your visit to Tolq were just too good to ignore. That's why I'm letting you live until we put into orbit. It's my little way of saying thanks."

"Next time," she said, "just send flowers."

"There isn't going to be a next time," he told her, and then motioned for Marty to take her away. "See you around, lover."

"You'd better hope not," she replied.

∽

MARTY HERDED HER back to her cell, then locked the door behind her. Although it was as black as space in the tiny compartment, Ammas showed up on the infra-red. He was huddled up on one of the pull-outs, hard and fast asleep. Jillian was glad that he was out, for while she was now lucid enough to see that blowing *Zeph* wouldn't have made a lot of difference in this debacle's evolution, she wasn't quite ready to forgive him for not doing it anyway. He should've gone down swinging, she thought, as she explored the cell for exploitable fingerholds. He should've done *some*thing.

There was probably a little guilt by association involved here, too, she thought. Freakin' Tark. She should've killed him when she had the chance. But he was just so damn good at what he did. The lying bastard. Not only had he sucked her in—again. He'd suckered everybody in sight.

Everybody but RK, that is. Roadkill had seen right through Tark from the very start. Images of her brother rippled through her thoughts like raucous laughter, exhuming her biggest regret: she'd never come right out and told him how she felt about him. How she loved him. Even now, she found it hard to admit, because he was—had been—such a seriously *strange* individual. She didn't even know how to mourn him. The oceans of tears that she'd shed for Myla were impossible now, and Roadkill would've scorned them anyway, just as he'd scorned everything else sentimental. Nor would he have approved of the guilt that was gnawing at her now.

Despite her grief, she managed a half-smile for that fallacy. RK would have *loved* the guilt. He would've reveled in it. He would've exploited it until he had, through sheer unmitigated obnoxiousness, cured her of it. Affection swelled within her then. It felt like the strumming of a cruiser's drive-generator.

"Captain?" a voice whispered then.

"What?" she said, a monotonic stiff-arm.

"You made a noise just then," he said. "What bothers you?"

The question both angered and amazed her. Here she was on death-row with a ship full of ghosts to her name and no freakin' cavalry in sight, and he wanted to know if there was something on her mind. Sweet, suffering mother! The man was an idiot. And she was pleased to tell him so.

"My brother's dead," she hissed. "So is another man whom I once loved, not to mention Micca, Tobia, and countless others whose names I don't know. Your uncle had a hand in every one of those deaths. That bothers me, Ammas. That bothers me *a lot*."

"I share your dismay," Ammas said then. "My uncle is a liar twice removed and a traitor to everybody who held him dear. I'll have no more to do with the man, and I mean to tell him so the next time we meet."

Jillian was on him in an instant, pinning him to the pull-out with one upper arm and shoving her face up close to his ear. "You'll do no such thing, Ammas su Xamar," she whispered fiercely. "You won't even speak such a thought aloud."

"And why not?" he asked.

"Because you're the only one who can stop Ross now. You're the only one who can make him pay for his many crimes." Sensing the what-about-you in him, she added, "I'm slated for execution as soon as Ross puts the cruiser into orbit."

He made a tiny, stricken sound. "I don't want to disappoint you," he said. "But I don't want to live lies like Tark does, either. I was taught to hold true to my principles."

"Is that what you were doing when the tribunal sentenced me to the desert that day?" she fired back.

"Pain has made you cruel," he told her. "Otherwise you wouldn't jab your finger into the most shameful hours of my life. I was wrong then. I admitted it, and apologized. Have *you* never made a mistake?"

Although he posed the question as rhetoric, it struck her deeply, rousing multiple guilts. She shifted, a vague concession to his point. He pressed his advantage.

"And besides," he said, in a whisper so faint that it could have been telepathy, "it may be that Ross won't have time to execute anyone." She shot him a quizzical look. A twinge of boyish pride tugged at the corners of his mouth. "While I was on the bridge, I found the comm-tech's mind and forced him to send a message to Station Control. *Ross in Tolq space, come quick, do not reply.* I didn't dare say more."

Well, color her surprised. After his pathetic performance aboard *Zephyr*, Jillian would've never guessed that he had that kind of gumption in him. It wouldn't do *her* any good, for even the cruiser had instantaneous-comm, which it didn't, it would take at least two days for a ship to get here from Station. But she was glad that he'd made the effort just the same. It restored a measure of her faith in him.

"Ross will kill you when he finds out," she warned.

"He won't find out," he assured her. "I made the tech forget about the message as soon as he sent it."

"Maybe I'll tell him. Maybe he'll spare my life in exchange

for the information," she said. He gaped at her as if she'd just sprouted a Gorgon's head. She realized then that he was right: she had indeed grown cruel. And now it was her turn to be ashamed. "Don't worry," she assured him. "I'm not about to do the bastard any favors. And he wouldn't spare me now if I could teach him how to raise the dead. But if you're going to play these kinds of games with him, be very, *very* careful. He won't spare your life just because you're Tark's nephew."

"I know," he said, rubbing the kidney that Marty had bashed. "But in this case, the game was worth the risk. We need to—"

"Not *we*," she said bluntly, "*You*. Help is still two days away. By the time it gets here, I'll be—"

Just then, a faint scraping sound registered in her ears. Footsteps. And they were headed this way. She raised a hand to Ammas, a command to stay put, then stood up and plastered herself against the wall next to the door. This could be her chance, she thought, as she listened and waited. Her only chance. The steps stopped then, but the door didn't open. Instead, a tray of food came sliding into the cell through a shielded slot at the floor. The footsteps began to recede then. She bit back disappointment, then brought Ammas's dinner to him.

"I don't want it," he said.

"Eat it anyway," she replied, and plunked the tray down in front of him.

He prodded a processed meat bar as if it were his appetite, then abruptly shoved the whole tray to the floor. It landed with a clatter that sounded louder in the dark than it would've in the light. Over that pseudo-din, he muttered, "What's the point?"

She squatted down in front of him and framed his face in her hands. "You can't give up now, Ammas," she said, in an urgent whisper. "Otherwise, both Tark and Ross will go unpunished for their crimes. And just think of all the people they've killed—RK, Tobia. Micca."

"Micca," he said, with unexpected vehemence, "is better off dead."

"How can you say that?" she demanded, although she was amazed to find herself jumping to Micca's defense. "You saw how she was after she discovered the truth about her gift. She was happy. Ecstatic. For the first time in her adult life, she knew a purpose greater than making people miserable in the name of H'Nath."

"You of all people should know better than to speak to me of H'Nath," he said, turning suddenly hostile.

The swiftness of his mood swing left her perplexed. "What do you mean by that? Is it Ni H'Nathelek for me to speak of your god now?"

He bolted upright and began to slash his hands through the air as if he were trying to brush away cobwebs that only he could see. "H'Nathelek. Ni H'Nathelek. They're just words, meaningless words."

"Wha—?"

"*I was in the hallway, Jillian.* I heard you and your brother talking." He raked her face with agonized eyes, then blurted, "H'Nath is nothing but a parasite."

Her mouth fell open, but no words came out. The first thought that came to mind was: *so that was what was bothering him.* He'd given her plenty of clues: the sickness that he'd never quite shaken and the collapse of his boyish grin, his sudden reticence and the haunted look that stole into his eyes when Micca entered a room. But she'd attributed these symptoms to stress, fear, and even love. It had never occurred to her that he might be mourning the death of a god. What a horrible ordeal to go through alone, she thought. She had made him afraid to believe, and afraid to doubt. And now he had turned to her for help. Comfort perhaps, or—stars forbid!—guidance. She didn't know what to say. Her casualties were all mortal. But as inadequate as she knew herself to be, she couldn't leave him to suffer by himself.

He was curled up on the pull-out now—a defensive huddle of elbows and knees. She sat down beside him and began to knead his shoulders. He tensed, but made no move to shrug her away.

"Ammas," she whispered, groping for words, "I'm very sorry you overheard that conversation."

"I didn't mean to," he said, sounding bitter now as well as aggrieved. "I would've rather walked into a nammaden than heard the truth about the *thing* that my people have worshipped from the dawn of our civilization."

"I understand," she crooned. "But maybe you don't know as much of the truth as you think you do. Maybe you took the right facts and jumped to the wrong conclusions." He shifted then, turning ever so slightly toward her. She took that as permission to go on. "Take those test results that you heard us talking about as an example. They prove that I now have a parasite in my head. And since I didn't have pyrokinetic abilities prior to my infection, it's logical to assume that the parasite is, in some unknown way, responsible for them. But it's possible to own that assumption and still believe in H'Nath. Because who among us can say what form a supreme being may choose to take, or what tools he may choose to work through? The test results prove nothing either way.

"There are also several other things that the tests can't explain. Like the madness that came over me at the gathering. It's said to be incurable, but I don't have it anymore. Where'd it go? And what about me happening upon Tobia in the middle of a sandstorm? How likely is that? And then there was Micca's ability to far-sense through wyrm-space. She never would've learned the true nature of her gift if she hadn't decided to come with us, and that never would've happened if things hadn't happened the way they did. Now, I've seen a fair share of coincidences in my lifetime, but never so many strung together so concisely in such a small span of time. Could a mere parasite cause all that, too?" When he didn't reply, she made one last, unpremeditated pitch. "Form is relative, Ammas. The important thing is the spirit that dwells within the form. If you can believe that, then H'Nath doesn't have to be a thousand year old lie."

He rolled over then, and scanned her face with red-rimmed eyes. It was a reading both hungry and fearful. "Do you really believe what you just said?"

She thought about that for a moment, then let out a surprised laugh and said, "As a matter of fact, I believe I do. Is that a problem?"

"You are so kind," he said, and reached out to caress the flat of her cheek. The gestured both thrilled and daunted her in a chemical sort of way. "And so much more."

His hand slid down to cup her chin. Before she could pull away, he leaned in and kissed her refabricated lips—a faint, lingering pressure that stirred nothing but memories and regrets. Afterward, he tried to pull her close. She eluded his embrace with a sorry shake of her head.

"You know what I am," she said.

"Yes, Jillian, I know what you are," he replied, with unnerving intimacy. "I also know that I'm locked in a prison cell far from home with little hope of seeing my friends and family again. My companions are dead, my uncle is a traitor, and the god that I've been raised to adore may be nothing but a fluke. You are all that is left of my heart; and before we, too, part company, I'd like to join with you, if only this once."

"But—"

He hushed her with an upraised hand. "It's not the form, but the spirit that dwells within the form that matters. Right?"

Before she could make an exception of herself, he pulled her close. Objections— physical and aesthetic technicalities— raced through her mind, but she made a conscious effort to let go of them. If he was willing, she decided, they could pretend just this once. And she knew ways to make it more convincing. Then, in a silent rush, her apprehension disappeared, caressed from the darkened back-rooms of her mind by a will not her own. Moments later, rapture took root within her, and began spread like a slow, delicious burn. She gasped. Ammas gasped, too. He was part of her now—more intimately linked than any corporeal lover. He drew her beyond the boundaries of flesh and into an otherworld of unmitigated union. And when it finally came for them to climb back into their separate shells, he was not alone in feeling faint.

Chapter 13

JILLIAN WAS TRYING to figure out a way to jimmy the door when she felt the cruiser's drive-generator strum to a lazy stop. That would be Ross putting into orbit, she guessed. And: *it wouldn't be long now.* In a way, she was glad of the impending deadline. She was getting restless here in the semi-darkness, trying to break out of an escape-proof cell. She wanted to *do* something, even if it meant dying.

Ammas shared her restlessness. Indeed, she feared that she had infected him with it during that incredible union of theirs. They'd kept nothing back from each other then— no feelings, no thoughts, no secrets. So she wasn't entirely surprised when he blurted out his position on pretending to join his uncle's conspiracy.

"I won't do it," he whispered. "I can't. I'd rather die with you."

"How sweet," she said, in a waspish tone. "But you're no good to me or anyone else dead. So just buck up and play along."

"If I do that, I'll be no better than my uncle."

"In this case, the end justifies the means, Ammas."

"I'm sure my uncle would say the same about his case."

That brought her up short. But before she had a chance to work her way past that ethical switchback, the cruiser shuddered. An instant later, she heard a muffled boom and then a cacophony of sirens. Over that din, an amplified voice urged all personnel to their stations. "This is *not* a drill."

"What's going on?" Ammas asked.

She laughed, then swept him to his feet and into a brief embrace. "We're being attacked!" she said. "Someone out there likes us."

The cruiser shuddered again, with less intensity this time. And the accompanying boom was barely audible at all. By that, she knew that the cruiser's shields were up now, and that its aggressor was either very far away or very poorly armed. Her glee gave way to apprehension. Who could've managed to catch a police cruiser unaware? Who would try, when all they were armed with was the equivalent of bare knuckles? And why wasn't Valiant returning fire? She strained her senses for the feel of cannons going off, but all she picked up was the dull crash and rumble of deflected plasma shot.

Just then, the cell-door whisked open. She whirled, then squinted at the blur that blotted out a man-sized chunk of flashing red and yellow light. Tark's features hazed into focus an instant later. "Hurry," he said, without a shred of his usual insouciance. "There isn't much time. Your brother and the others are alive and aboard your ship. If you wish to save them, you must act now."

An urge to charge past him and into the corridor tore through her. She tripped it up with a jaded thought—that would be *so* like Tark. "So I'm to be shot while trying to escape. Is that it?"

"Please, Captain," he urged, furtively glancing over his shoulder, "come with me. *Hurry. Zephyr's* first shot jammed the towing mechanism, but Ross's men are working to fix it already. And when they do, Ross is going to set your ship adrift and then blow it up. We must act before then." When Jillian didn't budge, he glanced past her at Ammas. "Please, nephew. I'm trying to save your lives." He hesitated for a moment, then added, "I know you didn't faint from the pain on the bridge today."

Before Ammas had a chance to reply, the leathery clatter of booted feet on the run pre-empted him. Then someone shouted, "There he is! You, Sand-Man—hit the deck!"

Tark made a move as if to bolt. At the same moment, the deceptively soft bark of an assault rifle defiled the air. Tark staggered backward. A look of surprise spread across his face as he clutched at the red, raw-meat hollow that had once been his chest. Then his eyes rolled back in his head, and he slumped to the floor with a heavy thud.

Although astonished by Tark's murder, the shock didn't impair Jillian's reaction time. She slung Ammas beneath the meager cover of a pull-out in one instinctive move, and flattened herself against the front wall in the next. Tark's killers were working their way down the hallway now. She could hear their boot-falls over the sirens. There were two of them hugging the near wall, one behind the other. One stopped three meters or so from the cell-door. The other crept on—a slow, circuit-wracking advance. Jillian forced herself to wait. Now that the time for action had come, she needed to pick and choose her fights.

Then an assault rifle's blackened snout appeared in the doorway.

She grabbed the muzzle with her left hand and gave it a single, powerful tug. Its startled owner came stumbling through the doorway and into her waiting fist. Plasti-steel knuckles and a bony chin collided with a hard crack. An instant later, she hit the gunman again—a vicious shot to the nose that drove splinters of bone into his brain. He released the rifle with a lurid gurgle, then dropped to the floor alongside Tark's corpse. Panicked footfalls broke out in the hall at that. Jillian shouldered the confiscated rifle, then stepped out of the cell and targeted the gunman's fleeing partner. Her aim—instinct unhampered by conscious thought—was deadly.

"Great H'Nath," Ammas said. He had crawled out from under the pull-out sometime between the first casualty and the second, and was now gaping at the corpses. His eyes were round with horror. His face was the color of ashes. "You killed them."

"That's right," she said, and then tried to hand him the rifle. "Here. You're going to need this."

"I—I can't," he said, recoiling as if she were trying to press a venomous snake into his hands. "You know that." Then he turned his gaze back to his uncle's sprawled body. "Dear god! Look at all the blood. I never knew—"

His voice trailed off then, but Jillian barely noticed. She was too busy mapping out her strategy. The way she saw it, her only hope of salvaging anything at all from this mess was to get to Ross before he got to her or *Zeph*. That meant fighting her way to the bridge. And that meant leaving Ammas here. He would only be a hindrance otherwise, a straggling distraction that she could neither disregard nor protect. He'd be safer where he was—out-of-sight and out-of-fire. She couldn't bear the thought of seeing him fall to an AP bolt.

So less than a moment after he'd stepped out of the cell, she drew him back in and then pressed him into a corner. His jaw was slack. His eyes still looked like ground-zero. On any other day, she would've stayed while the fall-out cleared. But not today. Alarms were still blaring, *Zephyr's* barrage was growing weaker, and somebody knew that Tark wasn't where he was supposed to be. All she allowed him—or perhaps herself—was a parting touch to the cheek.

"If Ross's thugs find you before I get back," she said, as she headed for the door, "tell them that you refused to go with me. Tell them you're loyal to Ross."

Her detachment seemed to siphon off some of his shock. He looked her way, then reached for her like an abandoned child. She stepped back and triggered the lock.

"Wait!" he said then, but it was too late. She was already on her way.

∾

SHE MOVED THROUGH the ship with urgent efficiency, following the route that she'd learned from that bastard Marty on their last jaunt to the bridge. It was a roundabout way, she soon realized, one designed to keep her out of sight. She figured that Ross wanted to keep her identity as close to himself as he could. The less people who knew, the less who could testify against him at a trial later. Furthermore, some of his crewmen might freak if they knew there was a cyborg on the ship. Whatever his reasons, she wasn't complaining. The main corridors would be chockful of people on full-scale battle alert right about now. She could travel farther and faster this way. And she needed to get as close to the bridge as she could before Ross discovered that she was loose. Because from then on, the going would be rough.

A lift loomed ahead—no fast-track to the bridge, but a lower-decks transport. She opted to use the service tube instead, reckoning that there'd be less chance of her running into anyone that way. And less chance of being trapped. So she climbed, monkey-quick, from one deck to the next. As she did so, she listened to the echoes of *Zeph*'s cannonade. They sounded bigger and better than life within this confined, ear-canal-like space. They filled her with fierce pride. *Way to go, RK,* she thought. And: *fuck you, Ross.* She'd bet a dozen years of pro bono work that he hadn't anticipated this little turn of events. She'd bet fifty years that he was spitting glass right now. But as much as she liked to think of it, she knew his fury wouldn't last. *Zephyr*'s shots were growing few and far between. The cannons would all be spent soon. Worse, the cruiser would be out of its detonation zone. Ross would blow it then—unless she got to the bridge first.

She crept out of the tube then. But even as she started down the new corridor, she heard a sudden noise—the sound of people on the move, weapons rattling to the meter of their unsynchronized steps. They were headed her way, too many for her to handle alone. She ducked into the nearest doorway, but apparently not fast enough. Just before the door closed after her, she heard someone hiss, "Look, over there! I thought I saw something!"

Shitshitshit. She didn't have time for a game of search-and-destroy. But even as the thought crossed her mind, she looked around for a hiding place. Nothing presented itself at first, for the room that she'd ducked into happened to be the galley. There wasn't an inch to spare amidst the food-prep appliances, and the storage compartments were all properly locked up. The only thing that resembled a bolt-hole was the walk-in cold-room at the far end of the kitchen, and that could turn into a dead-end fast if things went screwy on her—as things were wont to do these days. Still, she was in no position to be choosy. So she let herself into the locker, then wedged the door open with her feet and kept watch from the crack.

A long moment later, three of Ross's troopers infiltrated the gallery: two men, one woman. All three were armed with AP rifles. Their hyper-wary glances into every nook and corner told Jillian that they didn't know she was here. She waited until the door slid shut behind the last of them. She waited until they were all in the open, and too far away from the door to bolt. Then she kicked the locker door open and squeezed off three quick shots. Two troopers dropped: a man and the woman. The third threw himself behind the counter's edge and returned fire. One shot whistled past her and into the locker, the other slammed into the wall with a Crack! and a spray of red-hot shrapnel. Jillian targeted him again only to find that her clip was now empty. She cursed roundly, then pulled back into the walk-in. As she did so, the butt of her rifle struck something behind her that clinked a protest. She took a quick look, then did a quick double-take. Corellian champagne? It was just like Ross to have the best on hand, she thought, even in the badlands.

Then inspiration seized her.

"Hey, you out there!" she shouted. "I give up. My rifle's empty."

"Throw it out," he called back. "The cartridge in one direction, the stock in the other." She complied with elaborate care. The rifle, then its clip went skittering across the floor, stopping well beyond her reach. "Step out where I can see you," he ordered then. "Slowly. With your hands on your head."

So far, so good. She pulled her neckline down as far as it would go, then grabbed a bottle of champagne by the neck and slowly emerged from the locker. As she came into view, so did the trooper. He was crouched behind the counter with his rifle pointed at her heart. He was square-faced and swarthy, and he had definitely noticed her reconstructed décolletage.

"What's that in your hand?" he demanded, as soon as he caught a glimpse of the champagne.

She flashed him the old Jillian's most winsome smile, then held the bottle out for his inspection. "Nate and I go way back," she said. "I was hoping that he'd let this be my last request."

The trooper loosed a derisive snort, then emerged from cover. "I don't think the chief does last requests, bitch. Now set the bottle down on the floor and then hit the deck yourself."

She dropped to her knees like a petulant child, then started to set the bottle down. At the very last second, though, she chucked it at the trooper instead. He reacted to the sudden motion by firing a shot, but she was already in the process of somersaulting out of his sights. And before he could even think about getting another shot off, the heavy glass bottle hit him between the eyes. The cork popped. Champagne geysered. He stared at her for a disbelieving moment, then slowly pitched forward with a star-shaped dent in his brow. She confiscated his rifle, then headed for the door, regretting nothing but the waste of good wine.

Only then did she realize that she wasn't hearing the echoes of *Zephyr's* barrage anymore. Indeed, the whole cruiser was eerily quiet. It was, she thought, the sound of Ross looking for her. He'd be wanting to put the icing back on his cake right about now. He'd be wanting her dead.

As if in response to that thought, something slammed into her left shoulder-blade. An instant later, her left pectoral region burst forth from the front of her like magma from an erupting volcano. The whole arm went instantly limp. That made no difference to her, though. She turned and fired one-handed —*zing, zing, zing*. Two troopers dropped. A third turned and ran. *Zing*—she shot him in the back without a qualm and then continued on her way. As she ran, she marveled at her capacities as a killing machine. It was easy, a mere reflex. She was the legend of Targon reborn. But unlike Targon, she knew what she was doing, and that she could stop at any time.

And Ross had tried to kill her first.

She was approaching the secured lift now, and judging by the number of voices that she was hearing, Ross had beefed up the watch. Any hopes that she might've had about him not knowing that she was on the loose faded then, but she didn't let that turn her back. She had to get to the bridge. *Had to*. And with only one arm, the only way there was via that lift.

The only question left was: how was she supposed to take the guards? There'd be at least four of them against one of her at very close range—only a berserker would go for those odds. She needed an edge. Or a miracle. Or, she thought, as inspiration struck yet again—perhaps a little of both. So she drew as close to the security station as she could without being seen, then clenched her will and imagined herself on fire from head to toe.

With a silent whoosh, it was so.

She let out a blood-curdling howl then. A moment later, she went staggering into the open, begging for help. The sentries leveled their rifles at her, but didn't shoot. Their faces were a collage of surprise and horror. And before they had a chance to realize that she wasn't really burning, she shot three of them. The fourth threw his weapon down and raised his hands. As she bore down on him, shedding as she went, she recognized him as the guard who'd averted his eyes from her earlier. She decided to turn him into an ally— whether he wanted the job or not.

"Just do what I say," she told him, "and you won't get hurt."

"What *are* you?" he asked in reply.

"Crazy," she said, and ordered him to turn around and face the lift. He did so slowly, like a man expecting to be shot in the back. She pressed her rifle into his ribs, but then slid two-thirds of the barrel past his underarm and told him to hold it there. When he did as he was told without a fuss, she put him in a mild chokehold.

"Feed your access code to the security grid," she told him then. "Get it right the first time or else." He did as he was told. "If there's anyone in the lift when it gets here," she said, "I'm going to shoot them. If you try to warn them in any way, I'll pop you, too."

"I understand," he said.

As it happened, though, the car was empty. She tapped the quot'tl bead that Saj had given her as if in thanks for the bit of luck, then muscled her hostage aboard. Thirty seconds later, she hurried him into the bridge's antechamber

"Hold your fire," she warned, as the security detail moved to cut them off, "or I'll snap his neck."

The guards exchanged a look, then raised their rifles and started firing. One bolt thudded into her hostage's chest. Another took him in the groin. As he slumped dead in her chokehold, she thought, *so much for allies*, and was truly sorry for having caused his death. But that didn't stop her from using his corpse as a shield as she sprinted across the antechamber. She felt one shot smack into it, then another. Then the airlock to the bridge whisked open and she went charging in. As she did so, Ross swiveled his chair around to see what was going on.

Their eyes met. His backbone stiffened with alarm. But before he could call for her arrest, she slung her human shield at the comm-tech and then launched herself at him. The pained grunt that he let out when she landed gave her a visceral sort of pleasure. So did grabbing the neck that she'd wrung so many times in her dreams. She gave it a good, hard squeeze as the security team rushed onto the bridge, and then said, "Tell these boys to drop their pieces, Nate. Maybe they'll listen to you. Then again, maybe they'll shoot you like they did the last poor bastard, and save me the trouble."

"Do as she says," he told them, trying to sound dignified instead of half-strangled.

"And she says *disarm*," she said. "You know the drill—clips in one direction, rifles in the other. You, too, bridge crew," she added, as the troopers grudgingly began to comply. "When you're done, leave your stations and join the security team over there on the staging area."

A clattered ensued—the sound of various bits of weaponry hitting the floor. Then the comm-tech got up and started toward the staging area. Something about him snagged Jillian's attention. Unlike his fellow techs, who were broadcasting anger, resentment, and uncertainty on all frequencies, he was sauntering along with his hands in his pockets as if this were just another day. So she told him to hold up and clamp his hands over his head, then turn a slow circle for her. When he balked, she squeezed a "Do it!" out of Ross.

The tech reddened, but followed her instructions. The last vestiges of his phony nonchalance burst into rancor just even the laser pistol holstered to his left hip came into her view.

"Set it on the floor," she told him. "Now kick it this way."

The weapon skated across the floor in skittish circles, then came to a stop by her feet. She forced Ross to lean over and pick it up. "By the barrel, thank you," she said, as he reached for the grip. "That's right. Now put it in my hand." As soon as he did so, she switched from a stranglehold to gunpoint so she wouldn't have to go cheek-to-cheek with the bastard until the very end. "If anyone else had the same idea," she said then, "I would advise you to reconsider it *right now*. Because if I catch you holding, I'm going to shoot this man with your weapon."

Two more pistols hit the floor. She cast Ross a look of mock horror. "I've never seen so much hardware on a bridge before. What are you guys— pirates or something?"

"Or something," he drawled.

"All right then," she said, when everyone was massed in the staging area. "On the count of three, you're all going to go charging out of here. Your sneaky-pete comm-tech is going to lead the way. Ready? One—"

"But I could get shot!" the comm-tech bleated.

"That's definitely a possibility," she admitted cheerfully. "But if you refuse to go, I'll definitely kill you where you stand. Your choice. Two—" She stretched the count out as far as it would go, then added, "One last thing before you run. Tell all your mates that I'll blow this whole ship if they try to rush me. I'm RIM-sick, so I really don't give a fuck if we all die.

"Three."

The crowd surged toward the airlock, pushing the comm-tech ahead of it. "Don't shoot!" he shouted, as the door whisked open. "Crewmen coming through." A shot rang out then, but it must've missed or just nicked him, because the last thing that Jillian heard before the door slid shut again was his voice. "I said—hold your fuckin' fire!"

"Quite a pragmatic bunch you've got there, Nate," she remarked. "You must be *so* proud." Then, before he could answer, she gave him a hard shove. "Now get out of my chair."

As soon as he stood up, she kicked his feet out from under him. He landed on his back. She flipped him onto his stomach with another kick, then planted a boot across the back of his neck. A voice urged her to step down then, step down and crush him like the vermin he was, but she couldn't bring herself do it—not in cold blood. The mere thought generated an almost palpable feeling of discomfort in her. So she just kicked him instead: once before she sat down, then again afterward. Then she clamped his head to the floor with her boot. It was, she thought, a surprisingly satisfying act.

"Give me your access codes," she said then.

"I could," he said, in a mushy, half-muffled voice. "But then I'd have to kill you."

"I figured you'd say as much." She set the pistol down on the console, and began to scroll through his command files. Almost as an afterthought, she jammed her synthetic toe into his temple

"Ow! Damn you, Jillie! That hurt."

"That's *Captain D'Lange* to you," she said, and kicked him again.

"*Ow!* Stop that. I'm starting to think that your comment about being RIM-sick wasn't just a bluff."

"I woke up from reconstruction with the RIMs," she said, telling him the absolute truth and then one thing more. "What I am is what you've made of me."

"And is that really so bad?" he asked. "I mean, look at you. Look at that hole in your shoulder. A year ago, you would've been already been dead for an hour from that. Now, you're merely inconvenienced."

"Again, thanks to you," she said, and then blurted, "Oh, good," as she found what she'd been looking for. "Just like it's done on my ship."

She transferred scanner-output to the command console. The first thing that came on-screen was a surveillance grid. It contained a solitary, off-kilter blip that could only be her ship. A side-bar graphic accompanied the grid. It showed how much time the cruiser had left in *Zeph*'s detonation zone: twelve point two six minutes. That would do for now, she thought, and began lowering the cruiser's defenses as quickly as she could find them. Ross seemed to have a remarkably good feel for his ship, for as soon as she dropped the shields, he knew it.

"What do you think you're doing?" he asked.

"I can't blow this rig up without the proper access codes," she replied, "but I can blow *Zephyr*. By remote," she added, thinking, *what was one more lie at this point?* "And if *Zeph* goes, we go. Now, let me see if I can get us a little closer."

"And what if your rodent-brother decides to fire a few shots our way?" he asked, as she fiddled with the helm controls. "He already took out the tow-beam. Another shot to the same spot could breach the hull."

"That would just suck, wouldn't it?" she said, enjoying the chance to mock him. But while the probability of RK having any ammunition left was low, and the probability of him hitting the same spot twice was next to nil, she transferred comm-function over to her console and placed a call to *Zephyr*. When no one responded to her ping, she was automatically rerouted to the message nexus. Mostly sure that Roadkill was screening, she went ahead with what she had to say.

"This is Captain Jillian D'Lange, calling from the bridge of the unidentified guild cruiser on your screen. At the moment, I am in control of this vessel." Ross snorted at that. She mashed his face into the floor like a spent nic-stick, and then continued. "Do *not* shoot unless I give you the word—"

Just then, the lift doors parted.

Quicker than thought, she grabbed the pistol. An instant later, Ammas stumbled onto the bridge. His hair was disheveled. Blood trickled from his mouth and one nostril. And the muzzle of an AP rifle nestled in his ear. He cast her a look teeming with regrets, then winced as his captor reined him in by the hair.

"Let the chief go," Marty said, leering at her over Ammas's shoulder.

"Eat shit," she replied.

Marty gave Ammas a shake as if to make him more visible to her. "You know me, bitch. You *know* I'll kill him. And an AP bolt to the head is messy. Are you sure you want to see your friend's brains splattered all over the bridge?"

"I'm sure they'll look great next to Ross's," she said.

"That's tough talk, Jillie," Ross said then, "but I know you better. You've always been sentimental about your friends. Unfortunately, my security advisor doesn't have that problem. He won't even bat an eyelash if you decide to pop me. He'll just go ahead and drop the kid."

"So what's stopping him now?"

"I haven't paid him for the month yet." He paused for a moment, then said, "You know you can't win this, Jillie. You *know* it. But if you give this thing up now, I'll spare the kid. I give you my word on that. And knowing what you do, you have to admit that that's a pretty fair deal."

She rolled her eyes, thinking, *as if.* As if he'd keep his fucking word. As if she'd just go belly-up and surrender. That would be a crime against everybody who'd already died by Ross's hand, and against everybody who was still slated for slaughter. But sweet, suffering mother! She didn't want to be the one to sacrifice Ammas. She didn't want to see him die. It was as Ross said: she cared, and Marty did not.

"How 'bout it, Jillian?" Ross prompted. "Are you going to let me up?"

"Don't do it," Ammas said then, in a strained, faraway voice. "This man cannot hurt me."

She took a hard, fast look at him then. His eyes were focused on some distant point. The color had drained from his face. Marty had probably mistaken these for signs of fear, she supposed.

But she knew better. She recognized the look. And now it set her free.

With a hard, downward cut, she cracked the back of Ross's head with the butt of the pistol. He let out a moan, and went suddenly limp. She started across the bridge then. She had Marty's forehead in the pistol's sights. His sneer served as a model for her own.

"Let him go," she said. But her eyes dared him not to.

He went with the dare—she could tell by the cruel turn that his mouth took then. But when he tried to squeeze a round off, something went wrong. She suspected that his trigger-finger wouldn't work. He tried again, to no avail. Confusion turned the cruelty in his expression to fear.

"Technical difficulties?" Jillian asked, as she closed in on him.

He sputtered a curse, then shoved Ammas toward her and bolted. She sidestepped the still-entranced Tolq with a passing *sorrysorrysorry* and went racing after Marty. The door was already starting to open for him. She could see an anxious crowd milling in the antechamber beyond.

"Attack!" Marty urged his mates. "We can have everything back if you rush her."

At that, all of the grief and rage and hate that he'd inspired in Jillian came roaring to the forefront of her mind. It was a volatile combination. She was in a volatile mood. She grabbed him by the back of his flight-suit as he was clearing the door. The fire that already shooting down her arm quickly infested his clothes. He started to flap and squirm a moment later.

"Stay back," Jillian warned his horrified shipmates. "Stay back, or you'll all go up, too."

She dragged Marty back toward the staging area then. No one came rushing to his rescue. Indeed, no one moved at all—leastwise not while the door was still open. And by the time it slid shut again, he was already beyond any mate's help. His clothes were gone, reduced to ash. His flesh was shimmery and discolored, semi-molten fat on the bone. He tried to hit the deck and thereby smother the flames, but she was still beside herself with rage and wouldn't permit it. She caught him by the arm, then hauled him back to his feet as he screamed from the pain. Then she whirled him around and got right in his face. His fire didn't bother her. She was ablaze, too.

"This is how Denny died," she said. "This is how I died. How do you like it?"

His answer was a pathetic mewl.

Her fury curdled all at once, turning into profound disgust. She scorned him with one last look, then pushed him out of her way. As she did so, the fire disappeared from both of them. Marty whimpered again, and then collapsed with a meaty, well-done thud. His skin was all blackened and blistered now. His hands had constricted into claws. He lay there on the floor in a twisted, smoking heap—and Jillian didn't care. She hated him more than ever for that. She hated herself a little, too, for stooping to his terrorist tactics.

That heavy-fisted feeling gave way to a horrible sense of fatigue. The feeling was so intense, she actually had phantom symptoms: nausea and muscle weakness, even some motor impairment. She tried to shake it off, but it was insidious stuff. She found herself thinking about sitting down instead.

Only then did she notice that Ross had resumed his seat at the command console again. He had Marty's discarded rifle now. She wasn't close enough to make a grab for it. And he was too close to miss.

"Game over, Jillian," he said, flashing his perfect white teeth.

"Your skull must be thicker than I thought," she said, stalling for time and perhaps inspiration.

"You're full of surprises, too," he conceded, glancing toward Marty's smoldering body. "Did you learn that little trick on Tolq, or is it a standard feature for cyborgs these days?"

She shrugged, refusing to arm him with that kind of information. His toothy smile turned wistful. "It's a pity I can't trust you. We would've made a formidable team. Tell me—are you any good in bed anymore?"

"Try me."

He laughed, then shouldered the rifle. "Good-bye, Jillian."

She tensed, intending to rush him—an all-or-nothing gamble with very bad odds. But before she could work up the ambition to move, a high-frequency hum filled her ears. Then a thin red stream of light shot past her and punched a tidy little hole in Ross's head. He slumped forward in his chair. The rifle slid from his hands. She fetched it, switched it to stand-by, and then slowly turned toward her unlikely savior. Ammas was staring at her from the corner into which he had crawled. His eyes were round with shock.

"I almost couldn't do it," he said, as she approached.

"But you did," she said. She eased the pistol from his trembling hand, then kissed him gently on the lips. "And I thank you."

Chapter 14

THE COMM-BOARD BEGAN to ping—incoming call. Jillian wanted to ignore it. She wanted it to go away. Then, because she knew exactly how far she was from being in a position to indulge such wants, she headed for the command console. Once she got there, she shoved Ross's surprised-looking corpse out its seat and sat down in its stead. Sitting down did nothing to ease her fatigue.

"Captain Jillian D'Lange here," she said. "State your name, and the reason for your call."

"You *know* my name already," a familiar voice replied. "I'm calling to see why the hell you cut me off."

"I didn't hang up on you, RK," she said, "Ross did. We had a situation here."

"Oh. You resolve it?"

She glanced from one corpse to the next. "Sort of. Ross is dead. But I still have a whole crew of hostiles waiting for me on the lower decks."

"How is it that they haven't stormed the bridge yet?"

"They think I'm the second coming of Targon The Terror."

"I wonder what could've given them that idea?"

She was about to make some flippant reply when the surveillance grid caught her eye. And it caught her eye because a new blip had just popped up on the screen. It was big and fast, a real space-eater. The sidebar graphic identified it as another union cruiser.

"Shitshitshit," she said. "RK, you seeing what I'm seeing?"

"Yeah," he said, after a pause. "But that's a good thing, right?"

"Only if it's on our side. Ross was planning to invade Tolq right about now. That could be his reinforcements."

"Great." He sulked for a microsecond, then added, "So now what?"

"If worst comes to worst, you're going to have to blow *Zeph*," she warned him. "The access code is—"

"Your mother's birthday," he interjected. "Yeah, I know." He paused again, and then added, "Have I told you just how much this trip has sucked yet?"

"That's a negative, *Zephyr*," she replied. "Now play dead until you hear from me. Cruiser out."

She lapsed back into her seat as if it were a wallow. RK was right, she thought. This run had been brutal, every step of the way. And her next move was a fuckin' beaut. She brought Valiant's shields back to max-cap then, and armed a round of Sunbursts. It was, she thought, a fairly formidable threat display. She could only hope that the other cruiser was sufficiently daunted by it.

"Check the other stations for stim-tab stashes," she told Ammas then. "They'll either be under the console, or in a pocket on the side of the seat."

He found a supply almost immediately, and then watched with worried eyes as she chewed down a whole packet. "Are you unwell?"

She shrugged as if it were no big deal for a cyborg to be fatigued. "I'm just a little whipped, is all," she said. "Must be time for a tune-up."

"That's possible," he supposed, and then glanced toward Marty's blackened body. "It's also possible that you're feeling the aftereffects of H'Nath's fire. I have never seen it used in such a way. I pray that I never see the like again."

"I'm in no hurry for a repeat, either,"she assured him. "But it was like the fire had a mind of its own."

She didn't want to think about what *that* might mean. But as the blip ticked closer and closer then still, it occurred to her that having a god wouldn't be such a bad thing—if he did requests. Like: *make that freakin' cruiser go away.* It kept on coming, though. And it wasn't running ID. Not a good sign, she thought, and hailed the ship as soon as it came into range. She went with audio only so the other commander wouldn't be able to see how thin her bluff was.

"Attention, unidentified cruiser," she said. "Your presence here in restricted space represents multiple violations of Galactic Council treaty. I am ordering you to lower your shields and power down. Your commander-in-chief is hereby ordered to surrender immediately."

A moment's silence was shattered by a furious outburst. "This is President Barim speaking, comm-tech. Patch me through to the commander of that vessel at once. Ross, what the hell is going on here?"

Jillian had no doubt about the speaker's identity. No one could duplicate Barim's resonant baritone so perfectly. But she had to wonder why he was here. Had he heard the SOS and decided to break a whole stack of laws for one of his least favorite associates? Or was he rendezvousing with Ross? *Barim could be part of the problem*—that's what Denny had said. *Shitshitshit.* All she wanted to do was stand down and get some sleep.

"This is Captain Jillian D'Lange," she announced instead. "Nathan Ross is dead, Mr. President, and I'm in control of the bridge. Order your crew to power down."

This time, the response was immediate. "What's the meaning of this, D'Lange?"

"Nathan Ross was responsible for Denis Latimer's murder," she said. "He was also guilty of numerous acts of piracy, and a grand count of conspiracy against the Tolq government. I suspect you of being involved in these matters, too."

"Me? Involved?" he blustered. "What a preposterous idea. This is the first I've heard of any of this."

"And yet here you are, running without ID in restricted space, at just about the time that Ross planned to be here."

"I was looking for *you*, Captain," he said, waxing irritable now. "In case no one told you, you're supposed to be MIA. Now suppose you tell me what's going on."

"Suppose you surrender to me first," she said, sticking to her guns simply because that was all she had left.

"And if I don't?"

"I'll go at you with all I've got. I'll take both of these ships out if I have to."

"That's RIM-talk," he rumbled, and his deep-sea voice developed whitecaps. "I'd have to be mad to lower my defenses to a RIM-sick cyborg who's already taken control of one cruiser under mysterious circumstances. You'd kill us all."

"If I was RIM-sick," she said, "I'd be halfway down your throat already. As it is, I'm going to ask you nicely one more time. *Please* stand down. *Please* drop your shields. *Please* give me a reason not to take drastic action."

A long silence ensued. If she'd been able to sweat, she would've broken out in a cold one now. If she'd had nerves, they would've all been jangling. As it was, she rolled Saj's quot'tl bead between her forefinger and thumb, and hoped to hell that she was doing the right thing. If she guessed wrong—well, she remembered what happened the last time she'd pulled a tiger's tail.

Just then, the side-bar graphic on the surveillance screen flashed an update: the cruiser had killed its drive-generator and lowered its shields. She instantly did the same thing. For all she'd wanted was for Barim to show some faith. It made her much more inclined to return the favor.

"Are you screwing with me, D'Lange?" he asked then, reverting to an irritable tone. "Because if you are, I'll eat your first-class captaincy rating for breakfast, and have your refabricated ass in court before noon."

She smiled at the threat. That was Barim all the way: arrogant and overbearing and thoroughly up-front. He was incapable of sweet-talking her. She trusted that.

"I've got a full complement of renegade spacers below-decks, Mr. President," she told him, "and no one to take care of the problem. So why don't you send over a clean-up detail—ASAP? And while you're at it, send a shuttle around to *Zephyr*. There are a few people aboard who need rescuing. I'll let them know you're coming."

"Captain—" Barim said, imbuing both syllables with warning.

"You want to talk? Come and see me," she said. "Valiant out."

Ammas caught her attention then. He was holding his sleeve over his mouth and nose. When he realized that she was looking at him, his eyes turned worried, like those of a child who's just been caught nicking gluco-cookies. "Are we in trouble?"

"No more than usual," she replied with a snort, and then placed a call to *Zephyr*. As before, it was rerouted to the message nexus. "*Zephyr*, it's me, Jillian. Acknowledge, please." The comm remained silent. "It's OK, RK, this is your official all's-clear." Still no response. Pressure leaks came to mind then, and life-supports failing with no warning. "Roadkill," she barked then, "if you don't respond in the next five seconds, I'm going to tell everyone at Boom's that you're still a virgin."

"They'd never believe it," came his familiar sneer. "They all know that I've done it with you at least a hundred times."

Ammas shot her a horrified look. She assured him otherwise with a shake of her head, then proceeded to bring her brother up to date. When she was done, she said, "I'll see you soon, OK?"

"Anything you say, Capt'n," he said. "*Zephyr* out."

❦

THE DOOR TO the bridge snapped open, spilling a team of troopers onto the bridge. The first thing they did was ID themselves: "Housekeeping, Captain. Don't shoot." Then two out of the three men doubled over and gagged. The third one pressed his sleeve to his nose, then sank to a crouch alongside of Marty's corpse. A moment later, he looked to Jillian. "Sec-tech Guzman here, Captain," he said. "Do you know who this was?" She nodded. "A murderer."She saw the that's-not-what-I-meant dart across his face. He didn't say it, though. She didn't know why. Maybe the stench of seared flesh was distracting him. Or maybe it was the ragged, corsage-like hole in her shoulder. Maybe he was thinking: *uh-oh, cyborg. The poor bitch.* She didn't hold it against him.

"His name was Marty Conrad," she said. "Feel free to bag him before he causes a scrubber melt-down. I have another body over here, too."

Another team of troopers strode onto the bridge then. A short, balding man with penetrating blue eyes and a hawkish nose followed on their bootstraps. He was wearing a flak jacket and a sidearm, but he had his arms tucked behind him as if he were on a casual tour of inspection.

"Gawdamn," he said, as the charnel smell hit him. "Somebody turn the scrubbers up in here. And get that thing out of here—on the double," he added, pointing to Marty's corpse. Then, as his men rushed to his bidding, he turned to Jillian. "You've made quite a mess of this ship, D'Lange," he said, as he approached the command console. "I hope your explanation is in good order."

"You got here fast," she remarked, refusing to be brow-beaten. "Is the battle for the below-decks over then?"

"Mostly," he replied, with a careless shrug. "It seems that even the worst case of space rot prefers rehabilitation on a penal colony to immediate execution. If it were up to me, though, I'd maroon the whole lot of them on an airless—" He came to Ross's body then. His scowl turned thoughtful. "You tag him?"

She shook her head, then gestured to Ammas, who had instinctively closed ranks with her. "President Barim, allow me to introduce Ammas su Xamar, heir of Xamar, and nephew to the late Tark cis Xamar."

Barim's filter-feeder eyebrows arched as he took in the bedraggled, bloodstained Tolq, but his surprise had a short half-life. "I'm honored to make your acquaintance, sir," he said, offering Ammas a formal smile and an outstretched hand. "My apologies for any abuse that you might've suffered at my *ex-*chief of security's hand."

"You are most kind," Ammas replied. "And I assure you, everything that Captain D'Lange has told you about that man—and my uncle—is true."

"Well," Barim said, as he waved his sec-tech down, "she hasn't really told me all that much as of yet." Then, as Guzman began to bag Ross's body, he added, ""But I had my suspicions—leastwise about Ross. I just needed someone to smoke him out for me."

At that, Jillian rounded on the man like a gunboat turret. *"What?"*

"What do you want me to do with the commander, sir?" Guzman asked then.

"Vent him," Barim said. "In front of his crew."

As soon as the sec-tech was out of her line of fire, Jillian launched another round. "You bastard. You used me as bait."

He wagged a reproving finger at her. "You set yourself up with your mule-headed ways, D'Lange. I simply monitored the situation. And when Ross decided to Valiant out for *maneuvers* right after your brother's SOS came in, I knew I had him."

"Then where the hell were you when *Zeph* was getting pounded?"

"I was about to ask you the same thing," he said. "We couldn't have been more than four hours behind Ross, but by the time we got here, everyone was gone. We spent the past thirty-six hours sweeping this system for you only to receive word that your ship was putting out another SOS in a completely different sector of space. We were just on our way to investigate when you pulled us over.

"Care to explain that?"

"I'll give you a full and complete report once we get back to Circe's II," she told him, too weary and resentful to give him what he wanted now. "For now, suffice it to say that four hours wasn't a close enough margin."

"So it would seem," he said, and then shot her a sly, sideways glance. "I'm going to have to shake down my whole organization now, you know." At her shrug, he added, "I could use some help—help that I can trust."

"Like I said, I'll make a full report."

"I think you could make a more substantial contribution, D'Lange. I think you should become my new Chief of Security. The job offers top pay, the best equipment, and a fair amount of adventure."

She twitched him an insincere smile. "Sorry, Mr. President, but I'm a first-class freighter captain, not a headhunter. All I want to do is put my life back in order and get to work."

His gaze shifted toward the surveillance grid. Hers followed. For a moment, they stared at the sorry little blip that was *Zephyr*. Then a phantom smile tugged at the corners of his mouth, and he turned suddenly solicitous. "You must be tired after such an ordeal. I'm sure I can accommodate you and the rest of your crew aboard my ship. Or, if you'd rather, you can stay here and assume your new commission."

"I don't want the job, Barim," she said, straining the words through gritted teeth.

"There's no need to decide right away," he went on, as if he hadn't heard. "You can give me an answer later—perhaps after you've talked with your creditors."

Her jaw dropped, unhinged by incredulity and then outrage. All she could think to say was, "You are *the* pushiest bastard known to man."

"I know," he said, surprisingly smug. "And you're as stubborn as a tick. I think we'll work well together."

"I don't want the job," she insisted.

But she thought about it all the way back to Barim's cruiser.

જા

THE PROMISED ACCOMMODATIONS were strictly military issue: four bodies per plain gray room, with very little space for anything else. There were plenty of rooms to choose from, for Barim had sent half of his crew to man the other cruiser, but Ammas wanted to bunk with Jillian. Jillian didn't like the idea.

"Go and find one of the others if you want to share space," she said. "I'm used to rooming alone."

"I don't want to share space with any of the others," he said. "I want to be with you."

She ground her teeth against a sharp reply, then chose a room at random and went in. One of the live-ins had hung a mirror on the far wall. It now held her reflection.

And what a horrific reflection it was. She was flecked with dried blood and bits of gore. Her hair was matted, too. But that was nothing compared to the dish-sized hole in her shoulder. Jagged flaps of syntheskin curled outward from the wound like the petals of some syntheskin-colored flower; the protruding wires looked like stamens. And if she squinted, she could see right through herself. It was an eerie perspective, and one that did not sit well with her. This was *not* what Ammas wanted to be with, she thought. She had to make him see that here and now.

So she began to shuck off her outfit. She wanted to get it off quickly—to prove a point. But the job was easier said than done with only one arm, and she soon got tangled up with herself. And the harder she tried to free herself, the worse the snarl became. She was on the verge of shredding the uniform out of sheer frustration and spite when Ammas stepped in, uninvited, with a helping hand. She didn't thank him for his effort. Indeed, she went on ignoring him until she was stripped bare. Then, before her courage could falter, she turned around to face him.

"So what do you think?" she asked, half-expecting him to turn and run screaming from the room.

He looked her up and down—slowly, critically, taking in every scratch and dint in her reconstructed body. He was quiet for so long, she began to feel a bit foolish. Finally, she prompted him with a sharp-edged, "Well? Answer me, Ammas."

"What can I say that you don't already know?"

Her annoyance skyrocketed. "Look at me, you bog-headed son of a Tolq. I've got wires sticking out all over the place. Doesn't that bother you?"

"Under the circumstances, no," he said, remaining perfectly calm in the face of her discomposure. "I find the sight of blood and bones infinitely more disturbing." And before she could serve him up another slice of harsh reality, he framed her face between his hands and said, "I care for you, Jillian. And despite your attempts to get me to reject you, I know that you care for me. This should be a cause for celebration, not grief."

She pulled away from him. "It's better for us to endure a little grief now than to let the attachments we share grow any stronger. Because saying good-bye will hurt far worse later on."

"Then don't say it," he told her.

As if it were that simple, she thought. As if that were all it would take. *The man could be so freakin' naive sometimes.* But because he was a decent man, and because she did indeed care for him, she began to point out the things that he'd surely overlooked.

"I'm a spacer, Ammas. I can't change that about myself any more than I can change the fact that I'm cyborg. You, on the other hand, belong to Tolq. Your people will need you in the days to come, as they will someday need your heirs. And cyborgs don't come equipped for breeding."

"So?" he asked, and then pinched her lips closed before she could respond. "You forget: our minds have touched. I know you cannot stay with me on Tolq because it's not in your nature to stay anywhere for too long. But I also know that you'll come back from time to time, because you are a child of H'Nath now, and he will pull you home. On such occasions, I'll be on hand to meet your shuttle and then we'll be together until you decide to leave again. As for my heirs—if they're meant to be, they will be. And I'll make sure that she who bears them does not begrudge you your place in my heart."

"But it—"

She meant to say *won't work*, but he pinched her lips shut before she could get the words out. "Isn't my way better than the one that you've envisioned?" he asked, looking her straight in the eye. "Or must all your endings be unhappy?"

Up until then, it hadn't occurred to her that they could be anything else. *Always expect the worst,* Myla had said, *and all your surprises will be pleasant ones.* Jillian wondered if this counted as one of those surprises. She wondered if she could let herself count it as one. It was such a risk. And even she had limits as to the amount of pain she could take.

He touched her mind then—a fleeting reminder of what could be. All she had to do was trust it, she told herself. All she had to do was believe. And all of a sudden, that didn't seem so very hard. She kissed him then, on the mouth, because it seemed like the human thing to do. A moment later, a crisp rap at the door startled them apart.

"Who's there?" she called.

"Just a couple of horndogs looking for a good time at a reasonable price," came the reply. Although pitched an octave lower, she recognized the voice as her brother's.

"Just a tic, I'll be right there," she said, and then looked around the room for some kind of cover-up. Her unitard was out—she suspected that it smelled as foul as it looked. And there wasn't a blanket in sight. So she tugged open the nearest locker and pulled out the first thing she grabbed. It turned out to be a robe. Ammas had to help her into it. He did so with a broad, sugar-daddy grin. The door rattled again.

"I hope you don't embarrass easily," she said, and then hit the lock release.

Roadkill was the first one through the door. As soon as his lacquered gaze fell on Jillian and Ammas, he broke into a leer. "What's this, sister dear—a pretty, young boy to keep your gears greased? You *have* been busy, haven't you?"

The tips of Ammas's ears turned scarlet—just as Jillian

thought they would. She flashed him a smug, I-told-you-so smile. Or maybe it was a get-used-to-it grin. Then she pulled RK into an awkward, one-armed embrace. It was, she realized, the first time she'd ever done so. That was probably why it seemed so weird.

"You feel pretty good," he said, and then grinned at Ammas. "Beats a bio-plastic blow-up doll by a mile, hey, Ace?"

Jillian smacked him upside the head—a friendly, light-hearted swat that felt more comfortable than the hug. Then she noticed Micca and Tobia. They were standing in the doorway, huddled together like gate-crashers at some exotic party. The priestess came in at Jillian's urging, but Tobia didn't budge. He was looking past Jillian, past Ammas, as if he were expecting somebody to come strolling out of one of the lockers. His expression was a mixture of hope and fear. All at once, Jillian understood why.

"Oh, Tobia," she said, and he tensed like a foot-soldier who's just heard a mine go click beneath his heel. "I'm so sorry," she went on. "I should've sent word ahead to you. Tark was shot while helping Ammas and me to escape. He's dead."

The color drained from the Tolq's face, exposing a constellation of tiny scars. He clenched his eyelids. He gritted his teeth. Then, as Micca folded him into an embrace, he buried his face in the cushion of her shoulder and cried. Wracked by ambivalent feelings, Jillian looked away.

"We owe our lives to Tark," Roadkill said then, a hollow tribute. "It was his idea to send the shuttle out as a decoy while we hid ourselves aboard *Zeph*. *The shuttle won't be able to get far enough away to escape detection*, he said. *And if we're on it when Ross comes after it, we'll all die. I say we stay here instead, and send the shuttle out unmanned. Nate will believe me when I tell him that all of you were aboard when he destroyed it.*

"I didn't trust him at first," RK admitted, "especially when he got to the part about contacting Ross. But he said that that was the only way to stop him from blowing *Zeph*— and you—up on the spot. That sounded reasonable at the time, and since none of us were keen on leaving you behind anyway, we decided to go along with his plan."

"You could've let me know," she said.

"Sorry," he said, with an unrepentant shrug, "but we didn't have time to argue with you. And Tark said that your shock would clinch his story."

"It did that," she granted, in a semi-caustic tone, "leastwise for a little while. But if you were hiding on *Zeph* all this time, then how'd you know when to begin the attack? I'm sure Tark didn't have access to Ross's comm."

"He used his gift to contact Tobia," Micca said.

Tobia stirred then, moved to sing his father's praises. "It was a prodigious effort. Mind-speakers aren't noted for their range, yet he reached all the way across open space to reach me. I remember the message well: *the time is now, my son, and may H'Nath guide your hearts and hands.*" He faltered, bogged down by another wave of grief, but then forced himself to continue. "It didn't occur to me that those might be his last words to me. He had walked the desert seven times and come back every time. I just assumed that H'Nath would choose to send him back this time, too."

"Not even H'Nath can do much about an AP bolt to the chest," Jillian said. "But if it's any consolation to you, he died instantly, and knew no pain."

"Thank you, Jillian," he replied. "That actually is comforting in its own sad little way." His bloodshot eyes turned wistful then. "My poor, misguided father—murdered by his own friends. And all he ever wanted was for Tolq to take its place in the modern age." He shifted again, this time to entreat Micca. "Will you lead us through the Prayers for The Dead? I know Tark seemed ungodly at times, but H'Nath never fled his heart."

"It will be my honor to lead you," she replied.

Jillian and Roadkill exchanged a look, then headed for the door. Micca was quick to say, "You two are welcome to join us, if you so choose."

"Maybe later," Jillian said. For she had not yet to come to terms with the damage that Tark had done to her trust, and until she did that, if she ever did, her sympathies were with the living rather than the dead. "Right now, I'm in desperate need of a shower."

"Do you require my help?" Ammas asked, glancing at her shoulder.

"Your assistance is always appreciated," she replied. "But if you wish to stay here and pray, then please do so. RK can cover for you."

She expected him to join her. For he, too, had been abused by Tark. And he, too, had had his faith trampled. So she was surprised when he caressed her with a thought and said, "I'll see you later then."

Surprised and surprisingly pleased.

"You got it bad for that one, don't you, Jillie?" RK said, as they went in search of the lavatory.

She nodded.

He snorted. "A cyborg and a Tolq—now that'll stir a few tongues down on the docks." Then he stopped dead in his tracks, as if he'd just heard a click beneath his heel. "We *are* going back to Station, aren't we?"

She studied him for a moment. Delicate lines fanned from the corners of his eyes like spokes of distress. His mouth was taut with worry. He hadn't always been this easy to read, she thought. It seemed that this run had changed everyone in one way or another. Perhaps every*thing*, too.

"Yes, we're going back to Station," she said.. "But to tell you the truth, I have no idea what we're going to do once we get there. *Zeph*'s no good for anything but scrap at the moment. And my credit's shot."

"Jillie—"

"Barim kindly pointed that out to me during the course of our last conversation," she continued, too wound up to stop now. "He also offered me a job—as his new Chief of Security. I told him I wasn't interested, but so far, he's not taking 'no' for an answer. The pushy bastard. I hate that about him. None of this would've happened if he'd been just a tad less arrogant."

"Get real, Jillie," RK jeered then, shades of his old self re-emerging. "You were marked for something like this from the moment you woke up from reconstruction. But like I was saying—"

"You're right," she admitted. "I guess I'm just trying to avoid the issue at hand. Which is: do I take the job or not? It pays well enough. And an advance on my salary might keep *Zeph* from the salvagers. I could take you on as crew, too, although you'd have to conform to regs and—"

"None of this is really necessary, Jillie," he drawled then.

The condescension she heard in his voice peeved her. Because as appalling as the thought of working for Barim was to her, she was almost ready to take the hit and do it— not just for her sake, but for his and *Zephyr*'s, too. The very least he could do was show a little respect. Or gratitude.

"And why's that?" she asked tartly. "Do you know of a better way to stave off our impending poverty?"

"As matter of fact, I do," he said. "And if you'd shut your reconstructed flap for a minute, I'd be glad to fill you in."

Now peevishness gave way to true affront. She drew herself up to her full height, and stared down at him as if he were a bug in need of crushing. But her brother seemed more pleased with himself than concerned.

"Now work with me for a minute here, OK?" he said. She kept her reconstructed flap shut. He mistook that for consent. "Ross was the one who attacked *Zeph*, right?"

She shrugged, a silent *no shit.*

"And what was Ross?"

She shrugged again—deliberate obtuseness.

"He was a pirate, right?"

"So what?" she asked then.

"*So what? So what?*" He broke into a triumphant, half-moon grin. "So what do you think you've been paying insurance all these years for?"

For one stunned moment, all she could do was gape at him. Then, with a whoop, she swept him into a one-armed embrace and danced him down the hall. All of a sudden, it was oh-so-good to be alive again.

www.ingramcontent.com/pod-product-compliance
Lightning Source LLC
Chambersburg PA
CBHW030409030726
47497CB00002B/536